THE
FOREVER
HOME

BOOKS BY SUE WATSON

Love, Lies and Lemon Cake
Snow Angels, Secrets and Christmas Cake
Summer Flings and Dancing Dreams
Bella's Christmas Bake Off
We'll Always have Paris
The Christmas Cake Café
Ella's Ice Cream Summer
Curves, Kisses and Chocolate Ice Cream
Snowflakes, Iced Cakes and Second Chances
Love, Lies and Wedding Cake

Our Little Lies
The Woman Next Door
The Empty Nest
The Sister-in-Law
First Date

THE
FOREVER
HOME

SUE WATSON

Bookouture

Published by Bookouture in 2021

An imprint of Storyfire Ltd.
Carmelite House
50 Victoria Embankment
London EC4Y 0DZ

www.bookouture.com

ISBN: 978-1-80019-280-5
eBook ISBN: 978-1-80019-279-9

For my forever friends Justin Ryan and Colin McAllister, whose fabulous interior designs *always* blow my frock up!

CHAPTER ONE

It felt like a wedding. People panicking, flowers arriving, strangers in aprons running across my lawn. Champagne flutes teetered like glass towers on the verge of collapse as I jumped at a beeping horn from delivery vans pulling up too close to each other outside the house. Wandering around the front, I winced slightly at what looked like a seventeen-car pile-up, but apparently was just parking. I had to look away as a small lorry tried to manoeuvre around several other vehicles. Our narrow, winding lane was far too fragile for such activity.

It was late summer, the sun was high in a very blue sky, the salty air tingled with expectation. Life was good, and though I longed to stay in the garden, I felt guilty and went inside to see if I could help. It didn't feel like my house. We'd been invaded by 'party people', caterers working hard to provide this for me, for us. I was excited, and grateful, and stood in the kitchen, feeling rather useless as the experts did their job.

It was my silver wedding. Twenty-five years of marriage, two children and a beautiful home, perched – some said precariously – on the edge of a cliff overlooking the Atlantic in Cornwall. My assistance clearly wasn't needed here, so I wandered to the window and gazed out at the sea beyond the garden, my thoughts skipping between nervousness and happiness. Tonight, Mark and I would celebrate our marriage, and the life we'd made, and we'd drink champagne, our smiles wide as family and friends told us how lucky we were. But anyone who's ever been slightly successful at anything will tell you, luck only plays a small part, and hard work, planning and hope were my ingredients for a marriage. In fact, they were my ingredients for most things in life, tonight's party included, and I hadn't left anything to chance. I'd pored over every canapé recipe, polished every pane of glass, dusted the white shutters and styled the garden to within an inch of its life. Soon I would welcome our guests with a smile, a word and a drink, the perfect wife, hostess and mother, my handsome husband by my side – when he finally turned up.

Our story began miles away in London, where we met, but, for me, London was a pause, and my real life was resumed when we came back here, to Cornwall and my childhood home. This six-bedroomed, four-bathroomed white, art deco house had seen better days when I first returned, but over the years it became the canvas on which we'd painted our life. A labour of love for both of us, Mark had literally made a career from our home, transforming it from a beautiful old relic, to something contemporary, and visually stunning. He'd spent the first years of our marriage demolishing walls, while adding extensions, glass, light and space. Time, love, sweat and tears had gone into this house, and sometimes it seemed like we were woven into the very fabric of the building. We lived in it, and it lived in us; our roots were twisted through here, wrapped around the house, and each other.

'Mark and I are so different, and we often argue about what works and what doesn't,' I'd told a red-haired journalist only the previous day. The interview was for an interiors magazine, and I'd been flattered to be asked; my husband was the star. But Charlotte Cooper – the journalist who'd been sent to interview me – seemed keen to know where I fitted into things, both personally and professionally. She was young and pretty, close to my daughter's age, and pleasant to chat to, so I asked her to stay for lunch. Over home-made quiche and salad from the garden, I'd told her all about our lives, well the PR version of course. Then Mark came home early, and joined us for lunch and was soon centre stage, talking excitedly about his next plans for our home, and for the programme.

'A streaming service in America is interested in *The Forever Home*,' he announced, and she sat up in her seat, looked over at me for confirmation, and I smiled awkwardly. I didn't realise he was planning to tell anyone, least of all a journalist; it was, as yet, just 'talks' and I'd been sworn to secrecy.

'Ooh, America?' she sighed, gazing at him.

'Yes, we're really hoping this comes off,' I added, knowing she would be phoning this in to a tabloid within seconds if I didn't back-pedal slightly. 'Mark's always looking ahead with the programme, reaching out for new platforms,' I heard myself say, sounding like a bloody PR woman. 'He thrives on new ideas, contemporary stuff, always reinventing, designing new looks, whereas I love *old stuff* – vintage, shabby chic, and…' I'd started trying to get the conversation back onto design – which was, after all, why she was here.

'Er, when you say you love *old stuff*, I hope you aren't referring to your *husband*,' Mark had cut in, winking at me. We all laughed, and I'd watched as lovely Charlotte sipped her coffee slowly, gazing over the rim at my husband.

'It's true though, darling,' I'd said, smiling at him lovingly, 'you're always reaching into the future, but I linger in the past. I'm happy there. This house has preserved the past for me,' I added, turning to Charlotte. 'You see, when Mark had finished transforming our home, and we had the idea for him to work on other homes, this one stayed as it was. Yes, it's beautiful with its huge glass wall looking onto the sea, the high ceilings, the whitewashed curves of the exterior walls, giving a whole art deco vibe, but to me it's so much more. The scuff marks at the bottom of the stairs where the children raced to get to the bottom – or top – first, and the measuring chart on the wall over there.' I'd

pointed to the back wall where my pencil had charted the growth
of my two children. Tiny little lead snags, almost invisible, but I
knew they were there, a record of the annual countdown to my
babies growing up. Leaving the nest, and finding new places to call
home. For me, the house held onto the past; sometimes I swear
I heard the children's laughter running through the hall. Their
giggles chased me around rooms, and out into the garden, where
more memories would rush to meet me in a dizzy breeze of salt and
seagulls. It had always been a house full of happy noise, battered,
beautiful sofas, and windows so big and high my son once swore
he saw heaven. And in a way it had always been *my* heaven. The
house was *our* creation, a third child and mine and Mark's window
to the world. Our home spoke for us – on YouTube, television,
Instagram. We didn't need to tell anyone how achingly cool/happy/
wealthy/complete we were – because our very own beach house
in Cornwall said it all for us. Even if, at times, it lied.

Our marriage, like the house, had weathered storms, but we
were still together, unlike so many of our friends, who'd sadly been
abandoned or evicted from their own marriages. We were one of
the few couples left standing, and I looked forward very much to
marking this with those we loved, who would clink glasses and
marvel aloud at our fortitude. Let's face it, anyone who's been
married more than a few years knows it isn't the romance, the
passion or even the kids that keep two people together – it's sheer
bloody determination.

'Mrs Anderson?' I was suddenly awoken from my thoughts by
Ryan Jarvis, who'd come to help with the preparations. Jarvis &
Son had always had a great reputation locally, and Ryan's father
was the first builder we'd brought in on our home project years
before. Once the programme took off and was on TV, Mark
became the presenter/designer and replicated the show's formula
with other homes throughout the UK. By then, we had the
children, so I stayed home, still contributing ideas, helping Mark

with his scripts, et cetera. Meanwhile, the TV production team took over, travelling to locations with Mark, renovating 'forever homes' everywhere. Ryan's dad Ted went along as the off-screen builder on the TV series and worked with the TV team right up until his death three years before. Max, Ryan's brother, had taken over and continued to work with Mark, often travelling out to locations with him, while Ryan went off travelling, returning only recently to do the work local to Looe, here in Cornwall. I remember Ryan's dad saying he didn't like the TV cameras: 'My eldest isn't interested in being on the telly, Carly,' he'd said in his rich, Cornish accent, and Ryan spoke in the same, clotted-cream voice with the ghost of Ted's smile. I'd watched him earlier that afternoon as he'd carefully prepared the ground and instructed a small team to erect the marquee for the party, expertly co-ordinating all staff and equipment as self-appointed project manager. 'Is Mr Anderson here yet?' he was asking me now.

I shook my head. Mark had been due home about two hours ago, and I was trying very hard not to become anxious. After all, he was often late home from the studio. After a lifetime of living with someone who worked in TV, I was used to it, but today was different, and I wanted everything to be special. 'He won't be long now,' I said, more to myself than Ryan. 'I told him this morning we might be celebrating twenty-five years of marriage but if he isn't home by 4 p.m., we won't be celebrating twenty-*six* years!'

Ryan laughed. 'Oh dear, well I hope he does turn up, because the champagne's arrived. You can't drink it all on your own,' he said, smiling.

'You want to bet? I like a challenge.'

He smiled again. 'Well, you can't start drinking it yet – the delivery driver needs to park up. We could do with moving the car… do you have the keys?'

'Sorry! It's Mark's car. He probably has the keys on him,' I said, cursing my husband, who had no doubt absently put his keys in his pocket even though the production team were driving him to and from location. 'He should be back soon,' I offered, checking my watch; it was now almost 6 p.m.

'We might have to give it a push. Mr Anderson won't mind, will he?'

'No, and it doesn't matter if he does. Needs must, Ryan, and if there's a lorry full of booze, then I'm afraid that takes priority over his car,' I laughed.

'Thanks, Mrs Anderson,' he said, smiling at my joke. Ryan was good-looking, probably in his early thirties, with a little bit of a swagger. He smiled a lot. He smiled at *me*. He was very polite, too polite really – with his Mrs Anderson this and Mrs Anderson that.

'I've told you, call me Carly. "Mrs Anderson": it makes me feel ancient,' I called after him. Feeling ancient.

He stuck his thumb in the air and replied, 'Sorry,' without turning around.

The kitchen was getting busy, and I felt in the way, so wandered through to what Phoebe, our eldest, used to call 'the sunshine room'. Facing south, it was drenched in Cornish sunshine most of the day, and on summer evenings the walls turned shades of orange as the sun slowly set. The TV company used to love filming in here, and me and the kids would curl up on the cream sofas watching Mark do PTCs (TV speak for pieces to camera) espousing the new brickwork, the landscaped garden, the shabby-chic side tables, chosen by me, in an attempt to mark my territory. Shabby chic was all the rage in the late nineties, and Mark would laugh affectionately at what he referred to as 'Carly's artsy musings'. But that was where we differed: I saw the house as a living, breathing thing to be nurtured, added to, whereas Mark saw it as something to transform, to make over, do up. He could never stand still, and once he'd painted the walls in the latest shade, he had to move onto the next latest colour. Only a couple of weeks before the party he'd suggested we change the faded stripes, white shutters and pale-walled interiors from Cape Cod Beach House to 'something more edgy'.

'What?' I'd said, laughing.

'Edgy, industrial, bare brick walls and…'

'No Mark,' I'd cut in, horrified at the prospect of living in an industrial chic warehouse, not to mention the upheaval just ahead of our party. 'Why do you always do this – we love this beachy look, it's fresh and clean and suits the setting. We've finally got it just how we want it – but that's so typical of you, as soon as everything's perfect, you want to change it.'

'We can't rest on our laurels now, darling,' he'd said, kissing me on the lips, his way of trying to seduce me into the idea of exposed brickwork, rusty pipes and cold concrete flooring.

I smiled now, as I wandered through the house plumping cushions, running my palms along the folded throws in shades of blue. I gazed around me, looking at my home as a mother would gaze at a loved child. It was perfect, I was happy, and I'd been right to fight Mark to keep the fresh, summery look of pastel linens and white shuttered windows.

I stepped out onto the decking, feeling the rush that only salty sea air can bring, and took a moment to breathe. But just then, my phone rang, making me start. 'Carly, are you okay? Do you need me to do anything, or can you cope?'

It was my best friend, Lara.

'No, I'm good thanks. I told you, I've got the caterers in.'

'What? Is that some euphemism for your period… or… oh God, it's not the menopause, is it?'

'No, actual *caterers*, I laughed. 'I said we couldn't afford it but Mark said we could.'

'Oh yeah, yeah. Thank God. I mean, at forty-seven you're young for the menopause, but…'

'Lara, can we not talk about the menopause? You and another hundred guests will be descending on me very soon, my front garden's a car park, and my husband is AWOL. The last thing I need is a hot flush brought on by suggestion.'

'Okay, but as you are always keen to remind me, I'm six months older, so if *you're* menopausal, that's scary, because it means that mine is imminent. God, the night sweats... all my silk nighties will be ruined!'

She continued to talk, and I listened, with one ear on a conversation between the waitresses, who seemed to think the champagne wouldn't be cold enough. My heart sank, *warm champagne*, then I got a grip and reminded myself I didn't want to sound like one of Mark's TV friends, who'd say things like, 'It's only telly – not life and death,' while chain-smoking and not believing a word they'd just said. I'd been in this rather privileged world a little too long if I was genuinely worried about the temperature of champagne.

'Anyway, I digress,' Lara was saying. I smiled; she always 'digressed'. Mark said she was too noisy, but I enjoyed her. 'As you know, I was hoping to be with you by now for moral support, but it's been a bitch of a day,' she sighed. 'Bloody clients banging on about needing tractor-inspired boots and blue bucket hats, I mean really. Last week, they were clamouring for trench coats in sorbet shades. Somebody make it stop!'

Lara ran an online fashion website, and spent most of her time sourcing the maddest items of clothes for wealthy women with nothing better to worry about.

'One of them was in tears, in actual tears, because I'd sold out of the hour glass nano croc-effect leather tote bag.'

'I'm not even sure what you just said,' I laughed.

'Balenciaga,' she replied, like that explained everything.

'Trust me Carly it's a fabulous thing, especially in bubble-gum pink – but *not* worth dying for. I spent an hour on the bloody phone to her, I felt like a therapist! God, they're all just so attention-seeking. Where's my "me" time?' she sighed theatrically, but before I could respond, she was off again. 'And now Erin's just called, saying, "OMG, Mum, I need to talk to you as *soon* as you get home. It's *urgent!*" I'd only just left the office, and what's the betting it's something really *urgent* like… "Mum, I've got a date, we so need to discuss what nail varnish I should wear tonight."'

'Yeah, it's tough being twenty-four and beautiful with bare nails,' I laughed.

'Anyway, I'm so sorry, I can't be there yet, but I promise I'll be as fast as I can. I've been looking forward to my best friend's wedding anniversary, and happen to know she's ordered several crates of champagne,' she said, 'and after today I'll need several crates all to myself.'

'I just hope it's cold enough,' I said, echoing the waitresses.

'Jesus, Carly, who cares? Having waded through a delivery of statement handbags, Grace Kelly headscarves and an *urgent* talk with my over-anxious only child, I'll be drinking straight from the bottle regardless of how cold it is. See you ASAP.'

With that, she clicked off, and I returned to the silence, pierced only by seagulls. Lara was just what I needed at that moment, someone to drink with, make me laugh and tell me it didn't matter if the bloody champagne was warm. I really wished she could have come early, as planned, but it sounded like her day had been pretty chaotic, and now poor Erin was having another drama. She was a complicated girl, quite beautiful, in a fragile, blonde way, but seemed to pick unsuitable boys to fall in love with, which often resulted in heartbreak and angst.

Poor Lara, I thought as I pushed my phone back into my jeans pocket. I'd met her at the nursery Erin and Phoebe, my daughter, attended and as the girls were now twenty-four, that meant I'd known her almost twenty years. We'd been through a lot together, and when she'd lost her husband, thirteen years before, she leaned on me a lot, and I was glad to be there for her. In the years since Steve's death, Lara had worked her way through several boyfriends, and though her relationships with men hadn't lasted, our friendship remained solid. She often said she wished she'd married me. 'I wouldn't fancy you, but at least we'd still be together,' she'd joke.

We were quite different, Lara and I. She was loud, unafraid to say what she thought, and usually the centre of attention. I, on the other hand, was the calm, quiet one, who was there to step in and take over when Lara couldn't. She was either very up or very down, and I'd had to rescue her through break-ups and caring for Erin when life got too much for her. Lara was, at times, rather flaky, especially when it came to timekeeping and childcare. When Erin was younger, she'd often fly off at a minute's notice to source fashion items for her business from some souk in Marrakesh, or an Ibizan hippy market. I'd always been happy to look after Erin in her absence, and in her way, Lara had been there for me. Like tonight, at the party, I knew she'd calm my nerves, make me laugh, and probably make me drink too much. Lara always put things in perspective, stopped me from stressing about things – and tonight, that was just what I needed,

I was especially nervous because friends and neighbours made up only a third of our party guest list. The other guests were Mark's, the glamorous colleagues and new best friends he'd picked up on his showbiz journey. His world of TV fame was brimming with people on the edges of success, who thought by merely being close to someone like Mark, a sprinkling of stardust would land on them. Mark would chat for hours, give advice, even sometimes invite practical strangers for dinner. He loved including people; there was always someone new and interesting at Sunday lunch. I was used to it now, but when we were younger, I'd be horrified when he turned up with someone he'd met on the nearby beach, or at the pub, and tell them to take a seat at our table. I remember it as extra work, an intrusion. 'We can't afford to feed every Tom, Dick and Harry you get chatting to,' I'd said.

'But he was such a nice bloke,' he'd say, or, 'But they're a lovely couple and you'd made plenty of food.' I'd realised then that to stop

Mark was to change him, and one of the things I loved about him was his kindness. I'd also loved the way he loved me back then. It wasn't conventional perhaps – nor was it perfect – but when it came to us, particularly in those early days, he was imaginative, exciting, loving.

It was hard to believe Mark and I had been together for so long. It was twenty-five years since he'd carried me over the threshold of our home. This house was where we'd made our family and, apart from student lodgings in London in the mid-nineties, the only home I'd ever known. The house had grown along with me, and from the moment we met, I knew I wanted to bring Mark back here, to Cornwall, to my childhood home above the beach.

Mark loved to tell everyone, 'I was admiring her underwear when we met.' It always got a laugh, and it was true, in a way, because we met at my graduate art exhibition, and my final body of work was called 'Knickers!' It was a rather earnest attempt to show how women's underwear illustrated 'the continuing female struggle with body consciousness in a post-feminist, end-of-millennium era'. And when Mark wandered through the exhibition on the way to meet his girlfriend, our eyes met over my lacy briefs. I was just twenty-one, and Mark, the 'older man', at almost twenty-six. We chatted, he told me my work was new and different, and he loved the tongue-in-cheek aspect, which, in truth, I hadn't really meant. But he waxed lyrical about 'the depth and flair' of my work, 'ribboned with humour', and seemed to know what he was talking about. I was enchanted, and when, within just a few minutes he'd offered to buy all my pieces, because he loved them so much, I was completely in his thrall.

He invited me for coffee, where, over a millionaire shortbread and a skinny latte, he beguiled me with his gorgeous face and irresistible charm. A few hours later, I was naked in his cramped flat in Crouch End, and that was it. Twenty-five years on, we had two children, a lifetime behind us and were, tonight celebrating with *possibly* warm champagne.

Meeting Mark had changed my life in so many ways; it had taken me from the path I was following, a career in art, but had given me back the home life I craved. Within weeks, I was pregnant, and abandoned my plans to become the next Tracey Emin and returned to Cornwall. This time, I took Mark with me and announced to my widowed mother that a wedding was on the cards. After the initial shock, Mum began sewing my dress and making big plans with the vicar.

'We still joke about the fact Mark never actually asked me to marry him, but, to his credit, it was never a question,' I'd told Charlotte, the lovely magazine interviewer, the previous day.

'You have the most amazing life, Carly,' she'd sighed, after Mark had left. But I could tell by the way she said this that what she really meant was that I had the most amazing *husband*.

'I do,' I'd said with a smile. 'I have two perfect kids, a great husband, and this –' I'd gestured around me, 'this house, which I'm privileged to spend my days in,' I paused a moment. 'But,' I'd added, leaning forward, my fingers looping into the handle of my now empty coffee cup, 'we never take any of it for granted, Charlotte.'

She'd leaned in. Like everyone, she longed to know my recipe for success – the colour palette of my life, the intimate secrets of my marriage, how I raised my kids and folded my towels.

'Mark and I have to work at our marriage like everyone else. It isn't always perfect. This morning we had a huge argument,' I'd started.

Her eyes had widened – was I about to reveal something juicy, scandalous, were things not so perfect after all? She was trained to seek the truth, to spot the flaws, the real lives beneath the glossy, household interiors, and probably felt wasted on DIY journalism.

All Charlotte needed was one celebrity scoop to escape from typing endless stories on paint shades and fancy flooring.

'An argument? You and Mark?' she'd murmured. Her journalist tongue licked her lips, shiny red fingernails now twitching for her pen, which lay tantalisingly at the far end of the table.

'Yes, it was quite the row. I'm glad we don't have neighbours nearby,' I'd said, still fiddling with my coffee cup. Still enjoying the game. Mark had taught me all I knew about the press. We'd discovered together after the first flush of celebrity that our lives were fascinating to others. My husband's prime time presence had kept the interest, the questions, the probing, and we were constantly testing it. 'Yeah, we had this really angry exchange in the garden of all places,' I'd said, pausing. 'He wants to turn our beautiful, rugged, sea-swept garden into a *contemporary space* – fake grass and structured plants.' I'd rolled my eyes. The fire left Charlotte's eyes. She was hoping for something far more juicy. She didn't even reach for her pen, her disappointment was visible.

I thought now, as I wandered the garden, about Charlotte and all the others who'd wanted to know the secret of our success. From friends to family to news reporters, even chat show hosts, they all asked Mark, 'Where did it all go right?' A recent cover in a Sunday supplement was a photo of Mark and me sitting on the sofa, wrapped around each other, talking about twenty-five years of married bliss. The tease was a smaller photo of us, headlined, 'Winning at life'.

I was thinking about this as I almost collided with a stranger carrying a tonne of glassware through my garden. 'Winning at life'? Perhaps it looked like that, but I wasn't winning the battle to keep tonight's anniversary party intimate. It was beginning to look more like an awards ceremony than the celebration of a marriage. We were lucky, we had everything, but sometimes having everything could take you away from what you really wanted.

I continued down the garden, a last grasp at a few minutes of peace before the madness, and breathed deeply, stealing the summery scent wafting on the air. Escaping the clanking crockery, loud voices and tense revving of delivery trucks, I tasted the calm, salty tang that only the sea could bring. And standing high on the edge, I caught my breath as sharp spray from the waves spritzed my face. It revived me within seconds and reminded me of what I still held onto. Perhaps the magazine with its over-the-top declaration was right? Perhaps Mark and I *were* finally winning at life? The children had grown, and our nest was empty, but it was a beautiful nest. Despite my protests at change, Mark had recently installed a wood and glass-panelled extension, with breath-taking views and underfloor heating. Perhaps we'd stay home together more, like other couples? Things might calm down and our lives would make sense again after the tumultuous years of work and fame and child-rearing?

We'd come a long way together, and tonight we would show the world – our world – how happy we were. We'd laugh about that first meeting; Mark on his way to meet another girl, and me hoping to change the world with my political underwear. I often wondered about the girl he was rushing to meet when he'd bumped into me that day. How long had she waited before she realised he wasn't turning up, and how different would everything be if he'd gone to meet her instead?

CHAPTER TWO

It was almost seven when Mark finally arrived home from work, just minutes before the first guests were due to arrive.

'I know making television is life and death,' I said, joking sarcastically as he ran into the hallway, taking off his shoes, 'but this is our silver wedding. It only happens once.'

'Sorry, sorry.' He held his hands up in a surrendering gesture. 'You know what it's like, filming took ages!' He kissed me.

'Mmm, well, fortunately for you, superwoman was here to sort everything in your absence,' I said. 'As always.'

'Yes, you are amazing, but don't forget whose brilliant idea it was to get caterers to *assist* superwoman,' he replied, smiling.

'A brilliant, but *expensive* idea,' I countered.

He stopped in the hallway, brushed a tendril of hair from my face and looked into my eyes. 'But worth every penny?'

I felt a rush of something like love, and nodded reluctantly.

'Sherrie swears by them – "None of the stress and all of the nibbles,"' he said, standing in his socks at the bottom of the stairs. 'Oh, and by the way, she'll be along later,' he added, an apologetic grimace on his face.

'Great,' I sighed, my heart dipping. That was all we needed, his new co-presenter sashaying around the place. Mark said she was a bit full of herself and apparently treated the runners like rubbish; the producer had had to have a word with her.

He looked at me, holding out his hands helplessly. 'I know, I know, Sherrie can be a little… irritating, but I had to invite her. I've invited everyone on the team, it would be odd if I left her out.'

'She doesn't like me,' I said. 'She never even smiled at me when we saw her at the TV awards.'

'That's the botox. She doesn't smile at anyone,' he replied, with a shrug.

I laughed, feeling a bit mean, but she deserved it. At the very few social occasions I'd attended with the TV company, she usually managed to edge me out of a circle, pinning down Mark while putting her back to me. Everyone wanted a piece of him, and I guess, to people like Sherrie, I was just in the way.

'Sorry, babe, I know she's not exactly a laugh-a-minute, but I couldn't leave her out, could I?'

'No, of course not, it would be horrible and she'd be hurt, but I just feel…'

'What?' he asked gently, now standing halfway up the stairs as I looked up at him from the bottom.

'I just feel like tonight isn't quite what I'd thought it was going to be. You know I wanted an intimate gathering just for our friends and family, the people who know us and love us. But now it's less like our silver wedding and more like a TV wrap party.'

'But these *are* my friends,' he said.

'Yes, I know, and you're very kind inviting everyone on the team, but it's a *huge* team, and I thought we'd agreed it would be more of an *intimate* gathering.'

The crew and production team consisted of at least thirty guests, most of them strangers to me. To them, I was just Mark's appendage; Sherrie certainly saw me like that and would probably continue her determined campaign to keep me away from my husband – at my own party. Mark always laughed and said I was being paranoid, but she was just one of many women who salivated over Mark, batting their eyelids and thrusting their breasts towards him, as I stood by like a bloody wallflower.

'Go and get ready,' I said, trying to push Sherrie's breasts from my mind. 'It would be weird if I had to greet everyone on my own at our anniversary party – we're married, remember?'

'My darling, how could I forget?' He blew me a kiss and laughed as he wandered up the stairs.

'Oh, and your groupies will be here early, as always,' I called after him.

He stopped on the top step and turned around, with an exaggerated look of hope, his eyes darting everywhere. 'Groupies? Where?' He began to unbutton his white linen shirt. His face was brown from the sun, and a thick sweep of speckled silver hair fell across his brow. At fifty-one, he still had it, my husband.

'You know who I mean,' I teased. 'Your *groupies*… the local mummies who think you're God's gift to decorating? You insisted we invite them tonight too, remember?'

The groupies, as I'd christened them, were six mums I'd met at the school gate when Jake was five – he was now eighteen, and I'd barely seen them in the intervening years. I thought they were my friends, but I'd heard some things I wasn't sure of, and didn't feel I could trust them, so had kept my distance. But thanks to Mark's bonhomie when he'd met one of them by chance in a village shop the previous week, he'd reconnected us and we now had another group of virtual strangers at our celebration.

And tonight, some of those once-yummy mummies, would, fuelled by gin and absent husbands, be breathing fire into Mark's face and insisting he dance with them.

'Women adore him, and who can blame them?' I'd told Charlotte, the reporter.

'He *is* a very attractive older man.' She'd nodded her head vigorously

He was old enough to be her father, but few women were immune to Mark's charms.

'Aren't you scared of other women stealing him off you?' she'd asked.

'No, I'm not scared of other women stealing him,' I lied. 'It's me he comes home to at the end of the day, and even if he's tired, we still make time for each other... Do you know, after all these years, he still leaves me little love notes all over the house.'

'Love notes?' she sighed.

I nodded. 'He'd kill me for telling you this, but just this morning, I opened the coffee jar to find a note inside saying he loved me. He'd drawn this little heart...' I'd started, then rolled my eyes. I didn't want to come over as some self-satisfied, middle-aged wife. I'd been surprised to find the note; he hadn't done anything like that in years. I put it down to nostalgia. He was probably remembering us twenty-five years before.

'He left a love note in the coffee jar?' Charlotte had smiled, and sat back in her seat like she'd just completed a run.

With guests now due any moment, and Mark safely home and changing, I checked my hair in the hall mirror, glad I'd had my roots done; the grey was sprouting through the blonde more quickly these days. Wandering into the kitchen, I watched the chef scatter chia seeds onto dainty canapés, and gave a silent thank you to pert-breasted, botox-faced Sherrie. Mark's co-presenter may not have been able to move her face since 1998, but that woman knew a good catering company when she saw one.

My mind returned, as minds often do at birthdays and anniversaries, to the past and where it all began. Mark's TV programme, *The Forever Home*, started out in our back garden with me filming him working on the house, and little Phoebe playing in the background. To our amazement, the idea had, over the years, gone from strength to strength, and now Mark presented two series a year for the BBC, and was feted wherever he went.

What had been lost to history was that the idea was originally mine. The internet was still quite new, but as part of my art degree I'd done a module on video-making, so I'd downloaded the footage of my young, handsome husband single-handedly renovating our seaside home. Mum had given the house to me as a wedding present. My dad had died a couple of years before we married, and she felt the house needed a family. 'It's a home built for chaos and children,' she'd said before moving into her small retirement apartment on the other side of the village. Just a few years later, she died, and unable to cope with my grief, Mark became almost obsessed with transforming the house. But this had been my mum's home, all my memories of her were here, and I was still grieving for her. I always would.

Her death was devastating – she died of cancer, and I nursed her through those final months of her life until she couldn't take any more pain. 'I want to go,' she'd begged me, 'please let me say goodbye now.'

It was the lowest time in my life. I was a young mum, pregnant with my second child and too young to lose my own mother. I still needed her wisdom, her guidance, and her unconditional love; there's nothing quite like a mother's love for her children, I knew that too well. As an only child, I'd been incredibly close to Mum, and selfishly wanted her to hang onto life as long as she could, for me. It sounds terrible, but I resented her for wanting to die, wanting to be free of pain and the indignity of the final weeks, months. I just kept saying, 'Mum, you can't leave me.' But she did.

In some ways, not all good, Mum's death bonded Mark and I. But where losing her made me want to hide myself away and cry, it seemed to inspire Mark to start afresh, move forward. For him, her death was a watershed, and he wanted to change everything about the house, seeming to escape into the project, and leaving just the white shell, like a hollowed-out egg. I wasn't ready for that, but being tired and pregnant with a toddler running around,

I didn't fight it, and agreed to the transformation. He told me it would be 'an obituary to your mum', and though we both knew it was less about Mum and more about Mark, I hoped perhaps the project would free me from the syrupy grief and guilt I was wading through in the aftermath. But, in reality, the sanding of walls and floors felt like my childhood was being erased, and each blow of the hammer seemed to take me further from who I was.

On a practical level, the whole venture was a worry; Mark was an architect, but hadn't completed his training in London when we moved to Cornwall, so he had no job, and we had little money, just what Mum had left us. I was pregnant with Jake, our second child, and concerned about the future, but Mark was consumed with the idea of turning our home into an installation on the cliffs.

'People will see it for miles, it's going to transform this town,' he'd said. 'This will be my business card, and I'll be offered lots of work.'

I had to admire his optimism, and in a desperate attempt to support him, and try and find a way to pay for all the raw materials, I downloaded the footage of Mark working and talking through what he was doing. I tagged all the DIY stores where we'd bought our stuff, hoping they'd appreciate the mention and perhaps offer to help for a mention on our social media. It was the very beginning of 'influencers', in fact people like us didn't even have a label, but before long, companies responded, sending us paint, wallpaper, and all kinds of building equipment. It was early days, we were a novelty, but as our following grew, we could put a company's product before a million people. We didn't have a detailed plan for our home, we just worked with what we had and what we were given, and just shuffled along, doing one project after the next. But it seemed people watching us could relate, and think; *If those two skinny twenty-somethings can work out how to build a brick wall, so can I.*

Then local builder, Ted, had offered his services for free if we'd feature his company on our videos. By then we had one million followers, a huge following back then, and I dared to hope we might get some interest from TV. So I came up with a format and sent the idea and some footage to various TV companies, who showed a great deal of interest. There was quite a bidding war, which was when Mark got more involved and found an agent, Estelle. And she schmoozed her way around the different TV executives, and within about a week we had a deal, and *The Forever Home* went from a TV pilot to a series.

I'm sure in today's busy reality TV marketplace, a man painting a wall while having a conversation with his wife isn't exactly 'warts and all'. But in pre-*Love Island* days, when sex with a stranger on TV would have been considered shocking, this fly-on-the-wall DIY seemed quite intimate. People loved the realness of it, the way this handsome, amusing young husband and father was, magician-like, turning a tired old cottage into something spectacular. The viewers loved to share our triumphs and tragedies, our minor victories over a load-bearing wall, and the devastation when what promised to be duck-egg blue paint was green when painted on the wall. One newspaper described it as, 'making DIY drama out of a crisis,' proclaiming Mark to be a charismatic TV personality, destined for great things. Viewers adored him, they also loved the family dynamic, and the idea that Mark's blood, sweat and tears had gone into improving the house for us, his wife and kids.

My art degree was also utilised in murals, paint effects, patterns for soft furnishings. But there was no doubt Mark was the star. Branded as 'the decorating woman's crumpet', the TV company paid him well to keep him. Back then, we laughed at his new sex symbol status, but, I have to confess, it made me feel slightly insecure in the early days. I spent a lot of time worrying – as Charlotte had suggested – that he might leave me for someone more beautiful, more successful. But Mark reassured me as much as he could and, when asked about the success of the programme, would point out how my contribution at home had enabled his success. 'Carly carried all the weight,' he'd say. 'I owe my success wholly to her, because while I was messing about with renovations, she was doing the important stuff, as homemaker and mother to Phoebe and Jake.'

Looking back, I'm not sure that was strictly true. I did an awful lot behind the scenes *in addition* to looking after the house and kids. But I didn't have Mark's confidence on camera, so was happy to do stuff behind the scenes and always helped Mark with his words. He liked to do dramatic introductions, and describe things a certain way, but didn't quite know how to put it. He always said I had a way of making poetry and insisted I write the opening script and make notes for filming. Even after the programme moved away from the house, and Mark and the TV production team travelled the country, I continued to write his words. Most of the time, I hadn't even seen the place he was working on, but I'd look at the recce shots and write the programme opening and notes, then wave him off, sometimes for weeks on end. I missed him, but I had my children, my home and the gorgeous Cornish coast. Now, Mark had just received the offer from a big US streaming company, making all those lonely nights worth the sacrifice. The TV executives said they could turn him into the next *Queer Eye*, or, as he was eager to point out, 'the straight, silver fox version'. And they'd offered three million dollars. We'd been comfortable for the last few years, but this was something else. Of course, it wasn't just about the money, it would involve all kinds of change, and I was excited to start this new chapter in our lives. With the kids grown, I could go with Mark to America. I would hate to leave this house, even if it was for just a few months a year, but it was an opportunity I couldn't miss.

I was suddenly shaken out of my thoughts by the sound of champagne corks popping.

'I may need to taste that champagne to make sure it's right?' I joked, walking over to one of the young waitresses in the kitchen.

She smiled and handed me a fizzing flute just as the doorbell rang.

I thanked her and headed down the hall, opening the door with one hand and holding my glass with the other. Phoebe and Jake stood on the doorstep, and as soon as they were inside, they hugged and congratulated me. Then they did what all young people do when faced with the prospect of free drink: they marched towards the makeshift bar. Phoebe worked in London on a women's magazine, while Jake was just completing his first year at Exeter University, and Jake had driven down earlier to collect Phoebe from the train station.

'Mum, you look great,' Jake said, as a waiter poured him and Phoebe a glass of fizz each.

'Yeah, that white dress looks good on you, really sets off your tan,' Phoebe added.

I put my arms around both their shoulders. 'My babies,' I sighed, kissing each one on the cheek.

'Where's Dad?' Phoebe took a sip from her glass and looked around expectantly.

'Oh, you know your dad, late home, still getting ready upstairs as guests arrive downstairs.'

'Classic Dad.' Phoebe shook her head, smiling indulgently at her dad's complete inability to play by anyone's rules.

The doorbell rang again. It was the first of the guests and, as I'd predicted, I was greeting them alone. I placed my champagne flute down carefully on the kitchen island, put on my brightest smile and headed for the door, fully expecting to open it and see the yummy mummies standing there. They'd always been first at all the school events, and I could only imagine how keen they'd be to party here, especially with Mark.

But I was surprised to see a young red-haired woman on the doorstep.

'Hi Carly,' she said, rather awkwardly.

It was Charlotte, the journalist who'd interviewed me and stayed for lunch the previous day.

Smiling, I gazed questioningly at her. I wondered if perhaps she'd left something behind – her pen, her notebook? Had she forgotten to ask me a question? She was wearing a long, strappy dress, her hair curled, full make-up on, as if she were going to... a party?

'Mark... er, Mr Anderson invited me. He thought it might be good for me to see "the other side", so it's less about work, more about the family... in a relaxed environment... to add some background to the piece I'm writing?'

'Oh.' He really was too much sometimes. Inviting all his TV colleagues was one thing, but turning our wedding anniversary into a PR event was bloody irritating.

'I'm sorry, Carly, I should have checked with you first,' she sighed, clearly picking up on my surprise. 'I won't intrude, just wanted a bit of colour, but—'

I wished Mark had mentioned it to me, but it wasn't the girl's fault and I didn't want to make her feel awkward, so I nodded vigorously. 'No problem at all. Come and meet the children, they're far more interesting than me and Mark,' I said, smiling as I put my arm through hers and walked her into the kitchen, where Phoebe and Jake were starting on a second glass of bubbly.

I introduced her and the kids immediately made her welcome. As they chatted, I abandoned them, to answer the door again, while silently cursing my husband, who still hadn't made an appearance.

I swear I could smell the perfume from down the hall before I'd even opened the door to the school gate yummy mummies. I painted on my smile as they stood expectantly on the doorstep, resplendent in glitzy designer dresses, their expensive platinum highlights suggesting they all had the same hairdresser.

'Long time no see,' I exclaimed, as *The Real Housewives of Cornwall* moved as one into my hallway.

'Carly!' they all said in unison as they embraced me with firmly gym-honed arms.

'You look gorgeous, lovely,' one of them said, I'm not sure which one, they were interchangeable in their strappy dresses revealing deep, golden tans, telling of a summer spread across Cornwall and the Caribbean.

Gemma, the only one I could accurately distinguish, as she seemed to be the spokesperson, led the way down the hall like it was *her* home, arm around my waist, continuing with the theme of how 'fabulous' I looked, while glancing around for the *real* star of the show. But Mark was still nowhere in sight.

Over the next half-hour, more people arrived, a few I knew and some I didn't, which made me even more angry that my husband wasn't there to greet them and introduce me.

'I'm so sorry, I, er…' was my opening line to a gaggle of beautiful strangers who filled my hallway with the heady blend of French cologne and sun oil.

'Carly!' someone screeched and I turned around. 'Haven't seen you for ages, didn't recognise you.'

'Have I aged that much in just a few months, Sherrie?' I asked Mark's co-presenter, in mock alarm, as she swept me into a too-tight hug.

She giggled, and released me, so I made a quick move and guided her to the kitchen, where I hoped the kids might rescue me. 'Thing is,' she said, taking a glass from a passing waiter, 'when I think of Carly Anderson, I always think of the young blonde with the long legs on the very first series *all* those years ago. God, how long ago was that?'

'About a hundred years?' I said, not wanting to dwell on how much time had passed.

She laughed. 'No. More like twenty years. I was a *child*,' she added, her head to one side, her face a study in pity. 'You were gorgeous, running along that beach in shorts, making sandcastles with the little ones – I bet they're unrecognisable now too?'

'Yes, they're all grown up – just like me,' I said, forcing a smile, but wanting to slap her. 'They're just over there,' I added, pointing over to Phoebe and Jake, chatting with Charlotte at the far end of the kitchen.

Sherrie smiled and raised her eyebrows just to humour me; she wasn't interested in my kids, she was only interested in Sherrie. I wished she'd wander off and make someone else feel rubbish, but tonight it was my turn. I consoled myself that at least she'd acknowledged my presence.

'Oh wow,' she said slowly, and clutched both my upper arms, holding me at length, surveying me from a distance.

'What?' I tried to smile, I really did.

'You look *so natural* – I have to rely on Doctor Botox, but you don't, do you?'

I shook my head uncertainly. Was she saying I looked natural, or naturally old? I hated this fake world of TV, where looks and youth were prized above everything else – even talent, where Sherrie was concerned.

'If ever you decide to start fighting it, give me a call. I'll give you the number of my doctor, he's fabulous!' She gestured towards my face with long pink nails.

I looked around for an escape. Phoebe had left the kitchen and Jake was in deep conversation with the gorgeous redhead Charlotte, so not a hope there. To my deep relief, I suddenly felt Mark's presence, as he landed by my side, showered and smelling of fresh leaves and lemons. He kissed me on the cheek, then embraced Sherrie, who turned to face him, and started talking intensely. It was all just approval-seeking noise about their work, in-jokes about colleagues and 'hilarious' things that had happened on various shoots. As I never went on location, I couldn't join in, and the more she talked, the more she shifted round until her back was facing me.

I was about to wander off when Phoebe came over and tapped her dad on the shoulder. *That's my girl*, I thought, *the cavalry has come to save me.* She hugged him, then reached out to pull me in for a family hug, and poor old Sherrie was the one suddenly left out in the cold. It was deftly done, and Mark hadn't even noticed – but Sherrie had, and flounced off into the other room, taking her fake breasts and plastic personality with her.

'Carly, you shouldn't be hiding in the kitchen,' Mark said, 'come and mingle.'

'I would love to mingle, but I was talking to Sherrie – until you came along.' I rolled my eyes at Phoebe, who was open-mouthed.

'Dad, Mum has been greeting *your* friends for the past half-hour – she's been mingling!'

'Sorry, my darlings,' he said, a middle-aged man caught in a pincer movement between wife and daughter. 'I just meant—'

'No, *you're* the one who's late, don't you *dare* chastise Mum. You've been upstairs since we arrived,' she laughed incredulously.

'Come on then,' I said, before a row erupted between them. 'Perhaps you could introduce me to some of *my* guests?' I added, grabbing his hand and leading him from the kitchen into the throng. 'Don't get too drunk, too early,' I said under my breath.

'Wouldn't dream of it, darling,' he said, with a wink.

We wandered through the main sitting room, and into the garden, where guests had started to gather. It was around eight and the sun was beginning to melt, casting orange stains through the sky. The sea, glittering in the distance, never failed to take my breath away. Living here in this house, I owned that view; it was all mine, whenever I wanted.

'You ready for a full-on performance?' I asked Mark, smiling through gritted teeth.

'If you are, darling.' He smiled back, leaning towards me, and we kissed, pulling away only when someone shouted, 'Get a room!'

'I think we should dance the first dance, just like we did at our wedding,' Mark whispered into my ear.

So I threw off my sandals, and we held each other and danced in the failing light, as our guests stopped talking and gathered around to watch us. I hated being on show. I only did it for Mark; he loved being the centre of attention, and people loved to watch him. He was a great dancer too, far better than me, and he slowly moved me around, his hips loose, his rhythm so in tune with the music. My bare feet felt the cool of the grass, and the sway of the music, and with Mark's gentle guidance, I soon believed I could dance. Just like the first time all those years before.

When the music eventually stopped, we were brought crashing back to the present, and I had to take a moment before moving into the throng now gathering around us.

'Darling?' That voice, all full and throaty. It was Mark's agent, Estelle – the way she went on, you'd think she was an actress with the RSC. 'You two are totally GORGEOUS!' she almost yelled in our faces.

I grimaced, and stood by as she swept Mark into her arms and then pushed him away, still holding him so she had his full attention.

'I thought we were meeting today to go over paperwork for the next series?' she said, in a faux sulky voice, her collagened lips pouting trout-like in my husband's direction.

'Sorry, kitten, I had a big meeting, couldn't make it.'

Kitten?

'Tomorrow?' she demanded sulkily. I watched this performance like it was a game of tennis.

'Sorry, bae, I have to…'

Bae? WTF? I almost laughed out loud – why was he talking like our kids?

'Estelle,' I said, 'so glad you could make it.' I reached to give her a hug.

She squealed. I'm not sure if it was in joy or horror; her reaction to everything was always inappropriately big. She then hugged me too tightly and told me how fabulous I looked while gazing in a different direction.

A few others gathered round to congratulate us, and we smiled and hugged and thanked them for their gifts, their compliments.

'You are both so lucky – all this and twenty-five years of wedded bliss too,' one of the yummy mummies oozed.

'I'm the luckiest, because I have this one,' Mark said, pulling me in with both arms and kissing me on my forehead.

'You're squashing my newly squashed hair, darling,' I laughed.

'So, what do you say to another twenty-five years, babe?' he asked, and everyone murmured their approval.

'Oh, go on then,' I replied, with a smile, and he bent down and kissed me on the lips.

Everyone clapped. I felt ridiculous, but with one arm still around my shoulder, Mark squeezed me gently, a reassuring gesture.

We continued to chat for a while, but Mark was soon swept up in a bubble of TV friends, and with only the Yummies around, and no sign of Lara yet, I was sucked into their vortex.

'So, what's it really like to be married to the DIY Woman's Crumpet?' one of them asked; she was clearly a little tipsy already. 'Go on, spill the beans, we've all been married as long, if not longer – and I don't look at my hubby like you look at Mark.' They all giggled.

I blushed. 'Oh, I'm sure you do.'

'The last time I looked at him like that, he'd bought me a new car,' she said, laughing.

'No, really though, what's your secret?' Gemma cut in. 'Is he as perfect as he seems, or does he have a dark, naughty side, if you know what I mean?' She giggled, and winked at me.

'Honestly, girls, it's like being interviewed by the press. What can I tell you? He isn't a secret serial killer, he doesn't eat babies for breakfast, he's… lovely, he's… Mark.'

'I read somewhere that he still brings you breakfast in bed?' Gemma panted.

I nodded. I swear I heard them all purr, and was reminded why I hadn't kept in touch with them over the years. Why were people, especially women, fascinated by mine and Mark's private life?

I'd had enough, so told them I had to check on something, and escaped to the garden; no one had ventured out there yet, so I took the opportunity for a few seconds of solace. As always, I was drawn to the sea, and wandered slowly to the bottom of the garden, just to check it was still there. The sun had melted to make way for a white chocolate moon lighting the way down through the white hydrangeas, becoming almost luminous, as if they'd soaked up all the sunshine of the day to light the path down to the cliff edge in the semi-darkness. I tramped through the plants and sticky grasses, right to the edge, looking out in the semi light at the calm, grey-blue sea, the treacherous rocks below.

Where had twenty-five years gone? Were they swallowed up somewhere in the ocean? How that time had shaped us all – my little ones weren't little any more, and I wasn't the twenty-two-year-old in white lace who'd returned here with my handsome groom. I was older, stronger. I had more lines from twenty-five years of laughter, tears and everything in between.

I turned, my back to the sea, and looked back at the house, almost glowing in the fading light, remembering only the happy times.

Everything was so quiet and calm, the lull before the storm. I could hear the gentle throb of music, clinking glasses and the murmurings of our first guests, which reminded me I had to go back. I would be swept up in the whirlwind of fizzy wine and chatty friends, and it would be fun, and I was glad I'd had the chance for a few moments to gather myself together. But just as I turned to walk up the garden, I became aware of a rustle in the trees. Was it Miss Anderson, our white Persian cat? She was usually easy to spot in the dim light, but I wondered if she'd smelled strangers. Miss A, as she was sometimes known for short, didn't like strangers.

I bent down to look for her, and was about to call her, when I heard whispering coming from behind the trees. I couldn't make out words at first, just quick, rasping sounds. But it wasn't a cat, it was a voice. An angry voice.

'How *could* you?' a woman's voice hissed. 'You're a bloody idiot…'

I couldn't hear the rest, but waited in the stillness. Then I heard a lower, rumbling man's voice, but couldn't make out what he was saying. A couple bickering. I wondered which of our friends it was. He'd probably said something rude or insensitive, and embarrassed her in front of everyone – we'd all been there. A look, a remark, a compliment to another woman in the wife or partner's presence. 'You're making a big drama out of nothing,' was the clarion cry. Men could be so infuriating, and their blindness to what they'd done usually made things worse. 'What have I done now?' Mark would ask, hands out, totally unaware of the emotional and social carnage he'd put me through in front of others.

Now someone else was approaching; I could hear heavy footsteps marching through the garden. It was probably Mark coming to find me to ask me to mingle.

'Mrs Anderson?'

I turned to see Ryan Jarvis in the semi darkness.

'Oh, hi,' I answered quietly, not wanting to alert the arguing couple that I was nearby.

'Sorry, did I surprise you?'

The whispering stopped. Damn, they must have heard.

'It's okay, not your fault. I shouldn't really be here, I'm the hostess,' I sighed, glancing over to where the whispers had come from. Still silence.

'Can I get you another?' Ryan gestured towards my empty glass. I hadn't realised I was still clutching it.

'That's very kind. But I should get back,' I said, beginning to walk away, back up the garden. I was aware that the arguing couple had probably realised I'd overheard them, and might have thought I was listening. How awkward. I felt a bit guilty, but it had been too tempting not to linger, and try and work out who it was.

I wandered back into the main part of the garden with Ryan, making small talk about the number of guests and the way the weather had played in our favour.

'Thanks for all your help today,' I said. 'I bet your brother is glad to have you back from your travels?'

'Yeah, Max loves having me back to boss around. I'm starting some building work next week, think Max is going to carry on doing some work with Mark.'

'Yes, he's great on location, takes after your dad,' I said. 'When did you get back… it was Thailand, wasn't it?'

'Yeah. Beautiful place. I only got back last week, and I'm missing it already,' he added wistfully.

'I can imagine. Itchy feet, eh? Jake thought about going to Thailand and doing a gap year, but decided he couldn't bear to be so far away from home,' I said.

I'd always worried about my youngest; he wasn't academic, and he'd found school difficult, unlike his bright, confident sister. I felt that Jake sometimes struggled with having a successful father. When he was younger, he worshipped his dad, but the teenage years had put paid to any of that, and he seemed more embarrassed about Mark's fame. Mark had assumed Jake would do architecture as he had, after all Jake seemed interested, but he'd unexpectedly chose to do psychology. I'd been as surprised as Mark, but this was about Jake taking his own journey and not following in his father's footsteps – but they were big boots to fill. I remember Jake once saying to me, 'I'll never be Dad, I don't want to work late and leave my kids at home, and I'm not interested in people fawning over me at awards ceremonies. I'd rather stay home with a book.'

'Jake's such a homebird,' I continued, 'but I think university's given him some confidence, something to focus on.'

'Well, there's a pretty redhead who seems to be giving him something to focus on at the moment,' Ryan said, nodding in the direction of a small group standing in the garden, where Jake was chatting quite animatedly to Charlotte.

I was, as always, cautiously hopeful that this might lead to something more for my son. He had so much to give, but often fell for unattainable women – and always got his heart broken.

'So, Ryan, you're helping out, with the family firm,' I said, trying not to think about poor Jake being eaten alive by the gorgeous red-haired journalist who was probably less interested in him, and more in probing him about the Anderson family's secrets. I hoped she didn't probe too much.

'Yeah, I'm sticking around for the winter, want to spend more time with Mum. It's not been easy for her since Dad died.'

'Oh yes, of course. Poor Ted – he was a lovely man, your dad.'

We continued to chat as we re-entered the party area. I was finding Ryan easier to talk to than some of the guests.

'As a kid, I always wished I lived here, it felt... I don't know, like the sun was always shining, and everything was perfect,' Ryan sighed.

'Viewers love a happy family who live by the sea,' I said, with a smile.

'Yep, I bought it,' he laughed.

'So did everyone else, and that's how we can still afford to live here. It pays the bills, as they say.'

'Nice work if you can get it.'

'It has its downsides, Ryan,' I said, as I lifted a glass from a passing tray and took a large sip. 'People think it's all wonderful, but it isn't.'

'What do you mean?' He grabbed a glass off the same tray and took a quick sip, eager to get back to the conversation.

'Oh nothing, just the price of fame, I guess,' I said, and lifted my glass to his. 'Here's to anniversaries and homecomings.' We clinked glasses.

We continued to talk, slightly removed from everyone. I was always more comfortable talking one on one.

'It must have been quite tough being so famous. Are you glad you're not involved now, in the programme?' he asked.

I shrugged. 'Mark needed new projects, he couldn't work on this house forever and we couldn't all traipse up and down the UK, so I opted – happily – to stay home with the children. But even though Mark was away, some of his fans hung around on the off-chance he'd turn up. They were obsessed. One night, someone broke into the house while we slept. We woke the next morning to find fake rose petals and a "love note" for Mark. But the creepiest thing was that the rose petals were scattered at the bottom of our bed.'

'No. Someone had left them there while you were sleeping?' His brow creased, as he looked at me in disbelief.

'Yeah.' I shuddered.

'Christ, like you say, the price of fame,' he said, shaking his head.

I suddenly saw Mark's sister eyeing me across the garden then, and realised I had a job to do. 'It's been lovely chatting to you, Ryan, but I'd better play hostess and chat to our guests,' I said, moving away.

'Of course, see you later,' he replied, while I wandered away, steeling myself as I approached Mark's sister, Amanda, and her husband.

We embraced and made polite conversation, both recalling the wedding day twenty-five years before. 'Oh Carly, you were a mess – you cried during the reception,' she said, like I needed reminding of the mascara running down my just made-up face.

I could see it now, the expressions of horror on the faces of my family and friends as I walked down the aisle. I was about to point out I was very young, pregnant, and it had all been so quick, but I didn't need to respond, she'd already moved on to how bad my wedding breakfast had been. 'Ham. Salad. Enough said.' She pursed her lips and wrinkled her nose.

'It was my mother's choice,' I replied, hurt on her behalf.

Amanda raised her eyebrows in a 'so' gesture. And I realised it may have sounded like I'd apologised, and I wasn't going to apologise for my mum. 'As she was paying, she helped me choose the menu, and it was *nice* ham,' I added, like that would change her mind.

'Yeah,' she said, humouring me, and I felt rather foolish trying to defend the quality of ham served at my wedding more than two decades earlier. But, of course, it wasn't about the ham, it was about the way Mark's family had viewed me and my family. I think they considered us to be rather straight, and despite me being an art graduate, Mark once told me they didn't see me as being 'spontaneous' enough for him. If by spontaneous, they meant living like them, spending all the money they had when they got it, borrowing from the bank and maxing out the credit cards until they died, then no, I wasn't 'spontaneous'.

I knew the Andersons took delight in pitying my mum because she lived in a little cottage in Cornwall, whereas Mark's family had a big house in London. The irony was, when his parents died, it turned out that the house was rented; they had nothing – but what they did have was delusions of grandeur. Meanwhile, Mark's sister still behaved like a bloody countess – something I teased Mark about, because he too could be a snob when he wanted to be.

To my deep relief, in the middle of Amanda's usual listing of her children's stratospheric achievements, I saw Lara, like a beacon in the darkness. She'd finally arrived! She was tramping across the garden, clutching her cotton maxi dress high so as not to tread on the hem with her high wedge sandals. I had to smile. I could only imagine her screams if she fell; we'd end up laughing all night about her entrance. Meandering through the hydrangeas towards the house, she shook out her long, dark curly hair, and it suddenly dawned on me that she was coming up from the *bottom* of the garden. Where I'd been standing a few minutes earlier. Where I'd heard the argument. Had it been *Lara* arguing with someone, but who? It couldn't have been her she'd only just arrived – hadn't she?

I managed to break free from Amanda's monologue and excused myself. I marched across the grass towards Lara, arms outstretched, so pleased to see my friend, I didn't register the fact that my husband was following just a few feet behind.

CHAPTER THREE

'Carly! There you are,' Lara was saying. 'Someone told me you were at the bottom of the garden, so I walked down there – Mark had to rescue me. I didn't realise these sandals would be so treacherous on soft ground, and I almost ended up in the sea,' she laughed, opening her arms to hug me.

I hugged her back, grabbing a glass off a passing tray, and handing it to her as Mark trudged off.

'Are you okay?' I asked, as we sipped on our drinks.

'Of course I am, why?' she answered, a little sharply.

'Because you just almost fell in the sea, and Mark had to rescue you,' I said.

'Oh… yeah, I'm fine.' She took a huge gulp of champagne. 'Ah, that's better.'

I smiled at her, but she didn't meet my eyes, and I couldn't put my finger on it, but on that beautiful, balmy night in my gorgeous garden lit by lanterns and fairy lights, something wasn't right. 'Long day?' I asked.

'Yeah. Yeah,' she said, too brightly, and grabbed a second drink from a passing tray. 'This is wonderful, Carly,' she noted, looking around, raising one of her glasses to a local couple we both knew. 'Hope they don't come over,' she muttered under her breath, 'so boring.' Lara liked to choose her friends; she refused to be bothered by people who bored her.

'You're sure you're okay?' I asked again, wanting to get to the root of something I couldn't quite identify. I'd hoped Lara arriving would be my salvation, but there was suddenly a chill in the air.

'Yeah, bad day. I just need to get pissed.' She took another gulp and began to look around as if for the next drink when she seemed to remember why we were there. 'You having a good evening?' she asked, but I could tell she wasn't really interested.

I smiled. 'Yeah, thanks. I'm playing my usual role as Mark Anderson's accessory.'

'Yes, and a bloody gorgeous, priceless one,' she said loudly, and made a cheers gesture to a group of guests to her left, threw back her head, and downed the rest of her champagne from both glasses.

Lara was always confident, but tonight she seemed almost brash.

'Stop looking at me, Carly, I'm fine,' she almost snapped.

'Okay, okay. If you feel like talking, I'm here. You know that.'

'Yeah,' she softened, 'and it's so typical of you to offer to listen to me at *your* party. You're a kind and lovely friend.' Her eyes filled with tears, and she must have seen the concern on my face because she edged away slightly, shaking her head. 'No, I'm fine. Like I said, it's just been a shit day.' She gave me a half-smile, obviously not wanting to bother me with her problems tonight.

But it didn't matter that this was my party, she was my friend and I cared about her. I was about to gently pursue the matter when the catering manager appeared at my elbow.

'Mrs Anderson... the rest of the buffet... when would you like it?'

'Oh. Now... now... please,' I said absently. I'd been planning the menu with the caterers for weeks, and since Lara's arrival I'd almost forgotten about it. I was suddenly consumed with the need to poke around in my own head and locate exactly what was bothering me about the way she was behaving. I watched as her gold hoop earrings caught the light, bright orange lips pursing as she gazed around at the other guests. I took a sly glance to her right where Mark stood, talking to the Yummies. Something was nudging its way to the front of my brain, but I still couldn't touch it.

Even in the candlelit darkness, I could see Mark wasn't on form; he seemed distracted, going through the motions. He kept putting his hand to his mouth in a comforting gesture, something I knew Mark always did when he was worried.

And then I thought about the fact that Lara had emerged from the bottom of the garden with Mark. No one else had appeared from the shrubbery, so was it *them* arguing? But what would Mark and Lara possibly have to argue about? They barely spoke at the best of times. What the hell? Oh God, he'd bought me something horrific for our anniversary and he'd told her and she was telling him he was '*a bloody idiot*' for buying it. Then again, if he *had* bought me an anniversary gift, it would be the first time in years, but it was our silver wedding? I was still contemplating this when my cousin Lorraine and her husband wandered over to say hello, and Lara touched my arm and moved away. With both my parents gone, Lorraine was the only family I had, and I was pleased to see her and catch up.

'You had such a lovely wedding breakfast,' she said. 'Ham salad, what could be nicer for a summer wedding?'

'Thanks Lorraine,' I said, genuinely grateful for her comment, and made a mental note to have her over more often. We continued to chat a little, then they wandered off to grab a drink, and after some small talk with people I hardly knew, I looked around to see where Lara was, and if she was okay. I couldn't see her, and when another group of Mark's friends called me over, I joined them to talk polite, smiley rubbish for too long, all the time trying to work out what was happening here.

Earlier, in the garden, I'd heard a heated exchange that had a feeling of intimacy, not the words themselves because I could barely hear them – but the tone. Yes, it was the *tone* of their voices that bothered me. But if it had been Mark and Lara, why didn't she tell me? Why hadn't Mark come up to me and complained about her interfering, or being 'too much', as he often did? I felt a flicker of uneasiness as the dead body of a pig was wheeled out and someone sliced into it.

'Help yourselves,' I urged our guests, reminding myself I was the hostess and must stop overthinking something that might turn out to be nothing. But where was Lara? And for that matter… where was my husband? Gemma and the other women he'd been talking to were now queuing for the buffet, and he was nowhere to be seen. I was uneasy, and aside from my more personal fears, the caterers would be bringing out the silver wedding cake soon. I'd greeted most of the guests on my own, but I was damned if I was cutting the bloody cake on my own too; how would that look? So, as everyone descended on the food, I went back inside the house to see if I could find him – and her.

First, I went to the downstairs bathroom and knocked on the door, but a male voice responded, and it wasn't Mark. Then I headed for the kitchen, saw Phoebe, and contemplated asking her to cut the cake with me, but then thought that might seem even more odd than cutting it on my own. It would give out the wrong message, and in our world, before we knew it, someone would blab and we'd be in the news with rumours of marriage problems.

Walking from the kitchen diner through to the hall, I suddenly heard voices in Mark's office. What the hell was he doing in there while we were celebrating our twenty-fifth wedding anniversary? Whatever was happening, I had to know, so I took a deep breath, gathered myself together and walked in.

What greeted me in the room was odd. Lara was sitting on an easy chair cradling a large glass of whisky, and Mark was leaning on his desk holding an equally large glass. This didn't make any sense, the two of them only tolerated each other for me, and yet here they were drinking, alone. I looked from one to the other, confused.

'You guys opened a private drinking club?' I asked, half-smiling, but not sure quite what I'd walked into. I continued to walk across the room and stood near the desk, just a few inches from Mark. But neither of them seemed to acknowledge my presence; their lack of response was bewildering. Like I was invisible, a ghost.

I glanced over at Lara, the half-smile fading on my lips when I saw she'd been crying. Now my heart started thumping, strong and steady, gaining momentum in anticipation of what was about to happen here.

'What's the matter? What *is* it?' I urged, panic rising.

Mark stirred, moving his legs but staying on the edge of his desk like he couldn't leave.

'Mark?' I said, moving closer, looking into his face for a clue. But he didn't respond.

I turned to my friend. 'Lara?' My voice was shaky, unsure. 'It was *you* two arguing at the bottom of the garden, wasn't it?'

Lara looked away, so I turned to my husband, clutching his glass of whisky like it was all he had to hold on to.

'Mark, what the hell's going on?'

He took a deep breath, and lifted himself off the desk to stand up, and as he did, I reached out with one hand and rested it there to steady myself. The wood grain under my palm felt comfortingly real when nothing was as it seemed.

'Lara and I have been… talking,' he started.

'Just tell her, Mark, stop being a bloody coward,' Lara spat, without even looking at him.

I turned to Mark, my mouth dry.

'Oh Carly,' he said, taking another deep breath. 'I don't know where to start…'

'Well, *I'm* not doing your dirty work for you,' Lara hissed, 'it's time you stopped sneaking around and faced up to your mistakes.'

He didn't even acknowledge her; he was looking at me, a pained expression on his face.

'Is it money? You've been spending a lot lately, I haven't said anything because I didn't want to cause a row, but...' The day before he'd taken five thousand pounds from our joint account, I hadn't said anything at the time because I thought it might be for a silver wedding gift for me, maybe a deposit on that second honeymoon in the Maldives we'd often talked of. 'If you've spent it in the bookies, or the pub or on something else, then I'm pissed off,' I said, suddenly realising why he'd started putting love notes in the coffee jar. It was to appease me for whatever he'd been up to this time. 'But don't let it ruin the party Mark, we have safety money in another bank account...' I didn't want to say too much; it was humiliating for me to talk to him like his banker in front of Lara. 'Is it that the US deal hasn't come off and you feel you can't tell me?' It was the only thing I could think of, the only thing that would really upset him – his American dream collapsing. And when something like that happened to Mark, a visit to the pub, or to the bookies to put whatever money he had on a sure-fire winner at the races usually followed. 'Give me *something*, Mark,' I pleaded.

He was shaking his head. 'No, the deal's on, money isn't the issue.'

'*TELL* her,' Lara yelled at him, making us both start.

'Oh God! You're having an affair... you and... Lara?' I could barely say it. I'd left the obvious until now, tried everything else because I refused to believe that my husband and my best friend would do that to me. I was looking from one to the other, not knowing who had hurt me the most.

The colour had drained from Mark's face, his flesh now yellowy rather than the usual tan.

'Carly, I... I feel dreadful. I never planned for it to be like this—'

I put my palms on my ears. 'I can't hear this. Not tonight – not on our wedding anniversary,' I heard myself say. Like it would have been fine to tell me any other night.

'I love you, in my own way, you know that… always will. But she said if I didn't tell you, *she* would,' he said, glancing over at Lara, who looked so angry, so bitter, and at the same time like she was holding back tears.

'Christ, there are 120 people in the garden waiting for us to cut bloody cake, Mark!' I replied, irrationally, like the cake cutting was the issue here. 'What do I do… go out there and tell them my husband's having an affair with my best friend? Perhaps you two would like to cut the sodding cake?'

'No, Carly!' Lara's voice was raised.

'Darling, we can't let this get out, if it does everything's ruined,' Mark was saying, as he walked over to me still leaning on the desk, shaking my head vigorously, like it would somehow knock out all the thoughts I was having.

'Is that all you can think about?' I asked, incredulously.

'The tabloids would crucify me, we'd lose everything… the American offer would be off the table.' He was pleading with me, pleading for his life, his future – *their* future.

'You can't keep this one quiet, you snake,' Lara snapped. She looked like she wanted to punch him. Almost as much as I did. She stood up from the chair, finally able to face me. 'It isn't *me*,' she was saying gently, trying to control the wobble in her voice. As she walked, her arms opened out to me as though I were a wild animal needing to be calmed.

I edged back, opening the door, about to run, when Mark spoke.

'It's *Erin*,' he blurted, 'I've been seeing Erin.'

I looked from one to the other. 'Is this a joke? 'Erin, who's twenty-four, Phoebe's friend? Your *daughter* Erin?' I said to Lara, desperately hoping there was another Erin.

Lara nodded through tears. 'Carly, I'm so sorry. I only found out myself this afternoon. She called me in a state, I went to see her, and… I had no idea,' she said. 'But I feel as bad as if it were me – and I wanted you to know, you *should* know. You *have* to—'

'We can get through this, Carly,' Mark moved in. 'I love you and the kids and—'

'I knew you were a coward, but this is weak even for you,' Lara hissed. '*Tell* her!'

'Okay, calm down, Lara, for God's sake. Can't you see how upset she is?'

He and Lara were staring at each other, neither giving way.

Mark took a step towards me, and I lifted up both hands.

'No, you couldn't, I don't believe it – it's obscene, she's like a daughter to us.'

At this, Lara burst into fresh tears and stormed from the room, while Mark just kept repeating under his breath like a mantra, 'I'm sorry, I'm so sorry.'

I stared ahead, numb.

'Go, Mark.'

'I can't just—'

'GO,' I yelled, still unable to sully my eyes by looking at him. How could he do this?

'But… the party?' he said, looking at the closed door of the office that Lara had slammed in her escape. 'What will people think?'

'That phrase will be written on your grave, Mark,' I said, standing in the middle of the room, waiting for him to leave, but I could see he didn't want to. I knew then, as he stood there weak and pitiful, that however deep I dug, I couldn't find any more love for this man. Like a thief, he'd been stealing it from me for years, piece by piece, crumb by crumb, and now all that was left was a residue of hurt, a tidal wave of anger, and all the wasted years. I was finally done with him.

'I don't *want* to leave you,' he tried.

'You have to, I don't want you here. It's over, Mark, you've gone too far.'

'Don't say that, let's talk.'

'We've done all our talking. I want you out of my house and out of my life.' I turned to him.

'But the kids… what will you tell them?' he asked.

'The truth? But not tonight. I'll tell them tomorrow, or perhaps you should?'

He visibly shrank. 'I don't know if I can.'

'Coward,' I spat, as I moved towards the door.

'But what do I say?' He was pleading for me to deal with this, like I'd dealt with everything difficult in our lives.

'Tell them you're leaving their mother for Erin, the kid they grew up with, who they always thought of like a sister. Tell them you'd now like them to think of her as their father's girlfriend.' With that, I walked out of the room, grabbed a glass of fizz off a passing tray and, for the next few hours, laughed and danced and drank so much until I almost forgot. Almost.

CHAPTER FOUR

The morning after the party, Mark turned up at the house. I'd been awake all night, didn't even go to bed because I knew I wouldn't sleep. After bidding goodbye to guests around 1 a.m. and packing the caterers off with many thanks, I found myself alone. I don't know how I did it. I'd been operating on pure adrenaline or pain endorphins or something. I told anyone who asked that Mark was asleep upstairs, that these days he found parties too much, something I knew would upset him; he hated anyone to think of him as middle-aged. At forty-one, his 'showbiz age' was ten years younger than his real one.

And here he was now, the morning after the night before, on the doorstep of our home, looking at least 100 years old and asking to be let in.

I didn't want to discuss this latest crisis on the doorstep, so grudgingly allowed him in, asking him to wipe his shoes, like he was a stranger.

He followed me into the house. 'Do the kids know?' he asked.

'Yes. I told them.'

He looked away. 'What did you say… what did *they* say?'

'They were shocked, angry, upset. Phoebe cried. Jake did what he always does, pretended he was okay, when he really wasn't.' I'd told them over breakfast, before they headed off back to London and Exeter. They were both hurt and horrified at what he'd done, and concerned for me. But I pretended I was fine and would be happier on my own. I didn't want them to worry about me, but I worried about them. To endure the humiliation of their father leaving for one of their contemporaries must have been very painful. I suspected it would be something that would take a while for them to accept – if they ever did.

'Oh,' was all he could say.

'Why don't you talk to them yourself? You have both of their phone numbers,' I said challengingly.

'No… I'll leave it for now.'

Again, I saw his cowardice and remember thinking, how had that passed me by? God knows, he wasn't perfect, far from it, and like most wives of twenty-five years, if you asked me what my husband's faults were, the list would be long. But being a coward wasn't something I'd considered – it was a new one for my growing list. He hadn't argued too much about leaving the previous evening because he knew that in his absence I'd tell the children and clear up some of the mess he'd made. It was something I'd always done, not because I wanted to – but because he made a lot of mess, and he was incapable of cleaning it up.

He wanted to smoke, so we wandered through the sitting room and into the garden where less than twenty-four hours earlier I'd welcomed guests into our home to celebrate our marriage. Now that marriage had been packed away with all the glasses and crockery from the party, gone forever.

Once outside, I watched him spark a match against the bricks to light one of his filthy cigarettes. I won't miss *that*, I thought, as he leaned against the wall and sucked hard on the cigarette, looking at me like I was the problem. I stared back, imagining thick, toxic smoke, shrouding his lungs, choking the life from him, and tried not to smile at the image.

For a long time, we stood facing each other, gladiatorial in our stances, battle lines drawn.

'So, you and Erin. Is it love or mid-life stupidity?' I finally asked into the silence, punctuated only by the ripple of waves and the birds making their presence felt.

He looked down. 'I didn't expect this, not at my age. I didn't think I could ever feel this way again,' he said, slowly bringing his eyes up to meet mine.

'Wow.' I looked up into the sky. I couldn't look at him just then. I sighed. 'So you *do* think it's love then, this fling with a twenty-four-year-old?' I almost laughed out loud at the cliché.

'I don't *think*… I *know* it *is*.' He at least had the sensitivity to say this like it was difficult to say to his wife. Or perhaps I was giving him far too much credit, and it wasn't sensitivity, he just didn't want to leave himself open to another insulting remark from me. Considering the humiliation I was about to endure when all this got out, I reckoned I had every right to make him feel embarrassed about this. 'The thing is, being with you has emasculated me,' was his next line, straight out of *The Cheating Husband's Handbook*.

You really are a ridiculous and predictable man, I thought, mentally adding another two flaws to the list.

And as if on cue, he then added, 'Carly, I work long hours, I've given everything for my career – I've kept this house going, looked after you and the kids. But I *still* have to ask permission if I want to buy something – like I'm a child. And you even tell me off for drinking… "slow down, Mark," you say, if we're at a party and I'm having a good time. It's embarrassing.'

'Oh no,' I roared. 'You've been gone a matter of hours, and you will *not* rewrite history. Yes, I manage the money in our accounts, pay all the bills, and work out your expenses, but that's because you can't be trusted not to piss it away on a new jacket, a few shirts from Savile Row, or go on a bender for twenty-four hours and pay everyone's drinks bill!' I paused, taking a breath, then ploughed on. 'And you may have conveniently forgotten, but my mother left this house to *me* when we married, and on our first wedding anniversary I gave you half. Everything after that was – and I say this generously – a joint effort. I took care of the house, the kids—'

'But *I'm* the one who earns the money. I went out there and worked,' he whined.

'And I *put* you out there. Mark, I *started* your TV career, and I've maintained it. Jesus, I even wrote your scripts – I still do.'

'Yeah okay, but I'm the success here. I should be driving a decent car, but when I tried to, you put your foot down…'

'*That* car… that car you'd planned to buy was a £100,000 midlife crisis on wheels.' I could hear my voice rising to screaming pitch. 'You haven't a clue, you've earned a fortune over the years and pissed it away on drinking, golf club memberships, that flat in London, designer suits – all way beyond your means.'

'It comes with the territory. I have to look good, I'm selling a dream…'

'Now you sound like Estelle. For God's sake, Mark, you're a DIY man with a bit of pizzazz who earns decent money on TV, not some million-dollar film star. You don't *need* suits that cost thousands – who do you think you are?'

'Those suits are what got me the American deal – along with bloody hard work and *my* talent.'

That shocked me. The US deal was something we'd both dreamed about together, we'd made all kinds of plans, and now the kids were off our hands, I'd been keen to spend time out there. He'd agreed, even joked about me living in my LA pad with pool boys and cocktails. Obviously now we'd parted, the plan would change, and it would be eight-stone Erin lying by the pool in her tiny bikini instead. After everything I'd done for him, and his career, the minute he hit the big time, I wasn't just being dropped like a hot coal, I was also being written out of everything I'd worked for with him. But even if he'd chosen a new model more fitting to his new lifestyle in LA, surely I should have some credit?

'I know our marriage has been a compromise, but that was your choice,' I said. 'I would have carried on, we had a partnership of sorts. We could have continued, you didn't have to run off with some young—'

'Our life, what we had… it wasn't *enough* for me, Carly.'

We stood in silence as I digested this. 'It wasn't enough for *me* either,' I finally responded. 'Who wants to live like we did? It wasn't a *marriage*, but I was happy to keep the wheels on, get the kids safely into adulthood. I did the hard yards, the hungry years, we shared the work, I supported you as much as I could. I was there for the good times, and turned a blind eye when things weren't so good, and now, just when things are about to change and you're off to start a new, exciting life, built on *our* dreams, you dump me for a… a little girl?'

He sighed, finishing his cigarette, and dropped it on the ground, screwing his heel into it. 'She isn't a little girl, she's a woman, and mature for her age.'

That made me bristle. 'I really don't understand what's so special about her that you'd give up everything. Admit it, Mark, this is just a one-night stand that you can't shake off.'

'No, I…' He was uncertain, but he went ahead anyway. 'Erin isn't a one-night stand.'

'You *disgust* me,' I volleyed back, anger taking over again. My emotions roller-coastered between hurt and fury and I wanted to lash out. So I hit him where it hurt. 'The *Sun* called me this morning asking why you'd left your own party in a hurry.'

His face turned white. 'What? What the hell… How do they *know*? You haven't said anything, have you?'

'I was too upset last night to know what I said to whom,' I replied calmly, enjoying the horror on his face. 'But I doubt it. As you know, I'm *very* discreet.'

'So how the hell…?'

'There was Charlotte the journalist with the lovely red hair. She might have called them? I couldn't understand why you invited her, I thought she'd be too young even for you, but now I'm not so sure; she's older than Erin after all. And there were a couple of photographers hanging around the bottom of the road taking shots of the gaggle of loud Z-listers you also invited…' I offered, before adding, 'I think *you* call them "friends". Perhaps one of *them* is on speed dial to the press?'

'Bloody journalists make me sick.'

I laughed, bitterly. '*You* people make me sick, calling up the media when you want publicity, posing for any photographs to make you look good, visiting a children's hospital and begging the tabloids to turn up. But it works both ways, as you know, and those same tabloids, quite rightly, will turn up for the other stuff too; you don't get to choose. And you can visit a million sick children now for your photo opportunities, but you won't hide the fact you left your faithful wife for a twenty-something you used to babysit for.'

He began pacing around a small patch of garden, completely lost in panic, as I watched on, wearing a smug smile of mere bravado to cover all the hurt and anger I was feeling.

He was now biting his lip, clearly trying to clamp down his rage. Things usually went Mark's way in life, he made sure of it, he always managed to charm people into doing what he wanted, but this was different.

'Promise me you won't talk to the press…' he said, still pacing, looking at the ground, trying to come up with a deal, a plan, a way out of this. And it struck me he seemed more engaged, more passionately invested in this, than when he was trying to convince me of his feelings for Erin.

'Are you upset… do you feel jealous – about Erin?' he suddenly asked, looking up, emerging from his panic for a moment to have his ego stroked.

'Jealous? No,' I said quickly. In truth, I didn't know how I felt; it was too early to gauge my emotions. I just knew I was horrified that it was Erin, and having only been made aware of this a matter of hours before, I was still processing it. After the shocking revelation, my first instinct had been to make sure the children knew, and that I relayed the information to them as gently and as painlessly as I possibly could. After that, my second instinct was to keep my home and my heart intact. Analysing my finer feelings going forward, like pain and jealousy, was a luxury I hadn't yet had.

Mark was now on his phone. 'Estelle, I have to talk to you… There may be a problem with the press…' he started, and marched up the garden. He didn't want me to hear. I wasn't in his camp any more, and overnight had gone from most trusted aide to as big a threat as the tabloids. I was now a danger to him. I might give interviews, and might even tell the truth for once. He was nodding, animated, and I watched him desperately trying to save himself as he stood at the bottom of the garden, at the edge of the cliff drop. A storm was coming in, and the sea was swirling beneath him.

I moved inside as the skies turned black.

When he eventually got off the phone, the storm had moved closer, and lightning ripped through the sky as he pulled open the bifold doors and stomped inside.

'Carly, look, Estelle wants to set up a strategy,' he announced excitedly, his adrenaline clearly high after talking to Estelle.

'A strategy? Does she?'

'Yes, she should have thought this through before now, should have realised that given Erin's age, once I told you, the press…'

'I'm sorry I'm giving you and Estelle such a difficult day,' I sighed, stretching out on the sofa like a cat. I pretended not to care, but was surprised at the sting – even his agent knew about Erin and the end of my marriage before me.

'Your sarcasm isn't helping.'

'Neither is your infidelity,' I countered.

'Thing is,' he said, ignoring my comment, gazing out of the window, his back to me, running stressed fingers through his thick, silver hair, 'we need a narrative for this.'

'Oh wait, I have one.' I sat up, my hand in the air like a kid at school. 'You've been having sex with someone almost thirty years your junior, who you've known since she was born. And… you decided to break it to your wife during her silver wedding party…' I stopped for a moment and thought about this, then suddenly, overwhelmed with sadness, I asked, 'Mark, why did you do that?'

'What?' He turned to me; he looked defensive. There was something else, something he hadn't told me.

'Tell me at our anniversary party?' I pressed.

'Well, Erin told Lara about us yesterday afternoon and Lara went mad, said I had to tell you.'

'Yeah, but Lara's my friend, she wouldn't have *insisted* you tell me on my silver wedding anniversary, especially not at the party. Why was she so insistent you did it last night?'

He couldn't meet my eyes. And I knew, in that instant I knew *why* Erin wasn't a one-night stand. And I knew why Lara hadn't been able to sit on this to spare my feelings, even though she knew how hurt I would be. This must have been unbearable for her, torn between the feelings of her daughter and her closest friend.

'Erin's pregnant, isn't she?'

CHAPTER FIVE

SIX MONTHS LATER

It was now early spring, with a promise of blossom, and a tingle of warmth on the breeze blowing in from the sea. It had been six full months since Mark left, and I was finally starting to lift my head and feel like me again, a new me. I wasn't the me who'd sipped champagne and danced on the lawn with my husband the night of the party. I would never be *her* again. I'd done my apprenticeship in the career of 'wronged wife'. I'd lived the cliché of discovering that everyone seemed to know about this affair except me. I'd also heard second-hand from 'friends' about my husband and his girlfriend's cosy cottage by the sea, and lived through the agony of our kids' reluctant acceptance of his new relationship. I'd blamed him, her, me, his career – and me again.

As for the baby, I found that very hard to accept, especially with it now being due. *His baby. Her baby.* We'd only just begun divorce proceedings, and even though I had no real feelings left for Mark, I sometimes wondered what might have been. I grieved for the hope of those early days, when I thought he was perfect, and the future seemed to hold such promise. And as emotionally detached from him as I was, I found it hard to imagine us not being married. The idea of Mark as someone else's husband, and the father of a child that wasn't mine, felt unreal. In spite of what our marriage had become, Mark and I were bonded, we were a public couple, who'd shared much of our lives with newspapers and magazines. There was the house too, it held our past, and had made us what we were, on so many levels. But what really held us together, for better or worse, were our secrets.

The kids had just about coped with their parents splitting up. I assumed when children were adults they didn't feel the break-up quite so much, but as Phoebe said, 'It's still your family ripped apart, however old you are.' Phoebe came home from London every couple of weeks. I loved when she visited, but wished she didn't have such pity in her eyes. I usually spent her visits insisting I was fine and happy, while she looked doubtful. 'I hate him for what he's done to you,' she'd say. She couldn't bear to even speak about Mark, and referred to Erin as 'her' or 'it'. My daughter didn't mince her words and said her father had created 'a sordid mess' of all our lives. Once I would have attempted to paper over the cracks, and in an attempt to protect my kids, I'd cover for Mark, but not anymore.

Jake managed to avoid even mentioning the situation. I tried to talk to him, but he made it clear he was uncomfortable, so I decided to leave it until he was ready to talk, if ever. People process what happens in their lives in different ways, and Jake was more like me, he bottled it all up, until he couldn't and only then would he show his feelings. After Mark and I split, Jake had reluctantly gone back to his second year at university; he enjoyed the course but offered to take a year out to stay home with me. 'No, that would really make me unhappy,' I'd said, though part of me would have loved to have had him home. 'I want what's happened between Dad and me to impact yours and Phoebe's lives as little as possible.'

'I just worry about you and the house,' he'd said. 'When I get a job, Mum, I'll come back here and we'll make it like new again.' My son had always been a loving, caring child, and like his father, he wanted everything to be perfect. I worried he'd never find a girl that would be good enough for him, because he was such a perfectionist. Phoebe was single too, and I sometimes wondered if our kids had seen our marriage for what it was and subconsciously avoided relationships. Mark's betrayal and our subsequent split had made the fear deeper.

My own wounds were slowly healing, and showing the kids it was possible to move forward was probably the best thing I could do for them. So, feeling less bruised, if still tender, I was six months on from the split and ready to make some big changes. The first thing I did was to visit the hairdresser and ask for a total makeover. I'd always kept my hair shoulder-length with highlights, but Sally agreed I was ready for something fresh. I didn't need to tell her about my break-up; everyone in town had been talking about it.

'Of all the couples in all the world, I always thought you guys would stay together,' she'd sighed, as she lopped off most of my hair. I didn't say much, just agreed with her in all the right places.

An hour later, I was looking at a much younger woman, with a bleached-blonde short crop. 'I have cheekbones!' I exclaimed in wonder, turning my head in the mirror.

'You look fabulous. Now go get 'em, girl,' Sally said, laughing at my delighted surprise.

I was on my way to the till, when I spotted Gemma, one of the 'Yummies', having her highlights done.

'Hey, stranger,' she said, 'how are you?'

I wished I'd been able to avoid this encounter, and felt uncomfortable; this was one of the first people I'd seen who'd been at the party, and it brought back such painful memories. How I'd giggled with Mark about these women, but how Gemma and her friends must be giggling about me now.

'I'm great,' I said, feeling the flush of embarrassment creep up my neck, 'and you?'

'Better than ever,' she replied, smiling widely, her teeth too perfect to be real. Then, after a moment, she seemed to remember the situation, and the smile transformed immediately to a look of camp horror. Her hand shot out from under her salon gown, and grabbed my arm. 'Sorry… about you and Mark,' she said, looking up at me insincerely.

'Oh it's fine… I'm fine… honestly.' I tried to pull away, but she wouldn't let go. I was aware of long nails digging in my flesh.

'Are you sure?' she asked playfully, the dazzling, fake smile now restored.

'Yes, I'm *absolutely* sure,' I replied, desperate to get away. She was too intense.

'So,' she paused a moment, and focused her eyes on mine, 'you're finally leaving the way clear for the rest of us, eh?' Her eyes locked on mine, the hand still firm on my arm.

'I'm sorry?' I said, slightly confused.

'Your silver fox, he's now free to roam,' she smiled.

'I have to go—' I said, and pulled away.

'Yeah, I'll call by, Carly, we need a catch-up… how about next Tuesday?'

'Sorry, I can't,' I said, and was so eager to get away, I left the shop without even giving Sally a tip.

I almost ran home, feeling really unsettled. Gemma obviously knew we were separated, but apparently knew nothing about Erin. It looked like Mark and Estelle had done their usual PR magic and kept that out of the press and even off the yummy mummy radar. I couldn't believe the bare faced cheek of Gemma, telling me that the field was clear and presumably she would now be making a play for Mark. I wondered how many other women were waiting in line to step in? I remember Gemma turning up at the house once about 8 p.m., she had a bottle of wine and said she'd wanted to chat. I'd invited her in, and within minutes Mark appeared, and for the rest of the evening, I felt like a gooseberry. She'd clearly turned up to see him, not me. Well, she was free to go after him now, but I wouldn't be playing hostess any more.

I arrived home, tried to forget all about Gemma and called Ryan Jarvis. He'd been so organised and helpful at the party and mentioned he was doing building work, so I asked him to come over and give me some quotes on maintenance work for the house. He said he could come over right away, which was a great relief, because the house was in desperate need of some TLC.

In spite of my still slightly bubbling anger and resentment at my new-found status, the new haircut had given me confidence. I'd been covering myself up, hiding in Mark's shadow all these years, and was rather cheered by the prospect of taking back control. Until now, I realised I'd spent the recent years of my marriage with my life on pause, and it was exciting to be starting afresh with new possibilities. But as I waited for Ryan to arrive, I received an unexpected and not very nice reminder of that old life with Mark when a letter arrived.

It was a pale blue envelope, with my name written on, no stamp or address, so it had been hand delivered. As I'd cut myself off for the past few months, I assumed it was a friend, getting in touch, and was sorry I'd missed them. But when I opened it, the note wasn't anything like I expected.

Hope you're enjoying life as a single woman, Carly. But now you're living alone in that big house, you might want to double-lock your doors. Anyone could get in, and who knows what might happen?
It wasn't your Forever Home after all, was it?

Love x
PS. LOVE the new hair BTW!

I felt a prickle of fear sting my stomach, and immediately saw Gemma's face, her eyes locked on mine, the fingernails in my flesh. Who else could it be? She was the only person I knew who'd seen my hair. The thought unsettled me and I could feel my hand start to shake.

I used to rip up letters like this, when I was with Mark, so-called fans resenting me for being married to the man they felt was theirs. While he received women's underwear, and invitations to bed, I'd get nasty notes filled with bile addressed to me, from all over the country. Mark used to say: 'Be flattered – they're just jealous because you have a gorgeous husband and a lovely home.' Over the years, I'd received many letters telling me I was fat, ugly, punching above my weight, a witch, and the actual devil. But this one felt different. The threatening tone felt calculated, intimate even. It had been hand-delivered by someone who knew me and... had obviously seen my hair. It had to be Gemma.

I didn't rip it up, because it seemed more sinister than the usual celebrity stalker bile. I would keep it to show the police, and I was just picking up my phone to call them, when the front doorbell rang.

I froze. What if it was her? She'd threatened to call round, hadn't she? Perhaps she was pissed off because I rejected her suggestion about calling in the following Tuesday?

I didn't answer the bell, just held my breath, hoping she'd go away, but then rang again, and again, and in the end, I just picked up a bottle of wine, the nearest thing that was vaguely weapon-like, hid it behind my back, and walked into the hall, opening the door slowly, bracing myself.

I stayed well behind the door, waiting for Gemma's bright blonde smile, the insincere dazzle. But to my great relief, it was Ryan standing there. I almost hugged him because he wasn't Gemma.

'Hey,' he smiled, 'I was just beginning to think you'd gone out.'

'No... I was in the garden, sorry. I didn't hear the bell,' I lied, ushering him into the house, realising I was still holding my wine weapon, and felt rather foolish; living alone was making me paranoid.

'Thanks for coming round so quickly,' I said, discreetly leaving the bottle on the hall table. 'Considering Mark's job, you'd think our house would be perfect, but it's been deteriorating for a few years now,' I explained. 'The thing I'm most worried about are the cracks that have appeared on the outside.' I guided him into the kitchen diner, through the bifold doors and onto the patio, where I began running my hands along the once smooth exterior. 'I just hope they aren't serious,' I said. 'I only noticed them a couple of weeks ago, but I'm sure they're even deeper than the last time I checked.'

'They've probably been there a long time, you just didn't notice.'

'Yeah, I… well, I've been busy,' I said, avoiding his eyes.

He lifted his head in acknowledgement, but looked uncomfortable; he clearly knew all my business. It was a small town, we were well-known and there'd been lots of rumours. As Sally my hairdresser had pointed out, 'Everyone knows what happened, or think they do.' I hadn't been out much in town, just bought groceries and kept my head down, but it was clear from their reactions that the few people I had bumped into knew. They either tried to avoid conversation with me or asked how I was while gazing pityingly into my face like I was bereaved.

Fortunately, Ryan seemed more interested in the wall and wasn't too daunted by the cracks in the façade, which gave me some comfort. 'However bad they are, I'm sure we can sort them for you,' he said, with the confidence of a skilled surgeon addressing a rather nervous patient. I was grateful for his reassurance.

'Do you enjoy working in the building trade?' I asked.

'Yeah. Yeah. I just… it's hard work. We don't have as many helpers as Mark does on *his* show!' He laughed, then seemed to realise what he'd said and looked at me with a slight apology in his eyes.

'It's okay, I can bear to hear his name,' I said, rolling my eyes. 'You're right, he has an army of off-camera experts helping him.' I remembered our first programmes when we did the work together, just the two of us. They were happy times, mostly. I recalled them through a rather rose-tinted haze; our blonde-haired Boden-clad children and long-gone Lottie, our fluffy white dog, were regularly filmed trooping from the garden down the rocky path to the beach. Musical montages of me and our little ones covered in paint, 'helping' Daddy, Phoebe in a tutu chasing butterflies in the garden, sunshine on her hair, baby-teeth smiles, and of course the famous shots at the end of every programme of Mummy and Daddy carrying their little angels to bed. 'In the early days, there were no assistants, and just a couple of cameramen and a director,' I said. 'The children and I were the helpers then...'

'I remember. I was just a kid, but Mum loved watching the programme.'

'It was very popular, and to give him his due, Mark has moved it on; you can't stay in the past forever,' I sighed, thinking of my kids, silently grieving for their baby teeth, the days of shiny new school shoes, and the silence of their sleeping.

'Do you think you'll stay here, now...' he asked.

I was sure he'd just stopped himself from saying 'now your husband has left', but I rushed in before he could continue. 'Yes, I want to stay, it's my home.'

'You're not scared, here on your own?'

'No. God, you sound like my kids,' I said, laughing, putting my hands in my jeans pocket and alighting on the blue envelope I'd stuffed in there when Ryan arrived. My heart sank. 'I do worry, about people knowing I'm alone,' I sighed, 'especially Mark's so-called fans.'

He nodded. 'I remember you told me you had a break-in once. A stalker left rose petals on your bed.' He shook his head. 'That would freak me out.'

'Yeah. I was used to abusive notes from crazed fans, but the rose-petal stalker left a love note, a proper love note. it was so... intimate.' I felt a shiver run through me just thinking about it. 'I was more concerned for the kids; they both had problems sleeping for a long time after. Jake was about seven, and seemed to think it happened because his dad was away, but actually it was because his dad *lived* here,' I added, not really wanting to think about it. The whole event overwhelmed me still. 'Anyway, I'm fine, and enough about me, can I get you a coffee?' I asked, making a mental note to burn the contents of the blue envelope later.

'I'll have a coffee if you're having one,' Ryan answered.

'Always,' I said with a smile, and left him to look at the wall and work out what needed doing.

As I waited for the kettle to boil, I opened the drawer and put the envelope inside. I would leave it there for now and think about what to do – if anything. Had I overreacted? I would have been able to dismiss it if the note hadn't mentioned my hair, but whichever way I looked at it, Gemma was the only one who'd seen it. I tried to push these thoughts in the drawer with the note, and filled a tray with a cafetière and a plate of home-made lemon cake, and took it outside to Ryan.

Once outside, I studied him discreetly as he took out his notebook and made some notes. He wasn't smooth or educated like Mark, he was completely different. He was wearing jeans and a T-shirt, and I spotted a couple of tattoos on his upper arms, which were quite muscly; he definitely worked out. He seemed nice though, not full of himself like his brother Max, who'd always seemed quite brash, and loud.

'Is it terminal, Doctor?' I asked, as I put the tray on the outdoor table.

'I think she'll live,' he said, turning around, smiling. 'Oh, coffee, thank you.'

He immediately put away his notebook and joined me at the table, where I poured us both some coffee.

'I remember your lemon cake, it's delicious,' he said, taking a slice. 'When I was little and sometimes came by with Dad, you'd give us lemon cake. I loved it,' he added, through crumbs. 'I remember you baking one on the telly once.'

'Ooh, you are a hardcore Andersons' fan,' I laughed. 'I think I only did a couple of cooking segments. And that was very early on.'

'I remember, and the other time you made blueberry muffins,' he pointed to the little that was left of his cake, 'this tastes as delicious as it did when I was a kid.'

I think I blushed slightly, flattered he'd remembered. Visits from my children aside, I'd lived in splendid isolation for months, and it was nice to be appreciated by another human being. I offered him the plate, and he took another slice.

'I haven't baked for ages.' I gazed out onto the garden. 'Haven't done the garden either – haven't done a lot of things in the past few months, to be honest.'

He stopped eating for a moment, and put down his cake.

'You seemed to be okay?' he said. It was a question more than a statement.

'Oh yeah. Between us, me and Mark had been over for a while, I just don't think we realised. But we still love and respect each other,' I said, sticking to the script, using exactly the same phrase from the press release Estelle and Mark had created.

'Still, it's hard on you.' He continued to eat his cake, looking at me in a way I couldn't interpret, so I just kept on talking.

'It is hard, being alone, but it also has bonuses. I realised this morning that I've been married longer than I haven't. I'd almost forgotten how it feels to be...' I wasn't sure how to explain how I felt to myself, let alone a thirty-something man I didn't really know.

'How it feels to be *you*?' he offered, taking a sip of coffee.

'Yeah, that's exactly it,' I said, surprised at how intuitive this beach-bum builder seemed to be. 'I didn't have you down as the sensitive type, Ryan Jarvis,' I laughed, taking a sip of coffee.

'You think I'm just some hairy builder then?' he teased.

'No, I didn't mean… I guess I just didn't expect you to under-stand the complexities of being a suddenly single, middle-aged woman.'

'Oh, you'd be surprised, us surfer boys run deep, Mrs Anderson,' he said, and I noticed a twinkle in his eye.

'I've told you before, it's *Carly*, don't make me feel any older than I already do.'

'You're not old, *Carly*.' He pronounced my name slowly, then laughed. 'You've still got it going on,' he added, then seemed to realise he may have been a bit too complimentary, and looked away. I could feel my face burning up.

'Mmm, well just remember, call me Carly,' I said awkwardly, and tried to make myself busy gathering the plates together.

'I just find it hard to call you Carly,' he said.

'Well, if you call me Mrs Anderson, I won't answer,' I joked and, turning to look at him, saw his eyes hot on my bare arms. Ryan was having an effect on me that I found quite discomfiting. I wasn't sure what was happening; I didn't want him to feel he had to flirt with the old lady to secure some work. 'You know, I like the way the house is…' I said, turning back to the house, and keeping my eyes firmly on the brickwork. 'It needs some maintenance, which is why I asked you to pop over.' I kept talking. 'But there's nothing I'd massively change.'

'I think you're right, I wouldn't either.' We both gazed back at the house, and his eye seemed to catch on something. He stood up and wandered a little closer to the bifold doors on the back of the extension; he was checking the lock. 'Have you had a break-in?'

'No. Why?'

'Just – it looks like someone's tried to get in here.' He stood back slightly as I walked towards the area he was pointing to; the metal had been damaged.

'Oh God, looks like someone's tried to break the hinge,' I said, my mind immediately going to the creepy note I'd opened less than half an hour ago.

'It could just be that the door was open and the wind caught it,' he replied. I think he may have been trying to placate me.

But I didn't care, even if it *was* just the wind, first the note and now this – I was beginning to feel very vulnerable. 'Can you fix it, make sure it's secure?'

'Yeah of course, no problem. I'll secure it now temporarily, then finish it when I come back – that is if you decide to book me of course.' He was looking at me quite intently.

'Yes, I'm sure I will book you, Ryan, as long as you don't rip me off. I'm single now remember.' I wanted him to know I wasn't easily flattered by his intense stares; I was no pushover.

'God, I wouldn't dream of ripping you off, I wouldn't rip *anyone* off.' He looked so crushed, I completely backtracked.

'Sorry, I was joking,' I said, and changed the subject 'What do you think about the floor here in the sitting room?' I started, stepping inside, and he followed. 'Mark wanted to correct it.'

'Oh, the slope?'

'Yeah. Do you think it needs levelling?'

He shook his head.

'Good, because I like it, it reminds me of when the kids were little and they'd lie down and I'd roll them along the floor.' I giggled, glad there was something left for me in the rubble of my previous life. 'Mark was a perfectionist, hated anything out of place, anything slightly flawed,' I murmured, almost to myself.

'Shame he didn't spot the cracks on the exterior walls,' Ryan sighed.

'Yeah, well, this place has been a bit neglected the last couple of years – by both of us,' I added. Despite his earlier obsession with changing the house, once Mark had ripped down walls, added new windows, extensions, and anything else he could think of – he'd got bored and found other places to work on.

'Yeah, I guess he was too busy doing other people's houses to work on his. I've seen his new programme. Amazing how he turns people's old houses into these awesome builds.'

'Yeah, awesome,' I said, trying to sound like I meant it. 'Would you like some more coffee?' I offered. I'd had enough Mark talk for a lifetime.

'No thanks, Mrs… *Carly*,' he remembered, and we both smiled at this. 'I'm doing some more estimates today, so need to get going.'

'Oh. Okay,' I said, surprised at my disappointment that he had to leave.

I followed him through into the kitchen. When we reached the front door, before I could mention that you needed to twist and pull the lock, he'd done it.

'You know about the lock?' I said, intrigued.

'Yeah. From when I used to come along with my dad and give him a hand. I loved it when the telly people were here,' he replied, turning to look around the hall. 'I know this house like my own – every nook and cranny.'

I recalled the gangly youth who used to hang around with Ted; it was hard to believe he was standing before me now, over six feet, and he'd filled out a bit since then.

'I'll wait for your estimate,' I called after him, as he wandered down the drive to his van.

'Yeah, busy time of year,' he opened his van door, half in, half out, 'so let me know as soon as you can so I can book you in. I have a slot tomorrow, and the rest of this week if you're interested?'

This panicked me slightly, I didn't know if I could afford him, but didn't want him to get booked up either. 'Okay, start tomorrow, but just let me know how much it is first,' I said.

'Sure.' He lifted his hand in a static wave, climbed into his van and shut the door. I gave him a little wave back, and had turned to go inside the house when I heard him call me.

'Carly?' He'd started the engine, wound down the window and was half leaning out.

I turned and smiled.

'Are you *sure* you're okay out here all on your own?'

I was touched at his concern. 'I'm fine. I'm used to being here alone. It's my home.'

I closed the door, wondering why Ryan Jarvis was so concerned about my safety. And in light of the note, and the broken hinge on the bifold doors, I was beginning to wonder if I really was okay, out here all on my own.

CHAPTER SIX

The next day I decided to go into the town. I needed some groceries and a change from the faceless supermarket. I was also concerned about money; things had been really tight since Mark left. We were in the early stages of the divorce, so I had no idea how that would shake down. I'd been promised twenty per cent of the money from the American deal, but who knew if and when that was going to pay out? I'd started painting again, but due to my emotional bruising, my muse had left me for now, so I wasn't going to make any money from that at the moment. So, in order to make money to live on until the divorce and the American deal went through, I had to try and get a job. Spring was the perfect time to see if anyone had any work in the shops or cafes before the summer season took off.

I was just leaving when I spotted a blue envelope lying on the mat. At this, my stomach flipped. I'd convinced myself that if the last note *was* from Gemma, she'd probably sent it because she'd seen me that day. It was weird, and I didn't understand it, but it had probably been a one-off; perhaps seeing me at the salon had reignited some kind of jealousy for what I'd had before, Mark. But now, standing in the hallway looking at a second note, I felt sick.

I slowly bent down to pick it up. Yes, the envelope was exactly the same blue as the one I'd received the previous day, and I didn't know whether to read it, or just call the police. I was glad I decided to read it first, because when I opened it, I laughed with relief at myself and this strange paranoia that had hold of me. It was Ryan's estimate. Once I'd calmed down, I called him straight away to say the estimate was fine.

'Great, I'll start now,' he said.

'I'm popping out for the afternoon, so you won't be able to get in,' I replied.

'No problem, I'll come in through the side gate,' he said. 'I need access to the exterior walls, so don't need to go inside the house.'

I put the phone down thinking how easy-going he was, and how much I was looking forward to giving the house some much-needed repair and maintenance.

I hadn't ventured into Looe town much since Mark and I had split, but where else to find a job, and test my new haircut and rediscovered strength than there? Mark was the local celebrity, and naturally, as his wife, I was also known But I didn't want to hide away forever. I'd have to face people at some point, and today felt like a good day for venturing out into the real world.

It wasn't busy down in Looe. I popped into a couple of shops, the greengrocers and the cheese shop where I remember as a child my mother used to buy cheese. It felt good to be back, this was my home long before Mark Anderson came along, and I hoped that would continue long after he'd gone. I also went into a lovely shop which sold beautiful items for the home – cushions, soft furnishings, drawings and local pottery, made by local craftspeople, and they just happened to be looking for a part-time assistant. So, I filled in a form and handed it to the woman behind the counter who seemed warm and friendly. I left there feeling good; there were openings and possibilities for women like me, who'd abandoned their careers along with their dreams many years ago. I was secretly hoping that in the future, the shop might even take some of my paintings.

I walked around the town, marvelling at how life could change so quickly. I was here with Mark only the previous summer, having met him for lunch after he'd finished a morning's filming. After lunch, he had 'an important meeting' at a hotel in Plymouth, but I knew now that the 'meeting' had probably been with Erin. As we walked through the streets from the restaurant, I remembered him grabbing my hand, and I liked it, and felt like we might actually be on track to find each other again. Maybe he'd faced up to his demons, and we'd started to live in peaceful acceptance of what had gone before, while looking ahead to what was to come. 'Wow, you're being very romantic today,' I'd said, smiling.

'Well, we have to look the part, darling,' he'd replied, which crushed me slightly; did that mean he was just holding my hand because it looked good, not because he wanted to? We'd carried on walking, people stopping to chat to him, early holidaymakers asking for his autograph, or a selfie. It fed his ego, and me being there perpetuated the story, that we were happy and wholesome. Everyone wanted a little bit of Mark, even me, and after our rather rocky marriage, I'd begun to think that in spite of everything, we might just make it after all. What an idiot I was.

I dragged myself from the past when I found myself near The Silver Spoon Tearooms. I hadn't been there in a long time, and decided to go inside. I'd been visiting this traditional old Cornish tearoom since I was a little girl, when my mother would bring me for scones and clotted cream. I felt comfortable, and it was actually more pleasant to be here without Mark, because strangers didn't accost me when I was alone. It was so long ago since I'd been on the TV, no one recognised me, except for the locals, which was why I was surprised that two young women on the next table seemed to be talking about me. They weren't in my eyeline, but I heard my name and Mark's mentioned several times, and eventually glanced over to see Erin, sitting with her friend, both giving me daggers. It was like being hit with a blunt object. Even though I knew about the pregnancy, seeing her like that was a shock. And I was overwhelmed by sadness.

The last time I'd seen my husband's much younger lover was a few months before the anniversary party. Lara had called round to drop some plants off at the house; she was really green-fingered, and her own garden was like something from a magazine. She never wanted a moment of her life to be boring, and applied that theory to her garden, making sure it was always blooming, with no dull patches. Erin was waiting in the car as her mother handed me armfuls of bright green foliage wrapped in newspaper.

I'd invited her in, and told her to fetch Erin, so she beckoned her, but Erin had scowled, and in her usual sulky tone, said, 'No, Mum, we're in a hurry.' It was rude, but it was also classic Erin, and I didn't give it a second thought, but now realised the affair had been in full swing by then. I must have been the last person Erin wanted to see.

Even as a little girl, Erin had been quiet, secretive even. It was hard to reconcile that little girl with the very pregnant, round-faced young woman on the next table, carrying my husband's child.

'Seen enough?' I heard her voice; it sounded stronger, more aggressive than ever before.

I looked up to see her glaring at me, the other girl smirking.

'You've had your hair done, haven't you?'

'Yes,' I said, touching the back of my head self-consciously.

'Talk about mutton dressed as lamb!' she scoffed in her friend's direction.

I was crushed, I couldn't hide it. And she knew she'd got her bull's eye, which seemed to give her the confidence to push on.

'Aren't you going to congratulate me, Carly?'

The friend sniggered.

'Congratulate you on what, Erin?' I replied, gathering myself together for battle. I felt like a teacher steeling herself to deal with the problem girl in class.

'On mine and Mark's baby of course.' She gave a sly smile. God, she was so young, so immature. How could Mark tolerate such childishness? Presumably she compensated for that in the bedroom?

'Congratulations,' I said blankly, as the waitress arrived with my tea and scone.

Erin dragged her eyes from me to look the waitress up and down; obviously she wasn't quite sure where to take this now she'd started.

The waitress put down the teapot, then the cup and everything else involved with a cream tea. By the time she left, minutes had passed and I hoped the show was over. But Erin clearly had something else to impart.

'We're having a baby boy…'

'Really?' I said, slicing through the warm, baked scone with some vigour.

'Mark says I'm the love of his life.'

'I'm sure he did, darling… He says that to all his mistresses,' I murmured in a voice loud enough for her to hear, but hopefully not the rest of the café.

She was, for a second, taken aback. I supposed she too had believed the hype, that we were the perfect, loved-up couple, and Mark the perfect, loyal husband. But after taking a moment to digest what I'd said, she rallied quickly and, leaning over in my direction as far as her stomach would allow, hissed, 'Men cheat for a reason, Carly.'

'Yes, usually because they can't keep it in their pants.' I dropped a blob of blood-red jam onto my scone and, unsmiling, picked up the pot of clotted cream, slathering it on top of the jam, my eyes on hers, unblinking, throughout the process.

She watched me for a few moments, then turned to her friend and said in a stage whisper for everyone in the café to hear, 'The marriage was over long before I came on the scene – Mark says they hadn't been happy for years.'

'Your mother must be very proud,' I said in an equally loud voice. 'You destroyed a marriage, and broke up a family – well done,' I added, taking a large bite of the scone.

The café fell silent, save a few murmurings, with the sudden realisation perhaps of who I was and my connection to the great Mark Anderson, Looe's honorary son.

To my huge relief, Erin seemed to finish what she was eating, and called the waitress for the bill. I continued to eat, but the scone tasted to me of cotton wool now. I pretended to enjoy it, but my throat hurt to swallow, it was so closed up with anger and hurt.

Erin grabbed her shopping bags. I noticed a couple from the babywear shop that had opened last summer. It was French, expensive – thick linens and pastel hand knits. I remember saying to Lara, 'What kind of mother would be foolish enough to buy a pale pink linen dress at that price for a child under twelve months?'

'I know. For God's sake, they'll spew on it, or wee in it when they aren't dancing in mud.'

But here was her daughter buying the best French clothes for my husband's unborn baby, at eye-watering prices, while Mark dragged his feet over our financial settlement. And while they clearly were fine for money, I was out looking for part-time work, and hoping to God I could afford to keep my home – my childhood home. I discreetly watched her struggle to get out from under the table, while remembering how undignified pregnancy is. I wondered if she'd be quite so petty and mean after the birth and the stitches and the sleepless nights that awaited her.

I'd hoped she'd had her say, but should have known she wouldn't leave it there. And in a voice for everyone to hear as she headed towards the door, she said, 'Oh, Carly, you might have heard, me, Mark and our new baby are living in a tiny, two-bedroomed cottage, while you're rattling around in *his* great big house.'

'And?' I asked, taking a sip of tea.

'You should be ashamed of yourself – are you really so bitter? You won't be happy until we're on the streets,' she hissed.

I slowly put my cup back in its saucer and lifted my head to address her. 'So now you want my home? Haven't you stolen enough from me already? You dare come anywhere near *my* house and I won't be responsible for the consequences,' I spat, angrily. I didn't care who heard. The house was mine, it belonged to my family long before Mark came into my life, and I would rather die than leave it, or hand it over, to them. It was my home, and meant everything to me.

Trundling after her friend, Erin staggered through the door of the café and yelled, 'You're a selfish old COW!' She then slammed the door so hard the crockery rattled.

Everyone looked round, and then at me. My cheeks were burning, customers were staring and two of the waitresses were talking behind their hands. I wanted to die. For a moment, I contemplated throwing my money on the table and running out, but told myself I wasn't running away, I was stronger than that. So, I finished my scone and my tea and politely asked for the bill, like my husband's pregnant mistress hadn't just yelled at me in full view of everyone. Clearly Erin hadn't received Estelle's planned press release suggesting we inform the world that the break-up was amicable. Estelle's missive had been very Gwyneth Paltrow, describing my agony as 'a joyful uncoupling,' and both parties were showing 'the utmost love and respect' for each other. If this little fracas got out, Mark would have a bloody stroke, and Estelle would join him; all that about 'taking control of the narrative' had just gone up in a puff of smoke. In a matter of seconds, a chance encounter in The Silver Spoon Tearooms had escalated into something like the table-flipping scene in The Housewives of New Jersey. God, but she was unnecessarily nasty, and arrogant too – especially as Mark had betrayed me with her. Perhaps it's a generational thing, but usually when you steal someone else's husband, isn't it etiquette to show a little remorse, embarrassment, guilt even?

But this bad blood from Erin was all Mark's doing; it had had his fingerprints all over it. She'd presumably expected, or been promised, residence in our old family home, and in an attempt to appease her, and lay it on me, he'd told her I was refusing to move. He'd also let her believe the house was his, and the only reason they couldn't just move in there was because I wouldn't allow it, out of sheer bitterness and jealousy. But he hadn't reckoned on us bumping into each other, and her confronting me with the lies he'd told her. Nor had he reckoned on Erin's feisty nature, and her quick temper when she didn't get what she wanted. He would no doubt become acquainted with that soon enough, but for now they were in the honeymoon period, and I thought: *Let's see what happens when the honeymoon's over, and those baby stitches are pulling.*

Perhaps in time it would be wise to make friends with Lara again? We simply hadn't been in touch since the night of the party. I don't think either of us could face each other; she was probably too mortified, and I'd been too upset. But it wasn't Lara's fault my husband had impregnated her daughter. I missed her, and also, if Lara and I were friends again, Erin might think twice about any more public displays of hate. I sat for a while in the tea rooms, before paying the waitress with a generous tip and making as dignified a retreat as possible.

When I got home, I called Mark. He didn't answer, so I left a message telling him to talk to his 'little Rottweiler', and put her straight about the house, that it was mine, and she had no right to even suggest she move in, let alone virtually accuse me of bloody squatting. I may have raised my voice a little – and was just reaching the end of the message with, 'if that little madam ever does that to me in public again, she'll be sorry,' when I noticed Ryan, standing in the garden. Shit, the glass doors were wide open; he must have heard me.

He put his hand up in a sort of wave and I immediately ended the call.

'Oh hi, are you okay, Ryan?' I said, cringing.

'Yeah, yeah, great thanks, I'm just double-checking measurements and working out what I'll need paint-wise.'

Then he wandered round the back of the house and I didn't see him again.

I lay awake that night thinking about Erin and the way she'd spoken to me. I remember as a child Phoebe once saying she was mean and didn't play nice. She clearly hadn't changed. But it came from a deep-seated need for attention, and as a child, she'd do anything and say anything so adults would see her. Losing her father at eleven cut very deep, and though she was only a child, I think both her and Lara took on some of the guilt when he walked out into the waves that night. Lara would never talk about it; even when I asked her, she'd always say, 'Too raw, Carly, please don't.'

I think we'd all made excuses for Erin over the years, but now she was an adult, and though Lara may have contributed to the person she'd become, she couldn't be blamed for everything her daughter did. I knew Lara would be upset to think Erin was rubbing salt in the wound and trying to take my home from me. But that was never going to happen – over my dead body would Erin would get my beautiful home that meant everything to me. Over my dead body!

CHAPTER SEVEN

In the early morning, during half-dreams about Erin and a baby, I woke up thinking the smashing sound I could hear was me hitting Erin over the head with something. But it wasn't in my dream, it was real and coming from downstairs. I sat bolt upright in bed, my chest tight with fear. I glanced at the time: 6.17 a.m. What the hell was going on? As I now lived alone, I felt more vulnerable than usual, and was scared to go downstairs in case someone was there. I waited to hear if there was any more noise, but apart from the thudding of my heart, there was nothing. So after a few more minutes, I grabbed one of Jake's baseball bats from his bedroom, and slowly headed downstairs, creeping in bare feet one step at a time.

As soon as I walked into the living room, I turned on the light, and saw it. My favourite vase, a huge, handmade one that I'd bought from an art fair in town years ago. I loved that vase; it was more like a sculpture, rough in texture, blue and green and foamy, the colours and textures reminiscent of the sea. Now it was in a million pieces on the floor, and Miss Anderson was sitting daintily by the window watching me, like butter wouldn't melt.

'Oh bloody hell, Miss A, I *wish* you'd be more careful,' I said, upset about my vase, but deeply relieved. Then I realised I was talking to the cat and I needed to get a grip. My heart rate had now returned to normal, but what was happening to me? I was becoming a neurotic mess.

I was still sweeping shards of blue off the floor when Ryan arrived for work.

'You're early,' I said. It was only 7 a.m.

'Yeah, I want to make an early start,' he said absently, while watching me sweep the floor. I looked up and, before he asked, I told him, 'Miss Anderson, the cat, knocked a vase over this morning, and there are glassy bits everywhere – I'm still clearing it up.'

'It looks like it was a pretty big vase,' he replied, shaking his head. 'Surely it was too heavy for a cat to knock over?' By now Miss A was winding around his legs. 'You didn't do it, did you, Miss Anderson?' he said, bending down and picking her up.

'She likes to be called Miss A,' I said with a smile. 'Like me, she finds her full title very ageing.'

He laughed. 'I'm sure she does,' he was still holding her, stroking her chin. 'But she's refusing to take the blame for that vase. Big vase, little cat? It wouldn't stand up in a court of law, would it, Miss A?' he joked, putting her back down on the floor.

Thinking about it, he was right, the vase was really heavy and Miss A was very light, and though her nocturnal wanderings had caused some breakages before, it had only ever been a wine glass or something very small. But if it wasn't Miss A, then how *did* the vase fall?

We didn't get chance to discuss it further as I got a text just then from Mark saying he was outside. My heart sank. For months now we'd spoken only through solicitors and I still wasn't ready to see him in the flesh. But he was already knocking at the door. At least he hadn't just used his key, but then his manners were never the issue.

I didn't want him inside the house. I was just beginning to start afresh and I couldn't bear for him to bring everything into our home, and infect it with his ill-gotten happiness. Apart from the kids, and Ryan, no one had been to the house. I'd kept all the pain outside my door, not seeing people, not answering the phone or anyone's knock. A couple of friends had, at first, left a cake or a pie on the doorstep, like I was sick and needed nourishment. It was kind of them, but I didn't need their baked goods, I needed time and solitude to heal. Though we had our problems, Mark had been my husband, my companion for a quarter of a century; he was, I suppose, like all long-term partners, the devil I knew. It wasn't a marriage, it was a big agreement to differ – but it was still hard to detach myself. Like ripping a plaster off, I suppose.

What hurt me most and made me angry in the wee small hours when I was awoken by something and nothing was that I'd lost my future – the one I'd envisaged anyway. We'd planned for this, our third act in life – we'd talked often about the Maldives, the Canadian Rockies, an Australian odyssey. Anything and everything was possible, we'd bought the guidebooks, made lists of the places we'd like to visit. But first the plan was to go to the US, fly to San Francisco, and drive along the Pacific Coast Highway, landing somewhere near LA where we'd rent a place while Mark filmed the programme. At the risk of sounding bitter – and who can blame me? – Mark still *had* that future, the only adjustment for him was that he'd be accompanied on his journey by a different woman. But, for me, all those plans, all that big, wide open future, had suddenly shrunk. And it wasn't because I'd clung to my husband's career, or defined myself by him. I'd been part of his journey – I was the one who got him there. And here we were now, standing, oceans apart, in the doorway of the home we once shared, where we'd made love, celebrated birthdays, where our babies had become children, the place where we'd kept our secrets for all those years.

'Invite me in, Carly,' he asked without making eye contact.

'I can't.' I shook my head, my eyes so full of tears, I thought they might land on him.

'Please, let's not talk here. I need to see you. We need to work all this out.' His face was pleading.

'There's nothing left to work out.'

'Hey, Carly,' he said in that warm sing-song voice he used when he wanted something.

'No.'

But I knew I was being petty, so opened the door, turned my back and trudged down the hall like a sulky teenager. He followed behind. I plonked myself on one sofa while he sat down on the other.

'So what have you been up to?' he asked, like we'd met the previous week, like he hadn't ripped up my life and handed my future to another woman.

'This and that,' I said, with a tight smile. 'Oh, I had a lovely note from one of your fans, telling me I was basically going to be murdered in my bed, now I lived alone. That was nice.'

'Oh dear. Erin's getting weird messages on her Instagram too.'

'Oh, I'm sorry to hear that,' I said in a fake bright voice. 'Did she tell you we bumped into each other, stopped for a nice chat?' I said sarcastically.

'She mentioned something. And then there was the message you left on my phone about it.'

I smiled. 'My God, Mark, all the years you've tried to hide things, and in a matter of moments that girl will get you into all kinds of trouble.'

'Don't,' he said, and put his head in his hands.

'Oh dear, what a nightmare for you,' I said, my words laced with sarcasm. 'Is she not keeping to her script like I did?' What sweet justice that would be. 'You had something to hold over me, but not with her; she will sell you down the river the first time you cross her,' I warned, shaking my head. 'One false move and she'll be on that phone singing like a canary to the *Daily Mail*. And there you'll be, global at last – on the sidebar of shame.'

He sighed. 'Oh, it's all so hard, I don't think she understands what it's like for me.'

'For you?' I almost fell off the sofa. 'She tore me into shreds, in front of a whole café. I was mortified.'

'I know, and I'm sorry about… whatever happened when you two bumped into each other yesterday,' he said, wafting his hand dismissively.

'So am I. She was vile, Mark.'

'Yes, well in her defence, it might be her… condition. And she's very stressed about these anonymous Instagram messages she's been receiving.'

'Oh no. There weren't any nasty swear words in them, were there? I mean, she's such a delicate flower.' I covered my mouth with my hand in mock horror.

He shifted in his seat, clearly not amused. 'Look, don't take this the wrong way, Carly, but we wondered if… do *you* know anything about them?' He spoke gently, tipping his head to one side and adopting the 'pity' face others had recently when asking how I was.

'Piss off, Mark,' I spat, turning away. 'Of course I don't, I'm not twelve.' I could imagine them whispering about me, the two of them lying in bed wondering if I had lost it and started sending sweet little Erin cruel messages.

'I had to ask; it's an anonymous account, we don't know who—'

'Can you just stop?' I said, raising my hands, palms up. 'I *knew* I shouldn't have let you in. You've been here five minutes and you're already accusing me of—'

'Carly, I'm so sorry… it's just that we—'

'No. No you're NOT *sorry*,' I roared, stinging at the way he now used 'we' to mean her and him, not me and him, as it had always been.

'Carly… I—'

'Please don't speak, Mark. I need a minute to calm down.'

He did as I'd asked, and I got up and walked through to the kitchen area where I made some coffee. He followed me through and sat in silence, like a stranger in our kitchen, the one he'd built with his own hands.

'Why are you here anyway? I thought we were talking through solicitors?' I asked.

'I came to see if you were okay, if you're coping,' he said softly, like he cared.

'*Coping*? Without you, you mean?' My wall came right up. 'I'm doing great thanks.' I set three mugs on the kitchen worktop and spooned coffee into them while waiting for the kettle to boil.

'Have you seen the kids?' he asked.

'They call most days; they came for Sunday lunch last week.'

He nodded. 'All good?'

'As good as they *can* be. But I think it's time you made contact with them.

'It's a bit difficult…'

'You *have to* see them, Mark.'

'It's just… Erin would find it uncomfortable.'

'Wow,' I turned around and stood facing him, shaking my head, hand on hip. God, he was insensitive, and so selfish. How did I ever think this man was kind? He couldn't even put his kids before his new girlfriend.

'*She* would find it uncomfortable? *She* doesn't have to be there!' I hissed angrily. 'In fact I'm sure the kids would prefer that she wasn't, imagine how uncomfortable it would make them to have her there?'

'I know, I know, but she'd probably *want* to be there, she's a bit… insecure, with the pregnancy and everything.'

'I can imagine, poor lamb,' I turned back to make the coffee, unable to even look at him.

'Don't be like that, Carly,' he said dismissively.

'No, honestly. I'm genuinely sorry that my children make your woman-child feel so insecure. If it's any comfort to her, the new baby will, I'm sure, make your other children equally insecure.'

He didn't speak, and I began wiping down the kitchen counter wordlessly, as inside I raged.

'I don't want any – problems when the baby's born. I really don't want to hurt the kids,' he said eventually.

'I'm afraid that train has gone, Mark,' I sighed.

I turned back to the mugs, straightening them in a line unnecessarily. I couldn't bear to hear any more information regarding his new baby. I couldn't get over how much it stung, even now, when I thought I'd come to terms with the situation. But it was the kids I hurt for – my kids. No one hurts my kids. And for that I would never forgive him.

'I've dreaded coming to see you,' he said, as I poured boiling water onto coffee grains, wishing I could pour it on him.

'After what you did, I'm surprised you've had the bloody nerve to *dare* come here.'

'I didn't expect you to make me coffee either,' he remarked, taking the cup from my hands.

'You're lucky I haven't thrown it on you,' I said. The grateful victim act might wash with young, infatuated women, but I wasn't in the mood, and it was old. Very old.

'I forgot how feisty you can be.'

'Don't worry, I wouldn't waste good coffee on you now.'

'Charmer,' he said, and I couldn't help it, I smiled.

He saw this as his way in, his path to forgiveness. Mark had to be loved, by everyone, even me now after all he'd done. 'Let's talk this through like friends, not enemies, Carly. It will be so much harder if we hate each other – after all we had, we should be *kind*.'

'*Kind*? Did you just say *kind*?' His audacity was beyond my anger.

'I'm sorry, that was probably the wrong word—'

'I don't think *kindness* was on anyone's agenda when you and that… *girl* jumped into bed together.'

'No, I… It's just that everyone's using it, hashtag be kind, hashtag kill with kindness, and you know what a whore I am for a hashtag.'

'Hashtag whore?' I suggested, with a smile. 'Seriously though, Mark, have you any idea how ridiculous you are? You're the human embodiment of a midlife crisis.'

'I am only too aware of that,' he sighed.

His calm acceptance of what he was made me angry again. I wanted to lash out at him.

'You're superficial, materialistic, shallow, fake. Feel free to use all the above hashtags, you dickhead.'

'Do you feel better for getting that off your chest?' he said, seemingly unmoved by my attack.

'Yes, I bloody do.'

'Good… for a moment, I was impressed by your vocabulary, and you had to spoil it all with *dickhead*.' He had a pained expression on his face intended to amuse.

Once, that would have made me laugh, but not now. I ignored his attempt at humour. 'I have no feelings left for you, you do realise that?'

'I think you may have *hinted* at it, my love,' he joked.

'I'm not *your love*,' I snapped. It was too soon, and I'd been too humiliated for our bad marriage to become a good friendship.

'Why have you made an extra cup of coffee?' he suddenly asked, intrigued by the third mug sitting on the counter.

'Oh, I forgot,' I said, reaching for the mug. 'It's for Ryan Jarvis, he's doing some work – on the house.'

'The house doesn't *need* any work,' he said, bristling; he didn't like his territory being invaded by other men. How ironic.

'There are cracks all down the exterior – Ryan says it probably started years ago. You were too busy to notice,' I added, knowing this would sting far more than 'dickhead'.

'You should have asked *me*, I could have come over and filled it in, or at least got one of my contractors to look at it.'

'But you don't *live* here now, Mark. It's not your responsibility, so why would I?'

He shrugged, but I saw his jaw tighten; this had angered him. Good.

I left him to stew and carried Ryan's coffee outside to him.

'Aren't you going to join me for my coffee break?' he asked. It felt like he was flirting.

'No – Mark's here.' I rolled my eyes slightly, and he mirrored it, pulling an 'awkward' face.

I headed back into the house, but couldn't resist turning round to watch Ryan wandering down the garden to sit in the sunshine and drink his coffee. His T-shirt fit his firm, muscular body, and I realised I liked the way he walked, as though he had all the time in the world. How I longed to drink coffee outside with him, away from Mark and all the tension and resentment that he'd brought into the house and stirred up in me.

'How much are you paying him?' Mark asked when I stepped back into the house. He'd obviously been watching from inside. I hoped he'd seen our flirty encounter too – not that I cared, but I had an urge to hit him back. I wanted him to know that being flirtatious wasn't only for middle-aged men and younger women, it worked the other way round too. He'd done so much damage, and at times I just wanted to hurt him. I was surprised at my own feelings. Was I really so lacking in self-control that I wanted to throw hot coffee on him? Looking at him now, he seemed tired and old. How ironic that he'd swapped me for a much younger model in a vain attempt to recapture his youth. But Erin was no old man's darling, and after her previous day's performance in the tearooms, I could only imagine how high-maintenance she was, and how she had him dancing to her stiff little tune.

'So, how much are you paying him, the Jarvis lad?' Mark repeated.

'It's none of your business what I'm paying him.'

'I assume it's coming from our *joint* account?'

'Yes, the same *joint* account you use to pay that obscene monthly rental on the *country house* you've put your new child in. And her baby when it arrives,' I added.

'It's a tiny cottage, not a *country house*,' he snapped, but Phoebe told me she'd googled his new address, and it *wasn't* a tiny cottage. I guess it suited their 'narrative'. It would justify their 'Carly is rattling around that big house' trope they kept wheeling out.

'Oh yes, Erin made quite a thing about how small your rented cottage is when I saw her. And apparently I'm a selfish old cow for not just handing my house over to my husband and his lover.'

He looked embarrassed. 'Sorry, she shouldn't have said that.'

'No, Mark. *You* shouldn't have told her it was *your* house. I know exactly what you're up to, lying to her, lying to me, and we fall out with each other. Meanwhile, you sit shaking your head on the sidelines at *woman's inhumanity to woman*. You're such a manipulative bastard.'

'Ouch, Carly,' he said, playing the victim. Again. 'Anyway, she's right, our rented cottage is going to be far too small for three of us,' he went on, ignoring me.

I'd forgotten about that, how he never really listened, or paid me any attention. I hadn't noticed, I'd just grown accustomed to it, I suppose.

'Erin says she has some really happy memories here,' he continued. 'You remember how she loved playing in the garden, staying over… and look, I know you like living here, but what about somewhere new, somewhere a bit smaller that you can manage on your own?'

I simmered, just hoping he didn't say anything else because I might just boil over.

'Please don't even go there…' I started.

'Where?' he asked, playing the innocent.

'The land of make-believe, that's where! Don't *ever* think that you or her are coming anywhere *near* this house. We've already agreed that as soon as this divorce is finalised, I'm getting your half back as part of the settlement,' I said, with a warning look. 'And let's just rewind that last comment, shall we?' As sick as this sounds, I was actually starting to enjoy myself; this had been a long time coming. For years I'd just had to sit back and let things slide, for him, for the sake of his career, but not any more. 'Your girlfriend has some "wonderful memories"? I'm sure she does, of "kind, old uncle Mark" giving her piggybacks, throwing her in the air, teaching her to play cricket along with the other kids?'

He was about to smile in recognition of all this, then realised I was being sarcastic, and scowled.

'You have to admit, it's bloody weird. Do you think you might have… issues?' I asked.

'No, I don't,' he snapped. 'Erin's grown up now. I don't see the child, I see the woman.'

'I'm sorry, Mark, but I see only the child,' I said, wanting to hurt him, humiliate him as he had me. 'How do you wake up in the night, look across at the person next to you and *not* see that child?' I asked as I continued to twist the knife. 'You used to read her bedtime stories – honestly, it gives me the creeps.' I added a shudder for good measure, although in truth it wasn't much of an act.

'Oh Carly, you really do sound like some old fuddy-duddy now.' He rolled his eyes.

And I was so incensed by his dismissive attitude, he should have been so ashamed, I said, 'I was talking to a reporter, and he said the whole thing creeped him out too.'

The colour instantly drained from Mark's face, and all I could think was, *Bull's eye!*

'You haven't spoken… you didn't tell them…?' He could barely say the words.

I gave it a few seconds to torture him, then answered, 'No. Not yet anyway.'

'Don't threaten me.'

'Moi?' I put on a fake innocent face.

'You're being poisonous, Carly, it doesn't become you,' he spat. I'd finally touched a nerve; his public persona was all he really cared about, and for once, I held *his* fate in my hands.

I just shook my head. There were no words.

'It wouldn't be in your interests either for anything to come out in the papers,' he sighed. 'Remember, you're not exactly perfect yourself, are you?'

For a few seconds we just stared at each other across the kitchen, both keepers of each other's secrets. How long would this go on? Would there always be this stalemate?

'Anyway, now we've established that no one is running to the press, I've come to talk to you about far more interesting things.' He settled back in his chair, relieved I hadn't sung like a canary to one of Britain's tabloids. 'Firstly, the producer of the US show has sent me some scripts – but they're a bit… American?'

'And why are you telling me this?'

'Well, I could probably do with adding something of myself to them, you know, *my* personality, *my* little jokes… light and shade.' He shifted slightly as he said this; he knew what he was asking of me, and I was going to make him ask.

I laughed. 'You mean *my* personality, *my* little jokes… *my* light and shade?'

'Okay, okay. Anyway, I wondered if you'd mind looking over them, just a quick glance – see if there's anything… you'd include?'

So *that* was why he was here. He wanted something from me. I should have known, and to think I half-expected some kind of apology, atonement, but this was low, even for him.

I stood up, and walked across the room to take myself away for a moment.

'So? You *know* the way the scripts work – this is important, Carly. And I hoped you might just take a few minutes to look at them?'

'No,' I said, watching Ryan walk back up the garden, not even bothering to turn round and address Mark.

'What? Why?'

'For the same reason I haven't asked you to weatherproof the house – we aren't together any more, Mark! You aren't my responsibility now, you are someone else's – get Erin to give your scripts the once-over – I'm sure she'd be happy to.'

'You know she doesn't write. You had to virtually write her essays for her when she had homework from school.'

'Yeah, and look at the thanks I get.' I almost smiled at this myself.

He ignored my attempt at humour and continued, a little more tentatively. 'Thing is – she's tired all the time.'

'Well, as much as it kills me to be on team Erin, she *is* pregnant.'

He sighed. 'Yeah, but as you know, this is a really important time in my career – this is make or break. I need her to be at events with me, gladhanding the press, the producers.'

'I don't think "gladhanding" is Erin's forte.'

'I'm not sure what her forte is to be honest with you. She just spends an awful lot of time sleeping.'

'Oh no, she's not putting her unborn baby before your career, is she?' I shook my head in mock outrage. 'I always knew she was selfish! Next time you impregnate a young woman, ask to see their CV first. Looks like this one's absolutely useless.'

He made a grunting noise. I wasn't doing what he wanted; he'd thought he could sweep over to the house, ask me to write his scripts and I'd just do it. But in his absence, I'd grown, I used to be his support, the loyal wife he knew he could rely on, but now I was a loose cannon and it scared him. I liked it. I was now seeing him objectively, observing the dynamic of our marriage through his new relationship. Mark expected so much from his partner, assuming they'd feel the same as him, that his career was the apex of everything, including family. And when we were first together, I'd not only accepted this, I'd embraced it, put my own career on the backburner and gave everything to his. I realised now everything I'd sacrificed, everything I'd lost, was so he could gain.

'So you won't go over my scripts, even though this deal is the most important in my career?'

'I don't know,' I said in a small voice, luring him in. I now had something he wanted, and realised that us being apart had put me in the driving seat for the first time ever.

'Carly, please,' he said, then his voice changed. 'I need to impress them. We're almost inking the deal, but a couple of execs on the US side are still not sure, but if I have a good script…?' He sighed. 'I've already told the UK company that I'm going. They're looking for someone else now, I'm at the point of no return.'

'I know it's supposed to be a good thing, ambition, but it can also be a monkey on your back. It's a curse, you're never satisfied. What happens when you get to LA and you don't like the view, Mark?'

'I… I will, and the money will be amazing.'

'Yeah, I guess it will,' I sighed, 'but it isn't everything.'

'This time it's going to work out, it'll be everything I always wanted,' Mark replied.

I shook my head. I'd heard it all before: the next time would be the one, just one more bet on the horses, one more drink, one more ambitious career move. 'What's the phrase, this time next year we'll be millionaires?'

'Something like that,' he said with a smile.

'Good luck to you,' I said, and meant it. I didn't care about the money, I just wanted enough so I could keep my home. I wasn't going to pander to Mark's needs. This was my time now, and I was going to make sure I got what I wanted.

CHAPTER EIGHT

Mark stayed for at least an hour; he seemed reluctant to go. When he finally got up, I realised I hadn't asked when he'd be moving his things. I didn't want him to leave anything behind, it might tempt him to come back, and worse, bring his new 'little family' with him.

'So are you going to get someone to come over and shift your stuff?' I asked.

'No – er, as I said, the place we're in at the moment is small. Erin has nowhere to hang her clothes, we're sharing a rail. So if it's okay with you, I was going to store it here for a while, until everything's sorted?'

'Mark, it's been six months now. You need to take your stuff, it isn't fair.' His clothes were all that was left of him, they were the last to leave. I didn't need the reminders of our marriage, the ghosts of our life together, I just wanted them gone. 'You've always been a hoarder, there are two bedrooms filled with your clothes and books and everything else you ever bought. Which is a LOT!' I said grumpily, as I followed him down the hall, to see him out. 'I want to spring-clean, get rid of the cobwebs.'

'And the memories?' he said, almost regretfully as he turned around, glancing at himself in the hall mirror; he always did that. God, why did I never realise how vain and irritating he was? Perhaps I did, but chose not to dwell on it.

'Yeah, the memories are waiting in a dirty old skip. Now go, you vain bastard, you're steaming up my mirror.'

He laughed. 'Got to keep those groupies happy.'

'Sounds to me like you've got enough on your plate with the lovely Erin,' I said, scowling.

He stopped, and turned to me. 'Carly… About those scripts?'

Having worked on the treatment for the US show, I was in line for a decent pay-out once the contracts were signed and the deal went ahead. If the deal *didn't* go ahead, all we had was what was in our joint account, and that would be split on the divorce. Either way, I'd already done more than enough for his career, and now he'd found someone else to share the time in LA we'd worked for and dreamed of. So let him find someone else to write the little jokes and endearing comments in his scripts, which had earned Mark Anderson the tagline 'who every man wants to be and who every woman wants to sleep with'.

'Sorry, Mark, I'm not your scriptwriter, or enabler, any more.'

His jaw clenched and I saw the flash of anger in his eyes, and he opened the door, but must have realised he had one more favour to ask me, and tried to smile. 'Oh, Carly… just one more thing before I go. Erm, the US deal, if it comes off, it'll mean a lot of press coverage. And Estelle and I were thinking… there's still this issue of how we address… the end of our marriage.'

'Okay,' I said slowly.

'Thing is,' he leaned in conspiratorially, 'if you're happy to say you're fine with everything, that it was a mutual decision and we broke up *before* Erin and I got together – it will cover the tricky question of—'

'How you managed to impregnate a twenty-four-year-old while you were still married to me?'

'I wouldn't have put it quite so bluntly – but, as Estelle pointed out, if things start to look in any way… *unsavoury* – then—'

'Unsavoury? God forbid.' I gave a mock gasp.

'Look, you know what I'm saying, we need to manage this. There are rumours, but so far we've not gone public on anything.'

'Yeah. I know. I'm just keeping to myself. I don't want my business spread across the bloody news. Why don't we all just get on with our lives? Why do we have to make *anything* public?' I asked.

'You know why. No TV channel here or in the US will have me as their face if they think there's anything…'

'Unsavoury?' I asked, sarcastically.

'Oh, please stop being petty, Carly. We feel that for the American press, we may need to… tweak things a little.'

'You mean lie?'

'You might call it that. I call it tweaking the truth to keep a roof over our heads.'

'My roof is here, Mark,' I said, pointing at the ceiling.

'Okay, okay, and I know it's a big ask, after everything – but will you go along with the narrative Estelle's prepared and agree that we split up twelve months ago? Would you say you're happy for me and Erin, and that you welcome the new baby?'

'I already did. I congratulated her when I saw her in the tearooms, just before she called me a selfish old cow.'

He shifted awkwardly. 'I'm sorry about that.'

'So, you want me to welcome the new baby?' I said, pretending to think. 'I know, I'll go one better, I'll let them photograph me knitting baby bootees and say how delighted I am because it will be like having a grandchild.' I leaned on the door jamb, folding my arms.

'Stop it, Carly, and keep your voice down,' he hissed, looking round. He was so paranoid.

'I'm not married to you any more, so why do I have to lie? Why wouldn't I just tell the truth?'

He looked like he was in physical pain. 'Carly, for the sake of the kids, we need to keep this civilised, we don't want their lives ruined. Yes, it would be bad enough for my story to be plastered all over the newspapers… but what about yours? You wouldn't want that getting out, would you?'

I knew, in that instant, that I would never be free of Mark. He would still be threatening to expose me in years to come; my only escape from this would be if he died, and took what he knew with him.

'You'd never say anything… to Erin, would you?' I asked, my mouth dry.

He looked at me, but didn't answer. 'Better to say you're happy with everything. You don't want that bitter old ex-wife label, do you?' he said, and I got the message. I had to tell his lies or he'd tell mine.

CHAPTER NINE

I wandered back up the hall, his aftershave lingering, the imprint of our marriage still in the air. He used to say, '*One day* when we're retired, we'll take off every winter somewhere warm. We'll abandon the UK and rent a nice apartment with a pool. And *one day*, when we've got grandchildren, we'll take the whole family to France, rent a chateau and cook French food and the children can run wild in the grounds.'

'Or they could stay here and we could cook French food and they could run wild on the beach?' I'd say, happy at the prospect of grandchildren, and wanting to share this house and the beach with them. It was our One Day conversation, our shared dreams away from his TV life, like the second honeymoon in the Maldives, a road trip through America. It gave me hope, made me believe we had a future together, because, despite everything, I had loved him, once.

I'd naively thought, with my customary optimism, we could be fixed, renovated and perfected, just like one of his houses. But too much water had gone under the bridge, too many lies, too many secrets, and Mark never intended to be around forever; he'd been looking for a new model to spend his twilight years with. And when Erin Matthews appeared, all grown up and ready to embrace those daddy issues, Mark was waiting. And our *one day* never came.

I walked back into the living room, thinking about what had just happened. I spotted a glint of blue caught by the sun. I sighed as I bent down to pick it up; I'd probably be picking up pieces of my beautiful, broken vase for the rest of my life. I gazed around, scrutinising the floor for any more pieces waiting like sharp teeth for bare, fleshy feet. Looking up from the floor I glanced at the family photographs on the wall. Me, Mark and the children. I hadn't had the heart to take the ones of him down; I kept him on my wall for the children, one of the reasons I'd kept him in my life. I'd taken all the photos, and they were good, if I do say so myself, strong compositions, great light. I'd done photography as part of my degree and was proud of this curated time capsule of how my family used to be. But something wasn't quite right. I wandered over to the wall and I could feel the hairs on the back of my neck prickle. Two of the photos had been swapped.

But who could have done this? The only people who'd been in the house were Mark and Ryan, and neither of them would have done it.

I saw another glint of blue, another shard from the vase; if Ryan was right, and Miss A hadn't been able to knock it over, then had someone been in the house while I slept?

I kept looking at the photos, trying to believe I'd moved them all around so many times, I'd simply forgotten where I'd put them on the wall. Then I remembered I'd photographed the wall when I'd finished. I'd been so pleased I'd decided to put the 'gallery' on my Instagram. So, I grabbed my phone and went through my photos, eventually finding the one I was looking for, and enlarged it on the screen. My stomach dipped. The pictures had been moved around. I felt slightly nauseous. The only explanation I could think of was that Mark had done it, for fun?

I called him, and left a message, but it could be days, weeks even before I heard from him.

It was just like Mark to turn up as I'd started to lift my head in all this. He'd come along and stirred up all the sadness and resentment that had lain undisturbed like sediment at the bottom of the sea. I couldn't help but think back to the night of the anniversary, I'd been so happy then. It was a milestone, the silver wedding that would erase our chequered past. But just as our marriage was becoming bearable, it all ended in a puff of smoke.

I meandered through the house, reliving moments of my life, from my childhood, playing in the garden and on the beach, to the day I brought Mark here to meet my mum, and the day she told me the house would be her wedding gift to me. She handed me my past, present and future, and I couldn't have been happier, or more complete. Little did I know that the home I'd been so happy in, where the sun shone and my children played, would become a different place.

I went upstairs and, wandering into my bedroom, lay down. Just for a moment, I told myself. The sheets were cool and clean; they soothed the spikes of seeing Mark. I was exhausted, sad. Our marriage hadn't been perfect, but whose is? Over the years, we'd found a way of existing, side by side, and then, when the children left, we had to adjust slightly again. Mark continued to work away, and I'd relished my solitude, often just sitting for hours gazing through the floor-to-ceiling windows in the living room, from where I could watch the ocean changing every hour – like a moving picture. Late in the day, the buttery sunlight would fade, making room for dusk, covering the sea and sky in orange, then pink or navy blue or stormy grey. Sometimes, if Mark was home, he'd join me, and we'd curl up on the sofa, and marvel at the weather coming over the sea, find faces in clouds, sit through sunsets and storms. Once he even bought a huge bag of popcorn so we could pretend we were at the cinema. He could be so lovely, so loving. And at times like that, he could even make me believe we were as perfect as everyone else thought we were.

Mark's visit that day was a reminder that we'd lived through a marriage of sunsets and storms, and however much you want to, you can't erase a lifetime. The neural pathways in my brain where habits are formed all led back to Mark and our life in this house. I didn't want him back, but seeing him again, I was disturbed at how powerful and conflicting those feelings still were.

I fell asleep for just a few minutes, but it was disturbed sleep, and I was soon woken by the sound of something moving in the bedroom. I stayed very still, but opened my eyes. My first thought was rats. I have this real phobia, can barely say the word – once, I heard a rustling in the ceiling and became convinced we had them. I'd called Mark, he was working about an hour away, and I made him leave his hotel and drive through the night to go up into the attic. The kids thought it was great fun. Dad had come home and there were furry creatures in the house – it was a child's dream! It was 2 a.m. and he wasn't too chuffed, but as I pointed out, I was so scared of the little critters I would literally have to move out of the house if we had them. He'd yelled when he got up there. I was squealing in the bedroom, wrapped up in the duvet, trying to be funny so the children wouldn't be scared – but I was petrified. The kids were hysterical with laughter.

Mark had eventually poked his head round the bedroom door. 'I found something in the attic, you were right – it's furry with four legs.'

'I knew it, bloody rats!'

'I've got it here,' he'd said, still standing behind the bedroom door.

'Nooooo,' I'd screamed like something from a horror film and jumped under the duvet. When I'd eventually emerged, all three of them were laughing at the bottom of the bed, the children shouting excitedly, 'Mum, Mum, look!'

I'd pulled the duvet down very slowly to see Mark holding up Miss A, who'd somehow found her way up there. We'd all laughed; my laughter was mostly from relief. Then Mark made us all hot chocolate with squirty cream, and the kids asked him if he was going to stay. It felt like an episode from Mark's show, as I told them, 'Dad can't stay, he's working.'

But he'd smiled, and said, 'It's late – and I think Mum might want me here tonight after her fright.'

I remember them being so delighted at this, and it surprised me how much it meant to both me and the kids that he'd chosen to stay with us rather than drive back to the hotel.

One night soon after, when Jake couldn't sleep, he said, 'Why don't you phone Dad and tell him you think we have rats, he might come home then?' His little face was filled with hope as he clutched Dino, his raggedy old dinosaur.

I'd explained that would be a lie, and we mustn't tell lies. 'Besides, Dad's working a long way away this week, and he couldn't come home even if we *did* have rats.'

That broke his little heart, and he'd cried himself to sleep. When I told Lara about it, she'd said, 'When Mark isn't there, Jake probably feels like it's his responsibility to look after you and Phoebe. When Mark's there, he can relax.'

I'd mentioned this to Mark, and suggested that he stay home more often, especially if he was only a short drive away. He'd said he would, but he never did.

I'd been so distracted by the memory of my tearful son, I'd almost forgotten what triggered it, but hearing the noise again, I remembered. Perhaps it was Miss A again? But she was an old lady now and rarely ventured up the stairs.

I checked under the bed, and all around the bedroom. I'd been half-asleep, I may not even have heard anything, so I decided to forget it and take a shower. Heaving myself off the bed, I heard the noise again. I stood very still, and waited. And waited.

After a few minutes, I was cross with myself. God, this was ridiculous. I was being so silly. It was nothing.

I started taking off my T-shirt and jeans, then bra and pants, dropping them along the bedroom floor slowly, like a child. That was something else I could do without Mark around. He used to call me 'slovenly', but it was just comfortable not to be living in a bloody show home, where everything had to be in place all the time. 'You never know who's going to pop by,' he used to say. 'Can't have the Andersons' house in a mess.'

I took a lovely shower, and tried to wash that man right out of my hair, as the song goes. Then I realised I hadn't put the towels in the bathroom (okay, Mark would never have let that happen – there were plus points to his domestic perfectionism). I was padding across the landing, wet and naked, to get some towels from the airing cupboard, when I *definitely* heard something. My fingertips tingled. I had tried to pretend I wasn't bothered, but the blue envelope and broken vase were just beneath the surface of my brain. I suddenly heard a creak. Whatever it was, it was bigger than a rat.

I stood still on the landing, listening, but it was hard to make out. Then I spotted a shadow moving. What the hell? Was someone breaking in? I grabbed a towel that barely covered me and leaned over the bannister, to see if I could look into the kitchen. I estimated the heft of the table lamp nearby and, reaching for it, heard myself shout: 'Is someone there?'

Silence. The shadow stilled.

'Who is it?' I heard myself say, my voice more panicky now.

Nothing.

'Okay, I'm calling the police!'

And just as I was about to dash into my bedroom, grab my phone and barricade myself in, the shadow moved.

CHAPTER TEN

Someone was walking into the hallway, and I thought I was going to pass out there and then on the stairs.

'It's okay, Mrs Anderson, it's only me.' Ryan suddenly appeared in my line of vision, holding a mug, smiling.

'Oh my God! *Ryan*, you gave me *such* a scare. I thought you'd gone home.' I breathed a sigh of relief.

'I… No. I popped out to get some paint, but I'm back now…' As he came closer, he looked up at me, then quickly looked away.

I suddenly remembered I was in a miniscule towel that covered very little. I leapt backwards, out of sight.

'I could show you where I'm up to with the painting, if you'd like to check it over before I go for the day,' he said, now with his back to me.

'Okay, I'll get dressed,' I called, clutching at the tiny towel, mortified. How embarrassing! I didn't even want to think what he'd seen from the ground floor.

I ran into the bedroom and quickly threw on some clean clothes and headed downstairs two at a time.

'Sorry, I was just taking a shower,' I said, unnecessarily, as I arrived in the kitchen.

He was leaning on the island, the mug still in his hand, the sun behind him, and I discreetly took him in for a moment. He looked good. Messy hair, long in his neck, face shadowy with bristle, like he had so much testosterone surging through him he couldn't keep the bristles at bay.

In an attempt to stop thinking about Ryan's no doubt unending supply of testosterone, I walked into the living area, where my eyes alighted on the wall of framed pictures. 'Ryan, I know this is a mad question, but you haven't moved any of those pictures, have you?' I pointed to the wall.

As it was open plan, he could see from the kitchen area, and he looked over, shaking his head. 'Why?'

'I put them up differently... Mark probably moved them earlier. I think he forgot he doesn't live here any more,' I said. He was pissed off I'd brought Ryan in to work on the house, so probably decided to swap the photos around in a territorial way.

'Oh ignore me Ryan, I'm going mad,' I said with a smile.

'I hope you don't mind, I made myself a coffee?' Ryan lifted the mug to demonstrate.

'No, not at all,' I said, wondering if he had a girlfriend, and what she looked like, and fleetingly, shamefully, wondered if he liked her on top?

'Are you ready?' he asked.

'Ready?' Still thinking about Ryan and his girlfriend's sex life, for a moment I wondered what he was referring to.

'Yeah, to check the paintwork.'

'Oh yes... yes, I'm ready.' My face was hot, and not for the first time, I missed having Lara in my life. She'd know if this was a hot flush, or merely unrequited lust. She was an expert on these things.

'I like customers to see what I've done before I leave for the day, something my dad always did.'

I smiled, remembering Ted Jarvis, a bluff, overweight man, nothing like his son. I followed Ryan outside, admired his paintwork. In the middle of a discussion about rendering, I began to feel dizzy. I didn't want to be a drama queen, so discreetly leaned on the wall, hoping it would pass.

'Hey, you've gone very pale, are you okay, Carly?' Ryan asked, and my heart shuddered slightly. He reached out to me with his hand, like he was going to catch me. And I leaned on him. Then, to my own surprise, I just burst into tears.

'Aww, Carly,' he was saying, in a really soft, gentle voice.

He put his arm around me, and I tried to emerge from tears and mucus, telling him, 'I'm fine, honestly. So stupid. Don't know what's wrong with me – this is crazy.'

'Come on inside and sit down. Looked like you were going to faint for a minute there,' he said, his arm firmly around my waist now, as he helped me into the house.

I was perfectly capable of walking, but I have to admit, I liked how it felt to have him holding me, to be so close I could breathe in his warm, musky smell.

'Can I make you a coffee?' he asked, once I was sitting down.

'No, I'm fine thanks, Ryan. You've finished work, get off home, I'm fine.'

'I'm not leaving you,' he said softly, sitting down on the sofa next to me. 'Are you sure I can't get you a drink… some water?'

'I think I might need something stronger than water,' I said. 'Let's open the gin.'

Ryan got up and I directed him to the cupboard where I kept the bottles.

'I'm so sorry, I feel such a fool breaking down like that,' I sighed.

He poured tonic onto gin, threw in some ice and as it fizzed and clinked he handed me the glass.

'Would you prefer beer?' I asked, but he shook his head and, after making a drink for himself, sat down next to me. I could feel his warm thigh against mine, and I tried not to think about it because I might really pass out.

'I was worried about you,' he said, gazing into his gin.

I was touched. 'I'm fine, thanks. I don't know what came over me – it was just seeing Mark, I guess. I haven't seen him since… and it brought everything back.'

'I still can't believe what he did… and telling you at your party too – well, that's what I heard?' He trailed off.

I nodded to confirm this. I knew I was under strict instructions not to tell anyone the truth, but I was now a free agent, and there was something about Ryan that made me want to put my head on his chest and tell him everything.

'Unbelievable – what's wrong with him, is the bloke a sadist?' he said, tightly swirling the ice in his glass.

'Oh, I'm sure you don't want to know about your client's marriage,' I sighed, taking a large glug of gin, the cold aromatic liquid filling my throat with soothing fire.

'I don't usually want to know about my clients,' he said. 'I'm not being nosey or anything, but… but you're different.'

I was now very warm, and he was very close. 'Shall we sit outside?' I suggested. 'This room is so clinical, I feel like I'm waiting for a smear test.' I flushed – why on earth did I say that? As if this whole scenario of drinking gin with me wasn't awkward enough for Ryan, I had to add to his discomfort by conjuring up an image like that.

Before I could dwell on it, I got up and headed outside. He followed me into the garden. It was early evening, and quite chilly, but I was wearing a thick knitted cardigan, and he had a sweatshirt on.

We sat on the garden chairs. 'My mother planted this garden originally,' I said, eager to change the subject. 'She loved being outside. I'm the same, I never tire of being here. We're so lucky to live by the sea, aren't we? When I was younger, I used to take it for granted. I hated the small village, the church hall cream teas, the vicar's wife in her hat every Sunday. I wanted to tear it all down back then, hated the small-town attitude. As soon as I was eighteen, I was on a train to London.'

'Did you study there?' he asked.

'Yeah. Art. I had great aspirations – turned out to be less aspirations and more delusions of grandeur,' I laughed.

'Rubbish, I've seen your paintings. They're leaning against the wall in the garage, right? At least I think they're yours, you've signed them?'

'Yes, those are mine. I've only recently started to paint again, just views from the window,' I sighed, referring to my huge impressionistic landscapes of sea and sky, bright turquoise, daubs of orange, storms and sunsets on white canvas. My short-lived degree-show smashing of the patriarchy with pants was now a distant memory, and I was more fascinated by the unpredictable, moody sea. I loved and feared the sea. I'd seen what it could do, and despite its treachery, was comforted by the calm beauty of the ocean on a summer's day.

'Well, I think they're amazing. *Really*,' Ryan said, looking so deep into my eyes, I had to look away.

'What about you, what did you study?' I asked.

'Chemistry,' he replied, 'and when I finished, that's when the real learning began. I went travelling. Best thing I ever did – India, Nepal, Thailand.'

'Oh, I'd love to go to Thailand.'

'An amazing place, beautiful,' he sighed, lost in his memories. 'I'm saving up to go back there. I'm going to live in a shack on the beach, fish for dinner straight from the sea – you can live on nothing,' he said. 'A few baht for beers, sit on the beach under the stars all night…' He turned to me, smiling.

'I hope you can get there soon. Mark and I talked of going to that part of the world – I always wanted to see India too. We said we'd do a "middle-aged" gap year, five-star hotels and luxury travel to each destination. But, honestly, I'd have been happy with rucksacks and a youth hostel,' I said with a giggle, then felt a shadow come over me, another dream biting the dust. 'We never did get there.' I smiled, so he didn't think I was bitter. I was though.

'If ever you get the chance, you should go, it's life-changing,' Ryan was saying.

'I'm sure it is,' I replied, 'and I hope I do get there one day, but for now, I just want to be here. I need somewhere safe and familiar to lick my wounds, you know?'

'Yeah, I love this house,' he said. We were sitting facing the house, our backs to the sea, and he was slowly nodding, weighing it up with his eyes. 'This place is probably worth a bit too. A bit of paint and some general maintenance and it'll be spot on – even if the ground's shifted a bit over the years…'

'Oh God,' I sighed thinking of the news footage as cliffside homes were swept down into the water, gone forever. Being by the sea was a constant reminder of how everything we love is fragile, and life can never be taken for granted against the wild coastal backdrop. It could swallow us up at any moment.

'The house won't end up in the sea, will it?'

He laughed. 'No, not for a long time. You've got this big, long garden, and the movement will be miniscule in our lifetime. Hopefully you and I won't be here if it ever does fall off the cliff.' He gazed back at me intensely.

I clutched my chest. 'Life's a bit precarious as it is at the moment – that's *all* I need.' I looked back at the house, white and beautiful and proud, yet breakable, the foundations moving all the time, miniscule, but real nonetheless.

'I like the way it isn't completely symmetrical,' he continued, framing the back of the house with both hands.

'Isn't it?' I screwed up my eyes to work out the symmetry – or not – and eventually I saw it. 'Oh yes, it is slightly off, isn't it? Is that a mistake?'

He shook his head. 'It doesn't look like it – again, it might be due to the shifting ground it's built on, and the rear extension probably had some bearing on the wall. But it's nothing to worry about, even the Taj Mahal isn't totally symmetrical – and there's nothing wrong with that.'

'I never knew that – about the Taj Mahal,' I said, recalling the iconic, and very telling photo of Princess Diana sitting alone in front of one of the most romantic buildings in the world. I remember thinking that I would one day go there with the man I loved. I met Mark soon after, and despite talking about it, we never got there.

'Yeah, the Taj Mahal is pretty awesome, this guy built it for his wife who'd just died giving birth to one of their children,' Ryan added.

'Oh, how sad,' I sighed, and we both stared at the house.

After a few minutes of silence, Ryan shifted his chair slightly, turning it around to face the sea, and closer to me. I did the same, so I could look out at the blurred blue horizon. 'It's calm today.'

'Yes, like glass, so peaceful,' I said, feeling the warmth of the emerging sun on the back of my neck. 'I love it like this. Although electrical storms are pretty great from here too, it's a brilliant vantage point. Me and the kids would sometimes pull the big sofa over to the window, and watch the lightning over the sea. Jake was always scared and he'd huddle up close to me.' I was aware I was smiling at the memory.

'You miss the children, don't you?' Ryan asked.

'I do, like any mother I suppose. Sounds silly, but you think they'll be with you forever, and it's quite a shock when they go off and make their own way in the world.'

'Are you lonely?'

'No, not really. I'm alone, but not lonely,' I said, realising I was probably more lonely in my marriage than I was now.

'When a couple like you and Mark split, everyone panics, because you guys were goals – you know what I mean? "The Golden Couple", my mum always called you.'

'We weren't golden, far from it, more like gilt.'

'Oh.' He was looking at me intently.

'Mark wasn't… isn't what he seems. He may appear to be this amazing husband, father, TV star who can turn his hand to anything, but that's his TV persona; the real Mark is quite different.'

'In what way?'

I paused. The gin was making me say more than I normally would. Being married to Mark, everything I did or said had to be run by him or Estelle first. It was so liberating to be sitting in the dusk on a cool spring evening talking freely. 'Erin wasn't his first affair,' I heard myself say, and then after years of keeping everything bottled up, of telling lies to cover the truth, it all came tumbling out. 'Mark loved women, you see, he couldn't help himself. And it wasn't like it was something that crept up on him, the boredom of marriage or fear of growing old. At our wedding, he asked my bridesmaid if, after the honeymoon, she'd hook up with him.'

'No,' Ryan replied incredulously.

'Yeah, I mean, she didn't tell me until years later, and I thought perhaps she'd misunderstood. But deep down I knew she hadn't,' I sighed. 'Throughout our marriage, he had… *liaisons*. He was always discreet…'

'He never got caught, you mean?'

I smiled again, but this time it wasn't with fondness or nostalgia, it was to cover the hurt that still sat in my chest. Only me and Mark had known the truth of our marriage.

'Wow! But you guys were always so…'

'Perfect?' I gave a hollow laugh.

'Didn't he feel any kind of, I dunno, responsibility to *you*?' Ryan said, pouring us both another large gin from the bottle he'd brought out to the table.

'I… I don't know.' I was surprised at Ryan's comment and the fact he'd mentioned responsibility to *me*, something that never occurred to Mark. 'I shouldn't really be saying any of this.' I looked away.

'It's okay, you can trust me. I won't go blabbing to everyone.'

He seemed so genuine, so warm. I felt myself relaxing after keeping everything secret, bottled up all these years; this was a release. 'I was very young when we married, then my mum died when Phoebe was quite small. I think we just went different ways, and by the time we realised, it was too late.'

'My own father had never been a "family guy"; in fact, he was quite insular. He'd never really been involved in my life, and rarely engaged with my mother, so I had no role model. And if Mark took us all on a picnic, or a day at the beach, I thought that was amazing.' I looked at Ryan, who rolled his eyes. I almost laughed. 'Yes, but it was a low bar. I had nothing from my own dad, so whatever crumbs Mark threw my way I was grateful for.'

'I get that,' he said, looking down into his glass of gin. 'But other women?'

'I made excuses to myself at first, I'd covered for him,' I added. 'I took over care of the children and the household and business finances but in doing all that, I'd indirectly allowed him to abdicate all responsibility as a husband and father. Of course, I didn't realise that at the time.' I stopped for breath. I hadn't been listened to for a long, long time and I knew I shouldn't be spilling everything like this, but I couldn't help it. 'When I married Mark, I knew he wasn't perfect. I mean, he met me on the way to meet his girlfriend – and instantly dumped her. I should have known then really.'

'When you fall for someone, you see what you want to see,' he said.

'Yes, exactly – and I had this image of him that I'd held on to, but it wasn't really him, it was who I *wanted* him to be. For years I waited for that person to come back. But he'd never really existed.'

Ryan smiled gently. 'That's sad.'

'Yes, and stupid in retrospect, but I was young and naïve, and even when I thought he was playing around, I was never completely sure because if I confronted him… he'd deny it. He'd say I was paranoid, and become angry.'

'Wow! But why didn't he just admit it and get help, or end the marriage?'

'Because he had the best of both worlds, why would he leave?'

The grown-up me can now see how he manipulated my feelings, my vulnerability. I'd have done anything for him. I had no experience of life or men, and when I knew for sure he was being unfaithful, I blamed myself for my husband wanting to be with other women. I thought if I was prettier, sexier, more sophisticated, then he wouldn't need anyone else, he'd be happy with me. I spent my twenties and thirties waiting for him to turn up in the marriage. I'd try so hard to be perfect for him, a new dress, a new haircut, and we'd go out to some party or dinner and he'd whisper, 'Darling, you are the most gorgeous woman here tonight.' I'd glow, and then I'd come from back from the bathroom to find him cosied in a corner with another woman. It was like a compulsion with Mark, a constant need to feed his ego and prove himself. I suddenly remembered it was all over, and dragged my thoughts from the past, and into the present, and Ryan.

'Why did you stay?' he was asking, his eyes locking on mine.

There were things I couldn't tell Ryan. I could never tell him how Mark threatened to go to the police if I left him, how even *now* I worried he might betray me. But I *could* tell him other stuff, about my marriage, that I'd never told another living soul.

'I stayed because… he scared me,' I heard myself say.

'Mark *scared* you?' He looked at me in almost disbelief.

I nodded. 'I know. It's hard to imagine, isn't it? Affable Mark Anderson, charming, handsome… on the TV.'

'How did he scare you?'

'The first time, was when we'd been married about a year. We went to a friend's house party. I drove, he drank… and I *mean* drank,' I paused, wondering again why I was telling Ryan all this, but unable to stop. 'During the evening, Mark had been flirting with this girl, she was the hostess's younger sister, and about eighteen. He was teasing her, and she was enjoying the attention from a handsome, older guy and though I was uneasy about it, I didn't say anything. But when he asked her to sit on his knee, I felt he was going too far. It was embarrassing and hurtful for me, and I was becoming increasingly uncomfortable.'

'Didn't anyone say anything?'

'Well, everyone except me was drinking, and amused by a pissed Mark telling his hilarious stories. I was already upset, but then I saw his hand move around her waist, I thought I would burst into tears.'

Ryan continued to sit and listen as I spoke, reaching back through the years, unloading everything I'd hidden for too long.

'I didn't want to show myself up, but when he started bobbing her up and down on his knee, I couldn't take any more. I jumped up from my seat, grabbed the car keys, and told him I was going and if he wanted a lift he'd better leave now.' As I recounted this, I was surprised to feel my hurt and anger was as hot and potent as it had been all those years before.

'He looked at me everyone went very quiet, then he stood up quickly, almost throwing the girl from his knee. I remember his face, flushed with embarrassment, but he reached out and put his arm around me and said, "Oh sweetie, I'm sorry, I've been neglecting you, forgive me?"

I remembered being so angry, I'd pulled away, and marched out to the car, leaving him to say his goodbyes. Sitting in the car, I heard laughter – no doubt the laughs were on me – but I didn't care, I was humiliated and hurt, and bloody angry. He kept me waiting ages. I was sure it was deliberate, and imagined he made a huge deal about apologising for my behaviour, when he was the one who'd behaved badly. I was just about to drive off when he appeared, taking his time, wandering to the car, still waving and shouting to the others. We didn't speak all the way home.

'And… what happened?' Ryan was waiting for me to continue.

I took a breath. 'Once we got home, he slammed the car door and stormed into the house, and I followed him, slamming my own door and making my anger known,' but when I walked into the kitchen, he was standing there, waiting for me.' I hesitated, knowing I really shouldn't say any more. But I couldn't help it, I felt like I was releasing a valve that had been so tightly closed, I hadn't breathed properly for years. 'At first, he just let me talk, and I did, I told him exactly how I felt, how he'd shown me up, made me feel worthless, that he was embarrassing. I thought he was listening, taking it in, but when I'd finished, he just stared at me for a long, long time. I wondered then if he'd even heard what I'd said because there was nothing behind his eyes. Then suddenly, out of nowhere, he pushed me, so hard in the chest I fell backwards onto the stone floor. I hit my head, and could barely fathom what was happening, as he stood over me, saying in this really calm, weird way how I'd embarrassed him. He said "You're possessive and jealous and I don't even know why I'm with you. The reason I was flirting with the girl is because you're ugly and stupid – and you bore the hell out of me." And then he stepped over me, and went to bed.'

Ryan reached out and touched my hand in a comforting gesture.

'Was there anyone who could help you?'

I shook my head. 'There was no one, only Mum, but I couldn't call her in tears late at night to say my perfect husband had just hurt me. I didn't want to scare her too.'

I think he was too shocked to say anything. And we sat in silence in the fading light, our glasses empty.

I hoped that telling my story might free me, but it seemed to be pushing me deeper into the past. I remembered how the fall had banged my head so hard I couldn't hear properly for days, and my arm was dislocated; it was agony. That night, I saw Mark's true colours for the first time and I realised I was scared and alone, but there was nothing I could do. I was eight months pregnant with Phoebe.

CHAPTER ELEVEN

The dark side of my marriage was something I'd vowed never to reveal to anyone. To admit I'd stayed after the first time made me feel weak and stupid, and I knew I should have gone, but later it became far more complex than Mark losing his temper and being violent towards me. I became trapped; I couldn't have left; and we both knew why.

Ryan looked alarmed. 'Did it ever happen again?'

I nodded.

'So why didn't you leave?'

I shrugged. I couldn't tell him the truth, that there was so much guilt, so many lies and secrets wrapped up in our marriage, it was hard to disentangle myself.

I thought back to that first time; the idea that my husband, the father of my unborn baby, could hurt me was too much to take. But he was beyond remorseful: he cried for days, said he hadn't meant to push me, that he just wanted me to stop arguing. He said I fell because I was pregnant and unsteady on my feet. I thought perhaps he was right. He bought me flowers, promised it would never happen again, that he overreacted because he thought I didn't love him any more. It sounds crazy, but I ended up comforting *him*, after all, if he thought I didn't love him, then perhaps it was *my* fault for not showing it, and that's why he'd flirted with that girl? He said he'd only done it to get my attention, because he was scared of losing me. He said if I'd loved him enough, none of it would have happened. I was pregnant, tired and vulnerable, and as mad as it sounds, what my handsome, usually loving husband was telling me made a weird kind of sense.

A few months, maybe a year later, we were driving home from a dinner party, and I suggested that one of the husbands seemed jealous because Mark had talked to his wife all night. I also pointed out they were sitting very close, looking into each other's eyes and it was embarrassing. Again, the silence on the way home, and when we were back home, I started again.

'Is this about your weight, Carly?' he asked.

I didn't answer. I couldn't. But I knew he was building to something. I remember the fear creeping into me, as raw and fresh as yesterday, and I told him if he hit me, I'd leave him and take the children. I stood in the hallway, waiting for the blow, but instead, he circled me, and used words to hurt me. They left no visible wounds, but the scars were deep.

'Do you *really* blame me for spending the evening talking to Claire?' he'd spat. 'She's gorgeous – and when I have sex with you, I have to imagine women like Claire to get through it.'

He didn't hit me that night, he didn't need to because what he went on to say was more painful than any blow. And So, the next time he danced too close to someone, or was late home, or had spent money we didn't have, I said nothing. I didn't even comment at the click of the receiver when I answered the phone, or smelt another woman's perfume on his skin, because it wasn't worth the pain. And over time, I learned to "manage" him, keep the peace, and protect myself.

'I'm finding it hard to understand what you saw in Mark,' Ryan said, again dragging me back from my thoughts.

'I didn't always understand it myself, but now I'm out of the relationship I see things more clearly. It wasn't just about the times he hurt me, there was this constant threat hanging over my head that he might leave me for someone else. And that fear of losing him became the real force, it took over from love, but it happened so seamlessly, I didn't realise.'

'God, imagine if his fans knew about any of this?' he said. 'He'd never work again.'

'Yeah, and that was his biggest fear. The last thing he wanted was some police involvement or, worse still, press involvement – his career always came first.'

'You should have called the police on him.'

'I couldn't,' I sighed, 'apart from anything else, he said he'd make sure he got custody of the children, and I'd never see them again. He'd get the best lawyers, his agent would see to that.'

What I didn't tell Ryan was that all Mark had to do was tell the police what I'd done and I'd end up in prison, and he'd end up with custody.

Ryan was now holding both my hands in his. I hadn't even noticed. 'Did the kids know what he did to you?' he asked.

I shook my head. 'God no, but there were times it came close. It didn't happen often, might have just been a couple of times a year when he just lost control, but when he did it was scary. I remember one night he'd come home drunk, the kids were in bed, I was in the kitchen, and as he walked in, his phone pinged. I couldn't help it, I said, "Is that the woman you're sleeping with this week?" The moment I said it, I knew I shouldn't have. I'd just boiled the kettle to make some coffee, and I stood there, with my back to him, waiting. The silence was the worst part. I froze. I could feel him moving behind me, not knowing if he was going to hurt me or not. Eventually, he reached round my waist with both arms, and for a moment I thought he was embracing me, and I began to relax slightly, but as he kissed my neck, he reached for my hand… and pressed my palm firmly down on the hot metal of the kettle.'

Ryan opened his mouth, 'but you said the kettle had just boiled?'

I nodded, and he rubbed his cheeks with both hands, letting mine go, and I instinctively cradled the hand that had been burnt. The scars may have healed, but the pain will always be always there.

As I spoke, the memory of the burn seared through me. 'I was squirming in agony, but trying not to make a noise because I didn't want to wake the children. I held out for as long as I could, just whimpering quietly. Then, while still holding my hand on the hot metal, he flicked the switch on for the kettle to boil. I started to make a noise then, but he just kept pressing my hand down and, through gritted teeth, was telling me why he needed other women. "You're a lazy, dried-up shell, you do nothing for me, Carly," he was saying. By now, I was in so much pain, I almost fainted, and I remember hearing the kids coming down the stairs. He leaped back, and released my hand. I think it shocked him into realising what he was doing, and the minute they walked in, both sleepy in their pyjamas, he became fun Dad – just like that.'

'Did the kids see anything?' Ryan asked, horrified.

I shook my head. I remembered the tight-mouthed vileness transforming into a big smile. Straight into TV mode, like the cameras were on him: 'Silly Mummy burned herself on the kettle,' he'd said.

'The kids were completely unaware,' I continued. 'I stopped crying, and pretended I was 'silly mummy,' too, while he took them back to bed, making them giggle with his funny stories. I ran my hand under cold water and tended to my burn which was pretty bad, but Mark wouldn't entertain taking me to hospital and explaining what had happened. 'We don't want it all over the papers,' he'd said, and walked into town to the all-night pharmacy, returning with aloe cream. It really shook him up, he cried for days.' I paused. 'I remember him telling me something then that he'd never told me before. He said his father had a drink problem, and at night he'd heard his parents arguing, and looking back thought his father may have hurt his mother. He said he could sometimes feel the tension in the air, and his mother's fear, and he never wanted me or his kids to feel that. After the kettle incident, I realised things were escalating, so made a video, giving an account of what happened, showing the burn on my hand, and listing the other times he'd become violent. I also quoted some of the vile things he'd said, when he'd been drunk and out of control. And then I sent it to him. That was more than ten years ago, and he never touched me again.'

'Was that because he was horrified, at what he did?'

'Yes, it must have been a hard watch,' I said, with a shrug.

'Did the two of you ever talk about it?'

I shook my head. 'No, I told him I had kept a copy, and if he ever touched me again, it would be released online, and *then* I'd call the police.'

I'd also sent a copy to Lara, asking her not to watch it, just file it away, and if anything ever happened to me she must send it to the police.

'You were scared for your *life*?'

'Yeah, but it's only now that I can see how bad it was, and though it only happened a few times, it changed me.'

Ryan looked shocked; the fantasy of Mark Anderson had just been ripped apart and that's what the video diary would have done if ever it had been posted online. But he held my secret, and it gave him the power to do so much damage, that I had to find something to equal that. So, knowing about the video, he managed to control his anger, and stop hurting me, and we got through the last ten years of our marriage without any violence. We respected each other, and sometimes, even liked each other, but now I realise, it wasn't a marriage, it was stalemate.

CHAPTER TWELVE

The following morning, I woke, showered, dressed and wandered downstairs into the kitchen to make some breakfast. I stood in the state-of-the-art white kitchen diner that Mark had bolted on to the end of the house. I remembered him building it, and how he'd torn down the lovely, chintzy old cottage kitchen of my childhood. I'd wept like a baby; I didn't want him to make such drastic changes. It felt like he was tearing down my life.

Fortunately, my phone rang, taking me away from the bad memories for just a little while.

'Hey Carly, long time no see.' I didn't recognise the number or, at first, the voice.

'Hello?'

'It's Charlotte, the journalist? I came round to interview you a few months ago. Sorry, thought you had my number and my name would pop up.' She giggled.

'Oh, hello Charlotte, lovely to hear from you,' I said, wondering why she was calling out of the blue like this.

'I hope you don't mind me calling,' she said, 'but I am desperate. I've got to do an article on the décor in little fisherman's cottages, they are suddenly very chi chi.' She giggled again. 'I need a little fishing village, is there one near you?'

'Yes, actually. Polperro is near us, there's a lovely old harbour, little cottages, just what you're looking for I would think…'

'Yeah, yeah, yeah. Fab… Is Mark with you?' she suddenly asked.

I stiffened. I knew this script. 'I'm afraid not,' I said, unsure if she knew we'd split up.

'Oh, no worries, my editor wanted a word with him,' she lied. 'Anyway, I'd better get off.'

'Okay, nice to hear from you,' I said, certain that there was no article on fisherman's cottages and I wouldn't hear from her again. She was just another of Mark's groupies.

'You too, Carly, we must do coffee soon. Ooh meant to say, love the hair.'

I felt a punch in my chest. '*My* hair?'

'Yeah, you've had it cut really short, suits you.'

'It was *you* who sent the note,' I said, shocked.

'Note? What note?'

'Charlotte, stop playing games,' I snapped, annoyed at how all these women still thought I was fair game as Mark's wife?

'Carly, I can assure you I am not playing games. What the hell are you talking about?'

'The note, warning me about living alone; you said in the PS that you loved my hair.'

'Whoa, Mark said you could be a bit of a bunny boiler,' she said.

'*Me*? It's *you* who's the bunny boiler,' I snapped. 'I only had my hair done a couple of days ago; you must have been following me .'

'Er, hello 1950s, anyone heard of Instagram? I saw your photo. I follow the same hairdresser as you. Sally posted your photo on the salon account. God, Carly, get a grip!' With that, she hung up.

I felt so foolish, my face was burning. I'd just accused an innocent young woman of being a stalker. When she said she loved my hair, she was just being nice. I wanted to die – then again it was odd the way she cut me off to ask if Mark was there. Or was she telling the truth, and her editor *did* want to speak to him?

The mention of my hair in the note I'd received had made me think it had to be Gemma who'd sent it, because she was the only person who'd seen my hair that day. Now I knew that Sally the hairdresser was posting the photos, it could have been anyone who'd seen the picture on Instagram! So if it wasn't Gemma who posted the nasty note, who was it?

I was pondering this, when I noticed something on the floor of the living room and went over to look more closely. I wondered if it was yet another tiny shard from the broken vase, so bent down. The floor was covered in grains of sand. If Ryan had walked it in the previous day, I'd have seen it then. Besides, he'd been in the garden not down on the beach. It unnerved me slightly: had someone been in the house the night before, when I was asleep upstairs on my own?

'Are you using sand for any of the work on the exterior?' I asked Ryan an hour later, after he'd begun work. He was outside, with his back against the wall, but turned around, lifting one leg to rest his foot on the wall.

'No. Why?'

I explained about the sand on the floor.

'Really?' he said, looking at me quite intently. I felt slightly uncomfortable having drunk too much gin and told him my life story the previous evening. 'That's odd?' He was clearly as puzzled as me.

I was now beginning to freak out slightly. If it was nothing to do with Ryan, then what the hell was it doing there?

'The sand might have *blown* in?' he offered, probably picking up on my growing unease and trying to temper it slightly.

'I don't think so, it never has before…' I replied.

'Is it still there?' He glanced through the glass doors into the living area floor.

'No, I swept it up. But I took a couple of photos, just in case.'

'Oh, you're a detective in your spare time then?' he joked, making me feel a bit silly.

'Forget it, I'm just being paranoid.'

'Hey, Carly, I didn't mean…' He followed me into the house, but just at that moment, I heard someone in the hall. I cautiously walked across the room to where the sound was coming from, when my son, appeared in the doorway.

'Jake,' I yelped, delighted to see him, and swept him into a big hug.

'I wanted to surprise you,' he said, once I'd released him.

'You did, you nearly scared me half to death,' I said, laughing.

He nodded to Ryan, who nodded back, and then went back outside to continue working. 'How long are you staying, Jake?' I asked.

'I can't stay long, I've got a lecture later this afternoon,' he explained that he'd driven over from Exeter to get some text books.

Even now, in his second year, I still wasn't used to him being away. He missed home too and I wasn't convinced he needed the books; I think he just liked to come back and make sure everything was okay. Where Phoebe was never homesick and happy to go off to London and live in a bedsit, Jake loved Cornwall and the house as much as I did.

'Can you stay for lunch?' I asked, a rhetorical question for most mothers, and I didn't wait for an answer, but went straight into child-feeding autopilot. 'Cheese and chutney okay?' I asked, opening the bread bin and taking out a small loaf.

'Yeah, great Mum, thanks,' he said, then lowered his voice. 'So, what's Ryan Jarvis doing here?'

I explained about the work that needed doing.

'Good, but there's a lot to do, will he be able to get it all done? I was planning to stay in Exeter over the summer, get part-time work, but I could come home and help?'

'Well, that would be lovely, but you are not responsible for maintenance of the house, or checking up on your old mother,' I said.

'I know, but it's our home, I do have *some* responsibility.'

Mark's leaving had made both the kids feel like I needed looking after, and I had to keep stressing how fine I was to both of them.

'No, you must stick with your plans,' I said, surprised he was staying in Exeter for the holidays.

Jake sat down on a kitchen stool, and I placed a plate of sandwiches in front of him.

'A crisp garnish for monsieur?' I suggested, and threw him a bag of salt and vinegar crisps from the cupboard.

'Sublime,' he said, with a smile, tearing open the bag.

'And for dessert, would monsieur enjoy the delights of a rather special chocolate bar, grown from south American cocoa beans? It's called the Snicker bar?' I said in a French accent. It was a game we'd played since he was little, and the older he was the more ridiculous my descriptions had become; it never failed to amuse us. And we were giggling about it when Ryan came inside to wash his hands.

I offered him a drink, but I think he was sensitive to the fact my time was precious with Jake, and declined.

He was just heading off to his van when he said, 'Do you have those photos?'

I was puzzled for a moment, and looked at him, baffled.

'The ones you were telling me about before, the sand on the floor?'

I immediately saw Jake's face, and really wished Ryan hadn't said anything.

'What sand?' Jake asked, putting down the bag of crisps he was holding and looking from me to Ryan.

'Oh, I just noticed there was some sand over there this morning; it's nothing.'

'So why did you take a photo?' Jake said, not smiling.

'Because… Oh, I don't know, I just thought if… Okay, I wondered if someone had been here. I just wanted to take a photo in case I decided to go to the police.'

'The *police*?' Jake was alarmed. 'Let me see them, Mum.'

Ryan now seemed to have realised that this wasn't something I wanted to worry Jake about. 'Sorry, I just thought...' he said, looking uncomfortable.

'It's fine, it's fine. Come over here, Ryan, so you can both see the photos.' I laid my phone on the table where Jake was eating, and they both looked.

'Is that a pattern in the sand? Is it trainers... boots?' Jake asked.

'Not sure, could be, or it could be just the grain in the wood,' Ryan replied.

'Oh yeah, I see what you mean,' Jake said, sounding relieved.

'Yes, that's what it is,' I said, desperate not to worry Jake. And it seemed to work as he wolfed down his lunch without another word about the sand or any footprints.

When it came time for Jake to go, I walked him to his car on the drive.

'Look after yourself, Mum,' he said, hugging me.

'You too, sweetie, and don't worry, I'm great.'

'Be careful what you tell Ryan Jarvis too.'

'Why?' I said, surprised.

'Because you don't know him. You shouldn't have told him about the sand.'

'Jake, don't be daft. I had to tell him, I wondered if he'd walked it in.'

'Mmm, well, he was a bit too interested, if you ask me.'

'No, he wasn't. He's just trying to be helpful, that's all,' I said, feeling slightly unsettled by his words.

'Maybe,' Jake sighed, and got into his car.

It was only after he'd gone that I realised he hadn't taken his books. I guess he really had just come home to see if I was okay after all. And not for the first time, I felt so proud of my amazing kids, my caring, protective son, and bright, funny daughter. They made everything worthwhile.

'Thanks for dismissing the idea that the sand was a footprint in the photos earlier,' I said to Ryan when he'd finished work. He was wandering into the kitchen to wash his hands, and I was looking through the drawer for the blue envelope I'd received after my encounter with Gemma at the hair salon.

'No problem. Sorry, I didn't realise you hadn't told Jake.'

'He worries,' I said. 'I don't want to add to it.'

I was now almost face deep in the drawer, but couldn't find the blue envelope. I'd put it from my mind, and almost forgotten, but the sandy footprints had made me feel a little uneasy. I wondered if I should call the police, just to be on the safe side, but I could hardly say, 'I'm reporting an incident of sand on my floor.' After all, I lived near a beach! But I figured I could tell them about the letter too, the smashed vase, and that the lock on the back door had been broken – having discovered it, Ryan had now fixed it, but still. But now, even as I moved stuff around and opened the drawer right out, I couldn't find the envelope. There was nothing for it but to empty the drawer.

'What are you doing?' Ryan asked, as he leaned against the sink, drying his hands with a towel.

'Oh, looking for an envelope. I put it in here, but now it's gone.' I looked up. 'The only problem with living alone is you can't blame someone else when stuff goes missing,' I said. I emptied the drawer – all the takeaway leaflets from the past couple of years, some pots of glitter, a lipstick, and all kinds of treasure – but no luck. I checked behind it, to see if the letter had slipped, but nothing. I was puzzled. I'd been tempted to burn it, but I definitely hadn't, had I?

I was in the process of trying to push the drawer back in the casing, which was proving far more difficult than taking it out, when Ryan put the towel down and came over.

'Why did you take it out?' he laughed. 'Don't you have any other envelopes?'

'Oh, no, it was an envelope with a letter in…'

'Oh?'

'A fan letter… sort of,' I said. 'I just wanted to reread it.'

'You wanted to reread your fan mail?' he teased, as he slid the drawer back in with ease.

'Wow, thanks Ryan,' I said, watching the muscles in his arms as he adjusted the springs or knobs or whatever a drawer has.

'So, you still get fan letters?' he asked, as I put everything back in the drawer.

'Mark does, but this one was addressed to me. It wasn't *quite* fan mail, though… it wasn't exactly *nasty*… more like a warning that now I live alone I should be careful,' I said. 'Something along those lines anyway. I've forgotten the exact wording,' I added, trying to downplay this. I really was beginning to wonder if I was imagining things, and I didn't want Ryan thinking I was mad.

'Didn't you take a photograph?' he asked.

'No. I'm not paranoid.'

'Well, you took one of the wall with the pictures on and the sand on the floor?'

I gave a nervous laugh. 'I just thought, along with the sand, the note might be significant.'

'Why?' he said, puzzled, and that made me realise that if it wasn't obvious, I was probably overthinking things.

'Because I'm bloody paranoid of course,' I joked. Still wondering if I actually might be.

He smiled at my comment. 'I don't think it's anything to worry about,' he said, then he seemed to hesitate slightly. 'Carly… if you're ever worried, and you're on your own, call me. I'm only a few minutes away.'

'Thanks, Ryan, I appreciate that,' I said. 'I was just going to have a gin and tonic, would you like one, finish the day off before you go?' I felt slightly uneasy after finding the sand, and had been glad to have Ryan around, and as dusk settled, I didn't want to be alone.

Again, he hesitated, then said, 'Yeah, yeah, thanks.'

I grabbed two glasses and started preparing the drinks. 'This is getting to be a habit, you and me drinking gin at the end of the day,' I laughed.

'Yeah, and I like it,' he said.

'Me too.' I sliced into a lemon, filling my nostrils with the fresh, tangy spritz.

'I never drink gin. I usually have beer, or wine – I like gin, it feels a bit decadent,' he said.

'*Deliciously* decadent. Like a celebration,' I added, aware of a hint of flirtation in my voice.

'What are you celebrating?' he asked me, and I saw a glimpse of the dimple in his cheek.

'I don't know.' I stopped for a moment to think. 'Oh, I know, I'm celebrating getting through the first six months of being single,' I said.

'I'll join you in that. I didn't realise being single was a reason to celebrate,' he laughed.

'Yes, it is.' I handed him a glass. Not that you'd know about that, I'm sure you have lots of gorgeous women on the horizon.'

'No, not one. And what about you?'

'Sadly no gorgeous women on my horizon either – or men,' I added, with a smile. 'But at my age, what can I expect?'

'What do you mean "at your age"? You could have any man you want, Mrs Anderson.'

'I've told you, call me Carly. This is starting to feel like a scene from *The Graduate* – you know, Mrs Robinson?' I laughed.

He smiled, but I don't think he understood, probably too young. Perhaps it was just as well.

'I'm telling you, Carly, you could have anyone you wanted,' he said, looking directly at me.

I felt a flush creep up my face. 'You're very sweet, but you don't have to say that.'

'I mean it,' he said, putting down his glass.

'Oh, I'm sorry, you must want to get off.'

'I don't *want* to – but I *have* to, promised I'd pick Max up, his car's not—'

'God, Ryan, you don't have to explain to me. I hope I haven't been rambling on,' I said. 'I'm sorry... last night, I drank too much gin and told you my life story.'

'Don't apologise...'

I didn't wait for him to finish, just carried on talking to cover my embarrassment. 'You probably think I'm a lonely old woman who forces workmen to drink spirits with me in the afternoon for company.'

'You're *not* an old woman,' he laughed.

'But I am forcing you to drink spirits with me.' I touched his arm, hoping it felt motherly rather than cougarish, but have to confess, my pulse was racing.

'Quite the contrary,' he said, 'it's my pleasure,' and our eyes met. For a moment, just a fleeting moment, I thought we might kiss, but I brushed it away. I was being silly. I had to get a grip. God, he was young, single, attractive, of course he wouldn't be interested in me. I'd spent the previous evening regaling him with tales of my unhappy marriage, not exactly a come on. It was just the fact of me being on my own for so long; it was starting to have a strange effect. Maybe it was the menopause after all?

But as I turned to move away and put my glass in the sink, his hand caught my wrist. Electricity ran up my arm with such a jolt, I couldn't speak, and we both stood facing each other. The way he was looking at me, I thought my heart might stop. I had no idea what was going to happen next, until he slowly, gently, pulled me closer, reeling me in, and then his mouth was on mine, the bristly skin on my soft flesh. I could so easily have sunk into this and taken it all the way, but instinct told me this was too much, too soon. And too dangerous. I hardly knew him. So, reluctantly, I pulled away.

'Sorry…' he said, but he was smiling. I wasn't sure why.

'That's okay.' I heard my own breathless voice. I was somewhere high above, watching this. It didn't feel real. I was Carly Anderson, Mark's wife, mum to two golden-haired kids. What would people say?

'See you tomorrow.' Ryan gave a slight nod, and grabbing his keys, left me standing there, wondering what had just happened.

CHAPTER THIRTEEN

The next day when Ryan turned up for work, I felt rather awkward. It was hard to judge how he was feeling. If he was embarrassed about the kiss, he didn't show it, but stayed outside all morning, and didn't come into the house.

By late afternoon, when I hadn't seen him, I thought he must be avoiding me. He probably regretted what had happened between us. I felt so bad; I'd told him so much, too much, about Mark and our marriage, and I remembered what Jake said about not telling Ryan everything. Jake was right – my kids were often wiser than me these days. I felt such an idiot, and wondered if Ryan had picked his brother up last night and laughed about what had happened.

Just before four when I was in the kitchen washing up, there was a knock on the door that made me start. I turned and saw Ryan standing there, and felt a rush of adrenaline course through me.

'Hope you don't mind, but I'm leaving earlier tonight,' he said, no twinkle in his eye, no sign of the slight dimple in his cheek that emerged before, or in place of, a smile.

'Yeah, of course, up to you. It's all great,' I said, trying to hide my devastation. The kiss had meant nothing; he wasn't interested in me at all.

'It's just that… a storm's been forecast. I'd like to get home.'

'Of course,' I said, knowing a storm would not be something that scared Ryan Jarvis. He'd spent his life by the coast: surfing, sailing in boats, he'd travelled the world. It was probably just an excuse to get away before I offered him any gin and he'd feel obligated to kiss me again.

After he'd gone, I sat for ages by the big window looking out at the Atlantic. The sun had disappeared, leaving a cool, grey mist; the little glimpses of the summer to come were fleeting and fragile. I wrapped a woollen throw around me, warmed my hands on a big mug of coffee and in an attempt to shake off any pointless feelings I may be developing for Ryan, I thought about Mark. We'd had plenty of phone calls in the six months since the night of the party, some angry and shouty, some more calm and considered, but seeing him made me realise I was finally beginning to accept what had happened. With someone like Mark, this ending to our story was inevitable. It was my fault as much as his for putting up with the way he behaved, and, in the end he'd done me a favour, I was so much happier on my own. I couldn't deny that the frisson of having Ryan around had helped, but now it looked like his presence was going to be an awkward embarrassment until he'd finished working on the house.

I stayed on the sofa, watching the sea turn from pale grey, to charcoal, to black, and I reminded myself that the only person who had my back was me. I didn't need any man. I was so much better without. Mark had made a complete fool of me, and if I'd cared about myself more, I'd have seen it sooner and moved on a long time ago.

I was startled out of my reverie by a call from Phoebe. 'Hey, Mum, are you okay?' she asked. She'd been busy at work, and I hadn't spoken to her for a couple of days. 'Jake called me last night.'

'That was nice, he came over yesterday to collect some of his books, but then he forgot them. I texted him; he said he'll be back again for them. I think he just wants to keep popping home,' I said, smiling.

But then she explained that Jake had told her about the sand on the living room floor, and she sounded concerned.

'Oh, we worked it out. Ryan had been using this plaster that…
dries as sand,' I lied, 'and he'd walked it in without realising that's
what it was.'

'Ryan Jarvis?'

'Yes,' I said, as innocently as I could. 'I told you, he's doing
some work for me.' I felt my face go very red and was glad she
wasn't there to see it. Phoebe would have known straight away that
something had happened, even if it was just a kiss. Most likely
she'd be mortified.

'You don't think he's gaslighting you, do you, with the sand?'
she said, laughing.

I laughed too, rather awkwardly.

'We worry about you, Mum,' she suddenly said.

'Well don't, I'm fine. You know what Jake's like, he's always been
so protective. He worries when there's nothing to worry about,
and then he calls you and you worry.'

'Jake said Ryan's very much at home there.'

'Oh darling, my goodness, I never allow the help in the house, what
do you take me for?' I said sarcastically, in a Home Counties accent.

She laughed. 'Yeah, yeah, but you don't want him to get too
comfy.'

'Perish the thought,' I said, remembering the warm dampness
of his lips on mine.

'Mum, you know what I'm saying. The Jarvis boys have a
reputation, and you're going to come into some money when
Dad's US deal goes through.'

'Oh Phoebe, Jake's completely misread the situation and built
up quite a picture. Ryan's just working on the house, and he's doing
a great job, whatever his reputation locally,' I said, pretending to
brush this off, but wondering if he might be a gold digger; he seemed
very interested in hearing all about my life with Mark a couple of
nights before. And I came back to the same feelings that he was
young and good-looking and what did he see in me – was it money?

'Just don't want you at the mercy of some sweet-talking penniless builder,' she said, laughing. 'The last thing you need now is some weird, dysfunctional fling with a much younger guy.'

My heart sank. Was that how it would look to everyone? That I was some sad, deranged woman who'd been dumped by my husband and was now being taken for a ride by the local gigolo?

'I remember Ryan Jarvis,' Phoebe was saying, 'he's very easy on the eye, and you're a lonely divorcee.'

'I'm not divorced yet, your father's still dragging his heels on that one,' I said, which gave me the opportunity to change the subject. I told her that her dad had been to visit, then regaled her with the encounter with Erin in the tearooms. I hadn't planned to tell her about that, but needed to talk to someone about it, and was keen to stay off the rather awkward subject of Ryan.

'You are kidding me, how dare that… that… nasty little cow speak to you like that! Honestly, Mum, I could throttle her,' she hissed. 'I hate her *so* much… I mean, who the *hell* does she think she is, saying that shit to you?'

'Don't worry, I gave as good as I got, and—'

But she was furious, I don't think I've ever seen her as angry. 'I'm going to call Dad now, and tell him exactly what I think of him and his little—'

'No, no, love, I'd leave it for now,' I said, attempting to calm her down. 'Dad's going to have a word with her,' I lied. 'Let him sort her out.'

'Hmm, well if she says anything else to you, ring me straight away and I'll sort *her* out,' she spat.

I loved the fact my children were both so protective of me, but I didn't want them worrying about me or fighting my battles. I was the grown-up. I would take care of things.

*

Later that night, I received my 'instructions' from Estelle, Mark's agent. Her email was curt and to the point, telling me that I had her sympathies, but we now had to ensure that anything that may have happened wasn't twisted by the press.

> *I'm sure you will understand, the US deal is almost inked, and we need to think ahead. The announcement is imminent, and we all need to be together in this, in order that the deal goes through. Mark's image is that of a wholesome family man, and despite recent events, it is in everyone's interests to maintain this narrative both on social media and to all members of the press. As you know, the media can be unforgiving, as can the viewers – and unfortunately, if not handled correctly, could mean Mark losing lucrative contracts. With Mark's approval, I have therefore written a press release, including a comprehensive list of answers you may require, if questioned by the press.*

She was always a bit sniffy, old Estelle, and positively resented some of her clients – particularly the female ones. Anyway, to cut a long email short, Estelle and Mark had come up with quite the story. Apparently, as a former art student with a brilliant career predicted, I'd grown tired of playing second fiddle to Mark, and despite us both loving each other and having two beautiful children, I'd decided I wanted a divorce. Mark, was, according to the press release, the most amazing, caring husband who'd always respected my talent. He was also grateful for the sacrifices I'd made to raise our children while he worked.

> *'With much love and kindness between them, Mark left the marital home some months ago in order for Carly to pursue her career. "Carly allowed me to chase my dreams, and I agreed to leave so she can chase hers," Mark said.'*

I shook my head; they were unbelievable, making me look like some spoilt wife who threw him out so I could paint pictures, whilst ensuring Mark looked like a bloody hero.

> 'Mark has since formed a relationship with Erin Matthews and the two decided to settle down and try for a family. To their joy, they are about to welcome a baby boy any day now. "What began as a heartbreaking time for me has turned into something amazing," Mark said. "This is my second chance at love; Erin has saved me."'

I wanted to vomit. It read like a Mills and Boon, all love, heartbreak and joy. Unsurprisingly, there was no mention of Erin's age or the fact Mark used to babysit her. I didn't want to fight; if I objected, Mark would be difficult over the settlement. And then there were our children to think of: if their mother's dignity was intact and their father's penchant for younger women was somehow made slightly more respectable by being something he only indulged in after he and his wife had parted, then perhaps it was a good thing. I also thought of Lara. She had clearly been devastated about the whole business, and I know how I'd feel if it was Phoebe. I wouldn't want her name dragged through the mud for having an affair with a married older man. It couldn't be a proud moment for any mum, and Lara had known Mark years, so his shortcomings weren't even compensated by his celebrity or his building work. So I told myself I was going to let this go, not for Mark, not for me, but for my kids, and my once best friend.

I then went to bed, but barely slept and, at about 3 a.m., went downstairs to make some tea. I put the kettle on and, while I was waiting, looked out the big glass windows.

It was raining hard and was difficult to see anything else beyond the blackness. I could make out a tree, moving in the wind, but my own image was clearer, so I did an inventory of myself. I didn't look too bad. I was still fairly slim, and in spite of Erin's nasty remark about my hair, my hairdresser had said I looked ten years younger with my new haircut. Ryan said he liked it too.

Ryan. My heart sank; what *was* his game? Having come on quite strong, he had clearly regretted it and I was surprised at how disappointed I was about that. I suppose my ego was hurt, the ego I was currently trying to nurture back to health after its recent bashing.

Phoebe's gold-digger comment had given me food for thought too. If my own daughter thought someone like Ryan would only be interested in me because I might, some day in the future, get some money, then it was probably all a bit mad. Perhaps, like everyone else, Ryan thought because I'd been married to Mark, I was rolling in it. And, come to think of it, he had asked me a couple of times how much the house was worth, which I thought he was asking as a builder, but now made me wonder. Maybe it was just as well that he'd gone cold on me, but I didn't want any awkwardness while he finished off what he was doing.

What had happened between us was probably far bigger for me than for him. Ryan probably kissed a different woman every night, whereas I hadn't kissed anyone but Mark for over twenty-five years. To me, the kiss had meant something, but to Ryan I was probably one of the many middle-aged divorcees for him to toy with. Well, not this one, I thought. I wouldn't be played. I'd spent my adult life being manipulated by Mark and those days were well and truly over. And, to quote Phoebe, the last thing I needed now was some weird, dysfunctional fling with a much younger guy. However attractive he might be.

I poured boiling water on my teabag and breathed in the deep, sweet, earthy aroma of camomile. I closed my eyes, and when I opened them, there was someone looking in at me through the window. Suddenly two hands appeared on the glass, palms flat. I couldn't move.

My whole body was shot through with adrenaline. I felt sick and dizzy. My vision was blurring and I couldn't make out who was there, but I saw the face closer to the window. My grip loosened on my coffee mug, and it dropped to the floor with a shattering smash. The next thing I knew I was falling, putting my arms out to stop myself.

Then nothing.

CHAPTER FOURTEEN

Half an hour later, I'd cleaned up the broken mug, the spilled tea, and was sitting trance-like on a kitchen stool when the police finally arrived. Two officers in uniform checked the house, the garden – none of which gave us any answers. I told them about the sand, the letter in the blue envelope, the photographs, and by the time I got to the smashed vase, I could almost see it in their eyes – 'we've got a right one here.'

'Could we see the note?' one of them asked. I knew he wasn't interested, and when I told him it had gone from the drawer, I might as well have just said, 'I'm mad, I'm mad as a hatter. I just called you for company in the middle of the night.'

There was nothing more they could do then, though they assured me they would 'follow it up', by which I understood they'd probably go back to the station and have a good laugh about Mark Anderson's crazy wife. Because, in truth, that was what they were most interested in – Mark and the house, and the fact it was 'famous'. With my permission, they even did a nice little selfie in the middle of the living room.

When they left, I couldn't go to sleep, I just curled up on the sofa, covered in a huge throw, with a baseball bat hidden underneath. Because I knew, whatever reassurances the officers had tried to fob me off with – it was a stormy night, it was probably just a tree in the distance, a shadow of a branch – I *knew* someone had been out there, looking in at me.

I was keeping my eye on the glass doors when the front door-bell rang. I didn't move. I glanced at the time. No way. I had no intention of opening the front door to anyone at 7 a.m., and just stayed very, very still.

I waited in silence, and even though I was expecting it to ring again, when the doorbell rang, the sound pierced my chest. I tried to distract myself and absently noted that the early morning was breathtaking over the sea. But I refocused on the glass, not what was beyond, figuring if someone had put their hands against it, there might still be marks. The police officers hadn't really even inspected it, let alone looked for fingerprints.

I got up off the sofa, still clutching the bat; if I could see finger-prints, I'd know I wasn't going mad. I could call the police again and this time I'd have concrete proof someone had been in the garden. I moved towards the window and put the baseball bat down, placing my own hands against the glass on the inside. Everywhere was still and quiet and I concentrated really hard, desperately trying to see something. Suddenly I focused, as two eyes stared back at me. I screamed, grabbing the bat and pointing it in a threatening gesture, as I saw the hands raise, but this time, they were surrendering.

'Ryan, what the hell?'

He was standing exactly where whoever it was had stood just a few hours before, then came round to the door, which I unlocked to let him in.

'I'm so sorry, Carly, did I scare you? I thought I'd make an early start,' he was saying as he walked in. 'I've been ringing the doorbell for ages. Whoa, what's going on?' He looked at the bat, still in my hand. 'You can put *that* down for a start.'

I felt very foolish. 'Sorry. I'm a bit freaked out.'

'Why, what's happened?'

I made coffee first and, after the first few comforting sips, told him what I'd seen, and how I'd called the police.

He seemed genuinely concerned. 'Shit, the police? You must have been so scared. Carly, I really don't think you should be here on your own. It's remote and at night, anyone could break in. No one would hear or see anything. You're completely isolated.'

'I realise that, but I've been here all my life. I can't be scared in my own home. I won't!' I said, trying desperately to convince myself I wasn't scared, when really I was.

'You know, you don't deserve any of this,' he said, putting his arms around me.

I reciprocated, telling myself this was a friendly hug and I needed it. But it was giving me so much more, and when I eventually pulled away, he was looking at me with such tenderness, I wanted to bury my face in his neck.

'I want to protect you. You bring that out in me.' He paused. 'I want… to kiss you,' he murmured.

'Are you sure… you aren't just saying that out of pity, are you?'

He didn't answer me directly, just shook his head. 'I feel that you and me have a connection. I think about you all the time, Mrs Anderson, and trust me it isn't pity I'm feeling,' he breathed.

And this time, I kissed him. It was passionate, with no awkwardness. Having not kissed anyone but Mark for more than twenty years, it felt like fire. I'd forgotten the power of first kisses, the sheer intensity was overwhelming, and after a few minutes I had to pull away.

'I don't know what's happening here,' I said, but he pulled me in again, his tongue pushing between my lips, his breath hot, his face prickly with stubble. This was going to go further and we both knew it. I felt like I'd taken illegal drugs but couldn't stop and was heading straight for something my rational mind wasn't completely sure about. But my body wanted this more than anything, and when Ryan pushed me onto the sofa, I knew I had to have him. But then, the doorbell chimed again.

'Leave it,' he mumbled, holding me tighter, pushing his face into my neck.

'I have to answer it…'

'No, don't leave me,' he begged. I could feel his energy throbbing through us both, and as much as I wanted this, I knew this might be a sign that I should take a step back. I was heading for dangerous territory.

'Sorry,' I said, pushing him away with force, and feeling like I'd just landed back on earth with a bump.

He smiled, and flopped down onto the sofa.

'Let's talk about this in a minute,' I called behind me, as I ran from the room, straightening my hair and opening the door.

There was a delivery man bearing a big cardboard box, which I signed for and carried back through to the living room.

'This looks interesting,' I said as I made my way over to Ryan.

'Leave that,' he said huskily. 'Open it later, I want to pick up where we left off.' He tried to pull me down onto the sofa next to him, and as much as I wanted to go back to the kissing, I was dying to know what was in the parcel.

'No, let's open it,' I urged. 'I wouldn't be able to concentrate for wondering what it is.'

'Okay,' he sighed, reluctantly sitting up from his recumbent position, reaching out his hand for me to sit next to him.

I sat down, and ripped off the parcel tape, quite excited to see what I'd been sent. 'Who can it be from? No one ever sends me gifts,' I said, pushing my fingers under the flaps of cardboard to open the lid. We both peered inside, almost bumping heads. It made me giggle. 'You're almost as excited as me!'

Ryan nodded vigorously, still looking at the box expectantly. But inside was *another* box. This one was white, with a matching white ribbon.

'Is it something from The White Company?' I said, half to Ryan and half to myself. I shook the box – it was bigger than a shoebox, but not huge. 'It's very light. It could be a silk scarf?' I guessed, although I wasn't sure who would send me a scarf or why. It wasn't my birthday, Mother's Day had been and gone, and I wasn't one to get gifts unexpectedly, that had always been Mark. Some of the things he got sent beggared belief, but I'd checked the name and this box was definitely for me.

'Too heavy for silk. Any sign as to who sent it?' Ryan said, putting his hands under the box to feel the weight. 'It could be from an admirer?'

'I don't have any.'

'You have *one* at least.' He looked at me and smiled; his dimples appeared, and I almost forgot the parcel.

I could feel myself blush. 'You don't have to say that.'

'I know,' he said.

'Could be from Jake, or Phoebe... Ooh, I wonder if it's *Erin*,' I said, glancing over at Ryan, and raised my eyebrows while trying to undo the ribbon which was tightly tied.

'Erin... Who stole your husband?'

I nodded, my eyes still on the knot, waggling it with my finger and thumb. 'I saw her in the village the other day, she was pretty vile – might be a peace offering? Or it could be Mark?'

'Why is *he* sending you gifts?' Ryan asked, and I heard the irritation in his voice.

'Who knows, perhaps it's to say sorry and we're finally on the road to a happy divorce?' I suggested doubtfully. 'Ahh, finally.' The knot eventually loosened, and I carefully folded the ribbon and placed it on the arm of the sofa.

'Come on, you're driving me mad, open the bloody box, woman!' Ryan said, pretending to be annoyed.

'Sorry, I'm infuriating,' I acknowledged, giggling as I slowly lifted the lid off the box. It slid up easily, and inside was white tissue paper, which I began to remove slowly.

'Rip it,' he commanded. 'Go on, just rip it off and delve inside.'

I did as I was told, and excitedly ripped the tissue paper off, throwing each layer in the air, until the tissue paper further down seemed to turn pink, and then deeper pink, then red. And sticky.

I couldn't work out what it was. A red candle that had melted? Sticky strawberry sweets that hadn't survived the journey? Then it came to me, in complete horror.

'It's BLOOD?' I cried.

'What the…' Ryan was now standing up, like he didn't want to be close to whatever was in there.

But I was compelled to keep going, driven to prove myself wrong. It wasn't *that* – it couldn't possibly be blood. So I just kept lifting the tissue paper bit by bit. I refused to believe it could be anything horrible, and if I kept on, I'd be rewarded by a wonderful gift. That was me, ignoring the signs, always hoping for the best. But the tang of metal had already reached my nostrils, and when I lifted the final red-soaked sheet from the 'present' inside, I gasped, in sheer revulsion, and knocked it to the ground. The look of disgust on Ryan's face said it all.

'Get it out,' I yelled. 'We have to get it outside.' I was shaking, as we both stared at the raw, bloody meat lying on the pale sheepskin rug. Maggots were feeding on it, a white mass crawling all over it, devouring it, the movement making it seem like it had a life after death.

Ryan kicked at the meat with his foot, sending the maggots scattering through the rug, and as I grabbed one end of the rug, I yelled at him to grab the other. With blood now seeping into the fabric of the white rug, we lifted it, and both ran into the back garden, hurling it as far away as we could. But the maggots continued, relentless in their pursuit, moving as one across the grass, back to their host.

'What the hell IS that?' Ryan said. He was really shaken; so was I.

My heart was pounding and I started to retch, as thousands of maggots continued to swallow the meat, a moving, consuming white entity.

'Who… who?' so horrified he was unable to say anything more.

'I don't know, I don't know,' I replied, tearfully, shuddering, as if the maggots were eating my flesh. Ryan walked down the garden, and inspected the horror from a safe distance. 'We need to get rid of them,' he said. 'What about bleach?'

But I knew that would ruin the grass and might kill some plants, so for the next half an hour, I boiled the kettle and pans of water and Ryan simply poured the boiling liquid on the whole horrible scene.

'That meat's fetid,' Ryan said, wandering in with yet another empty pan. 'I think the maggots have all gone now, because I could finally see what the "meat" was.' He sighed, and walked towards me, putting both his hands on my shoulders. 'Don't freak out, Carly, but it looks like someone sent you a dead rat.'

CHAPTER FIFTEEN

'I'm scared to death of rats; anyone who knows me knows that,' I cried, unable to get the feeling of blood off my hands and the sight of that writhing mass out of my head.

'Yeah, I remember you telling me the other day, about when Mark teased you, that he'd found one in the attic,' he said. Then he hesitated, and his eyes locked on mine. 'You don't think he...'

'I don't *think* so. He'd have no reason to... would he?'

'I don't know,' he said, but there was doubt in his voice.

'I'm so confused, Ryan, things keep happening, and I feel like I can't trust anyone.'

'You can trust me,' he sighed, putting both his arms around me and drawing me close to him, resting his chin on my head. '*I'd* never do anything to make you scared.'

I relaxed in his arms, then I lifted my head and looked up at him. 'Who would do something like that, Ryan?'

He touched my hand, laced his fingers through mine, and gently guided me into the house where we sat down together. 'I don't know, but they must be very sick.'

'Thanks for clearing the garden,' I said. 'I couldn't face it.'

'I think I've got rid of everything now, it's all in the bin. I might take it to the tip tomorrow. The binmen aren't due for a few days and if it gets warm...'

'Yes, not a pleasant thought,' I shuddered, 'but really, Ryan, you don't have to go to all that trouble.'

'I *want* to,' he said, and in spite of what had happened, or perhaps *because* of what had happened, it felt so natural sitting there together. I got the feeling that Ryan wanted to be my protector, that he liked looking after me.

I leaned my head in the crook of his arm; the feel of his brushed cotton checked shirt on my face was comforting. I breathed him in, washing powder and aftershave, not French or expensive, just clean, honest, no pretentions. Surely the kids were wrong to think he might be after money? I didn't know him well, but I knew when a man was a cheat and a liar – I'd been married to one long enough. To me, Ryan was none of those things, and perhaps it was time to trust my own judgement and make my own choices? This was about being me again, and doing what I wanted to do, which might mean taking some risks, diving into an unknown ocean. And any mistakes I did make, I'd be the only one to pay for them.

'You said – before, about Erin, that she was vile to you. Do you think it was her…?' I heard him say.

I kept my face half on his chest, didn't want to leave. 'I don't know, but I wouldn't put it past her.'

'What did she say to you, when you saw her in town?'

'Oh, just stuff about me being jealous, crowing about the baby and Mark. It was water off a duck's back,' I lied. 'But as she slammed out of the tearooms, she yelled that I was a selfish cow living here, while they live in a little cottage.'

'But why would she say that?'

'She seems to be under the impression from Mark that he owns the house. And I'm *rattling* around in it, apparently. She thinks I'm the bloody tenant and should leave so they can move in.'

'You're not, though, are you?' he asked. 'It's *all* yours, is that right?' He was looking at me, his eyes full of interest in what I was saying, and I thought about my telephone conversation with Phoebe. *Gold digger.*

Was he just sticking up for me, or was he keen to nail down the fact that *I* owned the house?

I nodded, slowly. 'Yeah, I thought I'd told you – Mum moved out when we got married, and gave it to me.'

'Good, so, Mark and Erin don't have any right to it,' he said indignantly.

'Well, it's not that straightforward, some of it belongs to Mark,' I said, trying to gauge his reaction. 'I gave half the house to him as a gift on our first wedding anniversary.'

He raised his eyebrows. 'Wow.'

'Yeah, I know,' I sighed. 'I thought we'd be together forever and Mark had said he felt uncomfortable living in *my* house, so I went to a solicitor and gifted half to him. It made sense, at the time. But, trust me, once I get that half back from him in the divorce settlement, it's staying firmly in my possession.' I watched for his reaction again, but it was hard to decipher. After that conversation with Phoebe, I was overthinking everything he said, which wasn't fair; he'd been nothing but kind and helpful to me. 'Same goes for the business, The Andersons Ltd – I still own half of that, and it's staying with me too. I managed it, and did all the accounts – until he left. I think his agent does all that now; she's welcome to it, but I'm still determined to get my share of what I'm owed.'

'Will you stay here, once everything's finalised?' he asked.

'Yes, this is my home, I love it here. I can't imagine living anywhere else.' I looked at him. 'And I can't imagine any other woman living here – apart from Phoebe of course. I want to hand this down to the kids, like my parents did for me.'

'I understand why you'd want to stay here,' he sighed. 'I mean, it's a beautiful house, and the location – well.'

'Yeah, who can blame me for feeling possessive? I don't want Erin moving into my home; she already took my husband. Besides, she wouldn't appreciate it, not in the way I do,' I added. I never failed to be taken aback by the panoramic view; the sea was stunning, there was nowhere quite like it. The house had been featured in lots of glossy magazines over the years and we'd been contacted by people offering huge sums of money for it. Mark wanted to sell a few times, but I wasn't prepared to, at any price. 'It's a family home,' I'd said, 'and it's staying in the family.'

'Ryan, do *you* think Erin has a point, it's a big house – and now the kids have gone—'

'No. It's *not* selfish to want to stay in your own home. Especially because he was the one who cheated. He can't throw you out, can he?' Ryan looked alarmed.

'No, that's why I've asked for the other half back in the divorce settlement.'

'Good. I was worried for a minute I was putting all this love into your brickwork only for *him* to move back in. If he did, I'd take a hammer to it, pull the lot down,' he said. And I think he meant it.

I laughed. 'No, he won't be coming back here.' I patted his arm to reassure him. His interest in the house was about protecting me; he wasn't interested in what I was worth. But he did seem to be slightly jealous of Mark, which was actually strangely nice.

'I remember Erin,' he suddenly said. 'She was a weird kid. You might not remember but my mum was a childminder, and sometimes we had to have Erin at ours after school when their *au pair* was off, or had been sacked or whatever.' He said au pair in a funny voice; it made me smile. 'Never liked her. I was in my teens by then. Mum had always looked after kids and they were okay – no problem. But Erin, she was something else. I remember she once smashed a plate and blamed it on another kid. She always made the little ones cry – I could see it and I told my mum, but she just used to say "poor Erin".'

'Yeah, she wasn't a happy child,' I sighed.

'Yeah, and she's grown into a spoilt adult. Max, my brother went out with her, a while back. He really fell for her, they talked about moving in together, then she dumped him.'

'Doesn't surprise me, she just thinks she can have anything she wants, and she takes it, like with Mark. But, then again, it takes two. Mark is supposed to be the older, wiser one, after all.' I shook my head, still shocked at the depth of their betrayal. 'I treated her like she was one of us, and she could be difficult, but I never reprimanded her, just tried to understand her, especially after what happened with her dad.'

'Yeah, I remember her father drowning; the lifeboats were out that morning.'

'God yes, that was a horrible day. Lara was a mess. Mark was close to him too, I don't think I've ever seen him so upset.'

'Someone told me Lara was leaving him, that's why he killed himself.'

'No, that was just a rumour. They were happy, Lara adored him. She said he'd had depression on and off, I think it just got him in a grip and he couldn't cope,' I said, remembering the agony Lara went through when she lost him. 'He was a good man, I wouldn't have put him with Lara, he was quiet, and seemed too sensible for her. But I think he was a calming influence, and for a while after he died, she totally lost it. She locked herself in the house with Erin and wouldn't let me see her, wouldn't even answer the phone to me. She said she just needed time to heal. Everyone deals with grief their own way, don't they?'

'Yeah,' Ryan sighed, then paused before asking, 'Do you think she'll be okay, Erin I mean?'

'Erin?'

'With Mark. I mean, he hurt you – do you think he's hurt her?'

'I don't know, I hope not. People change, don't they? He's older now, he might be different with her?' In truth I hadn't really given any thought to this, and I was surprised Ryan had.

We sat in silence, both thinking about the implications of this, and then he smiled at me. His eyes were a soft deep brown – kind eyes, I thought.

'You are lovely,' he said.

I blushed like a teenager.

'I really like you, Carly. I've always…' he paused, 'had a bit of a thing for you.'

'Really?' I was amazed. I'd never really given him much thought; he was a teenager, and I was a young mum.

'Yeah, when I used to come here and help my dad. I was in my teens and just thought you were so beautiful. I used to love watching you play with the children in the garden. Your hair was always really white in the sunshine. Once, you gave me a glass of lemonade, it had a sprig of mint in it…' He put his head down.

'What?' I asked, bemused.

'I don't know why I'm telling you this – it's stupid, but I kept that sprig of mint for ages. I pressed it in one of my schoolbooks.'

'Ahh.' I was so touched. 'I was younger then, just a girl.'

'You're still that girl to me. You were my first crush.'

'It's so lovely of you to say that, but I'm not that girl any more—'

Before I could finish, he leaned over, took me in his arms and kissed me. I knew there was no escape from this, it was what my mind and body were crying out for, and this time, it was me who took *his* hand and guided him upstairs to my bedroom.

Later, we lay together on my bed. I felt different – it sounds dramatic, but like I'd been reborn. I'd never imagined I'd ever sleep with anyone but Mark, even after he left. This was the loveliest, most wonderful surprise.

'You're not scared, are you?' Ryan's voice was gentle.

'No, why?'

'The parcel that came earlier, I keep thinking about it.'

'Oh?' After everything, I'd almost forgotten about the horror, what had happened with Ryan almost erased the revulsion and fear, but now it was slowly creeping back. 'It's probably meaningless,' I sighed, and turned to rest my head on his warm chest. It felt good to have him to hold.

'I was thinking,' he said, 'it might be a warning? Mark and Erin want you out of the house and think if they make you scared here on your own, you'll move?'

Lying there in his arms, I felt reassured, safe. I could think things through more clearly than when I was alone and scared. 'They may have sent the note too,' I offered.

'And Mark has keys, he could have let himself in late at night?' Ryan added.

'Yeah, but it's not really his style. I can't see Mark getting involved in something to scare me, he'd be too worried about getting caught, and ending up on the front pages.'

'That *would* be funny,' he sighed.

'Also, they've gone to a lot of trouble to piss me off. They've sourced a dead rat and wrapped it all in posh tissue and ribbon. Mark wouldn't touch it, the blood might stain his suit. And gift-wrapping companies don't usually wrap rats,' I added, with a smile.

'Yeah, you're right. The last time I needed a dead rat wrapping, I had to do it myself.'

'Exactly,' I laughed. 'I think Erin's capable, and probably disturbed enough, but she's about to give birth. And – a dead rat in beautiful wrapping, it's a bit mafia, isn't it? I mean, what next? A horse's head in my bed?'

He laughed, softly kissing the top of my head.

'What a morning it's been,' I said, 'one minute we're kissing, the next we're killing maggots together, then we're in bed, and it isn't even noon.'

'Yeah, for a first date, it's been a bit *Halloween*, hasn't it?'

I cringed, trying not to think about the white swarm curling its way along the rug.

'I tried to pretend I was this fearless guy and you could rely on me for anything,' he said.

'You convinced me,' I replied. 'You are my dragon slayer.'

'And you're the woman of my dreams,' he said, pulling me close. 'And you make me laugh.'

'Yeah, well, that's the joy of an older woman,' I said. 'We can always find something to laugh at – after twenty-five years of marriage and two kids you learn to have a sense of humour. It's not life and death, is it?'

The following morning, I woke to find Ryan had gone. His clothes weren't on the floor where he'd left them. I was new to all this, and wondered how relationships worked in the twenty-first century. Was this even a relationship? I might just be a one-night stand, a notch on his bedpost. I smiled to myself. Either way, he was a good-looking thirty-something, and I had nothing to be ashamed of. My mind was drawn back to the night before. Ryan's flesh tasted of sea salt, reminding me of all the boys I'd kissed by the cliffs as a teenager. He had a good body, firm, and slim, his muscles defined, and just thinking about it now, I felt an excited little giggle at the back of my throat.

If it never happened again, no one could take away last night, I thought, skipping into the shower. Yes, in spite of all the unpleasant things that had happened to me in the past few months, peaking with yesterday's 'gift' – I was happy. I'd discovered that there was life after my husband, and it felt good.

I dug out an old loofah and gave my whole body a scrub. Then, once out of the shower, I found an old pot of body cream that once belonged to Phoebe – and I slathered myself in it. I had someone to be soft for now. And slipping on a cotton floral dress, I took a look in the full-length mirror, something I'd avoided for a long time. *You go, girl*, I thought, as I twirled around, shaking out my wet hair, applying a little lipstick and mascara.

Happy with how I looked, I ran down the stairs to see if Ryan was around, and to my joy, I found him in the garden. He was sorting through a pile of bricks, and I took a moment to watch him. It was like I'd never seen him before. He was suddenly so much more – tall, tanned, strong. I wanted to skip over the grass barefoot, and run my hands through his thick, dark hair as I had the night before. But I resisted. I didn't want to come on too strong and scare him off, so I just opened up the glass doors and asked if he'd like a coffee. That way, he had options as to how he responded to me. Were we client and builder, or lovers?

'That'd be great,' he said, wiping sweat off his forehead with his sleeve, and I knew by the way his eyes swept over me that I wasn't his client. I was his lover; the thought filled me with happiness and the kind of thrill I hadn't felt in years. 'You look cute,' he said, looking me up and down.

I thanked him, and turned to go back in the kitchen, feeling a rush of blood to my face. I had to keep reminding myself I was forty-seven years old, not seventeen. I made the coffee, thinking how easily I could fall for Ryan if I let myself, but my mind wandered back to my telephone conversation with Phoebe, *sweet-talking gold digger, the Jarvis boys have a reputation*. Should I let my guard down so easily? I was insecure about handing my heart to the first man that came along after Mark. Besides, did Ryan even *want* my heart? If not, what *did* he want?

CHAPTER SIXTEEN

It was a couple of weeks after our first night together, and in spite of our age difference, I was growing more fond of Ryan. I enjoyed having him around; he was easy, and funny, and after all the drama with Mark, I just enjoyed being with someone who didn't seem to put themselves first all the time. I wasn't going to ignore Phoebe's warnings, but I *was* going to trust my own instincts. I'd *had* to stay with Mark. I had little choice, there were the kids and the house, and of course his career to consider. But this was purely no strings, no commitment, and if I suddenly felt it wasn't working, or Ryan wasn't who I thought he was, then it was over. For me, this relationship was restorative, it wasn't forever, we both had different paths to travel in the future. Meanwhile, Ryan was a lovely distraction while I recovered from what had happened before. My instinct told me he was a good person, and he genuinely liked me, and I was just happy to continue the casual, loving relationship for as long as it lasted.

It felt like my life was finally turning a corner; I'd been offered part-time work at the coastal interiors shop in Looe, and was due to start any day. And there'd been no more weird parcels or notes delivered, no more strange things happening in the house. Phoebe was happy at work, and Jake had met someone in Exeter and when I asked him about her, as usual he went all shy and said, 'Yes, she's lovely, but we're just taking it one day at a time. Calm down, Mum, don't get planning any weddings.' Delighted, I demanded he bring her with him next time he was home. So life was good, for now – and I was pondering this one morning as I brewed coffee for me and Ryan, who was working outside.

After popping some bread in the toaster, I switched the TV on in the kitchen. As I went to pour coffee into two mugs, I suddenly became aware of a familiar voice. Mark? I looked up to see him on the TV screen, handsome, smiling, a touch of silver in his hair. I was surprised to see him, I didn't know he was doing a TV interview, but then why would I? I hadn't seen or heard from him for a couple of weeks.

I rolled my eyes, knowing he was telling one of his tall tales for a pretty presenter, and I turned up the volume to hear him.

'Carly ended the marriage,' he was saying. 'She'd had quite enough of me, and I don't blame her. She didn't want to be tied to marriage, and all the baggage that came with that; she'd always been such a free spirit, wanted to discover herself, as women often do when the children have left the nest. She said being in the marriage had held her back, and I understand, she wanted to be free.'

I stood, teaspoon in my hand, listening to the story of my life according to Mark, who, as always, managed to sound self-deprecating and kind, while throwing me under the bus.

'So, let me get this right – after twenty-five years of marriage and two children your wife just announced that you had to leave?' The presenter, a pretty young thing with a shiny brown bob, was familiar. I'd seen her fawning over Mark at some of the few TV events I'd been invited to.

'Ah, yes, and I can't deny it was a surprise, but you see, Fiona, Carly was… is very independent, very confident. She never needed me, she was always so happy with her friends, her painting… She is a wonderful painter. She said I'd held her back and perhaps I *had*?' he mused, holding the thought for a beat, while the camera held the shot, letting this sink in with the viewers. It made my hackles rise, but when the camera then moved on to the concerned face of his young lover, I started to seethe.

'It's been a difficult time for him,' Erin sighed. 'He had nowhere to go, and that was his home, he'd worked so hard on that house, it was part of him, you know? And for Carly to just throw him out like that…'

'Just so sad.' The presenter and Erin were both very young, both completely manipulated by Mark's victim act, shaking their heads in unison at the fact a grown man didn't have a bloody roof over his head, which of course was a lie, because he did. His refusal to take any responsibility for his life, his behaviour, was shocking. 'So, through all the pain and heartache, you guys forged the most amazing friendship, which turned to love?'

Mark looked into Erin's eyes, and the camera came in for a close-up. I wanted to puke. 'Erin and I, we were just friends. When Carly ended our marriage, I was lonely. What can I tell you? Erin comforted me as any friend would; no one was more surprised than us when we fell in love.'

'Er… correction, your wife was probably even more surprised, don't ya think?' I muttered, as I stirred the coffee. Was anybody watching this and wondering why he had twenty-four-year-old women as 'friends'? But such was Mark's charm, his ability to perform, no one ever saw through him, even me – until now.

'And now the patter of tiny feet?' Fiona made a stupid little gesture with her fingers, and the camera went back to the gruesome twosome now making a mockery of my life.

'Yes, our little one,' Mark said, and they all looked down at Erin's swollen belly as she sat there, beaming. 'And it's amazing, Fiona, because I've known Erin's family for years,' he continued, trying to give a veil of respectability to his seedy little affair, 'and there she was, all the time. Sometimes what you're looking for is right there… Erin's my life.'

'And baby too,' Erin corrected, sitting there, both hands on her tummy, like a bloody minor royal.

'Of course.' He beamed.

Fiona gave a sickly smile, then leaned in for what I guessed would be – for her – a hard question. 'Can I ask… the baby's due in a matter of days, will Carly play a part in the baby's life? I know you guys have the most amazing relationship.'

This puzzled me. I walked closer to the screen.

'I'm sure she will, won't she, darling?' Mark said, clutching Erin's hand.

'Carly's been so kind,' Erin oozed, 'and I'm sure she's watching this morning. Hey Carly!' Now *she* gave an idiotic little wiggle of her fingers into the camera. I stuck two fingers up at the screen, and kept them there; it made me feel better. 'In fact – and I know she's sworn me to secrecy, but I want people to know how generous she is. Carly says it's too big for her, and she's too old to have any more kids, so rather than rattle around in there, she's giving Mark his house back.'

I gasped. The presenter gasped. 'You mean THE house, the *Forever Home* house?'

'Liar,' I hissed at the screen.

Erin nodded vigorously, while Mark looked like he'd just been shot. An excitable Fiona announced that there would be a break, followed by a 'fascinating item on what your fridge says about you!'

I was so stunned, my mouth must still have been open when Ryan walked back in.

'Have you gone to Brazil for that coffee?' he was saying.

'Sorry – I'm just – just SO bloody angry,' I spat and, handing him a mug of steaming coffee, regaled to him what I'd just seen and heard.

'That's tough, you okay?'

'No, I'm not okay. They've just told the whole of the UK that they're moving into my house!'

He put his arm around me. 'Hey, it's not going to happen. It's *your* house, they can't just move in.'

'No, but *legally* it's half Mark's, nothing's been signed. And Erin is quite the little go-getter – and until the divorce paperwork's completed, everything could be up for grabs.'

My phone started to ring. It was Phoebe, and while I took it Ryan headed back outside; he'd clearly given up on any promise of toast.

'Hello, darling, did you see your dad on TV just now?' I asked, trying not to sound upset, raging or murderous.

'Did I see him? You bet I did. We have TVs on the wall in the office and someone said, "Is that your dad, Phoebe?" and, you know, I wished I could say "no". I'm so ashamed, he's making such an idiot of himself – does he really think people believe that shit about them being friends?'

'I doubt it, but he does have a way with people; it's got him this far, love.'

'I could kill that bitch, sat there all smug and—'

'Try not to let it get to you, sweetie, there's nothing we can do to change things, we just have to get on with our own lives and be happy now.'

She was still furious when I put the phone down ten minutes later, and the more I thought about him, the more angry I became. How dare he embarrass my children with his sordid little TV interview, like the fact he'd got a twenty-four-year-old pregnant was something to celebrate. He'd replaced me, and now he was replacing his kids; we were all so disposable to him.

I stabbed Mark's number into my phone, and waited for it to ring, but as always the answerphone kicked in. When we were together, he'd only take calls from people he knew and liked, and now it seemed I was just another annoyance. But I wasn't going to let that stop me having my say.

'How *dare* you… how dare you and your… bit on the side go on TV and tell lies about me,' I hissed, aware that Ryan had come back in and was watching and listening, probably wondering what the hell he'd got himself into. 'You sit there smugly, touching each other and cooing and… it's disgusting! She was my best friend's daughter, and you're a *predator*. God knows how long you've been looking at her and imagining… That's what the *real* story is, not this love's young dream thing you're trying to peddle. And who… who is SHE – some uppity little brat barely out of her teens – to say how I *feel*? I knew we were going to tell lies to cover up for your disgusting behaviour, but what hurts the most, Mark, is that you let her speak for me, for you. How could you – have you not taken enough from me? Do you now have to steal my story too?' I switched my phone off, and then remembered I had something else to shout, so stabbed his number into my phone again.

'Babe, leave it,' Ryan was saying softly, but I shook my head and waited for the beep so I could leave another rant. He was standing close by, obviously concerned, but I didn't care about anything or anyone else in that moment. I was blinded by rage – and fear of losing everything.

'AND as for the house – *my* house,' I started, as soon as the answerphone kicked in, 'trust me, Mark, it will be a cold day in hell before *she* ever sets foot in here again. As for her plan to move in with her "little family" – it won't be the patter of tiny feet she hears, it will be the sound of me chasing her with a bloody baseball bat!'

CHAPTER SEVENTEEN

'I wonder if you should look at making things a bit safer here – CCTV or something, what do you think?' Ryan said later that day when I'd finally calmed down.

'That's not a bad idea. I might be able to check on rat deliveries, and all the other weird stuff that's been going on,' I said.

'Yeah, and being on your own here, you should have some kind of protection; you could be opening the door to anyone.'

'You're right, and it won't be long before the photographers start turning up on the drive, now Mark's gone big on his new "love story",' I said, rolling my eyes.

'Yeah, if you get CCTV, you'll be able to see most of the drive from inside the house.' He paused, seemed to hesitate, then added, 'And you can also see if someone's letting themselves in.'

I felt a now familiar prickle of fear. 'You mean at night?'

He looked at me, and nodded, very slowly.

In my mind I saw the sand prints on the floor, the broken hinge on the back door, shards of blue from the shattered vase... and that face at the window.

'Yes, things can't go on like this, I should get CCTV installed,' I said, thinking how I could catch whoever it was, and call the police with evidence next time and they'd know I wasn't mad.

'I know someone who could install a security camera. He'd do it cheap, mates' rates?'

'Oh, okay, thanks. That sounds great, I don't have much money so...' I said, making a point, and thinking if he was a gold digger surely he'd be off now.

'Good, I'll call him, ask him to pop over tomorrow if he's free?'

'Thanks. I'm so grateful. I don't know what I'd have done the past few weeks if you hadn't been around,' I said. 'And I should point out, my life isn't usually such a bloody rollercoaster – and I don't normally burst into tears, receive rats in the post or rant into people's voicemails.'

'I know, I know,' he said with a smile. 'But do you usually threaten people over the phone with baseball bats?'

'Oh – *that*. Well, yes, that I do partake of, on a regular basis,' I said, laughing. 'I usually borrow Jake's; he has a selection of them in his room.'

'I'll try not to annoy you then.' He paused. 'Seriously though, if you're scared, and you feel like you need some company, I can always stay over?'

Ryan shared a house in the village with his brother; he was a mile away at most, but the idea of having him staying over appealed to me – on many levels. But I was determined to take things slow and keep it casual. I wasn't diving head-first into a relationship; what Ryan and I had was good and I didn't want to think about anything more serious right now.

'Thanks, but I don't want you to just feel sorry for an old lady who might need protection,' I teased.

'Well, that's exactly why I offered,' he said, and I hit him with a cushion, which turned into a bit of a tussle, and we ended up kissing. And, in fact, Ryan stayed over that night, which made me very happy – so happy I almost forgot about strange notes and dead rats and sand prints on the floor of the living room. And for a little while, I didn't even think about my husband and his new girlfriend holding hands on the TV and regaling perfect strangers with every aspect of their lives – and mine!

*

The following morning, Ryan's friend Simon turned up to give me an estimate for CCTV. It wasn't exactly cheap, but I agreed to it. I felt I had little choice, I needed some security. Simon was delighted, and said he'd pop back within the hour to install everything.

'I don't understand why you don't just get on the TV yourself, tell everyone what Mark Anderson's really like?' Ryan said, as we ate sandwiches for lunch; he knew I was still seething over the TV interview Mark and Erin had done the previous day. I hadn't dared look in the tabloids that morning; I could just imagine the headlines.

'I agreed I wouldn't. If I keep my mouth shut, I'll get my house back. I have to be quiet until everything's signed. This is my home, and it's worth everything to me, even more than my reputation, I guess.'

He shrugged, 'It doesn't matter what people *think*, as long as those you care about know the truth. But I'm telling you, Carly, you wouldn't get me lying for an ex.'

I put down my half-eaten sandwich, and pushed away the plate.

'It's complicated, Ryan,' I sighed, 'you don't understand.'

'Oh, okay,' he said, finishing his sandwich and getting up from the table, clearing away the plates. 'Sorry, I thought I *did* understand,' he said, wiping his hands on a tea towel and going back outside to work.

I'd been slightly dismissive, and obviously hurt him, he'd been so supportive and listened to me, but the truth was, he couldn't *possibly* understand. On paper, he was right, it seemed like I just put up with so much, and received nothing in return, but a union of two people over almost three decades is far more nuanced.

It's hard to explain; he'd hurt me a handful of times in our marriage, and once was enough, but what I didn't tell Ryan was that when he hit me a second time, I left him. He'd slapped me across the face because I'd complained about him coming home very drunk, and very late on our wedding anniversary. He'd booked a table, I'd booked a babysitter, and I'd sat waiting, in my new dress all evening, but by the time he came home at 11 p.m., it was too late. I was upset and angry, and I told him how I felt, and his response was to tell me I was a nag and whack me across the face with the back of his hand.

I should have known after the first time that this was a pattern with him. But he'd convinced me, and I'd convinced myself that it wouldn't happen again. So when it did, I knew he wasn't going to change and wasn't prepared to live with the fear of what he might do when he'd had a drink. It was so random, he was fine for months and then suddenly, from nowhere, this monster appeared.

So, the next morning, nursing a stinging cheek and a broken heart from the hard slap he'd given me, I packed up the car, and moved to the next town. Jake was tiny, and Phoebe was a toddler, and we stayed in an out-of-season holiday let for a few days, until Mark came to find us.

'Come home,' he'd said, in his kind, honeyed voice, 'this is silly, darling. You and I can work through this. You know I didn't mean to. I'm just stressed, I've been working too hard and you've been so busy with the kids, I felt neglected.' I hated him for saying that. My children would always come first; how could I put a grown man before a baby and a toddler? I remember he tried to hug me, to cajole me, offered all kinds of promises about not doing it again, about 'being a better man'. But I was adamant. I wasn't buying any of it, and made that very clear, and when he realised he wouldn't be able to get round me with kindness, he turned on me. He started by threatening to take the children off me, which I almost laughed at.

'Don't be ridiculous, I'm their mother. I'll get custody – especially when I tell them you slapped me.'

He was, of course, horrified at the prospect of this getting out. 'I can do far worse,' he said darkly.

'Mark, it doesn't have to be like this. Me and the children can move back into the house, we'll get an amicable divorce, and live our own lives. I can't stay married to someone who hurts me. I won't live in the same house as you.'

He'd just stood in silence, glaring at me, and I thought for a moment, I might just be able to negotiate this.

'Look, if you let me stay in the house, I won't tell anyone you hit me.'

'You can say what you like, no one will believe you,' he said.

He was probably right. I had no proof. He hadn't left a mark on me; it was my word against his.

'I'll get custody and stop you seeing them,' he said, emotion in his voice.

'You wouldn't get custody, and you can't stop me seeing my own children.'

'But, Carly, I *can*.' I'll never forget the look on his face, triumphant.

I didn't understand, and looked at him, confused.

'You'll never be allowed to see them because I'll tell the police all about how you killed your own mother.'

It was as if he'd raised a gun to my chest and shot me. I remember crumbling, falling to the floor. I was well and truly lost. Because what he'd said was true.

CHAPTER EIGHTEEN

After Mark's threat to tell the police what happened with Mum, I had no choice but to move back and continue with our marriage. I couldn't risk losing my children, and from then on, I kept his secret, and he kept mine. It wasn't a marriage, it was a stalemate, but because of the TV show, everything appeared to be wonderful. And over the years, our lives were turned into an artist's impression of us – the *us* Mark wanted people to see – no stormy greys, or dark steel, just light and airy and… happy, I suppose. And if I'm honest, rather than fighting it, the easiest way for me to live it was to accept what we had, and count my blessings. There were women much worse off than me. I was one of the lucky ones – and if I ever doubted that, all I had to do was watch an episode of *The Forever Home*.

I wasn't unhappy for twenty-five years of marriage, it was more nuanced than that. Mark could be wonderful, kind, funny. It's hard to explain, because it was complex and Mark wasn't all bad, he was ninety per cent amazing, and only ten per cent villain; there was always light and shade. He wasn't impossible to live with when he was sober and things were going well. And though I felt I had little choice, I had to ask myself, was it worth ripping a family apart, when ninety per cent of the time, life was good? And when they were young, the kids adored him. He was the fun 'Disney Dad', always making them laugh, bringing home gifts, waking them up for midnight feasts when he got back late from location.

There were flashes of violence, shadows on the sun, but it was rare, and I learned instinctively how not to press his buttons. What I know now is that I lived how I felt I *should* live. I became what others expected me to be, but I was rarely myself until the violence stopped. But still, he continued with discreet affairs, and as he grew older, he was like an addict, needing the reassurance that women still found him attractive. But I always had a thread of hope, and wondered if one day the affairs might stop too, and Mark would come back to me.

Just before he'd left, we filmed a programme that opened with Mark and I walking the South West Coast Path from Looe to Polperro. We'd gone from Honeymooners to Empty Nesters, and wandered the tiny harbour shops together, looking for accessories Mark could use for his next house makeover. It was a montage of sunshiny shots of us eating a wonderful lunch, from everything the sea had to offer. Mark was on form, he was the man I'd met all those years ago in London, and I began to believe we might have a future together after all. I realise now I was fooling myself, we could never be the perfect couple we presented to the world, too much had been said and done. But nonetheless, the years had faded the hurt, and I was filled with optimism and happiness, perhaps the man I'd fallen in love with had come back to me after all? It was just a few weeks before our anniversary, and as we'd dined by the harbour, the sun high in the sky, our future was spread out before us. I remember smiling at him, and he smiled back, putting his hand on mine. What I didn't know, was that Erin was already pregnant.

More than a year on, I now stood at the bottom of the garden remembering, while gazing at the sea. The ebb and flow of love and life was like the tide, surging forward before sweeping everything away as it disappeared into the distance.

Eventually, I wandered back up the garden, and felt my heart flutter, catching sight of Ryan, painting the exterior walls brilliant white. I couldn't help it, I went behind him and wrapped my arms around his waist.

'Oh, it's you,' he said, and turned around, slipping both arms around my neck.

'When I said before that you didn't understand, it isn't because you lack understanding, it's just all so complicated,' I explained. 'I'm sorry if it came out wrong.'

'No, I'm sorry, I overreacted a bit. It's hard sometimes to hear you talk about Mark. I know behind the scenes it was quite different, but I can't ever compete with someone like him. He's rich and famous and…'

'Oh, that's all meaningless. You're kind and clever and young and very good-looking,' I heard myself say, and wondered where I'd got this new-found confidence.

'Okay, I'll take that,' he said, staring at me. 'Coming from a beautiful blonde, I'm flattered.'

I giggled, and was about to continue this flirty conversation when he suddenly said: 'Does he still have a key… Mark?' All the softness had gone from Ryan's eyes.

'Er. Yeah, I think he does. But he needs access – half his stuff is still here.'

'Yeah well, when this CCTV's been fitted, always check the porch camera before you open the door. One night you might see him or mad Erin staring back at you.'

'Mad Erin, eh? I'm not sure she's mad – just a little…?'

'Unhinged?'

'No, misunderstood,' I said, feeling generous.

Ryan leaned back against the wall. I was facing him, and he pulled me towards him, his arms now around my waist. He always seemed to reach for me when we talked about Mark; I thought perhaps he was a little insecure.

'I remember moaning to Mum about what a spoiled brat Erin was, but Mum said, "She has everything and nothing." I didn't

understand what she meant – it sounded like a riddle to me.'
He laughed. 'My mum still talks in riddles; she's probably being
profound, but I can't always understand her.'

'How is she?' His mother, Tina, had recently been diagnosed
with dementia.

'She's okay.' He took a deep breath. 'To be honest – some days
you wouldn't know there was anything wrong. Then she'll suddenly ask, "Is Ted home from work yet?"' I saw the sadness in his
eyes and my heart went out to him. The Jarvis family were good
people, and Tina had been a real hard worker, helping Ted with
the business, and working as a full-time childminder.

'She's one of those people who'd do anything for anyone, your
mum,' I said, touching his chest, a vague attempt to comfort him.

'Yeah, she's always happy to help. I think she misses taking
in the waifs and strays, and I worry because she's on her own.
But she's happy enough. I called in to see her yesterday. Me and
Max try and see her most days now, just to make sure she's okay.
I think we may have to think about moving her to sheltered
accommodation soon. I think she's confused, and sometimes she
doesn't make a lot of sense – yesterday she told me the next-door
neighbour's a Russian spy.'

'Oh dear.' I didn't know what to say.

'Yeah, we keep telling her that Auntie Kath's dead, but she
doesn't believe us. And last week, she called the police and told
them someone was living in her attic.'

'That's creepy – and if it's real to her, then it must be scary.'

'Yes, I guess so, but the next day when I mentioned it to her,
she hadn't a clue what I was talking about, and she's like, "Don't
be so stupid, Ryan, no one's living in the attic."' He laughed at
the memory, but I could see the sadness in his eyes.

'Poor Tina.'

'The doctor's put her on new medication, we're hoping that'll
help.'

'I could call in on her if you like?' I offered.

'No,' he said, very quickly, then saw the surprise on my face. 'I mean, I wouldn't... best not.'

I was a little crushed. 'Okay, I just thought—'

'It's... difficult. I wouldn't just drop in, you don't know how you'll find her,' he said. 'Besides, you've got enough crazy going on in your life without an encounter with my mum.'

I nodded. I would have liked to see Tina again. I was sure she'd love a visitor, and didn't understand why Ryan was so against it. In my current mood, I was questioning everything and everyone, and wondered if it was because he didn't want me to get too close. Or worse, perhaps he was afraid of what his mum might tell me about him?

The following day, I was 'all rigged up', as Ryan's CCTV-installer friend Simon put it. I had a camera at the front of the house, in the porch, so I could see anyone coming and going.

'It feels a bit sci-fi,' I said, when Simon showed me how to access the footage from my phone. 'I'm not sure I want to see the axe murderer as he walks up to my door.'

'It's not just for you,' Simon pointed out. 'It's an insurance policy – for example, if that axe murderer *did* murder you, the police would be able to access the footage and identify him. I mean, otherwise it could be anyone and the police might never find them. According to official stats, four in ten female victims are more likely to be killed by a partner or ex-partner; they could be the ones to call the police, and be all innocent. But if they are there on film, standing on your doorstep with an axe, or a gun, then, bam...' He clapped his hands and made me jump!

'Oh wow, well, I guess I'm glad I'm having this done,' I said, trying to regain my composure. This was a guy who loved his job, but his imagination was fertile – a little too fertile! He was almost too excited at the prospect of catching a killer or criminal mastermind with his cameras, and seemed to be positively *hoping* for an axe murderer to turn up and prove his point. I was happy to use the CCTV as a deterrent though. 'So, if someone walked up the drive,' I said, 'would they *know* there was a camera there?'

Simon was nodding vigorously, like he'd already anticipated this question. 'Come with me,' he said, thrilled to take me out to the porch to create 'a dramatic reconstruction', as he grandly referred to it. I just hoped to God this didn't involve any real weapons that he may have about his person, 'for demonstration purposes'.

Once at the front door, I was then instructed to stand inside while he rang the doorbell, and I had to watch him on the monitor. I really didn't need this 'masterclass', but I indulged him, as he pointed out every little facet of the equipment, until, several minutes later, I received the eventual answer to my original question.

'If they knew what to look for, they'd know a camera was here – and might cover the lens with something, but,' he held up his forefinger, '*not* before the camera caught them walking towards it. If they didn't know what to look for, they wouldn't know,' he stated, which seemed rather obvious to me as he stood, licking his lips, waiting for my amazed reaction.

'That's brilliant, Simon,' I said, trying to wrap this up. 'Thanks for everything. I'll just write you a cheque.'

I paid him, and he insisted on giving me a wad of his business cards.

'Any job, any time – tell your friends,' he said, and I glanced at the cards, which read, 'Every breath you take, every move you make, CCTV is watching you.' They looked like something from a Boy's Own annual, coloured drawings of criminals being thwarted by CCTV, with Simon's 24/7 phone number emblazoned in flames at an angle across the artwork. I was surprised there weren't a few machine guns and an artistic array of flick knives thrown in for good measure. 'I've done work for the government,' he was saying, tapping his finger to his nose to indicate the secrecy involved. 'Deep. State,' he said, and I tried not to laugh. 'I'm also head of security down the boatyard.' He sighed at the apparent weight of this responsibility, like I'd be impressed. But it was pretty run-down last time I'd been there. 'Yeah, I fitted all the cameras down there too, *big* job,' he added.

'That sounds amazing,' I said, being polite and humouring him.

I was so relieved when Ryan appeared from the side of the house; this conversation could have gone on for days!

After a few high fives with Ryan, Simon eventually left, still talking as he went down the drive and into his van. Even as I waved him off, he wound the bloody window down and said, 'What you have to remember, Mrs Anderson, is that you now have a visual deterrent to potential intruders – sending a clear message that nothing goes unseen.' With that, he turned his van around and, on screeching tyres, sped off down the lane, leaving me exhausted.

'Simon loves his work, doesn't he?' I said to Ryan a little later. He was rendering the side wall, his forehead sweaty, his shirt open, a sheen of sweat on his chest. I averted my eyes.

'Yeah, he is a bit full on, isn't he?' he laughed. 'He's not really a mate, just someone I know from school. To be honest, I feel a bit sorry for him, he was bullied at school, and even now he gets ribbed in the pub. But his heart's in the right place.'

'Well, I'm glad he installed the cameras, because now if ever I see *him* outside here again, I won't be answering,' I said, rolling my eyes.

Ryan laughed. 'I like to give him work when I can. He needs it, and you need the extra security.'

'You're kind, getting work for him,' I said.

'Sometimes people need sticking up for. "The world's a cruel place, Mrs Anderson",' he said in Simon's voice, which was slightly creepy. He winked, and continued to work on the wall.

I watched him, and I realised I shouldn't keep wondering at Ryan's motives for being here with me. Phoebe was just looking out for me, but I shouldn't try and read into everything, just accept that Ryan was a decent guy. He looked after his mother, and Simon, and perhaps I was just another person he'd added to his collection.

A week later, I still hadn't heard from Mark, or his floozy (as my mother would have referred to her). I'd left several angry messages on my husband's phone, emailed my solicitor to inform her of Erin's comments on TV about me allowing them to have the house and how I was deeply concerned that they may find a loophole and get her wish. I also fired off an email to Estelle, threatening 'her client' with legal action if discussing me on air without my permission again. I was woolly on the word of law, but I was sure there was something libellous in their conversation. Estelle had clearly been involved in their 'script' and was straight on the phone.

'Carly, my darling, thank you for your message, how gorgeous to hear from you! But what on *earth* is all this silly talk about legal action?' To think I'd once quite liked her, amused by her caustic wit and salty bitterness regarding anyone on screen who wasn't her client. Now I suspected I'd probably also been at the receiving end of some of those darkly humorous remarks, and that wasn't so funny.

'Estelle, this isn't "silly talk", as you put it,' I snapped. I was angry that she'd tried to belittle me so early on in the conversation. 'I have agreed to tell untruths, but only because I want to keep my home. However, if Mark or his... *girlfriend*,' I said, resisting anything stronger, 'dare to say anything – and I mean *anything* – that we haven't agreed on, or they are derogatory in any way, I will instruct my lawyers to throw the book at you.' I said this with confidence, though quite unsure of the legal terms and cursing my lawyer for not getting back to me with a list of long legal threats I could repeat to Estelle. I recalled she had a nasty little habit of putting the phone away from her ear and rolling her eyes to her assistant; she was probably doing that now. 'Are you hearing me, Estelle? One more word about my feelings, my happiness or *my home*, and I promise you I will come for all of you. And please tell that child my husband's sleeping with to back off with the dead rats and the breaking in and the weird notes. If she doesn't stop, tell her from me she'll be sorry!' I clicked off my phone before she could respond, feeling sick with anger, blood pumping through my body.

I leaned on the kitchen counter, exhausted, emotional, and suddenly aware of Ryan, watching me.

'Oh... you always seem to walk in on me yelling at someone down the phone,' I sighed.

He nodded, staying in the doorway, half leaning on the door jamb. 'Yeah.' He gave a nervous laugh.

'I don't even know why I said that, just then, about Erin... but I think you're right, about her trying to scare me and make me move. She's been around us so long she knows about my fear of rats.'

'Maybe. But remember what Simon said... it could be someone you know, someone *right* under your nose,' he said in a creepy voice.

'Stop it, Ryan, you're scaring me,' I said, giggling nervously.

For a moment, everything stood still.

Then he smiled. 'Sorry, I was just teasing you.' He moved from the doorway and put his arms around me.

'Well don't. You could be the axe murderer Simon warned me about,' I joked.

He gave a big sigh. 'Hey, in other news, I came to tell you, I found more bigger cracks on the outside wall, but perhaps now isn't the time?'

'Tell me, I love a tsunami of bad news, just keep it coming.'

'They're far deeper than we thought.'

'Great. What does that mean?'

'It depends how deep they go – and the implications for the rest of the building. You might need an RSJ – could be a big job.' He shrugged.

'Obviously if it means the house is going to fall down, then I'll have to find the money – but until the divorce is finalised, I'm a bit short.'

'Leave it with me. I have a mate who might be able to take a look,' he said.

'Is he as weird as Simon?'

'Yes, all my mates are weird.'

'Well, they say show me your friends and I'll tell you who you are,' I said, with a smile, enjoying his company, and appreciating his friendship.

I'd lost several friends since Mark and I split, but I missed Lara the most. She would have been the one I'd have turned to at a time like this, to make me laugh, put everything into perspective. Even the Ryan situation was something I wished I could share with her, and Lara would have absolutely loved that drama. Over a bottle of wine, we'd have discussed the pros and cons of a younger man, and I'd have shared my concerns about trusting him.

One thing was for sure, I trusted Ryan's security advice, and was glad I now had CCTV at the front of the house, and he'd fixed the broken hinge at the back. But my real and present danger was Mark and Erin. Did he want to recapture the heady days of *The Forever Home*'s success? Did Erin want to be the new cast-member in the show that had been the golden days of *our* youth? She was often around back then, even once appeared on the programme I thought, in the background.

I suddenly remembered something Erin once said. She would have been about seven years old and Lara had asked her, 'What do you want to be when you grow up, darling?'

And Erin said, 'I want to be Carly.'

CHAPTER NINETEEN

A couple of days after he'd installed the CCTV, I had a call from Simon.

'Hi Simon, everything seems to be working okay,' I said, hoping I wasn't in for a lengthy phone discussion on the new camera equipment.

'Good, good,' he said, then silence.

'So, can I help you with anything?' I asked, not quite sure what was going on.

'Yeah… yeah actually, it's all a bit awkward, Mrs Anderson. Thing is, I don't always take cheques – I've had them bounce in the past, and now people usually transfer money or use a credit card – but I took a cheque because Ryan knows you. And – well, who *doesn't* know you – I mean you're Mrs Anderson, I used to watch you on the telly…'

'Right…' I said, unsure where this was going.

'Thing is – your cheque bounced, Mrs Anderson.'

'Oh God, I'm sorry, Simon,' I said, embarrassed. 'There's money in there, it's probably a glitch. I'll contact the bank right away.'

I'd paid him from the joint account; there was plenty of money in there, so I wasn't worried, but would need to sort it out. Mark and I had agreed that until the settlement we'd both use that account for basics but leave the majority of the money in there, then settle up when everything was agreed. I called the bank straight away, and after being kept on hold for too long, a rather bubbly young woman called Faye answered the phone, asking how she could help. I explained the situation, and she immediately checked our joint account, saying, 'I'm afraid, Mrs Anderson, it says "insufficient funds".'

I assured her the bank must have made a mistake and asked if she could tell me how much was showing in my account.

'Two pounds and forty-three pence,' she said, in the same jolly tone she'd answered in. I asked her to repeat what she'd said, and she did and I thanked her and clicked off the phone.

I was convinced the bank was in the wrong, so logged on to the account online but, to my horror, saw exactly the same figure that bouncy Faye had reported over the phone. There had been thousands of pounds in that account only two days before, and now just £2.43.

I immediately went into our joint savings account, where between us we'd had over £75,000 in there. We'd agreed not to touch that, it was waiting to be split 50/50 when we divorced, so I was confident it would all be there. I clicked on the page, and gasped, unable to believe what I saw. The final balance was £500. Two days before, £74,500 had been withdrawn. I sat with my head in my hands, and cried. Mark had emptied our bank accounts.

'You are kidding me, Mum?' Phoebe replied incredulously.

'No, I'm not. He's taken everything.'

I hated laying this on my daughter, but as Mark still wasn't picking up, she was the only person I could share this with. And she was my only hope – because Mark wasn't going to return my calls or respond to any emails, voicemails or death threats. So, in my desperation, I was hoping Phoebe might offer to call him and ask on my behalf what had happened with all the money we had in the world. He at least might answer if she called, even if he evaded her questioning.

'I'll call him,' she said, as I'd hoped.

'Are you sure, darling? I don't want you to feel like you have to get involved.'

'Get *involved*? Bloody hell, Mum, that's half your money – it isn't *his* to take, and it sure as hell isn't *hers*. That snotty little bitch can sing for it. Honestly, if I saw her, I don't know what I'd do... I'd want to grab her by the throat and—'

'It is what it is, there's no point in violence. We're now at damage limitation.' I tried to sound calm, but I was on the verge of bursting into tears. 'Actually no, forget that, violence is the answer. Let's strangle her together.'

That made us laugh and we both calmed down a bit.

'I can't believe I've been so bloody stupid to leave the chicken coop open for the fox to get in,' I said. I could have kicked myself for being so trusting – the majority of it was Mum's money, which she and my dad had saved all their lives.

Phoebe rang off, so she could call her dad. And, just then, Ryan appeared at the glass doors of the sitting room, which led out onto the garden.

'I've asked my mate to come over tomorrow to look at those cracks...' He seemed to suddenly realise I was upset. 'Sorry,' he said, leaning into the room, 'are you okay? I can't come in – my boots are caked in cement.'

'I'm fine – it's fine,' I said, discreetly wiping away tears with the back of my wrist. 'Just money worries.'

'Oh?' he said, and looked at me questioningly. I had living expenses, the cost of maintaining the house, I owed Ryan money for the work he was doing, not to mention Simon. And how could I continue living here with no money? I'd been living from hand to mouth and the pittance I'd receive from my new job in the interiors shop wasn't going to compensate for the money Mark had taken from our account.

I'd have to speak to Simon, and explain to Ryan that I wouldn't be able to pay him straight away for working on the house. He might be able to find work somewhere else until I could find the money to pay him. I dreaded telling him. He needed the money, and I liked him being around, but it was only fair to let him go – I just had to hope the house didn't collapse in his absence. Then there was the lawyer's bill; the money for that was to come out of the divorce settlement. And *that* was the money Mark had taken from our joint accounts.

My phone rang, and I looked at Ryan. I would talk to him later, once I knew the score. I made an 'I must take this' gesture, and he closed the door and went back to his work.

'You really shouldn't have got Phoebe involved.' It was Mark, and he wasn't wasting time with niceties today.

'I didn't want to, Mark, but it was the only way to get you to respond to me. You must have known how upset I was, I've left enough messages.'

'Erin says it's harassment,' he replied flatly, ignoring the whole money issue.

'Does she? Well, she should know,' I said bitterly. 'You really need to keep her on a leash. But as much as her fishwife behaviour in a village café, libelling me on TV and sending a dead rat in the post deserves a mention, let's save that for the finale, shall we? The most pressing thing on my agenda is where the hell has approximately seventy-five thousand pounds gone from our joint account?'

He cleared his throat. 'I was going to speak with you about that.'

'I bet you were.'

'I *borrowed* it. I have some outgoings – but plenty coming in and as soon as I get my US payment, I'll replace it.'

'You *borrowed* seventy-five thousand pounds and you didn't think to ask me or assume I'd notice?'

'I'm sorry, but the point is I'm on the cusp of signing, and the minute the American money comes in, I'll put it straight back,' Mark replied defiantly.

'Timeframe?' I snapped.

'Any day now – I think.'

'Look, I will give you a week, and if that money isn't back in the accounts, then I'm going to my lawyer – and the press.'

'There's no need for that, Carly,' he sighed; this laid-back approach was infuriating.

'No need? There's no *need* for you to have seventy-five thousand pounds, but you took it. What did you need that kind of money for anyway? Is Erin demanding a sports car – for her Barbie?'

'I… I owed it,' he muttered.

'For what?' I asked, imagining a gambling bill or some other luxury expense he'd incurred.

'Erin needed baby stuff – the baby's been born, a boy.'

I didn't know how to respond to this, it still didn't feel real, nor did it justify him taking the money, but I had to acknowledge what he'd just said. 'Oh, I didn't know,' was all I could manage.

'Yes, it was all rather distressing. Her waters broke, I wasn't there, she couldn't get hold of me—'

'So just like when Jake was born?' I said, remembering how scared I'd been, how alone. 'Congratulations, I suppose,' I heard myself say, into the silence.

'Thank you.'

'But can we rewind a moment? I'm still trying to process what you said – that you needed the seventy-five thousand pounds for baby stuff. I didn't know she'd given birth to a prince!'

'Erin wants the best for Billy, nothing wrong with that, and… and she needed a car.'

'A bloody Lamborghini?'

'She has to get out, it's driving her mad living in that little cottage. It's so cramped. I don't expect you to show me sympathy – but Erin is quite, how can I put it… a bit high-maintenance?'

'She was high-maintenance when she was *five*, why are you so surprised?'

'I just didn't expect it to be so – relentless. She wants *things*, expects *things* – a car, a holiday… a big house. She isn't happy with the cottage, but I can't afford to rent anything more expensive.' He sounded tense, desperate.

'This girl will be the death of you, Mark.'

He sighed. 'I feel like I'm—'

'Her father?'

'*No*, I feel like I'm—'

'Her *grand*father?' I couldn't help myself; the scorned, bitter, middle-aged woman part of me was loving this conversation.

'She watches my every move, Carly… always accusing me of seeing other women.'

'Yeah, but Mark, you probably *are*,' I said, struck by the irony of it all.

'I need to go to LA to make the pilot soon, but we can't just fly off to the States with a young baby – and Erin is refusing to let me go without her, she literally grabbed my ankles this morning before I went out.' He sighed. 'And then there's the baby. I've told her don't expect me to be getting up at all hours, I need my sleep – I can't do a piece to camera on no sleep, Carly, you know that. At my age, HD is unforgiving.'

'HD is an infringement on a presenter's human rights,' I said, but the sarcasm was completely lost on him. When Mark talked too much about himself and his problems, I either indulged or ignored him, depending on my mood – a technique I learned early on in marriage. Now I was completely detached from his self-imposed misery, and it was liberating.

'She's just permanently stressed, Carly,' he continued.

'I can imagine. Husband-stealing is a stressful business.'

'I'm sorry… for everything, Carly,' he said slowly, letting my name roll on his tongue; his voice was husky with what I recognised as lust. I hadn't heard that longing in his voice for years, except when he was talking to other women on the phone, when he thought I was out of earshot. But, of course, I was 'other women' now, wasn't I? And, consequently, I was far more attractive to him than when I'd been his wife.

Then I dropped the bomb: 'If the money isn't in the account, I'm going straight to the press with my video diary, remember? The one telling the truth about you, the perfect husband… the one I made after you hit me?'

His charm offensive immediately slipped then. 'You really are a bitch, aren't you?' he started, 'but don't forget, I also know the truth about you, and if you force me, I will use it!'

And with one click, he was gone.

CHAPTER TWENTY

My mum was diagnosed with cancer on her sixtieth birthday. It was a brain tumour, and she was told to expect a matter of months. I wasn't with her that day, I was waiting at home to welcome her with birthday cake and the news that she was going to have a second grandchild; she said it was the best birthday present she ever had. She didn't tell me she'd just come from the hospital, and that the chances of her meeting her second grandchild were slim. Instead, she danced in the kitchen with a six-year-old Phoebe, blew out her candles with gusto, and laughed like she'd never laughed before.

A week later, she told me, said she'd had to get her own head around it before she told anyone, and what mattered to her most wasn't when she died, but *how*.

'I want to keep my dignity,' she said, sitting on a garden chair, freshly painted nails the colour of candy floss. 'I want to die at home, I don't want to go through chemo and pain and losing my marbles.'

I, of course, couldn't bear to think about her leaving and refused to even consider her plan not to have any life-prolonging treatment. 'Mum, you must have whatever the doctors tell you to have, and we'll keep you going until they find a cure.' I was already googling hospitals in America, new treatments, medical trials.

'Darling, it's too late for me,' she said, and I remember her leaning forward, touching my knee and adding, 'I need your help.' But I refused to take part in that conversation.

For the next few months, I cared for her; it wasn't easy with a lively 6-year-old and morning sickness. But I was with her every day, and often through the night, and watching my lovely, vibrant Mum deteriorate into a shadow was heartbreaking.

One afternoon, when she'd been ill for about two months, she was incapacitated, sleeping most of the day, and said she couldn't take any more. 'I'm in such pain, my darling,' she said, 'but more than that, I know I'll begin to deteriorate mentally. I'm forgetting things, my words get mixed up. Please don't let me lose my mind.' She reached out her hand, her fingertips dusky from lack of oxygen. She was ebbing away, and in that moment, I realised, as much as I didn't want her to die, I didn't want her to suffer. So we finally talked, and the following morning, as one of her nurses left, I told her Mum would need more pills because her pain was now unbearable. She gave me a prescription, and that afternoon I returned, with the pills, a bottle of gin, and a copy of *Jamaica Inn*, Mum's favourite book, and mine too. I held her hand, and read the book to my mother, as she'd once read it to me, a story of love and loss, smugglers and secrets set against the backdrop of a rainswept Cornish coast. By the end of chapter two, we'd said our goodbyes.

I know in my heart I did the right thing; it was what she wanted, to choose her own death, to have some control in the horrific throes of a terminal illness, and escape the weeks or months of endless suffering. I didn't intend to tell anyone, it was between me and my mother, but when I heard there was going to be a post-mortem, I was distraught. I was almost nine months pregnant, and in total despair – what if I ended up in prison? Who would look after the children? So I told Mark, who assured me I'd done the right thing, and came back to Mum's apartment with me, where we took away the bottle with the remaining pills inside.

Mum's autopsy showed a body ravaged by cancer, with high levels of morphine, but acceptable levels for a cancer patient in the final days of life. As sad as I was, at least the worst was over, little did I know it was only just beginning.

Later, Mark used the way she died to threaten me when I left him; it was all he had to bring me home, and he held it over me throughout our marriage. He'd said it just a few times, but it was always there, hovering like a dark cloud, tying me in knots.

Scared that I might spill the beans on his sordid love life, our strange marriage, and his inappropriate new relationship, he was trying again to hold this over me. By doing this, he'd tainted something quite beautiful, something between my mother and I –

a final goodbye without hospital gowns, machinery and busy nurses. Just a mother and daughter, a bottle of gin, and their favourite book.

I made coffee to calm my nerves, and wished my mother was with me now to tell me what to do. Thanks to my husband, I had no money, and at the end of the month I owed Ryan a month's pay. He was now putting in new windows, as the frames were rotting. I felt terrible. I now had to break it to him that I couldn't pay him yet, until I had the money from Mark, but knowing my husband, I wasn't holding my breath on this deal. TV programmes could be dropped in an instant, and the person fronting them was like the wronged wife – usually the last to know. But first I had to deal with the Ryan situation, so with a packet of custard creams, and 2 mugs of fresh coffee, I set off into the back garden with a small tray.

It was another lovely spring day, crisp and sunny, the sky a blue halo over the sea, and any residue of anger I'd felt towards Mark began to lift and fly away. By the time I reached Ryan, happiness had landed in my heart. His T-shirt rose above his stomach as he reached for the top of the window, strong, brown arms lifted the frame clean out of the socket, and I marvelled at the sheer beauty of him, young and strong, the sun behind him, life in front of him.

I put the tray of coffees and biscuits down on the outdoor table, aware I was about to burst this perfect bubble.

'Ryan, I'm so sorry,' I said, and blurted it out, 'but I'm going to have to lay you off.'

He stopped in his tracks. 'Why?'

I quickly explained the situation, but promised I'd pay what I owed him as soon as I could. He looked disappointed, upset almost, and stood for a while, staring up to the sky, like there may be a solution among the clouds. The silence was awful.

'I feel terrible, obviously if I'd had the slightest notion I'd be in this position, I wouldn't have booked you,' I babbled.

'Never mind,' he sighed, 'it was good while it lasted,' which made me feel even worse.

'I just don't know what to say. You must be so pissed off with me.'

'No, it's just one of those things,' he muttered, kicking at the ground now, reminding me of Jake when he was little, trying not to show his anger over a broken toy, a day out cancelled. Then Ryan looked at me, his eyes dark. 'I *hate* him, Carly – he had no right to take your money, it's not fair. And you can lay me off, but the house *still* needs maintaining, the window frames can't be left like that – this house is exposed to all the elements all year round. I can't just do a few weeks here and there and fill in the cracks, cover up the problems. It needs someone working on it long term.'

'I know, you're right.' I nodded, remembering how my own father spent all his spare time repainting, weatherproofing. 'I promise, as soon as I get the money, I will pay you Ryan.'

'It's not just the money, Carly, but then again, I have to eat.' He smiled. 'I just love being here, I want to be around the house – around you.' He touched my shoulder, and I felt a sting in my chest.

'I like being around *you* too,' I said, my chin trembling.

'I don't have to go anywhere if you don't want me to,' he said.

'Yes, but you need work, and I can't keep you here like my toy.'

'I could think of worse things,' he joked.

'It's just an impossible situation,' I sighed, handing him a mug of coffee.

We sat down at the table, and neither of us spoke. He wasn't looking at me, just looking down; I'd seen him like this before, brooding, dark, like a stormy sky. And suddenly he looked up and the clouds lifted.

'I could just carry on working until you *can* pay me?'

'That doesn't seem fair. You need an income – as you say, you need to eat. I can't always rely on Mark. When he says he'll put the money back by the end of the week, it could be next month, next year even.' I'd threatened him with the video diary, but in truth, it was an empty threat. I wasn't stupid. It wasn't in my interests to release it as the minute something like that went out, he'd lose the US deal – and I wouldn't get my money back in the bank, or any percentage. And he always had the comeback of letting out my secret, which would be much more damaging.

'Okay – well how about this? The guy who owns the house I rent with my brother has decided to put it up for sale, and wants us out as soon as possible so he can get it ready to sell. I don't fancy being there while prospective buyers trail through my bedroom, so instead of waiting for the axe to land, maybe I could stay here?'

'Here? Oh,' I said, caught off guard, imagining Phoebe's face if I told her one of the Jarvis boys was moving in.

'Think about it. If I stayed here, I could get work whenever I can, but do bits and pieces in the evenings and weekends. I'd have somewhere to stay, and we could call it rent, and then when you've got the money from Mark, you could hire me full-time?'

'I don't know, Ryan, it feels too much like *an arrangement*, and what if it doesn't work out? I don't want to commit to anything at this stage.'

He looked disappointed again. 'I understand.'

'It's not that I don't *want* you here.' It was one thing Ryan staying over the odd night, but I wasn't sure if I was ready for him to be a lodger.

'It's fine, honestly.'

I felt so bad. I'd booked him for several weeks over the summer, his busiest time, and now just dropped him. Then he'd come up with a solution, and I'd thrown it back in his face. I watched him sip his coffee and offered him a custard cream. He shook his head.

'Oh God, you are pissed off, you love custard creams,' I teased, trying to lighten the moment, but he looked at me and there was anger in his eyes I'd never seen before.

'Yeah, I am pissed off, Carly. I love being with you, and I'm gutted. I thought it'd be nice. I love it here and just want to help out.'

We both sat in thick silence, not meeting the other's eyes, just sipping our drinks. I pretended to look out at the garden, and he just looked down at the table. I heard myself say, 'You're right, it would be nice, and I need the work done. Why not?'

He looked up and his face broke out into a big smile.

'Shall we say you'll stay for a couple of weeks, and hopefully I'll be able to pay you something?'

'And if it works out, we can talk again?' he said.

'Mmm, but for now, let's keep it from my kids, eh? They might take it the wrong way.'

'Fair enough.' He shrugged. 'I'm trying to save up anyway, going travelling once the summer's over – so you can save it up *for* me.'

I was surprised at the little thump in my ribs when he said this. I don't know why. There was I kidding myself that he might not want to leave, but that's exactly what he planned to do. I reminded myself that this was about two consenting adults having a casual relationship, a mutually supportive, lovely thing – with no strings.

'Anyway, let's not worry about money and shit,' he said, pushing into my thoughts. 'I wanted you to see this.'

He reached for my hand, and I took his, expecting him to show me some extra cracks in the wall or yet another rotting window frame, but instead he guided me through the garden, and down to the thick hedge that ran down the side. It wasn't too far from where we threw the maggots, and for a moment my heart was in my mouth. Then he put a finger over his lips, and held back some of the foliage for me to see inside. He stayed an arm's-length away, and I didn't get too much closer, but I suddenly heard the chirping of hungry little birds, and saw the nest, precariously yet firmly balanced inside the hedge.

'I noticed it this morning,' he whispered, and we both looked at the tiny little heads bobbing up and down eagerly. My heart melted, not just at the baby birds, but at Ryan's face, filled with childlike delight. 'We'll need to keep Miss Anderson away from here,' he whispered, and I was warmed again by the way he never referred to her as 'the cat' – she was always Miss Anderson or Missy to Ryan. It sounds silly, but it was those little things that drew me to him. For all his charm, Mark was more likely to kick the cat when no one was looking. The only time he gave Miss Anderson any attention was when Estelle got her a 'modelling gig' for a pet food company – The Andersons' cat – she was quite the celebrity. But as for showing me a nest of baby sparrows in a hedge in our garden, it wouldn't have happened with Mark.

As Ryan watched the baby sparrows, I watched him. I wondered if I'd done the right thing in letting him stay at the house. He'd shared my bed, wandered freely around my house, but now I'd agreed to something that might, down the line, be difficult one way or another. I just had to hope it would be okay – but history had taught me that blind faith wasn't something I should rely on.

CHAPTER TWENTY-ONE

The following day, I called Jake, who was finally admitting that he was finding it hard to come to terms with the fallen hero that was his father. My son felt things deeply, but bottled them all up, until they eventually came tumbling out.

'I still can't get my head round it even now, Mum. Why would he leave you for her? She's just a spoilt pig.'

Jake, like many kids, had a rather idealised view of his parents' marriage, and I wasn't going to disillusion him. Our children had happy childhoods, and to tell them what was really going on in the background – while they ate picnics on the beach and danced in the waves – would have been cruel.

'People just grow apart,' I said. 'And I think he has this weird belief that she'll make him young again.'

'But you're all alone there, and after all that you've done for him, now he's about to come into the big time, he's dropped you.'

'I don't think it was quite like that, and the plan is, he'll give me the money for the US programme, and I can keep the house,' I tried to reassure him. I hadn't told him about the money Mark had taken from our joint savings; it would have upset him too much.

'But it's *our* house, of course we should keep it. He can't just sod off to America with that bitch and leave you,' he spat. Jake was like me, he put up with things until he couldn't any more, and then he blew.

'It will all be sorted in the divorce, Jake. Trust me, everything will be fine. And if I do have to sell the house, I'll get another one around here.'

'There's nowhere like our house though, is there?'

'No,' I admitted, 'there isn't.'

We continued to talk, and it turned out his sadness and anger might also be stemming from something else. Apparently things hadn't worked out with his girlfriend, but he didn't want to talk about it, so I didn't ask too many questions.

'I'm sorry, love, some things just aren't meant to be,' I sighed.

'I was punching above my weight,' he murmured.

'I'm sure you weren't, darling. Never forget, you're the handsomest prince in Christendom,' I teased. It was a phrase from a book I used to read to him when he was little. 'That used to make you laugh,' I said, trying to cheer him up.

'Yeah, like when I was five!' he said, though I hoped he was smiling. 'But she doesn't think I'm the handsomest,' he sighed, 'she's found someone even more handsome.'

'Impossible,' I replied.

'She says she loves him.'

'Oh darling, I'm sorry, but if she didn't appreciate how wonderful you are, she just wasn't right for you.'

'Yeah, yeah. I have to go, Mum, I've got a lecture,' he sighed, and we said our goodbyes.

My heart hurt for him. Poor Jake, he was so young, and I knew one day he'd find the girl for him, but right now he couldn't see that. I wished he was here at home with me so I could comfort him.

I felt sadness in the pit of my stomach. I wanted both of them to be able to come home whenever they wanted to, and when they both left, it never occurred to me that one day we might not have the house. Then I thought about the alternative, Erin and Mark living here, looking at the sea through my windows, planting their bulbs in my garden, inviting my kids to sleep in their old bedrooms. The Andersons together again – all except one – me.

'Ahh that's shit for Jakey, I didn't know it was over,' Phoebe said, when I called her straight after I'd called Jake. 'He seemed really smitten with this one,' she sighed, hurting for him as much as me.

'He never put pictures on his social media, did he?' I asked. I had an account, but never used it, and relied on my kids to tell me if there was anything I should know.

'No, I asked him about that, but she didn't like her photos being online,' she said, but was soon distracted from her brother's pain by her favourite subject. 'Urgh. Erin. That smug little prig. I was thinking about it and she must have been eyeing Dad every time she came over. And then she just turned up about two years ago. I hadn't seen her since we were at secondary school, but just before I went to uni, she turned up on our doorstep, you must remember. She said she missed us having such a great laugh together so thought she'd come over.'

'Yes, I remember, but what I don't remember is Erin ever having "a great laugh" about anything.'

Phoebe giggled. 'Nor me. But I bloody bought it, and let her back in, but all she wanted to do was wave her tits in Dad's face.'

'Oh Phoebe, I'm sure it wasn't *quite* like that,' I offered, knowing it probably was.

'She used to turn up in tight shorts and low-cut tops in the middle of bloody winter,' Phoebe almost shouted down the phone.

I had to smile at this. I'd also thought Erin's clothes inappropriate for the weather. I once asked her if she was cold, and would she like to borrow a jumper; she refused. I thought it was a youth thing – but actually it was as old as the hills. And like the lech he was, Mark had fallen for it, hook, line and sinker. I wondered if that was when the seed was planted? Perhaps not the affair, but just a frisson between them.

'Mum, can I come home for supper soon? Stay with you for the night?' Phoebe asked.

'Yes, of course,' I said, delighted. 'When? Tonight?'

'No – I can't tonight, I wouldn't get there before midnight now! But can I come down next week? I just think we need to spend some time together. I'll arrange to have the day off work so I can be with you by about mid-afternoon – we can catch up, and eat, and drink.'

'That would be lovely, I'll make one of your favourites,' I said, my mind already inside a cookbook.

I came off the phone feeling happier, a visit from my daughter was just what I needed, but then I remembered Ryan. And I wasn't sure when he was moving in. We hadn't really discussed any details or ground rules, like where he'd sleep and what he'd do when one or both of the kids came over. So I wandered out into the back garden to ask if it was possible for him to stay somewhere else when Phoebe or Jake came home.

I opened the glass doors to go into the garden, but before I stepped out, I heard his voice, and there was something about the tone that told me this wasn't a work call. And then he said her name.

'Erin, just grow up, you really think it was okay? That was personal stuff between two people... How could you?'

I went to put my foot on the steps into the garden, which caused a stone to land on the ground, and make a noise. Ryan stopped talking. I held my breath; if he saw me it would be quite obvious I was trying to listen in. I waited in the silence for him to resume his conversation. But then I heard him say, 'I have to go, Carly's here,' and with that he clicked off the phone.

What the hell? I stood for a few minutes. He was whistling along; he knew I was there, but was pretending to be hard at work. How did I deal with this? Should I ask him directly why he was talking to her? But I didn't want him to think I was listening in on his phone calls, nor did I want him to think I was being jealous or weird.

Just then my phone pinged, alerting me to a text. It made me jump and at the sound Ryan popped his head round the side of the house.

'There you are, thought I heard you. Come and take a look at the windows,' he said proudly. He seemed to think I'd be more interested in this than the fact he'd just been on the phone with my husband's girlfriend.

'Yeah, great,' I murmured, hardly able to engage with what he was saying, still going over his conversation in my head. Why wasn't he telling me he'd just spoken to Erin? The way he was talking to her sounded casual, like he knew her; there was an intimacy in his tone, or was it my imagination?

As he continued to chat to me about the walls and the weather, I tried to convince myself this was something that could be explained. We lived in a small village, they could easily just be acquaintances and he'd never mentioned it. Rubbish, we'd talked about Erin, about his mum being her childminder, and he'd never said he was in touch with her now. From what he'd told me about her when she was younger, he didn't even seem to *like* her – so why were they chatting on the phone?

And then there was the comment about 'personal stuff between two people' – what the hell was that about? The worm of worry that had been slithering around my stomach now wrapped itself firmly around my intestines. Ryan had been my sanity through all this, and I didn't want to even contemplate the prospect that he wasn't who I thought he was, a nice, easy-going guy with no complications. Perhaps Phoebe was right after all.

My phone pinged again, a reminder that a text message was waiting. I looked down; it was from Phoebe.

Trying to get some time off work so I can come and see you.
Will let you know! Love you P xxxx

It was so preferable to another piece of bad news or weirdness to add to the ever-growing list. I was deeply comforted to know my kids would always be there for me, and I texted her some kisses.

'Was that your friend just then?' I asked Ryan, with deliberate vagueness. He'd gone back round the house to continue what he was doing. I couldn't see his face.

'Who?' His voice drifted around the corner.

'Just then, on the phone? I heard you talking. You said you had a friend who could come and look at the wall, see if we need a JCB?'

There was a few seconds' silence, and I knew he was going to lie to me. After twenty-five years with the master, I was an expert.

'No… it wasn't him… it was just another mate, called for a chat.' Then he popped his head round the side of the house. 'Try not to worry too much about the house, we just need to keep an eye on everything.'

'Yeah, we do.'

Silence.

'Erm… I'm going to work in a bit,' I said.

'Oh yeah, you start your new job today. Good luck.'

'Thanks, I'm a bit nervous. Are you around for dinner later?' I asked.

'No, no, I won't be. I can't stay over tonight.'

'Oh.' I was disappointed; we could have opened a bottle of wine and I could have asked him about the phone call again.

'Yeah, got to pack my stuff. No point waiting, I might as well move in tomorrow, if that's okay?'

'Yeah, sure.' I hesitated, really unsure about this whole moving in thing, but I couldn't back out now. 'The spare room is total chaos, and the back bedroom is filled with Mark's stuff he's yet to collect. So I thought you could have Jake's room for now, till

I've cleared it out? I'll put some fresh bedding on and you can put your stuff in there.'

He looked surprised. 'Won't I be... with *you?*'

This was awkward. Hearing him on the phone had made me wary, and besides, I didn't want him to move in like *that*. As much as I loved spending time with him, it was far too early. I took a breath. 'I don't know, Ryan, this feels a bit different than when you just stayed over – and officially you're the lodger – so really you should have your *own* room.'

'Oh – I see. Fair enough.' He seemed embarrassed, and I felt bad, but he *was* being a little presumptuous.

I turned to go inside, suddenly feeling very vulnerable. Was I overreacting to an overheard phone call? I had to learn to trust again, and there was nothing wrong with Ryan being around the place; we were just enjoying each other's company. He was kind and had really been there for me recently.

I put it to the back of my mind and started to get ready for work. Today was important for me. I hadn't ever really had a proper job as such, since I'd married Mark and become a mother and later been taken onto The Andersons' role, and I wanted to prove to myself – and the village – that I could do this. I tied my hair up loosely, and threw on a white linen top and jeans, which I dressed up with a necklace of glass beads.

As I headed down the stairs, Ryan was standing at the bottom, smiling. 'I sometimes look at you and feel like I did when I was sixteen,' he sighed.

When I got to the bottom, I kissed him, and said, 'Thanks, but you really don't have to flatter me, Ryan, we've already agreed you can stay.'

He looked hurt, but I wasn't pandering to him, or letting him think he could win me over with charm – I'd been *there* before.

Now, in the hallway, I slipped my feet into sandals, picked up my handbag and headed for the door.

He stood there, his arms hanging by his sides. 'Carly, before you go—'

'Yes?' I turned around. I didn't want to be late on my first day. Given my current financial situation, I couldn't afford to get on the wrong side of my new boss.

Ryan looked uncomfortable. 'I'm sorry, I think I might have come over as a bit pushy – assuming I'd be in your bedroom… but—'

'You weren't being pushy – why *wouldn't* you think that? I haven't exactly kicked you out of bed,' I said. 'I think we just perhaps see things differently. I think for now it would be best if we just keep this casual?'

He didn't say anything at first; he looked confused, hurt. 'Yeah, yeah, of course, if that's what you want,' he mumbled, already heading off back down the hall.

I left the house, slightly troubled. I wanted to believe Ryan, to trust him, but his words on the phone to Erin kept coming back to me. Were they just friends… or was there more to it?

CHAPTER TWENTY-TWO

I arrived at the shop to be greeted by the lady who'd been in the day I applied for the job. No one had interviewed me, but this was a 'training day', which I think meant I was being tested. I was fine with that. The lady, Maureen, was the manager, and very kind and helpful. She talked me through working the till and showed me the stockroom, and how to price things. 'Then there's a stocktake at the end of each month,' she explained. Later, she made us both a coffee, and we sat in the stockroom and chatted.

'As soon as I saw you, I remembered it was Carly from *The Forever Home*,' she said. 'I told the owner, Mr Karliss, that you'll be great for business.'

So that's why there was no interview. 'Oh, I'd better be good then, high expectations and all that,' I said, smiling, a little uncomfortable at still being seen as the TV version of myself.

'A lot of people who visit Looe still come because of *The Forever Home* show; they sometimes come into the shop, just to ask directions to the house,' Maureen said. 'In fact, I don't think we'd still be open if it weren't for the house.' I got the feeling, reading between the lines, that business wasn't good. There was a lot of stock, and all afternoon we'd only sold a couple of packs of paper serviettes.

I'd had this dream of opening a *Forever Home* shop, for those who came in search of the house. I could sell the lifestyle all over again, reliving the nostalgia of a family, sunshine, beaches, and home. *The Forever Home* was a great brand, with a unique aesthetic, and I'd wanted to bring it all back in a boutique of whitewashed walls, big open rooms, shades of white and pale blues, muted pastels, and the rather empty promise that 'nothing bad happens when you live by the sea'. Thanks to Estelle, Mark had retained the merchandising rights to the programme, and I doubted Mark would share the rights with me, or even sell them to me, and if Erin got wind, she'd make damn sure I didn't get anywhere near.

But working at the shop that first afternoon had reignited a dream. If I had my own shop, I could sell my paintings, and sculptures, just like the ones I made for the house. I'd fill the shop with pastel throws and cushions, ice cream shades of paint and candles that smelled like the sea.

After work, I walked back through the town, waving to one or two people I knew, then suddenly my phone pinged; it was Phoebe.

Hey Mum! I got tomorrow off. Yay! I'll be with you in the afternoon. Can't wait! Xxx

She'd said it would be the following week when she came home, and as delighted as I would be to see her the next day, that was when Ryan was supposed to be moving in. I'd have to ask him to move in a day later. I didn't fancy explaining it to Phoebe, sure she wouldn't understand or approve. And now I knew Ryan was in contact with Erin, I was also beginning to wonder whether I'd made the right decision.

The next time I saw him I would just come straight out and ask him about it. If I didn't, I would constantly be questioning everything he said and did.

When I arrived home, I made a salad and ate it on the sofa facing the sea. I missed the noise and bustle of family life, but on evenings like this, the birds singing in the trees, daisies sprinkled across the lawn, the sea glass-like, I enjoyed the solitude.

After I'd eaten, I started sketching, and by the time I looked up, it was almost dark.

Suddenly into the dim silence, my phone began shrieking, making me start. I picked it up and saw an unknown number, so answered it.

'Is that you? Is that Carly?'

'Yes.'

'It's me... Erin?'

I felt instantly unnerved; why the hell was she ringing me?

Before I had chance to ask, she blurted, 'Are you sleeping with Mark?'

'Mark?' I asked, incredulous.

'Yes – your ex-husband!' She was tense and snappy.

'Well, for a start, he isn't my ex-husband, we're still married.'

'Only because you're dragging your feet...' she retorted.

'*I'm* keen to move on, Mark's the one who's taking his time. You can ask my lawyer.'

There was silence and then she said: 'He told me it was *you* who didn't want to divorce...' She sounded like she might cry then.

'No, Erin,' I said, 'I *want* a divorce, and if Mark is telling you differently, then he's telling you lies. In fact, he tells an awful lot of lies.'

'Is he lying when he says he's not with you now?'

'No, he's not with *me*.' God alone knew who he was with though. Mark was clearly up to his old tricks.

'Has he hidden his car down the road?'

I wasn't quite sure what she was talking about.

'He's hidden his car so I won't see it. He's in there now, isn't he?'

And all of a sudden, I realised what she meant. 'Erin, are you outside my house?'

She didn't answer, so I went to the front door, and looked at the CCTV monitor; a figure in black, hands dug in her pockets, head down, was pacing the front lawn.

Irritated by the intrusion into my evening, I opened the front door and she looked up and glared at me.

'For God's sake, Erin, why are you here? What *are* you doing?'

'I know he's here,' she snapped, marching past me, her eyes darting everywhere. She walked down the hallway, then stopped and turned to look at me, anxiety etched on her face. I saw the fear in her eyes, and realised I wasn't dealing with 'the other woman' any more, I was dealing with a vulnerable young girl.

I gestured for her to go through into the kitchen diner, suggesting she sit down, offering to make her some tea, but she shook her head like I'd just offered her poison. She perched on the very edge of the sofa, like she might run away any second.

'Is he in bed waiting for me to leave, so *you* two can get back to it?' The disgust on her face said it all, and I wondered for a moment if she might just run up the stairs to check.

'Calm down, there are no estranged husbands in my bed,' I said. 'Go and have a look if you want to.'

She didn't get up, but she didn't decline the invitation either. She was really wound up and clearly had created a whole narrative around her anxiety.

I took a moment to look at her properly in the lamplight. Her hair looked unwashed, she was wearing a thin T-shirt and jeans; it was chilly out, so she must have been cold.

'You don't have a coat or cardigan with you?' She must have run out into the night, jumped in her car and driven here. That's what Mark Anderson did to women, he messed with their minds, made them do things they would never have dreamed of doing. Just to keep him. I knew, because in moments of madness I'd considered going out into the night, searching for him, my kids tucked in bed. I never did though.

I handed her a throw and she took it, without saying a word, and wrapped it around herself.

'Did you drive here?' I asked.

She shook her head.

'How did you get here then? It's a long walk.'

'I like walking.' She couldn't look at me.

'Erin, what's all this about?'

'I know he called you, earlier. I heard him on the phone.' As she spoke, she was looking around impatiently, like she was waiting for him to pop up from behind a bookshelf.

'He hasn't called me today, it wasn't me he was talking to,' I said gently.

'It would be different if we lived here,' she sighed, as if she hadn't heard what I'd said. 'Mark would be content.'

'Mark will *never* be content,' I replied. 'He'll always be looking for the next adventure, the next house, the next... woman. And the only way you'll keep him, if you really want to, is to accept that, and make your own life alongside him.' I couldn't believe I was giving bloody relationship advice to the woman who stole my husband. But I was speaking from experience, trying to save her from years of pain.

She shook her head vigorously. 'I could never accept it. The thought of him touching... kissing... having sex with anyone makes me *sick* to the stomach,' she hissed through gritted teeth.

'Then leave him now, because that's what you're in for.'

She suddenly turned on me, fury in her eyes. 'You'd *love* that, wouldn't you Carly? Then you'd get him back and could keep the house and pretend to be the happy couple again.'

'No, no, Erin, you've got this all wrong. I am glad Mark and I are over. He wasn't good for me. And seeing you tonight, I genuinely believe that he isn't good for you either. Look at you. You're thin, pale, you look like you haven't slept. You're not well, Erin.'

'I'm fine,' she said, just staring at me. 'I just need you to get out of our lives. I need you to stop calling him up, pretending the bank accounts have been emptied, leaving messages begging him to get back with you, inviting him here then trying to get him into bed.'

I laughed at this, but the look on her face pulled me up short; she really believed it. 'Erin, he's telling you lies, that's not true, any of it—'

'I know what you're doing, you're trying to manipulate the situation – come between us. Mark says you're like that. Well, just wait till I'm living here and you've been kicked out!' She suddenly sounded mean, the fragile child replaced by a woman fighting for the father of her child. I wished she'd realise he wasn't worth fighting for, but she didn't want to hear it. She reminded me of how I used to be.

Gently, I explained, 'I'm not going anywhere, Erin. This house belonged to my parents. I gave half of it to Mark as a gift many years ago. He's returning it as part of the divorce settlement, and it will be back with me and the children. You'll have no right to any of it.'

She seemed so taken aback by this, I knew Mark must have told her the house was his, all a big show for the new girlfriend. But this girlfriend wasn't going to give up on anything easily – especially him.

'Okay, well even if that is the case, Mark wouldn't give up his half, because he knows how much I love this house,' she said, sounding like the petulant child she'd always been.

Her audacity was quite startling, but I could see in her desperation, she was trying to convince herself as much as me.

'I know what Mark wants, and he knows what I want. And I *won't* be leaving here, Erin.'

She gave a mirthless laugh and looked around. 'Mark *wants* to put a big, beautiful glass box on the back of this house. And he's going to cover the lawn with trendy tiles and artificial grass. It's going to look so modern and stunning.' She leaned towards me, and said quietly, 'I've seen the plans!'

I shrugged, like I didn't care, but what she said bothered me, and the fact he was discussing this kind of detail with her made me wonder just who he was lying to.

'I'd make some changes in here too,' she was saying, looking around. 'I mean, it's all so old-fashioned, isn't it? I'd take that stupid picture off the wall for a start.' She gestured in the direction of a huge black and white photo of us all – me, Mark, the kids, running along the beach, the sunlight behind us.

'It was used for the TV show,' I said, refusing to rise to her comments. I'd kept the picture up, because it was part of the myth of The Andersons. I wasn't going to be psycho about it and cut Mark's face out of it. I wanted to keep the kids' childhood alive, to reflect the good times.

'Yeah, I remember the day it was taken,' she said, tears forming in her eyes again.

'Oh? I didn't realise you were there.'

'No one did. Except the director, who told me I couldn't be in the photo. "Not family," he kept saying.'

'I'm sorry, I didn't realise,' I sighed, 'but in his defence, the director was probably told by Mark to get you out of shot.' I didn't want to hurt her, but she needed to face the truth that he wasn't Mr Charming all the time.

'You moved the sofa?' she suddenly said. All the resentment gone, back to the fragile child again.

'Yes, the forecast said there's a good chance of a storm tonight.' We were both sitting on the sofa, at either end, oceans apart, but looking at the same view.

'I always loved watching the storms on the sofa,' she said, sadly. 'I wanted to live here.' She turned to me. 'Whenever I had a wish as a child – you know, a penny in a fountain, or before blowing out birthday candles – it was to be an Anderson.'

'Well, looks like you're going to get that wish, Erin.'

She was gazing ahead, not really listening. 'It was always sunny, and you'd make picnics and we'd play on the beach. Mark would give us piggybacks. I never wanted to go home.' She continued to stare out the window. 'But... but it isn't like I thought it would be. And sometimes I'm not sure I want to be an Anderson after all.'

CHAPTER TWENTY-THREE

A few minutes passed in silence. Erin continued to stare ahead, her eyes ringed in black eyeliner. It should have looked pretty on her delicate young face, but was grotesque, like a sad clown.

'Where's the baby?' I asked, softly, suddenly scared she might have left him somewhere.

'With my mum… he's with my mum.' And then she just broke down, in floods of tears. And I couldn't believe it myself, but I moved across the sofa, and put my arms around her while she sobbed.

'So, living with Mr Anderson off the telly isn't as much fun as you thought it would be?' I said in a low voice.

She looked up, her cheeks wet, the eyeliner now streaking down her face.

'I used to feel like you do now. When I was younger,' I said, feeling this need to fill the silence, to share with this woman young enough to be my daughter. She'd stolen my husband to get my life, and was just beginning to realise it wasn't all it was cracked up to be. 'Mark was – and still is – the most charming, fun man I've ever known. And for much of the time we were together, he was amazing. But when I became a mother, and he wasn't the centre of my attention any more, he began to look elsewhere. Most nights, I spent alone with two little ones, wondering where he was, who he talked to in a low voice on the phone. He was often away filming, but on more than one occasion, someone from the production team would call. "He's on location," I'd say, "he's with you, isn't he?" Their silence spoke volumes. Sometimes I'd try and catch him out, call him on location, and sometimes he was there, but there were times he didn't answer for hours, and once I called his hotel room, and a woman answered. But everyone loved Mark, and his colleagues covered for him, and when he came home he'd tell me I was imagining it all.'

She pulled the throw around her, more for comfort than warmth, I think, and she listened, the way she used to listen on sleepovers when I read the children bedtime stories.

'So I know how you feel,' I continued. 'You can't put your finger on it, but you know you've been moved from the top spot, don't you? And you think I'm the one who's taken your place, but it isn't me.' I paused a moment; she needed to hear this. 'I don't say this to be unkind – but trust your instincts. If you think Mark's seeing someone else, he probably is,' I said, gently. 'Many nights he'd come home drunk, reeking of perfume, and sometimes I'd confront him. The first time, I was pregnant with Phoebe and...' I paused, realising that now I'd said this out loud to Ryan, it was somehow easier to say. 'He pushed me across the kitchen. He said he didn't mean it, that he didn't hit me, just knocked me, but I still felt it, both physically and emotionally.'

She didn't look surprised, just resentful, and so I asked her, 'Has Mark ever hurt you, Erin?'

She shook her head vigorously, like she didn't want to deal with this. And I knew then that he hadn't changed.

'He hurt me too,' I said gently, 'until I made him stop.'

She seemed to flinch.

Tears were running down my cheeks; the pain of my marriage had always been bubbling under the surface. But it was only now I could see how much I'd been in denial. I had, in effect, become another viewer, a smiling spectator seeing my own marriage through the lens of a TV camera.

'He didn't mean to,' Erin said. 'He had to slap me because I was becoming hysterical… he spent the night at a hotel, feeling terrible. He loves me so much, you see,' she said, echoing his lies, his excuses.

'The truth hurts, Erin, but it's not as painful as sticking around waiting for the next slap, the next insult… the next woman.'

'He doesn't… he wouldn't. I just need to be a better partner, more supportive—'

I couldn't believe what I was hearing. 'No, you have to accept that it's impossible for Mark to be faithful.'

Erin was staring down at the carpet; she seemed numb, lost, just as I had been all those years before. 'It's not like it was with you,' she mumbled. 'He wanted younger women then, and I'm younger than him, I'll always be younger than him. He won't *need* to be unfaithful, he loves me. I *know* he loves me.'

'He probably does, in his own way, and he'll tell you again and again that he loves you. But Mark's love is worthless, because it isn't exclusive.'

I was surprised to hear myself talking so candidly to Erin, the woman who'd stolen my husband from me and still seemed hell-bent on taking more from me. We shared something though. We both knew the conflict, the passion and the sheer bloody agony of loving a man like Mark Anderson. We'd both experienced his magic, the way he could make you feel like the most beautiful woman in the world, the way you'd wake to find him watching you sleep, and telling you how he couldn't live without you. We'd experienced the thrill, followed by the pain, and then the thrill again. Fear slicing into soft, warm love, knowing you shouldn't stay, but for so many reasons, being unable to leave.

'I read a magazine article recently that said some people are addicted to falling in love,' I said to her now. 'Apparently, they constantly seek the initial ecstasy of being with someone new, and all the highs that brings. I think that's Mark – he falls hard at first and it's genuine, but he has no desire to move to the next stage, so just keeps seeking the highs, with new women. It is an addiction,' I added, almost sorry for Erin, but so glad I was now on the other side and able to see everything for what it was.

'I won't leave him. I know what you're trying to do… you want me to hate him, so you can have him back.' She sounded almost hysterical.

I just kept shaking my head. Erin was so young, and so in Mark's thrall, she couldn't see how ridiculous that idea was. 'I don't *want* him, Erin.'

'Well, let's face it, I doubt you get many offers, and you're always meeting up with him under some pretext,' she spat.

'It's not true,' I said calmly. 'You've got it all wrong. I'm so over him, you mustn't feel threatened by me.'

'Threatened?' She gave a hollow laugh. 'You're no threat, Carly, if you were younger or prettier, I'd be worried, but not…'

She wasn't the sweetest of people, but I doubted that she was trying to be cruel; she was just confused, and threatened by every female he came into contact with. That's what men like Mark do to you.

'I don't know what he's telling you, but let me be clear,' I said. 'We don't meet up, hardly ever. And perhaps *I'm* not young or pretty enough to catch his eye any more, but there will always be *someone* younger and prettier. Do you really want to live like that, checking his phone, watching his car, following him? It's painful, and stressful, and it wears you out. I know this because I went through it too in the beginning. Until I realised I had to build a wall around me, and stop loving him. It was the only way I could protect myself.'

She looked at me, her eyes glassy, but finally the hate and fury had left them. Something I'd said had made a connection with her.

'He went out last night,' she started. 'He left me on my own, and Billy wouldn't settle. I was exhausted, couldn't sleep wondering where he was. I called and texted but it just went to voicemail and there was no response to my texts, he was ghosting me. So I phoned the pub, but they said he wasn't there, and I ended up in tears. Billy was crying too and I nearly called my mum, but I knew she'd blame Mark.'

'Well, it was his fault.'

'Yeah, but she has a real problem with him, always has, even when he was with you,' she said, tears filling her eyes. 'So when I heard his key in the door, I ran out of the bedroom and stood at the top of the stairs. I only asked him where he'd been, I mean, it was two o'clock in the morning, and by then I was totally freaked out. But he didn't even look at me, just said, "The pub," and went into the kitchen. So I ran downstairs, told him I'd called the pub, and he wasn't there, so where *had* he been?' She started to cry, quietly, and I reached for a box of tissues from the coffee table, and handed them to her; things were still too raw between us for me to hug her. 'He… he was just vile, saying I was obsessed, that I was stalking him, and he didn't know why he was with me. Then he said he wished he'd stayed with you,' she sniffled. 'Then when I saw your number on his phone, I thought you were back together; he told me you'd been begging him to come back.'

'He doesn't wish he'd stayed with me, he just told you that to make you feel insecure, it's what he does.'

From being a baby, Erin had spent a lot of time with people who were paid to care for her and almost pushed into other families where she didn't quite belong. It didn't take a psychologist to work out why she was with Mark. She'd watched the family, danced around the fringes of people's lives and chosen the Andersons.

'What do you think he'd *do* if I left him?' she suddenly asked.

I doubt it was what she wanted to hear, but I had to be honest. 'I think he'd lick his wounds, be sad for a while then move on.'

She shook her head. 'No. You're wrong. He'd realise what he'd lost. He'd miss me…' she said resentfully.

'Perhaps,' I humoured her, but I realised then she was beyond help, and as with my kids, I just had to let her find out for herself. Experience is a hard teacher, but in time, like me, she'd learn. I stood up and stretched. 'I'm going to make myself a cup of tea – would you like some?' I asked.

She half-nodded, without looking up, just kept staring out of the window at the night.

I went into the kitchen area, and while I made the tea, continued to talk. 'I understand how you feel, Erin. I loved him once just like you do,' I said, then, turning back to pour boiling water into the cups, I added gently, 'He lures you in, you feel so loved and happy, but that's when he lets go and suddenly you're flailing around.' I stopped for a moment, and staring at the wall for inspiration, I tried to explain to her the way he was without sounding bitter or divisive. 'He has this huge ego,' I started. 'His mother treated him like an absolute prince, she spoiled him really. She died before I met him, but if his sister's anything to go by, I can only imagine,' I said, laughing. 'I reckon it was his mother who instilled in him the belief that the people in his life are bit-part players, and he's the leading man…'

I turned for her reaction, but the sofa where she'd been sitting was empty.

'Erin?' I said, moving from the kitchen area into the section where the two sofas sat. But she wasn't there, so I checked the downstairs toilet, calling her all the time. I then went upstairs to see if she'd gone to check Mark wasn't waiting for me. But she wasn't anywhere – and I came back into the sitting area and saw the white muslin curtain blowing in the breeze. The huge, glass bifold doors had been opened – and she'd gone.

Was she bored of listening and just decided to leave? It was possible. Erin had never been big on manners. I popped my head out of the window to see if she was still around, but it was so dark and windy I could barely see anything, so came back inside, closed the glass doors and drank my tea. But then I started to wonder about her mental state and her safety. You only had to climb over a fence at the bottom of our garden to be on the cliff edge. What if, in her rather emotional, erratic state, she'd fallen, or worse, done something stupid?

I was now very concerned, so grabbed a torch and headed outside. As I stepped into the garden, thunder clapped in the distance; the threatened storm was on its way. Wading through the darkness, I was becoming quite scared. The possibility of Erin throwing herself from the cliffs was stark, and real. What if the pain of loving Mark was so unbearable, the only way Erin felt she could leave him was to end her life? And what if, in my attempt to share the truth, I'd actually metaphorically given her the final push?

The hawthorn rattled; the wind was getting stronger. I shuddered, not knowing what the hell to do. And now the rain started, and the further I went down the garden, the nearer I was to the sea, I could hear the waves roaring, and the air was tinged with salt and fear. The thunder boomed, and seconds later lightning lit the sky, flashing the garden with brightness, allowing me to see briefly beyond the meagre reach of the torch, but there was nothing but an empty vista.

I stood right on the edge of the garden, the sea swirling beneath me, the tang of salt on my lips from the spray, and I wanted to cry. I felt so helpless, but continued on, calling her name and flashing the torch. But the wind was whipping up now, and snatching my voice. I turned and looked back at the house; it seemed a long way away. But suddenly, I felt a lurch in my gut. Something, or someone, was moving behind the glass. Had Erin gone back inside?

I started to run up the garden towards the house, still calling her name, but losing it to the wind and rain. What if it *wasn't* her inside, and while I'd been out here looking for her, someone had got inside? As I approached the house, breathless from running, I saw the side gate was open – had the latch loosened in the wind, or had someone let themselves in? My heart began pounding. I needed to get inside and grab my phone, so I could call the police.

Taking a deep breath, I walked carefully onto the patio, trying to stay along the edge, so if someone *was* inside the house, they wouldn't see me. Slowly, I approached, holding my breath. I reached the glass doors, and stopped. They'd been closed. I'd definitely left them ajar. And my phone inside. And I was outside. I could see it now, through the glass doors, sitting on the coffee table, so near and yet so far. I barely felt the rain on my face, the cold wind now chasing me like a madman up the garden. I just had to get my phone.

I grabbed the edge of the door and, while keeping my eyes on every corner of the room, slowly started to open it. Gathering all my strength, I heaved the glass door open, trying not to make a sound, trying desperately to stay on my feet. Still holding the door with one hand, I leaned over, one foot inside, one out, and bent down to where my phone sat on the coffee table. I saw my own hand touch it, and just as I did, was aware of another hand reaching for mine. My scalp prickled as I slowly looked up.

CHAPTER TWENTY-FOUR

'Ryan?' He wasn't supposed to be here.

'Carly, what are you *doing*?'

'What are *you* doing?' I snapped, grabbing my phone. 'You'd finished for the day; I didn't expect to see you until tomorrow.'

'I came to see you – we left things on a bit of a—'

'Why didn't you *knock*?' I hadn't given him a key yet and was still creeped out that he'd turned up and just let himself in.

'Whoa, hang on.' He was holding his hands in the air like he was surrendering. 'I *did*. I knocked and I rang the doorbell, I even pulled weird faces into the camera – check your footage. I guessed you were in because your car's in the drive, but when you didn't answer, I came round the back. To be honest, when I saw the glass door open in this weather, I was worried.' He walked towards me, his arms outstretched, but I still felt rather prickly and moved away. 'What's *wrong*? I was worried. The curtains were flapping in the storm, your phone and keys on the table, you missing—'

I took a breath. 'I'm sorry, I just didn't expect anyone to be here.'

'I hope when I move in you don't get scared every time you find me in the kitchen,' he said with a smile.

'You're right, I need to get used to people,' I said, beginning to calm down but still anxious over Erin, where she'd gone.

Ryan stretched out his arms again, and this time I walked towards him.

'So, what's going on?' he asked.

'I'll explain everything, but first I need to make a call,' I said, finding Lara's number. I had to know Erin had got home. I wasn't sure if she was going back to Lara's or the cottage she shared with Mark, but she'd said Lara was looking after the baby, so I hoped she might have headed there.

I called Lara on her mobile, but it rang for ages, no answer. I considered calling her landline, but I didn't want to wake the baby, or alarm Lara unnecessarily. Erin was probably back with Mark at the cottage by now. And I could hardly call him. She would then definitely be convinced something was going on, and besides, I doubted Erin would want him to know she'd been here. I called Lara back to leave a voicemail, but after the beep, I froze. I didn't know what the hell to say. Lara and I hadn't spoken for months, the last time I'd even seen her had been at my wedding anniversary, and understandably neither of us had called the other since then. I hung up, hoping that Erin had simply walked out so that she could think on what I'd said and consider her next steps. I was pretty sure she'd fall for Mark's lies again – after all, I'd been the same once – but I hoped what I'd said would make her realise her mistakes sooner than I did. For now, though, I just had to let her find her way.

'I'm just going to dry off my hair a little,' I said to Ryan with a smile, kicking off my wet trainers and grabbing a towel from the kitchen area.

'I meant to say, when I came in earlier, I panicked when you weren't here, so ran upstairs. If you see wet footprints in your bedroom, they're only mine,' he said.

I rolled my eyes. 'Ryan, honestly, it's like having Jake back, he was always making a mess everywhere,' I sighed, realising I quite liked the idea of mess. I wanted the house to be lived in, and not the styled film set Mark had always insisted on. I wandered back through to where he was, while drying my hair with a towel.

'Sorry.' He smiled, looking up at me, and my heart melted. He was so good-looking, and again that shadow came over me; what on earth did he see in me?

He was relaxing on the sofa now, and I joined him there, pulling my knees up under me, sitting so close I was leaning on him.

'I'm not sure landladies should sit like this with their lodgers,' I giggled.

'Actually, I wanted to check in with you about that.'

As conflicted as I was about him staying with me, the thump of disappointment made me only too aware of how my heart felt. 'Oh? Have you changed your mind?'

'I'd still love to stay for a while, but I wanted to help out because you couldn't pay me. But now your hubby's in the money, does that still stand? I'm happy to keep to the arrangement if you're still up for it?'

I started, taken aback. 'What do you mean Mark's in the money?'

'Apparently he's finally signed the big deal in America. The *Daily Mail* says he's a bloody millionaire!' He took out his phone, found a news article and handed it to me.

'I didn't realise,' I said, reading it quickly. 'But it says here he signed it a few days ago, and he's heading off to Los Angeles next week?'

Ryan nodded.

'But he didn't tell me when I spoke to him, and Erin never mentioned it.' I shook my head as I read the story. Why hadn't he told me? I hoped to God he wasn't going to renege on our agreement.

'Erin? You've seen her?' Ryan raised his eyebrows in mild surprise.

'Yes, that's what I was about to tell you, it's why I was in the garden just now.' I explained about Erin's unexpected nocturnal visit and rather sudden exit. 'I was worried she might have fallen

– or worse. But she must have run through the side gate and down the lane back to the cottage.'

'That's quite a hike,' Ryan murmured.

'Yeah, it's about three miles. I did think of jumping in my car and trying to find her – but—'

'Why? You don't owe her anything.' He sounded irritated.

'She was in a state. I feel like I should have gone after her. I wonder if I should call Mark and see if she arrived back there?' I reached for my phone. 'I might call him—'

'Don't.' Ryan put his hand on my arm to stop me, then slipped his arms around my waist tightly. 'Do it tomorrow, give *me* some attention now.'

I was surprised by Ryan's neediness. I'd never seen him like this, and I suddenly remembered something.

'Did you say your brother once went out with Erin?' I asked.

He sighed, and pulled away from me. 'Many moons ago.'

'Does she keep in touch with him?'

'I don't know, you'd have to ask him.' He clearly didn't want to talk about Erin, or his brother. But I did.

'It's just that I overheard you – talking to Erin.' I wasn't going to mess about any more; I had to know before this went any further with Ryan.

'Yeah, she wanted to get hold of Max. I don't know why.' His whole demeanour changed; he suddenly seemed defensive, didn't want to elaborate.

'Is that all? Did you really not talk about anything else? It sounded like you were… friends?'

'Quite the opposite, she's a pain in the arse.'

'It's just that—'

'Carly, I am not friends with her!' he snapped. 'I'll call you over next time my phone rings so you can listen properly, yeah?'

'Don't be like that. I wasn't *listening*, I just happened to walk out into the garden and I heard you say her name.'

He sighed. 'She's just bad news, brings trouble wherever she goes. *Please* can we change the subject now?'

Perhaps she *had* just called him to ask for Max; perhaps what he said to her would make perfect sense if I'd have heard the whole conversation, in context. But I'd remembered exactly what he said – *That was personal stuff between two people... How could you?* – and however hard I tried, I couldn't make it fit with his seemingly innocent explanation.

CHAPTER TWENTY-FIVE

Ryan stayed over that night. And he slept in my bed. It just happened, and when, a little later, in the dark, he rolled over and ran his hands all over my body, I silently said yes to everything that led to.

In the morning, when I woke to find him gone, I was sad, and wished he'd come back to bed. I felt like a lovesick teenager. My concerns about the phone call with Erin now faded. I'd probably read far too much into it and, in the cool light of day, felt there was nothing to worry about where Ryan was concerned. I leapt out of bed and called Mark straight away, ostensibly to pin down times, dates and bank transfers, if the money had come in. I also had an uneasy feeling about Erin, and wanted to double-check she was with him and had arrived back safely. Of course, as usual Mark didn't pick up, so I left a message for him to call me. And, to my amazement, by the time I was dressed and on my way downstairs, he'd called me back.

'Congratulations,' I said. 'So, the US deal's finally gone through?'

'Yes, I... yes,' he said, sounding a little subdued, probably because I'd caught him out and he realised I'd be expecting my money sooner rather than later.

'Is Erin with you?' I asked.

'No. She, er... we had words and she's gone to her mother's.'

I walked into the kitchen. Ryan was there, fully dressed, making coffee, and my heart lifted just to see him – he handed me a mug, and I gave him a peck.

'Oh dear, what will the press say?' I replied sarcastically. I couldn't help but feel a little smug; here I was with Ryan whilst Mark's relationship was already on the rocks.

He didn't answer me.

'Mark, are you there?' I asked, rolling my eyes at Ryan and going to the sofa, plonking myself down.

'Yes – I'm here – and I'm not in the mood for your humour. Anyway, she hasn't left me, she just wanted to spend time with Lara. She's as excited as I am… we just had a little disagreement,' he said absently. I thought back to the previous evening and a distraught Erin. 'It wasn't "a little disagreement" to her,' I said. 'She called in here last night looking for you. She was upset.'

'Did she?' he said absently. 'I'm trying to sort out tickets – need to book flights urgently.'

'Mmm, that reminds me, before you leave the country, can we please meet with our lawyers as soon as possible?' I said. I hated to sound like a grabbing ex-wife, but it was my money, and as it was usually so hard to get to talk to him I had to take advantage. 'I'm desperately short of money, and our accounts need reimbursing after you drained them,' I said, glad he and Erin were off to LA. I genuinely hoped they'd be happy, and the bonus was I'd never have to see them again.

I smiled at Ryan, who was now buttering toast.

'Yes, yes, we'll sort something with the lawyers,' Mark sighed. 'I just feel… oh, I don't know, I wonder if Erin will survive in LA. She's already saying I can't leave her alone and go to work every day. I mean, why does she think I'm going out there if not to work?'

'Oh Mark, you really did land yourself in this one, didn't you?'

'And she wants a big, fancy house out there – well, so do I, but until we know this is going to be a success, we can't buy anything. But she doesn't understand… she's so… fragile.'

I had already done my marriage therapy for that week, and didn't want another debrief on their dysfunctional relationship.

'Anyway, look, about the money – the three million or whatever – we agreed twenty per cent?'

'What?' he challenged.

I felt a shadow cross over me. 'It's in all the papers, Mark, you have the US money?'

'It's agreed in principle. We don't have it in the account yet; we announced it early. Estelle thought it would be prudent to get it out there.'

'Okay, but I helped with the treatment, most of the ideas were mine – originally I was going with you – and it isn't my fault you *recast* me, Mark. I put the work in, so I want the money I'm owed as soon as possible.'

'I'm sure we can come up with something.'

'*Something*? This isn't a *gift*, you owe me the money!'

'I… Yes, okay, but I don't recall anything legally binding.'

'I hope you're joking,' I replied in disbelief.

'Carly, I'm not rolling in it. I owe a lot, plus I have another family to support now…'

'That's not my problem, you bastard. You agreed to this.' I had Mark on speaker, and Ryan was looking back in shock at what he was hearing. I just shook my head in despair.

'A discussion isn't legally binding, Carly.' He said this like he was tired of explaining something to a child that didn't understand.

'Stop patronising me. You are *not* just going to disappear to LA and wriggle out of this.' My heart was thumping; what kind of stunt was this?

'Look, as I said, I haven't even received the money myself yet, and everything's in the hands of Estelle and my lawyers.'

'Great, so she'll be salting it away and coming up with all kinds of little plans with your lawyers.' I hissed down the phone, 'You are a self-centred, lying, pompous—'

'Oh please, Carly, I'm not in the mood for one of your abusive phone calls today, you'll get some spending money, just calm down!'

'You condescending bastard – you—'

But he'd gone, leaving me clutching the phone, angry as hell.

'After everything I've done, after everything *he's* done – he talks down to me like that. Spending money? *Bastard!*' I yelled into the air.

Ryan was standing nearby, eating toast, just chewing and watching me.

'He's got his big American deal now, thinks he's untouchable,' I said, getting up and pacing the floor. 'Well, he isn't. I could ruin him. One phone call, that's all it would take – I could simply tell the truth for once about our marriage, his drinking, his womanising. And how he used to read bedtime stories to his current baby mama – twenty-seven years his junior!'

'Whoa, Carly, think calm thoughts, babe.' Ryan was pretending to be scared of me.

'He just gets me so— He's such a pig! He's the only person who takes me to boiling point – I could kill him, Ryan, honestly!'

I could see now that all the delays with the divorce settlement were planned. Mark had had no intention of giving me the twenty per cent he'd promised. He'd just told me that to shut me up, so it could all go through smoothly without me kicking up a stink. And thinking about it, Erin's comments the previous evening about taking down the family photo if she lived here were real.

'Mark *wasn't* going to give up his half of the house, he was planning for *me* to give up mine. He doesn't want me to have what's owed, he wants to give me so little that I've no choice but to sell up. And then he'll swoop. He wanted this house for Erin, to keep her happy. Neither his ego nor his US deal could take another relationship breakdown. They'll probably use the house as a second home when they aren't sitting in their luxury house in LA gazing out onto their infinity pool. Meanwhile, I'll be so desperate for money, I'll have to spend the rest of my days looking at the home I once owned from a rented flat nearby.'

'Hey, it's going to be fine, you'll sort it all out.'

'Ryan, how *can* I?' I asked, plonking myself back down next to him on the sofa.

He shrugged, and kissed me on the cheek. He wasn't taking it seriously, and why should he? Ryan would be off at the end of the summer; my life didn't impact his in any significant way. I was alone, and only I could sort this.

I paced the floor, working out how I could get what I needed. I didn't want Mark's millions, I wasn't greedy, just enough money to stay here in my home, pay my bills, and make my own life and have financial independence – was that too much to ask?

I was racking my brains for the answer, when my phone burst into life, making me jump, especially when I saw Lara's name on the screen.

This was going to be very weird; we hadn't spoken for months. I held my breath and pressed the answer button, putting the phone to my ear.

'Is Erin there, have you seen her?' she started, without any preamble. 'I had a missed call from you. Do you know where she is?'

'But I just spoke to Mark, he said she was at yours?' I replied, taken aback.

'She isn't. She didn't come home last night.' She sounded frantic.

My head started spinning, thinking a million different things.

'Carly,' she said. 'I'm really scared.'

My oldest and dearest – but estranged – friend, was telling me her daughter hadn't come home, and all I could see in my head was the open door, the sea, the storm.

CHAPTER TWENTY-SIX

'Erin was supposed to come back here, last night,' Lara was saying. 'She said she was meeting a friend. I was looking after Billy and she was going to collect him afterwards. But she didn't come home. I just assumed she'd gone back to him at the cottage...'

'But she isn't there...?' I finished her sentence.

'No, she isn't there now. I just called and *he* said he hasn't seen her since *yesterday*, but I don't trust a word *he* says.' She said *he* like Mark was dirt on her shoe; the new baby hadn't changed things there. 'I'm terrified something's happened to her. She's been getting nasty messages on her social media. Someone's really jealous of her. It's because of *him*, women actually think he's a *prize* – can you believe that?'

'No,' I lied, but I could, actually. There was always a woman somewhere waiting for Mark. Who hated the one he was with.

'I'm calling you because when I saw you'd called, I hoped you might... you might know where...'

She burst into tears and I tried to talk her down, saying stupid things like, 'I'm sure she's fine,' and 'She's probably with a friend.'

But Lara, understandably, wasn't listening. 'She's been behaving weirdly recently, the messages have been really nasty, and – I know this is crazy, but she thought *you* might have been the one sending them.'

'What? No – why on *earth* would she think that?'

'Oh, she got it into her head that you and Mark were secretly back together. Apparently the messages you sent—'

'I didn't *send* any!'

'Okay, okay – but some of the messages suggested you *might* be back with him.'

'Lara, you know me. You were there the night Mark told me. He slept with your daughter; he ruined our friendship. I could never go back to him. You must know that even if Erin doesn't?'

'I'm desperate, Carly. I can't think straight, I'm imagining all kinds of things. She's not answering her phone and... I wondered if you hated her for what she did?'

'No, I—'

'I know you were upset about everything. I wouldn't blame you if you did, just to get back at her... but, Carly, I'm worried, please, if you know *anything*...'

'Look, Erin *was* here last night,' I started. 'She came looking for Mark. I guess she told you she was meeting a friend, but she was coming here instead. I think she thought she'd catch us here, together.'

'What did she say? When did she leave? Carly... there must be something?'

I told her in more detail about Erin's visit, and how she'd virtually run away.

'Oh God, you don't think she ran down the garden and jumped—'

'No. no. I bet she'll turn up in the next half-hour. She might even have booked into a hotel to teach Mark a lesson?' I suggested, but I wasn't even convincing myself, and now I was really worried.

'Teach him a lesson? But you said he wasn't *with* you.'

'He wasn't, but from what Erin said, it sounded to me like he might have been with *someone* last night.'

'The little shit!' Lara snapped. 'I told her this was the biggest mistake of her life. Let's face it, he was the biggest mistake of *yours*.'

I didn't want to get into the mistakes of my life right now. 'Lara, what can I do?' I asked. 'Shall I come over?'

'No. No, really, it wouldn't help, but if you could check your garden again, and the… beach?'

'Yes, of course I will.'

'What *time* did she leave yours last night?'

'Oh, er, I imagine it was about 8.45ish… a bit later? As soon as I saw she was gone, I ran outside to see if I could see her but—'

'Okay,' she cut me off. 'I'm going to see *him* – if I don't get any answers, I'm calling the police. I honestly don't know how you put up with him for all those years. You were a bloody saint, Carly. After what he did to you, how he hurt you… If he's lifted a finger to her, I will… I'll…' She started to cry and then hung up.

I put down the phone; so Lara knew about the abuse. She'd watched my video, even though I asked her not to.

I was sure Mark would be upset that Erin was missing, but knowing him as I did, I knew he'd be even more concerned with how this would play out for his TV career. I doubted very much that Erin and their child were any higher on the food chain than the first 'Awesome Andersons'.

Erin was a loose cannon. Had it not occurred to him that she would want to be the centre of attention? She wouldn't be satisfied with a cameo role as I was. Erin wanted more.

When I'd called him earlier, Mark had been booking flights to leave the country having just pocketed three million pounds. And now his high-maintenance girlfriend was missing. I couldn't help but wonder if Erin had also stopped being an asset and become an obstacle in his life. And what lengths Mark might go to, to move on.

CHAPTER TWENTY-SEVEN

'So, any news on Erin?' Phoebe said, when she arrived for her overnight stay with me. I'd called her first thing to let her know; I wondered if she might have any ideas as to where Erin might be, but she was as stumped as the rest of us. I was so looking forward to seeing her – with Erin missing it made me want to hug my kids a little closer. I still didn't feel it was the time to reveal my 'lodger' plans to Phoebe, so spoke to Ryan and he'd agreed to hold off moving in until the following day. She'd brought a bottle of Prosecco and we were both sitting on stools at the kitchen island with a glass each while I told her in more detail about Erin's visit, and now disappearance. 'Let's hope she's left Dad and run away and we never have to see her again,' she said.

I raised my eyebrows in agreement and took a sip of Prosecco.

'Someone I hardly knew asked me the other day if you and Dad had been really married, or was it just for the TV,' she said.

That made me uncomfortable, but then we'd asked for it. Both me and Mark had put ourselves out there for the public's scrutiny, and they duly scrutinised.

'Well, it wasn't a conventional marriage,' I conceded.

Phoebe put down her glass, and turned to me. 'Oh God, Mum – please don't tell me you were swingers… or worse, Dad had three wives?' she teased.

'Not quite. We presented a united front, for Dad's career, and you kids, but your dad… went his own way, and I found it easier to live my own life. I realised early on that you can't change people – sometimes you have to adapt.'

Not much of a marriage,' she mumbled, fiddling with the stem of her glass.

'No, and now I'm on my own, I'm happier. But we had this unspoken agreement: he could live his life, and I'd be home with you and your brother. I was happy, and I think you and Jake were, and so was Dad.'

'Doesn't sound like a marriage to me,' she said, unsmiling.

'Sometimes the weirdest things on paper work in real life,' I said, trying to make this sound simple. I wanted to be honest with Phoebe, she was old enough to understand, but at the same time I wasn't going to tell her about the women, or the temper. Mark was her dad after all. 'It wasn't your dad's fault; he just wasn't the marrying kind.'

'He wasn't the fathering kind either. Big on the presents, but not on being there.' She took a large glug of her Prosecco.

Phoebe was right, he was the fun dad. It was all very superficial; Mark's real parenting credentials were rubbish. I'd covered for him often enough, but hadn't realised the kids saw it too. It made me sad to think maybe I'd let them down as much as he had, by allowing him to stay in our lives. I constantly told myself, *I stayed for the kids,* but perhaps I was just too scared to leave?

'Well, at least Erin's latest drama should stop everyone talking about you and Dad,' Phoebe sighed, climbing down from her stool, and taking the remaining Prosecco from the fridge.

'I didn't know they still did. I thought we were so last week,' I joked.

'The Awesome Andersons? Not likely.' She refreshed our glasses, and I lifted mine for a top-up, the bubbles hitting my nose. 'Nah, we were once famous for being the perfect family who lived by the seaside, now we're famous because you and Dad got divorced.

Middle-aged couples everywhere went "whaaat?" thanks to that little tramp.'

'I'm no fan of Erin, but it takes two, love,' I said, taking a sip, enjoying the lovely sting of fizz at the back of my throat. Sparkling wine always feels so celebratory, even when there's nothing to celebrate.

'Yeah, I know.' She paused. 'Dad's never really been the faithful kind, has he?'

She couldn't look at me, and I didn't know what to say.

'Well, Dad worked away a lot, and…' I was finding it hard to defend him, even to his own daughter.

'I remember girls at school telling me he *liked* their mums. One girl came up to me in the playground and said, "You're Phoebe Anderson from the telly, aren't you?" And I'd smiled. I was always proud to be an Anderson. I thought she might want to ask me about the programme, I was about twelve and thought I was quite the TV expert. Then she told me my dad had stayed over at their house when their dad was away, and…' Phoebe finally looked up at me. 'And he'd slept in their parents' bed with her mum.'

'Oh God, Phoebe,' I said, wondering, not for the first time, who he'd left me alone for.

She nodded her head. 'It was Jake who got the worst of it though – teenage girls can be *evil*.' I could see the dimples in her chin as it started to tremble; she didn't want to upset me further by crying.

'I'm so sorry, darling. That must have been awful for you both,' I sighed, putting my arm around her, both of us reeling in the wake of one man's hurricane.

'Worse for *you*, Mum.' She reached out her hand and put it on mine.

'You never said anything, darling, you should have talked to me!' I hated the thought that my kids had been forced to endure something so painful.

'I told Jake not to tell you; it would hurt you too much.'

I wanted to cry. There I was naively going through life think-ing I was protecting them. How foolish I'd been to think I could shield my kids from our unhappy marriage. While I was hiding Mark's infidelity from them, they were hiding it from me, all of us protecting each other, lies breeding more lies. 'We should have divorced long ago,' I sighed.

'Yeah, I guess,' she said. But being Phoebe, she tried to soften it for me and backtracked. 'You and Dad were happy *sometimes* though, weren't you? And in the last few years, he seemed more settled. The two of you had a laugh and might have turned a corner if that evil cow hadn't got her nasty little claws into him.'

I had to laugh at Phoebe's brutal honesty, and her optimism too. 'I don't think anything would have changed, love. Erin did me a favour. I'm so much happier now.'

'I'm glad… So you wouldn't get back with Dad then, even if *she* wasn't around?' I saw hope glimmer in her eyes. Despite everything, we were her parents, and in her mind, even as an adult, maybe she felt we belonged together.

I shook my head. 'Are you okay with that?'

'I don't know, me and Jake talk about you both sometimes and, well, you know what he's like, he idolises Dad. At first, we were desperate for you guys to get back together, and just stay in the house… Jake says you might lose this place. Is that true?'

I was about to explain, about the US deal and my theory that Mark might want to recreate what we had at the house for a new TV series with Erin, but I didn't get the chance, because at that moment, Ryan appeared. He'd finished for the afternoon and was sliding through the doors Erin had escaped from the previous evening. I thought for the hundredth time, what if she had just run through the garden and thrown herself into the sea? What if she'd run the other way to a different kind of danger, a man driving along the dark lane – someone she knew offering her a lift, a friend, Mark… *Ryan*?

As he wandered through the living area, my mind quickly did the maths from the night before. He'd turned up at the house not long after Erin left. If she did leave through the side gate and head off round the front, towards the road, Ryan would have been driving towards her, and would have seen her, surely? But he didn't, or he would have said. Wouldn't he?

I watched him disappear into the downstairs toilet, telling myself he could easily have missed her on the road, in the storm. And then further down that road, she could have cut across the fields, where *no one* would have seen her. She might have fallen. She might still be there. But then, if she were, someone would have found her by now, surely?

I stopped thinking about it when Ryan reappeared from the downstairs toilet, and walked into the kitchen. My heart sank, I now had this encounter to deal with. Phoebe had already warned me against any kind of 'thing' with Ryan. I had to make sure this looked completely innocent, client and builder.

'Hi,' he said, nodding to Phoebe, who smiled back.

'Ryan Jarvis?' she said. 'You used to come here with your dad – years ago?'

'Yeah, my brother was the film star,' he said with a smile.

'Yeah… Max,' she said. 'I remember Max. Actually, didn't he go out with Erin?' She was looking from Ryan to me, assuming I wouldn't know, and this might be of interest.

'I… think so,' he said, which puzzled me. He'd told me himself that Max went out with Erin; why would he be so vague? 'Last time I saw you, you were about this high,' he said to Phoebe, putting his palm waist height.

I laughed with them, realising at twenty-four, Phoebe was closer to Ryan's thirty-five than I was, which made me feel slightly uncomfortable. When Ryan and I were alone, the fact I was twelve years older didn't matter; I didn't *feel* older. I liked that he found me attractive, it was something I never thought I'd experience again. But seeing him with Phoebe made me think again, *Am I being a middle-aged fool to think there could be something between us?*

'We're just talking about Erin going missing,' I said. 'Have you heard anything?'

He turned his head quickly to look at me. 'No, why should I?'

I was a little taken aback by his response. 'No reason,' I answered, maintaining eye contact, trying to work out what I'd said to cause such a reaction. 'Just thought you might have heard something in the town.'

Then he seemed to relax and, pushing his hands in his jean pockets, leaned against the kitchen counter. 'No. How could I have heard anything? I've been *here* since...'

He'd clearly forgotten that we'd agreed his lodger status wasn't being shared with my kids, something I was even more keen to keep quiet after Phoebe's comment about his reputation. I had to shut it down, so I quickly moved the conversation on. 'Well, I haven't heard from anyone, thought my ex-husband might call,' I said, trying to sound formal, hoping Ryan would pick up on this – and Phoebe wouldn't.

'She'll turn up I'm sure – she's just looking for trouble, that one,' Ryan said, turning now to get a mug.

'Mmm, my sentiments exactly,' Phoebe said, watching him open the cupboard and reach for the coffee jar with thinly veiled surprise.

'Would you like a coffee?' he asked, directing the question at both of us.

Phoebe shook her head and gave me a bemused look that said *WTF? Mum, Jake was right about him settling in, he just marched in and offered us coffee – like he lives here.*

God, if only she knew.

I could feel my skin burning up as he opened the fridge, knowing exactly where the milk was, and then asking me, 'Have you made any more lemon cake?'

Flustered, I shook my head, aware that Phoebe was looking right at me.

A few minutes later, I watched her watch him wander outside with his mug and a small tower of custard creams, and she turned to me. 'Well, *he* certainly knows his way around your kitchen.'

'I hope that's not a euphemism,' I said, which made us both laugh, and as Phoebe was taking a final sip of her Prosecco, it went up her nose and she ended up with it everywhere. 'Lovely!' I said, grabbing a tea towel and wiping us down. 'You are one classy lady, Phoebe Anderson.'

'Seriously though, the way he was looking at you – I think he's got the hots for you, Mum!'

'No – don't be daft, he's only thirty-five,' I said, feeling slightly uncomfortable.

'Well, age hasn't stopped Dad making a dick of himself.'

'True,' I said, knowing her cutting words weren't meant for me, but feeling them just the same.

'And why wouldn't he fancy you? You're gorgeous,' she said kindly, the way daughters do to their mothers.

Hearing what I thought might be a note of understanding, I was about to tell her that we were in fact in a sort of relationship. I wanted to tell her how he made me feel young again and I had no idea what might happen, and I was scared and excited all at the same time. But then she spoke again, more serious.

'Just be careful, Mum.'

'What do you mean?' I asked.

'Oh, I don't know, bad boys? The love 'em and leave 'em type? I mean, his brother definitely went out with Erin. He was quite a bit older, about ten years.'

'That's a big gap,' I said weakly, thinking about the twelve years between Ryan and me. 'But from what I gather, Max is the troubled one. Ryan's the good brother,' I said, realising I didn't know Ryan or his family in any depth.

'Yeah, well, that's probably what he wants you to think. Like I said on the phone, a guy like that *might* be under the impression you've got money.' She didn't say anything else, just climbed down off her stool and headed to the bathroom.

I sat alone, glass in hand, realising I probably shouldn't have told Ryan about the money I was owed by Mark. Then I reminded myself that he didn't seem the type to be bothered about money. He'd spent years in Thailand on a beach, living off nothing. He wore old T-shirts and got excited about a bird's nest in the garden. He wasn't some gold-digging toy boy. But my mind wandered back to the phone call I'd overheard, with Erin, and why was he so vague when Phoebe mentioned the fact Erin went out with his brother? This led me to questioning even more – how he was moving out of his place very quickly to move into mine. Even now, I wasn't quite sure how I let that happen so easily. I just felt so bad because I couldn't pay him, and I went along with the idea before I'd had chance to think about it. I liked him, and I enjoyed his company, but had I been an idiot and let my heart rule my head?

When Ryan came into the house to announce he was leaving for the day, I held my breath. I prayed he didn't forget Phoebe was there and do what he often did, come up behind me, massage my shoulders and kiss my neck. I could only imagine the horror on Phoebe's face. So I was deeply relieved when he threw his jacket over one shoulder and said good night.

After he'd gone, I started cooking, and I was just putting the steaks on when my phone rang. I was nervous to see Lara's name on the screen; Phoebe looked up from the table mats she was laying out.

'It's Lara,' I mouthed, picking up. 'Is she back, have you found her?' I heard my words tumble out.

'No.' I could hear the tears in her voice, and my stomach dropped. Before Phoebe had arrived, I'd rechecked the garden and even been down to the beach. Everything looked so calm and untroubled out there that I just imagined Erin had taken herself away for a short time, needing space. It wasn't easy with a new baby and with Mark, and I'd told myself she'd be back by the evening, but this was getting scary now.

'I'm at my wits' end,' Lara was saying. 'I called the police. They've been here, took a statement. No one's seen or heard from her – and *he's* no use. He hit the bottle as soon as he knew she'd gone missing – typical!'

As much as I enjoyed the pastime, now wasn't the time to bitch about Mark. 'I was thinking, she might have gone back to your house over the fields. Phoebe's here, we'll take a walk down there, see if there's any... sign... of her.'

'Thanks, but the police are already looking, and I think having civilians around might be more of a hindrance. I'm furious though, Carly. At first the police wouldn't take her disappearance seriously, because, according to *him*, she's walked out before and gone missing overnight.'

'Really? Did you know that?'

'Did I *hell*. Since she got together with him, we've hardly spoken, and it's only now when she needs a babysitter she bothers to call me. She doesn't want me around, because if I knew half of what was going on there, I'd be at their door with a bloody shotgun. And she knows it. I'd blow his sodding head off, if I got the chance.'

'Get in the queue, love,' I sighed. 'Is there anything I can do, Lara?'

'No, no, it's fine, and it might be best you staying there in case she turns up again.'

'Yeah, you never know,' I murmured, doubting that very much. 'Are you okay there? Are you on your own?'

'I'm fine; the neighbours are popping in and out.'

'Good, well as long as you're sure I can't come over?'

'No, the police are still here asking tortuous questions; they've been here all day. My next-door neighbour's been a lifesaver though and come over to look after little Billy; he's good as gold.'

'So Billy's still with you? Mark hasn't taken him home?'

'Mark? Would you leave a tiny baby with that drunken knob?' she seethed.

'When you put it like that, probably not.' I paused. 'Let me know if you hear anything or if there's anything we can do.'

After talking to Lara, I called Mark to see if Erin was there, and of course it went straight to voicemail.

'I'm worried, Phoebe,' I said, putting the phone down. 'I was the last one to see her. I feel somehow... responsible.'

'Mum, she's a *psycho*. She turned up unannounced, then ran off into the night – as psychos do.'

'Darling, I think psycho is a bit harsh,' I said. One of the perhaps more trivial problems associated with Mark choosing this girl as 'the other woman' was I couldn't bitch freely because she was so young, and her mother was once my friend. He'd even denied me the chance to vent my spleen fully, about his wannabe wife.

'Dad's an idiot – but she's just a bloody stalker. I know of at least two guys she went out with from round here,' Phoebe was saying, 'and when they tried to finish with her, she threatened to kill them, then kill herself.'

'Okay, that sounds a *bit* psychotic,' I said, abandoning any pretence of restraint.

'Do you think she threw herself off the cliffs?' Phoebe asked, nodding her head in the direction of the garden.

'God, I hope not. But she's always been troubled,' I offered lamely, as I watched the steaks sizzle. 'Lara said the police have been at hers all day,' I added absently, thinking of my friend, and how awful she must be feeling right now. I knew how I'd feel if it was Phoebe.

'Shit's getting real,' Phoebe murmured.

'I couldn't have put it better myself. How would you like your steak?'

I never found out how Phoebe wanted her steak, because just as she was about to answer, the doorbell rang. I headed for the door, asking Phoebe to keep an eye on the steaks while wiping my hands on a tea towel, and looking at the CCTV monitor, it was a man and a woman. I opened the door, and was about to politely say 'no' to whatever it was they were selling, but the expressions on both their faces stopped me from speaking first.

'Mrs Anderson?'

I nodded.

'I'm Detective Sergeant Harefield, and this is Detective Sergeant Barker,' the man said. 'We're investigating the whereabouts of a missing person – an Erin Matthews? Lara Matthews – her mother – and your husband – Erin's partner – said that you were the last one to see her. May we come in?'

CHAPTER TWENTY-EIGHT

The two detectives walked into the house, and both remarked on the TV programme. DS Barker, 'Call me Sally,' was enthusing about the view, and DS Harefield, 'Call me DS Harefield,' was asking if it was an expensive house to maintain.

'Yes, it is. I have someone working on it now as a matter of fact,' I said, smiling weakly, and gesturing for them to sit down.

'Oh,' DS Harefield said, sitting down, pen poised, 'who's that?'

I gave him Ryan's name, feeling awkward, like he was a suspect. Harefield wrote this down carefully, and Sally, who seemed much more relaxed, told me how she used to watch the programme.

'Oh, we loved *The Forever Home* in our family, every week we'd sit round the telly – I can't wait to call my mum and tell her I've actually *been* here.'

I nodded, still finding words hard. I'd never been visited by detectives before.

Phoebe stepped into the sitting area, and asked if they'd like tea or coffee. They both asked for tea – which she made while they asked me about the previous evening.

'Before we start, do you mind your daughter being present?' DS Harefield asked.

'Not at all,' I said. 'In fact, Phoebe knows... well, *knew* Erin well, she might be able to help?'

Phoebe nodded almost too enthusiastically from the kitchen area.

'You say *knew* her… there's nothing to suggest Erin's dead,' DS Harefield said bluntly.

'Oh gosh, of *course* not. No, when I said "*knew*" her, I didn't mean she was… I meant that they aren't close any more,' I blustered, unsure why I felt so nervous; it wasn't like I had anything to hide.

'Not that we're *not* friends,' Phoebe piped up, and I wondered if my nervousness was catching. I'd never had two detectives in my living room asking questions before. It was quite intimidating.

'I'm surprised you're investigating so soon,' I said, in an attempt to climb out of the hole me and Phoebe had just put ourselves in.

They both looked up at me questioningly.

'I mean – I thought, unless the person was a high risk, the police didn't start looking until after twenty-four hours?' I don't even know why I said this. I'd read it on a website somewhere and was just trying to make conversation. But as soon as I heard myself, I realised I sounded dismissive, or worse, guilty!

'It depends,' DS Harefield said, looking at me intently. 'Erin Matthews is the mother of a newborn, and the fact she's missing is a concern. Her own mother, Mrs Lara Matthews, is also extremely concerned for the welfare of her daughter. She called us after phoning everyone she knew, and then all the local hospitals, so it is… something we take seriously. Very seriously indeed.'

'Of course, of course,' I agreed, blushing and wishing I'd never said anything.

Thankfully, Phoebe brought over two mugs of tea and put them down on the coffee table, which gave us all a welcome pause.

'So, you were the last to see her, Mrs… er… Mrs…' DS Harefield was clearly feeling uncertain now; he'd obviously read something in the Sunday papers about my husband's new woman, but for the life of him he couldn't recall her status.

'Anderson. I'm still Mrs Anderson, we aren't divorced yet,' I said, quietly.

He began to make notes. 'Okay, so can you cast your mind back to last night and tell us about her visit, Mrs Anderson?'

'Every detail, however small or seemingly insignificant,' Sally added, now taking out her own notepad in anticipation, as I began to tell them, in detail, about the previous evening. They both listened intently, occasionally sipping on tea, taking copious notes and asking for clarification as I continued.

'But when I turned round, the door was open and she'd gone,' I explained, reaching the end of the story from my perspective.

'Do you have any idea where she might have gone?' Sally asked, her head to one side, pen held poised above her notebook.

'No, she just disappeared, so I went out into the garden, looked everywhere, but it was dark and stormy – I couldn't see a thing.'

'Did you phone her?'

'No, no, I didn't. I was too busy trying to find her… Besides, I don't have her number.'

'But you're friends with her mother, Mrs Matthews, *surely* you have *her* number?' DS Harefield probed, and I detected something new creeping in.

'I *did* call Lara, but she didn't pick up,' I clarified.

'Did you leave Lara… Mrs Matthews, a message?'

'No, we haven't spoken for months. I didn't want to alarm her; I assumed Erin had gone home to Mark, or was staying at a friend's.'

'So you *didn't* leave a message,' DS Harefield reiterated, pen poised, judgement in his voice.

I put my head down. 'No. No I didn't. It was difficult. I didn't want to upset her, and under the circumstances, my husband… and her daughter… it was *difficult.*' I left it there and hoped I didn't have to spell this out.

Sally nodded, she got it, but DS Harefield just looked at me steadily, like he was waiting for a more detailed explanation.

'Look,' I said gently. 'I didn't think Erin was in any danger. I'm as amazed as everyone else that she's gone missing. If I'd had any idea this would happen, I—'

'But you went into the garden, you say? The edge of the garden is built on the cliffside, right? So it *did* it occur to you that she might have had an accident?' DS Harefield continued to probe.

'Yes, well, *anything* is possible, I suppose…' I answered, in a quiet voice.

'Mrs Matthews says she spoke to you this morning?' Sally broke in, bringing a bright tone and a welcome smile.

'Yes, yes, she did – I was a bit surprised when she rang; it was the first time we've spoken in six months.'

'Why is that? Had you had some kind of argument?' asked DS Harefield. For God's sake, wasn't it bloody obvious?

'It was just awkward… I mean it *is* just awkward,' I said, trying not to sound irritated. I could feel myself getting caught up in knots. I felt like everything I said was being scrutinised. 'Lara's daughter is with my ex-husband now, and so obviously it's difficult for Lara and I to be friends.'

'Her daughter's the same age as your daughter, isn't she?' Sally asked.

'Yes, she is. That's how Lara and I met. When the girls were both small.'

Phoebe, who'd been hovering in the room, sat down next to me on the arm of the sofa.

'She was probably sleeping with Dad when she was friends with me,' she announced.

Both the detectives perked up at this and I didn't feel Phoebe's comments were helping. She was trying to make them see that Erin was no innocent, but in doing that made it sound like Erin had become the enemy – which she had, I suppose. But I didn't feel it was appropriate to share these strong feelings with the two detectives trying to find her. Especially as I was the last one to see her.

'She's very young, it was his choice,' I said, 'but, naturally, Lara and I now have different loyalties, and sadly we aren't the friends we were. It happens,' I added, like it was unimportant. Like the fact my husband had not only run off with someone half my age, he'd chosen my best friend's daughter, thus denying me any comfort from my best friend at one of the worst times in my life, was inconsequential. If I resented anyone, it was Mark. Erin was just another of his toys who'd come along at an opportune time, just when he was looking for a new leading lady.

Eventually, after more difficult questions, they were ready to leave but took my mobile and landline and said they would need to speak to me again. And as I let them out, DS Harefield said, 'You have CCTV, Mrs Anderson?'

'Yes, just here and at the front of the house.'

'Not at the back?'

'No – I just wanted it at the front.'

'Why?'

I sighed. 'I don't *need* it at the back. I want to see who's at the front door, and choose not to open it if I don't want to.' I was rambling now.

'Have you had problems, with unwanted callers?' He was looking at me, pen poised.

'Well, yes. I had a weird parcel delivered a few weeks ago, and sand prints on the floor. A vase smashed, photographs moved too – oh, and a note.'

'A weird parcel you say?' DS Harefield pressed.

'Yeah, it freaked me out. When I opened it... it was a dead rat covered in maggots.' 'Did you call the police about this?'

'No, but I did call the police when I saw a face at the window,,' I said, sounding like an absolute nutter.

'Gosh, a lot's been happening, you must have been scared, someone at the window and a dead rat, that must have been distressing for you. I don't blame you having cameras fitted after that. Any idea who…'

'No. I think it might be crazy fans who still think Mark lives here,' I said, deciding not to mention Ryan's theory that it might be Erin. I didn't want to give them any reason to think I had a further grudge against her. 'It's happened before, years ago, the children were quite small.' I told them about the previous episode, and the petals on the bed.

'No petals this time?' Sally asked.

I shook my head. 'There are some lovely things about being part of a TV show, but there are downsides too, and over the years we've had all kinds of weird "fan mail",' I explained. 'Mark was always receiving letters from women declaring undying love; he got champagne and underwear on a regular basis; I got death threats. The recent stuff was addressed to me. I don't know why, anything can trigger them, and let's face it, "they know where we live",' I said in a mock scary voice, which I immediately regretted when neither responded.

DS Harefield looked at me like he was trying to work me out. 'Was there a note with the parcel?'

'No, nothing.'

'Mrs Matthews said her daughter had also received some disturbing messages on social media.' He began looking around like the sender might pop out any minute. 'Do you think it might be the same person?'

'I've no idea,' I said.

'Do you know anything about Mrs Matthews' messages?'

'No, I *don't*,' I replied, offended at the insinuation. 'But apparently Erin thought it might be me.'

I almost heard their eyebrows raise in unison.

'It wasn't me,' I said, feeling the need to state this for the record.

They didn't respond; it was like they hadn't heard me.

'We'll need your permission to take a look at the film from your CCTV,' DS Harefield continued.

'Of course,' I replied.

'Oh, just one thing,' she said quietly, 'we didn't want to say anything in front of your daughter, but Erin's mum has forwarded a video you sent to her… in the video you claim that Mr Anderson hurt you?'

My mouth went dry. This had all happened so quickly; it hadn't occurred to me that my video detailing the physical and emotional abuse would now have huge significance.

I started to speak… but couldn't find the words.

'We'll be in touch about that,' Harefield said, and I closed the door feeling very uneasy.

I walked back down the hall, thinking about the video, damning in itself, but now? I just hoped it would stay with the police; it would devastate the kids if ever they got wind of it.

I went back into the living room, where Phoebe was sitting on the sofa biting her nails.

'What the hell was *that* about?' she said, her face etched with worry.

'I'm not sure. I feel like I'm in a TV police drama. It's all really weird. I can't work out where Erin went last night, but I'm scared that somehow I might be implicated.'

Phoebe stood up, and put her arm around me. 'Don't worry, Mum, you won't be.'

I didn't *like* Erin, but I would never cause her any harm. The two detectives who'd been sitting in my living room seemed to have formed their own narrative though. Perhaps they saw me as the woman scorned, the jealous ex-wife? It was an easy, if lazy, connection to make.

But less than half an hour later, Lara called me. 'I think you should know, Mark's been arrested. He's at the police station.'

CHAPTER TWENTY-NINE

Phoebe and I sat up until late, downing another bottle of wine, and going through the different possibilities. I didn't mention the video to Phoebe; if Mark was charged, and it was used in court, I'd deal with telling the kids then. How could Lara *not* have given it to the police? I'd have done the same. I just wish she'd told me. It was a very raw, personal diary, and I would have liked to have some control over who saw it, and when. But that was the price I'd paid for being with Mark, nothing really belonged to me, even my personal life.

In the meantime, we were just waiting for news from the police. I'd called Estelle to see if she knew anything, but she wasn't picking up, and neither was Lara, so we just had to wait.

'Last time I spoke to Dad he didn't sound happy, Mum,' Phoebe sighed. 'He said Erin was difficult, that he wondered if he'd made a mistake…' Then the colour drained from her face. 'Christ, I hope nothing…'

'No, Phoebe, your dad wouldn't…' I paused, remembering the times his temper had got the better of him. 'We just need to wait and see what happens after Dad's been questioned.'

We were both so tense that when my phone rang, we jumped. It was Jake, who'd seen news on his phone that his dad had been arrested.

'Mum, you don't think he's… done something to her, do you?'

'Oh no, love, I'm sure it's all a big mistake,' I said, in a desperate attempt to convince myself as much as him. 'They often arrest people, and talk to them, then have to release them in twenty-four hours if there's no evidence,' I added, hoping the nugget I'd picked up in a recent crime drama was fact not fiction. Jake seemed happy with this, and after a quick chat with Phoebe, he asked us to let him know if there was any news and hung up.

'I'm sure it's nothing,' I murmured, like a mantra, as I put my phone down.

'I just keep thinking, what if they argued, and... something happened?' Phoebe said. 'In the news, it said he'd just had this massive pay-out too.'

'Yes, Estelle was crowing about it in the papers.'

'Estelle?'

'His agent.'

'Oh God, yeah – I thought he'd found someone else for a minute.' She gave a nervous laugh.

I felt another pang for Phoebe. My kids had seen through him as much as I had. Unfortunately, they *couldn't* let go like I could; he was their father, and they loved him, as much as they were conflicted by the past.

'You don't think he tried to dump Erin, do you, and she's done something to herself?' Phoebe asked.

'I don't know, Phoebe, I really don't know, but the tabloids will have a field day over this...'

In the past, Estelle had stamped down on the women who had threatened to kiss and tell. From overheard, hushed phone calls between her and Mark, I knew when something had gone on, but she protected him like a tiger mother. No way would she let some fame-hungry dumpee tell their sordid little tale to the tabloids and stop her star in his ascendant. However, after all the years controlling the narrative, even Estelle couldn't stop the reporting of Mark 'being arrested in relation to his missing girlfriend'.

So it proved the following day when I woke up to headlines offering a tantalising glimpse 'Inside the Troubled Marriage of

TV's Golden Couple', where 'betrayed Carly, 49, mother to Mark Anderson's two children' apparently lived her life like 'a recluse'. The 'dashing DIY man' dumped her after enjoying 'secret trysts' with her daughter's twenty-four-year-old best friend, 'who's now been missing for two days'.

'She wasn't my best friend! WTF?' Phoebe spat as we both sat, devouring the contents of our respective news feeds with mugs of coffee.

'And I'm not bloody forty-nine years old either,' I said. 'I'm only forty-seven!' That made us both laugh, in spite of everything. It was strange but liberating to think that after all the years of hiding, and lying, and me protecting Mark's image, along with fierce and frumpy Estelle, it was all flooding out anyway.

Mark's TV colleagues were talking, local people were talking. No one could keep their mouths shut. I imagined Estelle in her office batting away the phone calls, screaming at her staff. But I was taking no pleasure from this. I was genuinely worried about Erin, and the idea that Mark might have done something was really disturbing. This was the father of my children, and as bad as it would be for me, they would have to live with whatever had happened. But what *had* happened?

'God, I hope she is okay. She's Lara's daughter, and the mother to a new baby, it would be such a tragedy if…' I said, taking a screen break from my phone and gazing through the window.

'I can't get over the fact she was so toxic. She smashed this family into little pieces. I'm sorry, I can't feel sorry for her – whatever's happened.'

'Don't forget Dad in all this,' I said. 'He was the one that was married, not her.'

Phoebe didn't reply and I went back to the constant updated news on my phone. The press seemed to think Mark and I had had this blissful marriage, until he spotted Erin, and exchanged me for the younger model. I was 'bereft', 'distraught', and now the waitresses from the Silver Spoon Tearooms had waded in with their story about 'a showdown' between Mark's pregnant mistress and his wife, 'Carly, 49'.

'For God's sake, isn't it bad enough that they make me sound like the woman scorned, bloodied by betrayal, reeking of bitterness – do they really have to keep adding two years to my age? I'm just waiting for the paragraph on my menopause that spawns a million spin-off articles headlined with, "I had a menopause just like Carly Anderson".'

I had only just begun to appreciate the freedom of being me, and living truthfully, with none of the fiction dreamed up for the media. Here we were now, with everything up for grabs again, reminding me how exposed I used to feel. And then there was the time bomb of my video diary. I pushed that to the back of my mind; I'd deal with that when it happened.

'It's not looking too good for Dad, is it?' Phoebe sighed, looking up from her phone.

'It's too early to tell,' I said gently.

'I can't see Dad being involved. I mean, he wouldn't... he couldn't?' I felt her need for reassurance, but couldn't offer much.

'No, of course not,' I said, trying to sound like I meant it, but who knew what had gone on that night after she'd left my house? Their whole relationship was beginning to sound a bit rocky, if you listened to Lara's account. I knew from personal experience the switch in his mood and the difference between me and Erin, who was so needy and wouldn't let go. So if he'd hurt me, the more laid-back partner, what might he have done to the more abrasive Erin when she challenged him?

'Well, whatever's happened, this won't be good for his precious image,' Phoebe sighed.

'Phoebe, you're terrible,' I said.

'I'm only joking.' She winked, but I wasn't sure. 'I'm right though, Mum. Even if he hasn't done anything, and isn't involved, it still looks murky. And the press won't just let him off the hook.'

'Yes, and when we wrote the treatment for the US channel, we sold it on the fact he was the perfect husband and father. The big concern recently was reconciling that with the extremely young, pregnant girlfriend – but this is just beyond damage limitation, even if he's innocent,' I said.

Phoebe put down her phone and turned to me. 'He still owes you the money he took from your bank accounts; if he loses the contract, he won't pay you. Can you afford to keep the house if that happens?'

'I'll be fine,' I said, not wanting her to worry. 'I've got this new job, and I'm sure I'll get extra hours once the summer season starts.' I smiled. In truth I would have to sell the house; just thinking about it made me want to cry. If Mark wanted to ruin his own life that was up to him, but it seemed, even now, when I'd made my break from him, he was still in control of mine.

Later that day, Phoebe left. She offered to stay longer, but I knew she had to go back to work. 'I hate leaving you like this, with Dad at the station, and *her* missing…'

'I'm fine, Phoebe. This is Dad's drama – and for once he can sort it out,' I said, knowing I was already caught up in it, and perhaps there was worse yet to come?

'Yeah, you're right. It's just that you're all on your own.'

'Ryan will be around,' I started.

'And that's supposed to make me feel better?' she asked, with a warning smile.

'Honestly, you remind me of Grandma. "I won't talk to any unsuitable boys, Mum, honestly!"' I parroted in a little girl voice. 'Now, you get back and stop worrying about me.'

Ryan was packing to move into the house that day, so wasn't around. But later he'd turn up with his life in a van. At least Phoebe would be gone by then, and once he'd moved in, if he only stayed a few weeks, no one had to know.

We hugged and she grabbed her stuff and set off in her little car, waving and beeping as she drove off, leaving me to wonder who Mark was with when Erin thought he was with me. If he was seeing someone else, and they saw Erin as being in the way, then who knew what they'd do? Perhaps it was the same person who'd been sending her the messages? God, it might be the same person who sent *me* the note and the parcel? And if she'd hurt Erin, I could be next.

I called Lara to see if she'd heard any news, and if she needed me to do anything; we may have been estranged, but I still cared about her. And it was her daughter that was missing.

'That bastard's done something, I know it,' she hissed down the phone.

I didn't respond; I had nothing to offer.

'You know something, don't you?'

'No… Lara, I don't. I'm as much in the dark as you are. Do you need me to do anything?'

'Yes, Carly.'

'What?' I said, eager to help.

'Can I ask you not to call me again?'

'Oh.' I was a little surprised at her bluntness, but then again, under the circumstances, it was probably stressful to receive calls. 'I'm sorry, I imagine every time your phone rings you think it's someone with news?'

'No, it's not that. I just don't trust you,' she spat.

'What?'

'Erin was perfectly fine when she left here, supposedly meeting a friend. But she went to see you, and after that something happened and she didn't come home. I don't know what's going on, but I don't trust you – and I don't trust him. So, please don't call me with that "can I help" voice, because it doesn't wash with me, Carly.'

'Lara, I've told you and the police everything I know. And apparently you've given them the video.'

'Yes I did. Why didn't *you* give it to them?'

'Because I honestly thought she was hiding somewhere,' I said. 'But I don't know anymore – I just want *you* to know, whatever's happened, I'd never hurt Erin.'

'Carly, you've lied for him for years. I remember once when "a rumour" was about to hit the papers. Instead of telling them what a liar and a cheat he was, you stood in your back garden, holding a tray of coffee and feeding journalists lies and chocolate digestives. You posed for pictures with your arms around him, and all the time you *knew* he'd been with another woman,' she hissed. 'So forgive me if I don't believe a word you say.'

With that, the phone went silent.

I felt like she'd stabbed me. She was right, I'd lied for him, and I felt ashamed. In my defence, he had a hold over me. Mark was the only person in the world who knew about the circumstances of my mum's death and he used it brutally. He was reckless, and selfish, and one day, he'd tell someone, and my life would be over. As long as he lived, I would never be free.

CHAPTER THIRTY

After the phone call with Lara, I was hurt and confused, but I understood, this was about her daughter, and I'd be the same if Phoebe was missing, just desperate for answers and lashing out. I'd spent the late afternoon walking up and down the garden, going over and over the night Erin had gone missing and becoming quite agitated. So when Ryan arrived on the doorstep soon after, with his bags, boxes and guitar, I was glad to see his smiling face.

'Just to say thanks for having me,' he said, holding out a bunch of pink peonies.

'Ahh, thank you. But I should be thanking you too,' I said, leading him inside. 'After all, this is a mutually beneficial arrangement,' I added, as we walked into the kitchen.

'Yeah, it *is*,' he said, sliding his hand under my T-shirt.

I slapped it down. 'I meant... well, you know what I meant,' I said, filling a vase with water, and putting the peonies in. 'Now, come on, let's get you unpacked.'

I led him upstairs to Jake's old room, where I'd made a fresh bed, which he playfully pushed me down onto.

I sat up. 'No way, not in here,' I said, when he started to open my blouse. 'This is my child's room.'

He stopped, lifting both hands in a surrendering gesture. 'Good point, not exactly sexy for you in your kid's room. I'm not sure I'd want to either now you've said that.'

He started to unpack, while I sat on the bed. I watched him putting his clothes in the wardrobe and drawers, moving easily around the room, and I was glad he was here. The house needed new life, new memories, new stories, and I looked forward to him just being around, and doing nothing together.

'Hey, I heard about Mark – being arrested,' he said, his eyes wide. 'Is he still with the police?'

'As far as I know.' I nodded, running my palms along a T-shirt as I folded it, imagining him wearing it. Since meeting Ryan, lust had returned like an old friend. I'd forgotten what the feeling was like, but when I thought of him, it was always there to greet me.

'So, they think *he* did something to her?' Ryan was now standing by the wardrobe, attempting to put a jacket on a hanger.

I looked up. 'I don't know, I think they're just questioning him. I mean, anything could have happened, couldn't it?'

'I guess so – but it's not looking good for him. I read that they'd had this big row and she stormed out.'

'I don't know.'

'But she stormed out and came *here*, didn't she tell you what had happened?' He'd stopped trying to hang his jacket, and was now looking at me, waiting for my answer.

'She said the same, that they'd had a row. Look, it's not *me* who's a suspect,' I said, standing up.

'I just don't understand…'

'There's nothing to understand,' I snapped. Perhaps I was just at the end of my tether, but I'd had enough. 'Why are you so interested anyway?' I asked.

'Well, it *is* interesting, isn't it?' he said, without looking at me.

Yes, it *was*. A celebrity, his missing girlfriend, and a three-million-pound pay-out? The only problem the papers would have was how to get everything in one headline. The tabloids would pay a lot for inside information on this story; reporters and photographers had been gathering at the bottom of the road since yesterday. And, as much as I liked Ryan, he was almost too interested in the details, and I had to face it, one good titbit to the *Sun* could pay his ticket to Thailand, first class.

'I just thought you might know. That she might have said something to you about where she'd been, where she was going.'

'No – she didn't,' I repeated firmly.

'Okay, calm down,' he said, a trace of anger in his voice that lingered in the air as he continued to move clothes around.

This annoyed me, so I took myself off downstairs.

I'd hoped having Ryan around would be light relief; instead I felt like I was being questioned by the bloody police again. If he was going to keep going on about this, and sulking when I didn't answer his questions, this arrangement wasn't going to last the night, let alone a few weeks.

I pottered for a while, and eventually he came down.

'Sorry, didn't mean to piss you off,' he said, awkwardly.

'And I'm sorry I snapped. I just felt like you were interrogating me – and if I'm honest, I already feel guilty. Erin disappeared from here, and now I feel like even though Mark's the one who's been arrested, everyone's thinking I'm somehow in on it.'

'If he'd looked after her better, this wouldn't have happened, she wouldn't have turned up here in a state and you wouldn't feel like this.'

'Oh, there's no point in what ifs… who knows what happened or why?'

'Have the police said why he's been arrested?' Ryan asked.

He was asking questions again. 'Ryan, I only know what you do… and whatever's been said in the papers,' I said, exasperated.

'The police must have something, they can't just arrest him,' he continued.

But I was too embroiled in my own guilt to answer him. All I could think was that I *should* have run after her as soon as I saw she'd gone. I *should* have gone all the way down onto the beach straight away to check she hadn't gone down there.

He turned away from me and walked slowly to the big glass doors, and stared out. 'God, I just wish none of this had ever happened.'

'Me too,' I said, surprised again at his strength of feeling over this. But it suddenly occurred to me that his anger was on *my* behalf. Ryan liked to make things better, and he was angry because I'd been put in this position, and he couldn't help me. Perhaps I'd misinterpreted his interest, his strength of feeling regarding this whole thing? And as he turned to look at me, I felt this overwhelming need to hug him. I walked over and put my palm flat on his back, feeling the warmth of his skin through the T-shirt, wanting to put my hand under the cloth, touch his skin. 'I'm sorry if I snapped, Ryan, but your questioning made me feel defensive. I haven't had to answer to anyone for a long time, and I'm not going to start again now,' I said as softly as I could.

'Carly, I wasn't *questioning* you...' he cut in. 'This is... I don't know why I ever thought you and me could...'

I instinctively took my hand from his back, feeling suddenly on edge. This was reminiscent of Mark in the early days, just when I thought everything was wonderful, he'd start with the, 'This isn't working, Carly,' waiting for me to beg.

'What do you mean?' I asked.

'I'm just not *good* enough for you, Carly; you'd be better off without me.'

'I don't believe that. I love being with you and want to get to know you better.' We may not have started his move on the right foot, but there was no doubt I wanted him here.

'I want to get to know you too, but...'

'But what?'

'I know I might be a bit difficult to understand sometimes, Carly. But I feel things for you... and whatever happens, I want you to know, I really do care.'

I had feelings for him too, and even if this was only for a summer, I wanted us both to feel secure in this. He might have a reputation, and I might not understand him sometimes, but this guy went out of his way to make me feel good about myself. He was always telling me how beautiful I was and how much he wanted me. He also worked on the house in the same way he cared for me: gentle, loving.

We moved to the sofa, sat down next to each other and I rested my head on his chest. It felt good. Ryan was either a very honest man, or a very good liar.

Later, we opened a bottle of wine, and sat together, talking as the light faded over the ocean.

'This house is so beautiful,' he sighed. 'Sometimes I just can't believe I'm here, like this, with you.'

'Yes, it is beautiful. I feel part of it, not just because I was born here, but when Mark and I came back, married, I felt like I gave myself to it all over again. Like my blood runs through the walls,' I said, 'which sounds very dramatic, but sometimes I feel like I don't know if it belongs to me, or I belong to it.'

'This house takes you over. I can understand why you feel so passionate about staying here.'

'Yes, it possesses you, this house. When I first moved back in, with Mark, I hoped he'd feel the same, but he didn't. It was only when it started serving a purpose, making his name, that things changed; initially his keenness to work on the house was all talk, and I was so disillusioned. I remember standing in the middle of the kitchen one night, all those years ago. It was little more than a pile of bricks and rubble with a plug-in heater and countertop stove. It was winter, we were all freezing, there was no heating, no money, it was like living on the street. Mark would convince me it would all be fine and he'd take care of things, and back then I believed him. But one day it dawned on me, he couldn't be trusted, and not just regarding extramarital affairs. He gambled with mine and the children's lives to achieve his own personal goals, always telling me I worried too much, and "I've got this, Carly," when he hadn't.' I shook my head at the memory. 'Then one day, I pulled out the fridge to clean behind it, and found a wall of unpaid bills stuffed there.'

'They hadn't been paid?' Ryan asked, incredulously.

'No – he'd said he had, but he'd lied. God knows what he'd spent the money on. Then, soon after, I discovered he'd also taken on credit cards I knew nothing about, and racked up thousands. Huge amounts of money had been spent on fancy meals I'd never eaten, hotel rooms I'd never slept in and flowers I'd never received.'

'Did you ask him about them?'

'Yes, of course. At the time, they upset me more than discovering we were in horrific debt and in danger of losing our house. But he told me they were "clients", and he was doing it for "us".'

'Did you believe him?'

'I tried to. Because anything else would mean I had to kick him out, and back then I still cared. I knew the truth in my heart – but I couldn't prove anything, nor did I really want to,' I sighed.

'What did you do?'

'After I cried and ranted and railed? I fixed it. I took out a second mortgage on this house, and made sure any money we had went straight into a joint account so I could manage it. We already had the YouTube channel, so I then wrote a treatment for *The Forever Home*, sent it to all the TV companies.'

'And that's how it all started?' Ryan murmured, reaching out for my hand.

'Yeah, I remember how happy we were when the TV company got in touch said they were interested. I thought I'd solved our problems, but they were only just beginning. Mark now had an army of women to choose from.'

'That must have been awful for you,' he said.

I nodded, slowly. 'Yeah, but eventually I lived my own life, and didn't allow his behaviour to affect me. It never occurred to me that what he did affected anyone else. But yesterday Phoebe told me that she and Jake both knew about their dad's affairs,' I said into the silence, aware there were tears falling down my cheeks.

He pulled me to him. 'That must have been horrible for them.'

'Yeah, but I didn't see it. I didn't know my own children were suffering. I feel like such a bad mother. I had no idea.'

'Don't beat yourself up,' he murmured, stroking my hair, 'you had everything else to deal with.'

'Yeah, like keeping a roof over our heads. I took in washing and ironing, baked pies and cakes and sold them in the village; it was pretty desperate.' I smiled at the memory of the kids and I standing behind a trestle table groaning with home-made cakes and pastries. 'I made a few quid too, enough to help keep us going. When we got the TV programme, I suggested doing some cookery segments. Cornish pasties, scones, Stargazy pie, that kind of thing – just me and the kids. I mentioned it to the director, who seemed to love the idea. But Mark hated it, said it was "small-time and too colloquial for the programme" and shut it down.'

'Why would he do that?' Ryan asked.

'Well, at the time, I thought he was protecting the brand, and genuinely didn't feel that it would fit. But now I guess he didn't want to share the stage with me; he wanted to keep me as the support act. I think me and the kids were just window-dressing.'

Ryan was looking out through the window, clearly moved by everything I'd told him, yet somehow troubled.

'Are you okay?' I said. 'You've gone a bit quiet. Are you disillusioned that the Andersons weren't awesome after all?' It was my attempt to lighten the moment.

He appeared to be miles away, like he wasn't really listening, and then he said, 'Whatever happens, know I'm on your side, Carly.'

I was puzzled. 'Thank you, but what do you mean, "whatever happens"?'

'It's just… Oh, it's just a figure of speech. Who's questioning who now?' he said, smiling.

'Sometimes I wonder what goes on in your head.' I ruffled his hair and stood up. 'I'm going to make dinner,' I announced, and went into the kitchen to start cooking.

But as I chopped vegetables for dinner, I couldn't help but feel slightly uneasy.

CHAPTER THIRTY-ONE

I woke late the next morning, and Ryan was already up. I could hear him on the phone downstairs. I heard anger in the tone of his voice, like he was arguing with someone. Then I remembered Erin was missing, and everything else went from my head.

So I called Lara, who surprisingly picked up.

'I know you said not to call you – but, Lara, is there any more news?'

'He's still at the station, as far as I know,' she sounded so absent, so defeated.

'Can I do anything?' I asked, but she'd already put down the phone.

I felt numb, barely aware I'd even dressed myself as I walked downstairs and into the kitchen.

'Oh, you spoiled it,' Ryan said, standing in the kitchen; the comforting smell of coffee and toast filled the air.

'What?'

'I was going to make your breakfast, I thought... well, you seem so stressed.'

'Yes, of course I am. Erin's missing, Mark's been arrested, and the last person to apparently see her was me... Oh, and Lara's just put the phone down on me, again.'

'Carly, I didn't mean...' I saw a flash of anger; it was probably justified.

I sighed. 'It's okay, Ryan. I wasn't having a go at you, I'm just worried. I have this horrible feeling that Erin has done something bad. You know, hurt herself... or something?'

'It's fine,' he said, but I saw his jaw tighten.

I picked at the plate of toast he'd just put in front of me, as he wiped down the counter. 'Who was that on the phone before?' I asked. 'Sounded like you were having a row?'

'Oh… it was Max.'

'Were you arguing?'

'Yeah.'

'What about?'

'About… about him being a total dickhead. Do you want your eggs soft-boiled?'

'Yes please.'

He clearly didn't want to talk about the conversation with his brother, and I couldn't think of a way to press him on it. Perhaps that was all it was, one brother telling the other what a dickhead he was. But his reaction, and my instinct told me there was more to it.

Later that day, DS Sally Barker arrived without DS Harefield, but with several other officers, and announced they had a warrant to search my house and garden.

I almost collapsed, but how could I say no? It would make me look like I was hiding something. So I agreed and invited her inside, while the officers searched.

'How do you put up with that lot?' she asked, as she walked in, nodding behind in the direction of a group of photographers and reporters, who were still camped out at the end of my drive. My personal press pack.

'Oh *that*.' I rolled my eyes. 'Fortunately, the drive's long. The guy who's working on my house put up a No Trespassing sign yesterday, and they're okay, so far they seem to be sticking to the rules.'

'Well, let me know if you get any trouble,' she said, as we walked down the hall. 'I'll be happy to send a couple of lads over to scare them off.'

'Thanks,' I said, with a smile.

She seemed nicer on her own, without DS Harefield, or perhaps it was just an act to lull me into a false sense of security?'

We walked into the sitting area, and looking through the windows I could see Ryan standing around, unable to work with several men moving plant pots and checking every bloody grain of soil.

'Quite a search party you've got here,' I said, hoping the officers who'd gone upstairs weren't seeing Ryan's clothes in my bedroom and putting two and two together.

'Like I say, it's a high-profile case. And you know,' she shook her head slowly, 'it seems the more we look, the less we know. None of it makes any sense, we just can't find her – even if she isn't... alive.'

'I just want to clear a couple of things up,' I started, once I'd made her a cup of tea and we were sitting down on opposite sofas. I leaned forward and spoke quietly. 'I'll be honest... Sally, I'm worried that as I was the last to see Erin, I should have been more... proactive?'

'Do *you* think you could have been more proactive?' she asked, taking a sip of tea.

'Well, I don't know. She just disappeared, and I assumed she'd gone home, but could I have done more?'

'Do you feel you could have done more, Carly?'

This was starting to feel like a therapy session.

'I don't know – perhaps? But it's complicated. As I explained, my friendship with Lara has been non-existent since Mark and Erin... So when she didn't get back to me, I didn't keep calling her to tell her that Erin had run off. Nor did I feel that Erin was my responsibility. But now I wish I'd done something, you know.'

'Do you think she might have been running away from you?' Sally's head was to one side, waiting for my answer.

'No, definitely not! We were having a conversation... Erin has always been a bit frosty, but we kind of opened up a bit... I thought...'

'That reminds me,' she said, like she hadn't heard me. 'I wanted to show you something.' She opened up her satchel and produced a file, laid it carefully on the coffee table, opened it and then flicked through agonisingly slowly. What the hell was she going to show me? I had to put my coffee cup down on the table for fear she might see me shaking. 'This.' She finally lifted her head from the file and, looking straight into my face, laid a photograph down on the table.

I put on my reading glasses, held my breath, and picked up the photo. It was a picture of a blush pink knitted throw. I looked at Sally, puzzled. 'It's... it's a throw.'

She nodded. 'Recognise it?'

I lifted my head very slowly to meet her gaze. 'It *looks* like mine.'

She sat back in her seat, without blinking, and the bonhomie from seconds before burst like a bubble above our heads. '*Is* it yours?'

I looked down again at the photo. 'I have two of them, they're on the sofas,' I said, looking across both sofas, and with a jolt, seeing only one. How had I not noticed this before? But then so much had been going on I hadn't even thought to look.

'I gave it to Erin, she was cold.' I hoped, if nothing else, this would prove that I wasn't nasty to her, that I didn't try to hurt her.

But Sally seemed unconvinced. 'Okay...'

'Where did you find it?' I asked, dreading her answer.

'We found it down on the beach, just a few hundred yards from here.'

'So did she go down on the beach, did it fall...' I couldn't look at her, just kept staring at the remaining throw on the arm of the sofa, and wishing there were still two. My insides were churning; this didn't look good for Erin. Or for me. 'I don't understand.'

'Yes,' she said, looking into my face, 'it's been puzzling us too. Especially as it has bloodstains on it...' And before I could ask, she added, 'It's Erin's blood.'

My hand rushed to my mouth, then I remembered watching a TV programme where a police psychologist said that's what people do when they are lying, trying to stop the lies coming out. Thinking of this, I moved my hand away, aware Sally seemed to be watching my every move.

'So... it looks like Erin might have... fallen, from the cliffs?' I asked, horrified, and finding it hard to say the words. All I could think of was Lara, and how devastated she would be.

'Well, it's too early in the investigation to say. There are *a lot* of theories flying around. Your husband, for example...'

'Yes, I heard he was under arrest.'

'Not any more. We released him,' she looked at her watch, 'about an hour ago.'

'Oh, so, he isn't a suspect?' I couldn't help the disappointment; after all, if he wasn't under suspicion, that made it point all the more to me.

Sally shrugged again. 'Well, he had an *alibi*, and, as he pointed out, it isn't in his interests for anything to happen to Erin. He says her disappearance will have a negative impact on his new TV programme in America.' She began putting the photo into the file, then stopped. 'Will it have any impact on *you*, Carly?'

'What?' I asked.

'If the programme doesn't go ahead?'

I suddenly saw a way of proving I hadn't done anything to Erin. 'Actually yes, it isn't in my interests either for Erin to be missing – because if the programme's cancelled, then I won't be getting the percentage of money I'm owed.'

'Oh, I see. Thing is, we've now viewed the video Mrs Matthews... Erin's mother, sent to us.'

'Oh. Okay.'

'And Mr Anderson seems to think you made the video to try and stop him from leaving you.'

'I made that video more than ten years ago!'

'Yes and according to Mr Anderson, it was around then he wanted to separate, and that's *why* you made the video. He says none of what you say in the recording is true.'

'Well, he would say that wouldn't he? It isn't *lies* – I made the recording because he hurt me and I wanted him to stop.'

She nodded, but I wasn't sure she believed me. I was one half of the golden couple, and who would ever believe that Mark Anderson the perfect husband and father, could do something like that? She looked back at her notes. 'He says… you once kidnapped the children?'

'Kidnapped?' I was horrified.

She looked at me apologetically. 'Yeah. He says you hid the children in a rental cottage, and wouldn't tell anyone where they were.'

'Whoa. It wasn't *like* that. I was staying away from *him*… I wanted a divorce, I was desperately unhappy…'

'But you went back to him?'

'Yes, I went back *home* with him.' *What was Mark doing to me? And why was he doing it now?*

I couldn't tell her about the hold he had over me; and if he could make me leaving with my children sound like kidnap, he could easily convince them I was a murderer. He once told me it would be easy to convince the police that I benefited financially from my mother's death. Just thinking about this made me start to cry, and I reached for a tissue to wipe my eyes.

'You told us previously that you'd had a nasty note, a rat delivered, and someone's face was pressed against the window.' She continued, listing this in monotone, making it sound far-fetched even to me.

I nodded, listlessly; how could I deny it?

'Carly, tell me, are you upset about the fact that Mark and his new girlfriend are about to come into some big money? If it were me, I'd be furious,' she said, pulling what I can only assume was a 'furious' face.

'No! I'm *not*,' this was all getting a bit scary, what did they think had happened?

'Mr Anderson also seemed to be of the opinion that you are still angry about their affair,' she looked back down at her notes, 'and about them having money you felt was *owed* to you?'

'Yes. It was… it *is* owed to me,' I stressed. Why was he playing games? The money in our bank was half mine, and he knew it.

'So you *are* angry? Jealous even?'

'I'm annoyed about the money. But *jealous*? No. I was upset when I found out about the affair, who wouldn't be? He'd been having a relationship with Erin behind my back, and she was pregnant. She was like a *daughter* to us.' I heard my voice crack. I kept thinking about the blood on the throw; I couldn't get it out of my head.

Sally pulled a face, suggesting that she sympathised. 'Of course, I can see why you'd feel weird about that.'

'I don't feel *weird*… exactly, just let down, by both of them.' I was scared to say anything now. Mark had apparently painted me as the jealous, greedy ex-wife and with his alibi in place, the police had obviously turned their attention to me.

Sally moved in her seat, like she was making herself comfy to chat with a friend. 'I'm a bit confused, Carly. You see, Mr Anderson said *you* were the one who left him. And I seem to remember reading in the paper that in fact you left him ages before he met Erin, because you were *looking for yourself* or something?' She said this like it was the most ridiculous thing she'd ever heard. It was. Because it was all lies. All part of Mark and Estelle's narrative.

'*Finding* myself,' I corrected gently, 'though God knows why, because that wasn't what I was doing, that was what Mark and his agent *told* me I was doing. And I did *say* that – but the truth was that Mark was having an affair with Erin, and she was pregnant. Thing is, we didn't always tell the press the truth. And it was decided in this case it would be best for all of us to pretend it was me who wanted to end the marriage.' I was aware how this showbiz arrangement might sound to Sally, and in truth I felt foolish for going along with it. But because I told him about Mum's death, he always had that hold over me, and as long as he lived he would *keep* that hold over me.

'Men are bastards,' she sighed, shaking her head. 'My ex ran off with a younger woman, a few years ago now, but I remember how it felt – and, between you and me, I could have killed her.' She looked at me, waiting for my response.

I feigned surprise.

'Yes – me – a detective, I'd have *killed*,' she said, 'and I'm not proud of it – just being honest with you, as I know you're being with me.'

'Yes,' I heard myself croak.

'It was bad enough for me, but for you… well, you had a lot more to lose than I did. I wouldn't blame you for *anything* you did.' She looked at me questioningly, sympathetically, seemingly waiting for me to admit something.

'I didn't—'

'I mean, here you are struggling, trying to keep this place going. Jarvis & Co aren't cheap either – he must be charging you way more than you earn at that shop?'

I could feel myself blush. I didn't know they knew where I worked. And did Sally know about me and Ryan? Not that it was relevant, but it might make things awkward.

'And all the worry of making ends meet, while Erin Matthews is sitting pretty with your husband's millions, the millions *you* worked for? That he's now telling *you*, you can't even have a little slice of? I know what I'd do if it were me – and I tell you,' she looked around, and leaned forward, before saying under her breath, 'honestly, I couldn't guarantee she'd come out alive.'

Now she was playing me, she wanted me to nod and confess, but it wasn't like that.

'I don't… don't *resent* her. And I don't want *his* money, I just want what's *mine*,' I said, desperately trying to keep the irritation out of my voice.

She looked disappointed. 'Fair enough. Well, you're a better woman than me, Carly.' She smiled. 'Now, just one more thing.' She took out a tablet and clicked it on. 'Thanks for sending us your CCTV footage. I presume you checked this yourself?'

'Yes, there was no sign of Erin.'

'No, but we have the technology,' she said in an American accent. I humoured her, and smiled, while cringing at her attempt at humour.

She placed the tablet on the coffee table in front of me.

'We've got this CCTV wizard in our department,' she started. 'She really is a genius, and she's cleaned up the footage, and you're right, there's no sign of Erin, but take a look at this.' She pushed the tablet towards me, and as my eyes focused on a black and white image of the front of my house, she pointed at the large rhododendron bush at the end of the drive. 'Can you see? There's someone there,' she said, her finger still pointing.

I leaned in to try and focus, and suddenly became aware of slight movement, and yes, someone was pacing outside.

'If we look at the time Erin *arrived*,' she was saying, looking at a sheet of paper with timings on, 'and the time this person turned up – they appeared *straight* after Erin went inside your house.'

The consequences of this may not have been good for Erin, but it might mean they'd found the real suspect, before they'd started digging up my bloody garden.

I almost hugged her with relief. 'So someone was *waiting* for her?' I asked, feeling a prickle of hope. They knew I had nothing to do with it now, didn't they?

'Looks like it, but he seems to disappear down the side of the house, towards the back garden, see… now watch,' she said, and zoomed in. 'Do you recognise that man?'

It was still slightly blurry, and dark, but as she zoomed in, it became clearer, and the more I looked, the more I didn't believe what I saw. My heart began thudding; my mouth was dry.

'It looks like Ryan…' I said. 'Ryan Jarvis.'

CHAPTER THIRTY-TWO

I didn't understand. The night Erin ran out of my house, Ryan wasn't there. He turned up later, about half an hour later, after I'd been out looking for her; he was inside the house, said he'd just arrived. He made out he wasn't even aware that Erin had been there – so why did he lie, and what the hell was going on?

Just then, one of the officers stood at the glass doors, holding something in a clear bag. I couldn't see from where I was what was in it, but he was gesturing for Sally to go out to him.

'Excuse me, Carly, I won't be a minute,' she said, and disappeared into the garden.

I felt breathless. I wanted to be sick; was this real? Had Ryan done something to Erin? Had he followed her here, to my house that night? Everything was tangled up in my head, and I couldn't straighten it out.

And what was happening now, in the garden? Had the police found something of Ryan's that was incriminating? Sally was walking down to the bottom of the garden to greet two police officers who'd come into the garden from the beach below.

I had to do something or I might explode. I was so tense, and so very nauseous, and carried the cups to the sink, where I washed them carefully, trying not to shake. Then I threw up.

I managed to clean myself up and was sitting back on the sofa with a glass of water when Sally returned, marching in through the glass doors, where Erin had left. She looked pale; there was no jauntiness, no more acting my friend, just a serious detective face, when she said, 'I am sorry, Carly, I'm going to have to ask you to come down to the station with me.'

I couldn't speak. I had so many questions, but everything became a blur as she read me my rights and I was escorted to the police car parked outside.

I don't remember the journey to the police station, I just remember the ball of fear sitting in my throat, threatening to erupt into sobs at any moment. I'd only ever been in one once. I was eight years old and Mum and I went there to report our missing cat. This was very different, and I didn't know what scared me most, that Ryan had done something to Erin, or that they thought I had.

After being checked in – a mortifying experience – I was soon sitting in a room with Sally and another female detective plus a duty solicitor called Peter. He seemed kind and calm, but was probably as nervous as me, which made me wonder what he knew that I didn't. He smiled politely while the two women detectives made small talk that I couldn't help but feel was some kind of warm-up act. Watching them, I doubted if Peter had the knowledge, the gravitas – or quite frankly, the balls – to support me adequately against two alpha females?

'It must be lovely living in that house, on the cliffs, above the sea,' Sally was saying, as she gathered her notes together. 'If I won the lottery, I'd have a house just like it.' She turned to DCI Choudry, her partner in the interview. 'It's the original *Forever Home*, the very first one, before Mark Anderson started doing other houses up, it's gorgeous,' she said, in hushed tones.

They both raised eyebrows to each other, presumably to signal envy – or was it perhaps a secret detective signal to say 'she's guilty' or 'she's an idiot, that murdering toy boy played her for a fiddle'? By then I was completely paranoid; my husband had told them I was a jealous liar, my boyfriend was on CCTV lurking in the driveway, and my sofa throw had been found on the beach, covered in Erin Matthews' blood. And just when I thought things couldn't get any worse, it looked like they'd found something incriminating in my garden.

Sally turned on the tape and they started the interview, asking exactly the same questions I'd been asked before. I just told them again what happened and what I knew. Meanwhile, Peter, who looked barely older than Phoebe, squirmed in the seat next to me. It seemed that this fight was mine, and I was on my own in it, so rather than wait for my cue from him, I dived right in.

'Look, I realise potentially something terrible might have happened, and I also feel that, in retrospect, I *should* have done more. But you're asking the same things over and over. How many ways can I tell you… whatever's happened to Erin Matthews, I wasn't involved?'

I was tired, and becoming tearful, and Peter finally intervened to ask if I wanted a rest. I shook my head and he offered me water, but I refused.

'I just want to go home,' I said. 'Have you asked Ryan why he was there? He might know something?' I said, still clinging to some hope that Ryan was innocent, and his weird, unexplained presence at the bottom of my drive might be my salvation.

'Ryan Jarvis is here now,' Choudry responded; she seemed cooler than Sally, more businesslike.

'Has he been arrested too?'

'No, he came here with some information.'

'Oh?' I murmured. 'Can you tell me what…?'

'I'm sorry, I can't,' she said tightly.

What the hell was Ryan up to? What information did he suddenly have? Why was he standing in my drive that night? Had he given himself up, or had he thrown me under the bus too? Could I trust *anyone* any more?

'Now,' she said, shuffling papers, 'can we please just go over this again? Your husband said you made threats on the phone…'

I shook my head, confused. '*Threats*? What kind of threats?'

'Threats to his partner, Erin Matthews,' she said, unblinking.

'No – no I *didn't*.' I was alarmed. Mark again, my God. I would make him pay for what he was putting me through.

DCI Choudry breathed out loudly, and looked down at her notes. 'In a telephone conversation with Mr Anderson on Wednesday the nineteenth May you said—' She paused for a moment, then read slowly in a monotone, '"It won't be the patter of tiny feet she hears, it'll be the sound of me chasing her with a bloody baseball bat!"'

Shit. I could remember saying that, Ryan and I even joked about it, but it wasn't a threat – although now, in this context, it sounded exactly like one.

'I take it you were referring to Ms Matthews when you said that?' DCI Choudry pressed.

'Okay – yes, I was. And I can see why that *might* sound vaguely threatening, but—'

'*Vaguely?*' Choudry said.

I felt like I was drowning. Surely they knew as well as I did it was an expression, a way of venting my anger. I didn't mean it literally.

'We also have statements from two waitresses at the Silver Spoon Tearooms,' Sally piped up, shuffling yet more papers. My whole bloody life counted out in sheets of A4. 'They say there was an argument between you and Erin there?'

'I guess you could call it that, but—'

'And you said,' she looked at her notes, '"Haven't you stolen enough from me already? You dare come anywhere near my house and I won't be responsible for the consequences."' Sally looked up. Choudry looked up. Four enquiring eyes glaring at me. Waiting. Wondering how the hell I was going to worm my way out of this.

'She… she'd just told me she wanted my *house*, how I was alone and didn't need the space, that I was being selfish… I'm sure you understand how that would feel, Sally?' I said, turning my gaze to her, desperately trying to connect with her as someone who'd had experience of a cheating partner.

She looked slightly uncomfortable at my direct plea, but nodded. 'Yeah, yeah sure. I mean, it would make me bloody angry – like you obviously were…'

For a second, I was relieved, then realised I was being walked back into quicksand. 'Yes, I *was* angry – but it was in the moment. I wanted to stop her from *entertaining* the idea that she could take my home from me.'

'So, it was a temporary anger, and you didn't resent her for being with your husband, or want him back?'

'Exactly. And as for my husband spouting theories about me still having feelings for him, he wouldn't know – he hasn't *listened* to me since about 1998.' It was a weak joke – but not far from the truth. He hadn't a clue about me; it seemed he'd created this idea in his head that I'd do anything to get him back, including murder. Either that or he was suggesting this as a distraction, to cover for something *he'd* done. Did people even do that in real life, or was it just in TV crime dramas? Either way, I got the feeling the police were buying his theories – I was the woman scorned after all, and could easily have pushed Erin off the cliff that night. 'Mark doesn't know anything about me now, he has no right to suggest I want him back. In fact…' I hesitated, I really didn't want to bring Ryan into this, but I was fighting for my life here. 'I'm seeing someone, I've moved on. I'm very happy.'

They glanced at each other, and as I'd expected asked who it was.

'I'd rather not give his name, but needless to say, I'm over my husband, and had no reason to harm Erin.'

'Carly, it would be really helpful to us – and for you – if you told us his name. It doesn't mean he'll be implicated.'

I wasn't convinced. I thought it would make Ryan *and* me look very *implicated*. I'd only told them this to make it clear I wasn't jealous; I had no intention of revealing his name. And knowing he'd been on the CCTV and was now being questioned put a whole different light on our burgeoning relationship. In my head it was already over.

'He has nothing to do with this,' I said, though it was looking very much like he did.

'Okay, well in that case there's nothing to worry about and it may help to clear a few things up,' Sally said pointedly, but with a smile.

'It's not really a relationship – I mean…' I tried. But they were both looking at me, pens poised. So I took a deep breath. 'Ryan Jarvis,' I said.

I saw a look pass between them, so continued to try and downplay it.

'He's just been working on the house, and he's – well, a friend, but only recently it's become something more. So, you see, I've moved on, and it's not true what Mark said about me being jealous. I don't hold a grudge against Erin,' I said, desperately trying to get back to defending myself against Mark's ridiculous claims.

DCI Choudry sighed, and Sally wrote something down. Then they asked me details like how long I'd known Ryan and when had the relationship changed. And then they continued asking me the same things again and again, until I wanted to scream.

They seemed to take a deep breath at exactly the same time.

'Carly.' Sally leaned forward, speaking quietly, going for a softer approach. 'You can see our problem, can't you, love? We've got a missing twenty-four-year-old woman. She's your husband's girlfriend, and was last seen at your place – and now she's disappeared. Your CCTV shows her arriving and knocking at the front door, but it doesn't show her leaving…'

'No, it won't because she must have gone out through the back garden and if she walked close to the wall, the CCTV wouldn't have picked her up,' I said, wishing I'd been able to afford CCTV at the back of the house and I might be able to prove my innocence. Because that's what this was turning into – me desperately trying to convince the police of my innocence.

'Okay, but then we find your sofa throw, covered in blood – Erin's blood – on the beach.'

'But I told you, that could easily have been put there by her to make *me* look guilty.' How many times did I have to say this? Surely they could see that someone was trying to frame me? But who? Mark, Erin… Ryan?

'And then today, we find bits of wool *from* the throw on the rose bushes in your garden, and the rocks beneath your house…'

'Oh?' Even Peter reacted to this, as he shifted in his seat, and I took it as a sign that things weren't looking good for me.

'…And her phone smashed up and shoved behind the garden shed.'

'Christ.' I threw my arms onto the table and buried my head in them.

In the silence, I suddenly heard DCI Choudry's voice: 'Do you *still* think you're being made to look guilty, Carly?'

I slowly lifted my head, tears now filling my eyes. 'I don't *KNOW*,' I yelled.

They didn't flinch, just sat and waited for me to calm down. Then eventually Sally started talking to me like a primary school teacher. 'Carly, thing is, we're at a loss, because none of this is adding up, and everything keeps coming back to you and your home.'

'I know, I know. And I wish I *could* explain it to you…' I began earnestly, 'but I don't understand it myself. I've no idea why her phone was there, or why the throw or—' I glanced over at Peter, who I think was about to drop off. He certainly didn't look as if he was going to come in and save me any time soon, in fact it didn't look as if he believed me either.

DCI Choudry took a breath. 'So, you said Erin came to your house that night, hoping to catch you and Mark together?'

I wanted to bang my head on the table. This was a never-ending loop of the same questions. If I'd been guilty or was trying to hide something, it might have worked, but I wasn't. As we were going around in circles, I was about to start saying 'no comment' to everything until it stopped, but just then, a police officer knocked and came into the room.

He whispered something to Sally, which I couldn't hear, but I did hear her murmur, 'You're kidding?' then 'Shit,' under her breath.

What the hell had happened now?

Sally looked at DCI Choudry, and asked her to turn off the tape. 'We are stopping the interview. Would you be kind enough to wait here, Carly? We just have something to attend to.' And with that, they both left the room.

'Are you okay?' Peter asked.

I just nodded; I didn't want to get into any conversations with him. Besides, they might be watching us behind a two-way mirror, trying to catch me out.

We waited a long time, me tapping my fingers on the desk, him opening his briefcase, taking out an apple and crunching loudly into the silence. It was torturous; my life was hanging in the balance. I didn't even know if the thing they had to 'attend to' had anything to do with Erin. It could have been something relevant that implicated me, and I'd be jailed for the next twenty years while my kids fought the courts to prove my innocence – if they even believed my innocence, if the evidence was that damning. Or it could have been a completely different case, and they would leave us here, me and Peter and his big, crunchy apple – only to return refreshed and ready for another round?

Oh God, I couldn't take it. I hated Mark for putting me through this – just by having her in his life he'd brought all this on me. How dare he get himself into some hopeless relationship and imply to the police that *I* might have done something to his mistress! My head was a whirl, I couldn't think straight and was beginning to feel nauseous as I hadn't eaten for hours and I was scared of going to prison for something I hadn't done. I tried not to think about my kids and what this would do to them, because I'd just start crying and not stop.

Then suddenly, after about an hour, the door opened, and in came DCI Choudry, alone. She sat down, and looked at me. I desperately searched her face but she remained impassive.

The door opened again and in came Sally, who joined DCI Choudry. 'So…' she started. 'Erin has been found.'

'Oh God!' I almost collapsed on the chair. Erin's body had been found. This was the worst news, and I started to cry. 'Where was she found?' I asked, through tears of sadness and exhaustion.

'We can't say.'

'Do you know who… killed her?'

'Oh, sorry, love – no, she's not dead.'

'She's *alive*?' I asked, just to absolutely make sure I'd got this right.

Sally nodded. 'Alive and well.'

'But… what happened?'

'Well, at this stage it's confidential, and we don't actually have all the details. I'm sure in due course you will find out exactly what happened. But now you're free to go.'

As desperate as I was to leave, I felt like after all I'd just been through, I was owed some kind of explanation.

'Can't you even tell me where she was *found*?'

Sally shook her head; she had a pained expression on her face like she really wanted to tell me everything, but wasn't allowed to.

I stood up to go, my mind wild and frazzled with what might have happened. Had she been attacked and left on the beach? Had she gone away for a few nights and put everyone through hell? Mark and Estelle were now probably conjuring up some Hollywood-style story, ready to sell it to the highest bidder. 'This just feels weird, going back out there like nothing's happened.'

Sally gathered her papers and stood up, walking with me to the door. 'Oh, stuff's happened, you can be sure of that. Sorry I can't be more specific, but until people have been charged… I can't…'

'Okay, I understand.'

'But Ryan Jarvis is just outside,' she said, and looked at me meaningfully. 'I'm sure *he'll* explain everything.'

CHAPTER THIRTY-THREE

Leaving the interview room, I signed my release papers with the desk sergeant, feeling like a different person to the one who'd arrived hours before. It was now dark outside, and walking through to the exit, I saw Ryan leaning against the wall.

As soon as he saw me, he reluctantly pulled himself away from the wall, and instead of his usual bright smile, the cheeky wink, he just rolled his eyes slowly.

I walked towards him, and we hugged, half-heartedly. I didn't know what to expect. 'Why are you here? Sally said you know what happened with Erin.'

He nodded and, taking my arm with one hand, opened the door with the other, leading us outside.

'So what's happened? She's okay, isn't she?'

'She's fine,' he sighed.

'Why were you outside my house the night she went missing?' I asked, 'You were on the CCTV Ryan.'

'Let's just get in the van and I'll tell you what's been going on.'

Once inside his van, he handed me a bottle of water. I twisted the lid, I was so thirsty, and glugged about half the bottle in one go. 'So, *tell* me,' I said, wiping my mouth on my sleeve.

He took a deep breath. 'I feel terrible; this is so difficult, Carly. I don't want you to hate me.' He turned to look at me, his eyes filled with pain.

My stomach dipped. I couldn't possibly imagine what the connection was between Ryan and Erin. 'Okay, what?'

'It wasn't me on the CCTV, it was my brother.'

'Max?'

'Yeah, people say we look alike, and from a distance...'

I nodded; they did, that made sense. 'But why?'

'I told you that Erin used to go out with Max. It was only for a few weeks, and it was ages ago. I never really understood it, never liked her, felt she was using him.' He paused for a moment, clearly trying to work out how to best tell me. 'Anyway, when she dumped him, he was *really* gutted. It took him a while, but I thought he'd got over her, especially now she's with *him* and had the baby and everything.' Ryan was leaning on the steering wheel, gazing ahead, like he was trying to remember. 'But seeing her with him, on the telly and in the papers, I think it reignited something with Max, he still had feelings for her. Anyway, a couple of weeks ago, I saw them in Looe, having a drink together, and it looked like... well, more than just a drink.'

'Oh?'

He nodded. 'Yeah, so I asked him about it, but he said they were just mates. I knew he was lying, but probably because I'm with you, and he worried it might get back to Mark. And Erin had told him she thought you and Mark were seeing each other. I didn't put any of this together, until I went to see Mum, and she kept talking about "the little girl who lives upstairs". Now, I know Mum has dementia, but she seemed worse than usual, really agitated. She kept asking me to make sure the little girl was okay, and turns out "the little girl" she'd seen was Erin. Before she went missing, she'd been at Mum's with Max, and the other morning when he called me and you heard us arguing, I'd asked him if he knew anything about Erin. He went mad, just really angry, upset, thinking I was accusing him of hurting her.'

'And when *Erin* called you a few days ago, when you were at the house working?' I asked.

'Yeah, as I told you then, she was trying to get hold of Max, but I stuck my nose in a bit. I said didn't she think she'd done enough stealing someone's husband, why try and break my bro's heart again, was one man not enough for her? Thing is, she can't be trusted. She told everyone about how sex with Max was rubbish – personal, nasty stuff, you know? And I called her out on that.'

I nodded; so Ryan had been telling the truth about that call.

'So, on the night she went missing, she'd asked Max to drop her at yours, park down the road, and wait for her,' he continued. 'She'd said she was scared if Mark was there, and scared if he wasn't because either way you were so jealous you'd probably lash out. She'd made this sound so real that Max was worried about her, so wandered up to the house in case she was in trouble; that's when he was caught on the CCTV. And when she did eventually run out that night, she called Max from your garden to meet her on the beach, then threw her phone away so she couldn't be traced. He then ran through your back garden to meet her on the beach, where apparently she was sobbing, had blood all over her, and said you'd attacked her in a "jealous rage".'

'Which explains the sofa throw on the beach. She must have cut herself to put blood on it, making it look like I'd done it,' I murmured, shaking my head in disbelief.

'She really planned this, hooked Max in saying she needed somewhere to hide from you because you'd threatened to kill her. So, naturally, he took her back to Mum's.'

'She went through all that just to implicate me? But she must have known she'd be found eventually?' Besides, I thought, she would want to see her son surely?

'Seems she genuinely thought Mark was seeing you, and when he wasn't with you at the house, she decided to disappear to scare him into giving her attention and at the same time drop you in it. She thought if she told Mark you'd attacked her, he'd stop seeing you. Then, if she was found, or decided to reappear, she said she'd had to go into hiding because you'd threatened to kill her.'

I was just listening, open-mouthed. I resented Erin, I didn't like her, but the hate she'd clearly felt for me was unimaginable, and all because of Mark.

'Anyway, I'd almost given up on it, until today, when I went round to see Mum. She was still talking about "the little girl upstairs" and I suddenly thought, what if Mum recognises her as the little girl she used to look after? She'd remember her as the child, because Mum's long-term memory is still quite good; it's what happened half an hour ago that she *can't* remember. So I asked her where the little girl that she used to look after was and she said, "here". He turned to look at me, taking his arms from the steering wheel. 'So… I pretended I needed something from upstairs, and went into Max's room to see if there was anything in there that might give me a clue. I couldn't see anything obvious, so opened the wardrobe, and heard something behind me, and when I turned around a pile of coats on his bed were moving. I freaked out, couldn't believe it – there she was – the woman whose face was in every newsfeed. Erin – hiding under a pile of coats in Max's bedroom.'

I gasped. 'How could she put us all through such hell,' I said, thinking mostly of poor Lara.

'I don't know why you're surprised, Erin doesn't think of anyone else.'

'No, you're right. So, when you found her, did you call the police?'

'Yeah. She begged me not to, but I wasn't taking any shit.'

'Wow,' I sighed, appalled at how Erin was still trying to ruin me, but relieved it was all over. My exhausted mind could barely comprehend everything Ryan had told me. I resented the way she'd tried to drag me in, but at the same time, I understood her dynamic with Mark; Erin was trying desperately to get his attention, to be relevant to him, to make him love her and be faithful. But he couldn't.

Ryan was shaking his head. 'Erin's really stupid, she hadn't thought it through, and when I found her huddled under the coats, she pretended to be scared!' He gave a hollow laugh. 'Like Erin Matthews has ever been scared of anyone. *She's* the scary one.'

'Yeah, she's pretty scary,' I murmured.

'She told this long story about how you'd attacked her when she went to your house that night. She said you were screaming at her, chased her out into the garden, and in her apparent "desperation", she climbed down the rocks and ended up running along the beach.'

'She probably *did* run along the beach – but I wasn't chasing her, she'd gone on ahead, minutes before while I was making her a cup of bloody tea,' I said, still shocked at this.

'Erin used Max, and as he's still smitten, she knew she could trust him not to tell anyone. And he didn't, the idiot. But when she'd gone missing, I knew something wasn't right, that's why I kept asking you about it.'

'Sorry, I just thought it was odd, you seemed obsessed.'

'Well Max hinted that you were still seeing Mark. I was confused.'

I smiled. 'But you *knew* how I felt about Mark.'

'Yeah, but what Max said made me feel insecure, and when Erin disappeared…'

'I know, I know, we were all the same, feeling like we couldn't trust anyone,' I said, reaching for his hand.

'Yeah, thanks to her we've all been through it, looking over our shoulders.'

'Well, now it's her turn to go through the police questioning and mind games.'

He smiled; 'Yeah, she'll be charged with wasting police time at least. But she's dragged Max into it too – whatever he tries to say, he went along with it all. Even when he *knew* she was missing, he didn't tell the police where she was. He broke the law, thanks to that stupid cow.'

'And your mum,' I said, suddenly remembering poor Tina caught in the middle of all this. 'Is she okay?'

'She doesn't really understand, but obviously having the police there upset her. She's very fragile, it's like trying to explain something to a child. Everything scares her. That's why when you offered to go and visit, I said best not to, she can get really upset even if someone just knocks on the door.'

'I understand now, so all this must have really unsettled her.'

'Yeah, and I'm angry with Max for putting her through it.'

I just sat there, my mind still in a whirl. 'Mark caused all this though, Erin was reacting to his behaviour,' I sighed. 'And then he tried to pin it on *me*.'

'I'll be honest with you, Carly,' he said, resting his hand on my knee, 'I even wondered myself.'

'No,' I was horrified, 'you didn't think—'

'You said yourself, we don't know each other that well, and you had plenty of reasons to want Erin off the scene one way or another.'

'I guess so, and if I'm absolutely honest, I did wonder about *you*,' I said, pulling an awkward face.

He looked surprised; 'Really?'

'Yeah, and when I saw who I thought was you on the CCTV, I nearly died,' I said. 'And you were really vague about Max going out with Erin when Phoebe asked you.'

'Yes, I knew something weird was going on, I just didn't want Max to be connected with her. Looks like we both lost the plot,' he said smiling. 'Shall we go home? You must be starving, I know I am.' He kissed me, started the car, and when we got back to the house, he cooked supper, and held me all night.

*

The following morning, I still felt bruised from the whole ordeal, but thanks to Ryan, I was calmer, and more hopeful. I thought about Lara and how happy and relieved she must be now Erin was safe, and I longed to call her, but decided it was best to send a text saying what great news, and I was happy for her. A little later that morning, though, she was on the phone.

'Carly, I feel terrible,' she said, her emotion clear. 'I said some things in the heat of the moment… I even told the police you might have done something…'

'I know, I know, but the main thing is that Erin's okay.'

'Can you ever forgive me?'

'Of course, I understand how upset you were. I'm just glad for you that Erin's safe,' I said, though my feelings were still conflicted. I was surprised to feel quite hurt that Erin would do all that to get at me.

'No thanks to that despicable ex-husband of yours. He wasn't exactly out searching, was he? Just holed himself up in the cottage drinking himself to oblivion.'

'In his defence, he was arrested for at least a day when she was missing, but far be it from me to defend him,' I said. 'And sadly he isn't my ex – he's *still* my husband,' I sighed. 'I have been pushing, but getting him to do anything is always a nightmare and this divorce is dragging.' The last couple of days had put into perspective how much I needed this all to officially be over and Mark and his drama to be out of my life.

'I'm sorry, Carly, but as far as I'm concerned, I hope it drags even longer. I'm desperately hoping Erin comes to her senses before you're divorced and won't end up married to the bastard. You'd have thought this whole episode would have cooled things off between them, but she's back there now, and he's declaring his undying love.'

'I'm afraid Mark doesn't know the meaning of such things.'

'Well, *you* know that, but she's twenty-four and he has her wrapped round his little finger.'

According to Lara, Erin had spent several hours at the police station once she'd been 'found', and after being put in touch with social services, was asked where she wanted to go. Much to Lara's horror, she'd asked to be taken back to Mark rather than back to Lara's where her son was. I found it hard to be apart from my babies for just a few hours when they were small, but she'd been gone for *days*, surely she wanted to see little Billy? Then again, she was Lara's daughter, and that was where the issues began, Lara was someone who often put her child last on her list.

'The police called me to say she was safe,' she said, 'and I just assumed she'd come to me, but she called from the cottage. I could hear him in the background telling her, "Don't say too much, be careful." Bastard!'

'He probably won't let her talk to anyone until she's done an exclusive interview with *Hello*,' I said cynically. 'Estelle will be negotiating a fee as we speak.'

'I *hate* him, Carly. I hate what he's done to her. He'll ruin her life. He's not who she thinks he is, he's vile.'

I tried to reassure her that if she left things for a little while, Erin might come to her senses. 'We can't tell our kids what to do – *we* have the experience to know when they are walking into walls, but the more you try to stop them, the more they keep walking.'

'I adore little Billy, but just wish there wasn't a baby involved. If it was just Erin dealing with her daddy issues for a few months, then I could live with it.'

'Yeah well, if that's *all* it was, she's still left some twisted wreckage behind,' I said, pointedly.

'Sorry, Carly, that was insensitive of me.'

'No, it's fine. I just feel like – after everything, I was just getting my life back. Having the police search my house, question me for hours and accuse me of attacking Erin, *plotting* with Mark…' I left that hanging on the line. If we were ever going to be friends again, I had to make her and her selfish daughter realise the collateral damage that had been caused.

'Yes, and I'm sorry you had to go through that, Carly. But in Erin's defence, being with Mark and having the baby has put her under such stress.'

'She could have left, Lara, she didn't have to drag me into it. She deliberately came to see me that night, so she could leave from my home and implicate me. It wasn't random, she planned it all. She even cut herself so she could leave my bloodied throw on the beach.'

'I haven't spoken to her yet, as I said, she hasn't come home, but when she does we'll have a long talk,' she said, like that would make any difference. 'Carly, I hope you can forgive her, she's been through so much, vile parcels in the post, and nasty messages online. She even received this revolting box of spiders... I was with her when she opened it, thinking it was a gift, beautifully wrapped. They all came running out.' She shuddered audibly. 'She was a mess!'

I was annoyed at Lara pinning the victim card on Erin, and hadn't forgotten her words the other day. 'You virtually accused me of being the one leaving those nasty messages,' I said, still hurt.

'No, no, I didn't, I just asked if you knew about them.'

'Same thing,' I said. 'I assume you thought I'd packed a box of spiders and sent those along too?'

'I only thought it might be you, because not everyone knows she has a fear of spiders. It has to be someone who knows her.'

'Yes, well, I think whoever it was, they know me too. I had a parcel delivered – a dead rat... you and Erin *both* know I'm scared to death of rats, but I haven't blamed you. And there was weird stuff going on in the house, like someone had broken in. I haven't had anything happen for a while but—'

'Oh my God! Really? Sounds like someone you and Erin both know… God, I feel cold just thinking about it. Have you any idea who it could be?'

'No. It crossed my mind it might be Erin – or Mark. It made sense, they both wanted me to leave the house. I thought they might be trying to scare me… but if Erin was getting stuff too, then God knows who it is.' I felt a shiver go through me.

I heard Lara sigh. 'I'm so sorry, Carly, for everything you've been through. I've been a shit friend, but I had to try and be a good mother and… Yes, if I'm honest, I wouldn't blame you for sending messages. If someone ran off with my partner, I would; you know how feisty I am.'

'Yeah, I can only imagine the scenes if someone tried to cross you,' I said, laughing. 'But you can rest assured I didn't send anything to Erin. Besides, you know I hate insects too – I'd be too scared to touch spiders – imagine *me* trying to get a load of spiders in a box?' I rolled my eyes. 'I'd be in therapy for months!'

She laughed at this. 'Oh Carly! I've missed you. Let's get together? Just you and me? Can't we put everything aside and be friends again?'

'I've missed you too,' I said, honestly.

I agreed to meet for coffee very soon, once the dust had settled, because I just knew this wasn't over, there was more to come.

Erin had played with fire, and I wondered just how she'd be slithering her way out of this one – and what kind of script Mark and Estelle would be writing for *her*. I didn't have to wait long to find out, because later, I turned on my phone, and pictures of her were everywhere, along with the headline: 'Celebrity's Girlfriend Forced into Hiding in Fear of Vengeful Ex-Wife!'

CHAPTER THIRTY-FOUR

Reading the newspaper story about Mark's 'Vengeful Ex-Wife', it was clear they'd gone with the 'blame Carly' option. Erin was still telling lies and taking no responsibility for her actions, and Mark was telling lies and taking no responsibility for causing her to do what she did.

> *Erin Matthews, 24, partner of TV's Mark Anderson, today spoke of her deep fear of Mark's former wife Carly, 49, and explained how this fear forced her to leave the tiny cottage she lived in with the handsome TV presenter and their son, after bitter ex Carly refused their half-share of the house. 'I have lived in fear every day since I moved in with Mark,' new mum of one, Erin, told the Daily Mail. 'Carly ended the marriage, but as soon as he started seeing me, she became jealous.' Strange parcels started arriving at the £400,000 rented cottage the couple share, and Erin said she was very scared. Just a few weeks ago, when Erin was still heavily pregnant, staff and customers at The Silver Spoon Tearooms in Looe were horrified to hear the women trading insults, and when Erin disappeared recently, Carly was the number one suspect.*

My mouth was dry. I didn't know whether to cry, or break plates in anger. It just wasn't true. I wondered again about my video diary. The police hadn't leaked it after all; I almost wished they had. Then again, if it did get out, I shivered just imagining Mark's retaliation, how he'd 'repackage' my mother's death for the police – and the press. It didn't bear thinking about.

Ryan was reading the same thing on his phone, and looking from me to the text. 'Can't you get lawyers onto this – she can't say these things, can she?'

'Well, she *has*. And as much as I'd love to get a lawyer onto it, lawyers are expensive, and Mark would just go bigger and better. Estelle would turn it into a circus, I just want a quiet life,' I added.

'Bloody newspapers!' he said.

'No, I don't blame the press, I blame Mark – and Estelle – and Erin!'

So, call me predictable, but I did what I always did in times like this. I called Mark, yelled at his answer machine for a while, said mean things, swore a lot, and felt much better. I put down the phone, and Ryan was watching me.

'You're *really* pissed off, aren't you?' he said.

'Yeah, I could kill both of them – and smack Estelle hard across the face. Like really hard,' I said, flopping on the sofa next to him. 'But what's the point? I'll only drive myself mad with all this. There's no point in taking it any further, it's already out there. I just hope that by not responding publicly or getting lawyered up, the whole story will die a natural death.' I said, reminding myself that it wouldn't do to wind Mark up too much, as he might finally do what he'd been threatening for years and call the police about my mum's death. Erin was going to be the focus of the press for a while, and I worried he might even use my story to detract from his own sordid life. Even apart, the problems he created followed me and caught me tightly in their grip. How many more public humiliations could I take? I felt bruised and battered, and in my mind's eye was making a noose and hanging my husband very, very high.

*

The next few days I spent regrouping. After everything else, the press mauling had left me feeling battered, and I just wanted to ignore everyone and everything – except my kids and Ryan. Being on the other end of Mark's lies to the press made me realise he'd used them as much, if not more, than they'd used him. All those years when I lived in fear of the press, and all the time, they weren't the problem – *he* was.

I spent the time trying to get back to where I was before the whole Erin ordeal, and heal by painting, planting bulbs in the garden, and working in the shop, which was proving to be a breath of fresh air and a break from all my problems.

Once I felt able to cope, I met with Lara in a hotel and we drank chilled white wine overlooking the beach. The bar was too dark for a sunny spring day; it smelt of old beer and one-night stands between middle-aged couples married to other people. But Lara liked it there and it wasn't too far for me to walk. I'd both looked forward to and dreaded this meeting. I knew it would probably revive a lot of painful memories for me, but I needed to let go, and knew that meeting Lara would be good for me.

'This is nice, like old times,' I said.

'Yes it is. I've missed you so much, Carly.' She squeezed my arm, and smiled into my face.

'How's Erin?' I asked, not really wanting to know.

'She's good,' Lara said, not really wanting to tell me.

We sipped on our drinks, and she gazed around.

Eventually Lara said: 'I do admire you, you're so bloody resilient, you've come through the marriage and all the shit he's put you through.'

'I'm trying to be the bigger person, trying hard to forgive,' I sighed, without adding, 'but I'll never forget,' which was the truth.

'Well, you're bigger than me. I hate him, always have – and the fact he's now with my daughter, it couldn't be worse. It's a nightmare.'

'You've never liked Mark, have you?' When I'd first introduced them years before when Steve, Erin's father, was still alive, I'd invited them both over to dinner, and we all just hit it off. Even Mark and Lara got on with each other back then, and we did a lot of things together as a foursome, and with the kids too, but then when Steve died everything changed, and it was back to just Lara and me. I wasn't aware of how much Lara hated Mark until, at the wake after Steve's funeral, he tried to comfort her, just said a few kind words and put his arm around her. I remember her pulling away and being quite rude to him. I actually felt quite sorry for Mark; he wasn't used to being treated like that by anyone. Afterwards, I subtly asked her about it, wondering what Mark had done to offend her, but she just said he was 'a sodding narcissist'. I wondered if perhaps losing her husband meant she found it hard to see other couples together, so after that I just saw Lara on her own, without Mark.

Little did we know, he'd one day be the father of her grandson.

'I always knew he was a womaniser,' she said. 'I spent years worrying about you, and now I'm going through it with my daughter – it's awful, Carly, and we'll never be free of him now, especially with the baby.'

I sympathised with her; I knew how I'd feel if Phoebe started going out with someone I knew was bad for her. Like Mark. 'Oh, love, just try not to think about him and wait for her to come home. Because she will.' Though I didn't point out it may not be Erin's choice, it may be because another blonde, or redhead, had moved in.

'I sometimes felt like he flaunted it in your face, like he wanted to get caught almost. Do you think he did?' she asked.

'Perhaps? Without ever talking about it, we just agreed to live our own lives. I didn't want to know what he was doing, or who with. I was in effect his enabler, but it was easier for both of us to leave it in Pandora's box.'

'But what kind of marriage *is* that?' she said. 'Christ, you were with him for twenty-five years and he just took the piss.'

'It may have seemed that way, but I could have divorced him, I just didn't want to leave the house, break up the family, and neither did he. Not good for his image,' I said, raising my eyebrows.

She seemed to hesitate, then put her hand on mine. 'Carly, I wanted to say sorry about the video. I had to send it to the police. I know you told me not to watch it, and for years I didn't, I promise. But after Erin became involved with him, I had to know what was on it, what it was that you felt you had to record.'

I shrugged. 'I understand, I'd have done the same if I thought Phoebe might be in danger. I just needed something to stop him, to put an end to the possibility of him hurting me too much, going too far.'

She rubbed my hand. 'I wish I'd known, back then. I might have been able to help you. The injuries you photographed… but you should have called me, I could have helped. I'd have gone to the police, told them everything and—'

'Just him knowing it existed was enough, and knowing someone else had a copy scared him. He stopped,' I clicked my fingers, 'just like that.'

She bit her lip angrily. 'Funny how he could control himself when his precious career was involved, isn't it?'

I nodded. 'Always.'

'God, I wish *he'd* walked into the sea that day instead of Steve,' she suddenly said.

'You must still wonder why?' I said, referring to Steve's suicide. We'd never really discussed this, it was too difficult for Lara, and I just took my lead from her, and was there to support her.

She nodded, tears in her eyes. 'He's been gone thirteen years now, and I wake up every morning and he's the first person I think about, and then the guilt kicks in, and I hate myself all over again.'

'You can't blame yourself, he had his demons,' I said.

'No, no… you don't know. I hurt him. Steve was a good man. He didn't deserve what happened to him.'

'No, he didn't. We used to have some laughs, didn't we, the four of us?' I said, trying to lift her spirits.

'Yeah, I guess so, but Mark was always so full of himself, wasn't he? I think Steve felt like a loser next to him.'

She'd never said that before; perhaps that was why we stopped seeing them? It was so long ago, I barely remembered. Mark did have a tendency to take over, to charm all the women in the room, and other men didn't always find that comfortable.

'Mark's just very confident, always has been, and it sometimes makes others feel intimidated, but he's all talk,' I said.

'Don't apologise for him, Carly, and don't ever forgive him,' Lara replied bitterly.

'I don't. He's hurt me too much – all the nights I didn't know where he was, all the whisperings on the phone, the looks of sympathy from other people when I turned up alone and he joined me later. I know most of the time it was work, but I spent so much of my marriage alone,' I sighed.

'Yes, but work was an excuse, wasn't it? I remember your thirty-fifth; he hadn't been there for your thirtieth, said he was working, so promised when you were thirty-five he was going to push the boat out. But what happened? He sent you a bunch of lilies,' she said, 'and told you he was working late, couldn't make it home. And all the time he was down the road, in *this* hotel with someone else…' She stopped herself.

'I didn't *know* that,' I said, surprised at the sharp sting this information had caused. I was imagining him with one of the blonde, well-preserved groupies he kept close to home, like a stable of expensive horses. I didn't think after all these years that hearing something from the past about my husband would hurt. But it did.

Seeing my face, Lara was clearly surprised too. 'I thought you were over him?'

'I am, but sometimes it feels raw, you know, even now?'

'Yeah, men like Mark can hurt forever, can't they… the gift that keeps on giving!'

All the pain from that birthday now reached out over the years and squeezed my chest, like it had just happened. Would I ever be free of him?

Lara could see I was upset. 'I'm sorry, love.' She reached out to touch my hand, but I slowly pulled it away. I was beginning to realise the significance of what she'd just said.

'You *knew* he was with someone else on my birthday and you didn't tell me?'

She sighed. 'God, Carly, I'm sorry.'

We both sat, numb, and I felt saddened, let down – was anybody ever on my side?

'Love,' she started earnestly, 'you *knew* what he was like. It's all in the past, let's order more drinks and forget about him.'

My thirty-fifth birthday, he was just minutes away in this hotel? He'd hurt and humiliated me, and didn't even have the respect or decency to keep it from my doorstep. As Lara went to the bar, I tried to soothe myself; *it was twelve years ago, a lot of water under the bridge, but who was it? Who spent my birthday with my husband in this hotel?*

I took a large glug of wine; it soothed the prickling pain that had been dredged up again, but it didn't eradicate it completely. Something was gnawing at me, but I couldn't quite work out what it was, and though I stayed another half-hour, with Lara, talking about old times, something didn't feel right, like a shadow had crossed the sun. When it came time to leave, Lara offered me a lift in her red sports car. 'I'll keep the roof down, we can play Thelma and Louise?' she said, but I didn't want to spend any longer with her.

'Thanks, but I fancy a walk,' I said, and promised to be in touch, knowing I probably wouldn't.

Lara waved and beeped her car horn, soon disappearing into the distance, a flash of red, as I walked in the opposite direction back home. The weather was warm, but fresh with a salty sea breeze. I hoped the walk would shake off the feeling that had enveloped me in the rather dim hotel bar, but something weighed heavily on me. I couldn't quite put my finger on it.

I walked through the village, and up towards the house. Reaching the brow of the hill, I was faced with the last person I wanted to see. She was walking in my direction, pushing the buggy with his baby in. And judging by the look on her face, and the diamond on her finger, she was back to feeling pretty good about life. As we got closer, she started to describe that feeling without being asked.

'Hey, Carly, I've just been to take a look at the house. I think I'm going to have slatted blinds fitted on the front windows when you move out, what do you think?'

I was still walking towards her, as I had no choice; it was the only way home and she knew it.

'Glad you got to spend some time outside, Erin. Better than sitting huddled under a load of coats at your old childminder's, while your poor mother is frantic and the rest of us are being questioned by the police.'

Her face tightened.

'You really didn't think that one through, did you?' I pressed.

'Yeah well, it brought Mark to his senses, made him realise how amazing we are together.'

'I'm very happy for you, but you'd better make room, Mark's bed can get pretty crowded,' I said, and moved on, without even thinking about asking to look at the baby.

An hour later, Estelle called. 'Darling, how are you, my sweet?'

'Okay,' I said, wondering what the hell she was calling about. She never called me now if she didn't have to.

'It's just – oh dear, this is rather delicate, but Mark just phoned me, said you've been leaving messages. On his phone?'

I had to think for a moment, then recalled the diatribe I'd left a couple of days before. 'Yes, I have. Listening to recordings of my caterwauling seems to be his preferred method of contact these days. It must be, because he never calls me back.'

'Ooh, don't shoot the messenger, lovely. He's such a busy boy at the moment, he barely gets time to answer his calls, but he just asked if I'd call you after you left some pretty unsavoury comments on his voicemail—'

'Yes, they were *deliciously* unsavoury,' I said proudly. 'And it's funny that he's so busy but has the time to call *you*, to say I called,' I snapped.

'Oh sweetie, don't take it to heart, there's really no need to be jealous of little old me.'

'I'm not. That isn't what I meant!' I said, frustrated, knowing full well she knew exactly what I'd meant but had decided to turn it into something else. I may find myself in the next day's papers, at this rate: *'Estranged Celebrity Wife in Jealous Phone Fracas With Agent!'*

'Ooh, it's your birthday soon, isn't it?' she oozed. 'Have a *very* happy birthday, I'll send your usual white lilies,' she said in retaliation. No one but me would see the hidden darkness here, but Mark always sent me white lilies. That was Estelle's way of telling me he didn't even do *that*. I should have guessed she'd been the one sending them on his behalf. Every time we had a row or I found out he'd been with someone else, a bouquet of white lilies would arrive. He must have discussed every row, every whisper with her, and along with everything else that had been wrong with me and Mark – to quote Princess Diana, 'there were three of us in the marriage'.

'Apart from calling to reprimand me for leaving messages with your client – who, by the way, is my husband, and old enough to fight his own battles – to what do I owe the pleasure of this call, Estelle?'

She made a weird laughing sound; laughter didn't come easily to her. 'Oh Carly, my love, none of my bloody clients are old enough to fight their own battles – that's why they have *me*. You know what they say, an agent never sleeps; it's like dealing with petulant toddlers, I tell you.' Then she took a breath, like this was going to hurt. 'The thing is, gorgeous – your messages – they are very, how shall I put it? Visceral?' She paused for effect. 'And might in… a certain context sound bitter? Can I say that, is that fair, darling?'

'You can say bitter if you like.'

'And how shall I put this, the phone messages, which are, of course, still on my client's phone, have hurt him deeply. And may be deemed abusive enough to, dare I say, require police intervention?'

'Okay, message received, Estelle,' I said calmly, 'and in response, would you pass on this message with my best wishes? *"I am incandescent with the lies, the humiliation, the cheating, and the physical abuse I received from my husband. I'm finally ready to talk to the media."* Is *that* fair, darling?'

A nervous giggle emerged from somewhere in her throat, and I knew I'd hit her where it hurt. 'You are hilarious. I'm always saying to Mark, I miss your humour. It's funny, I always thought *you'd* be the star,' she suddenly said.

'Mmm, I'm sure you did,' I said doubtfully.

'No, you had it, my love, you were gorgeous and great in front of the camera.'

'I couldn't get anywhere near the camera, my husband was always elbowing me out of the way,' I said.

'Oh, you're so naughty, stop making me laugh, this is serious,' she said, and I wondered just who was being sarcastic with whom. 'Thing is – Mark says these messages are bordering on – hate to use the word – but *stalking*.' I swear I heard her salivating on the other end of the phone.

'*What?* You're telling me his ego is so big that he thinks I'm *stalking* him? He really doesn't get it – I don't want him anywhere near me, I just want money. *My* money!'

'I might also remind you that *my* calls are recorded, sugarplum.'

'Good, perhaps you can forward the recordings to him? Because he promised he'd repay what he took from our bank. And then there's the money for the US deal too?'

'I hear you, sweet cheeks… and that's what this phone call is all about. Mark will shortly be in receipt of the US money, and would like to make you an offer. If you accept, we can put this straight through to the lawyers.'

'Good. That sounds good,' I said, hoping we could finally say goodbye forever.

'So, let me just find the paperwork… Ah, here we are. Mark wants me to express his fondest wishes and to extend to you the rather generous offer of £5,000.'

I almost choked. 'For what?'

'Good will, dear. I happen to think it's very generous.'

'And I happen to think it's a joke! We agreed on twenty per cent, and that is *not* £5,000, that doesn't even cover the money he took from our accounts – let alone anything else. This has never been about "good will", it's about me collaborating. I came up with the original *Forever Home* concept, the American idea, the treatment, the—'

'That's his final offer, my darling. My hands are tied… and no, it isn't a joke. I *never* joke about money. Love and light, Carly!' She hung up. Estelle was like a jelly baby – all sugary and sweet on the surface but there was often a bitter aftertaste. She was clearly the sentinel at the gates of presenter hell, and wasn't going to let me anywhere near Mark, nor was he going to face up to his responsibilities and pay me back.

I just stood in the kitchen and cried with frustration. What the hell was I going to do? In my heart, I knew then I had no choice. I'd have to sell my childhood home, and as joint owner he had first refusal. He and Erin would buy my forever home and use it as they wanted, even though they'd be based in the US. I'd have to live in the village, watching my home be changed, as she stripped the walls and he added more glass monstrosities to the back.

I suddenly heard a noise behind me, and 'Happy birthday!'

It was Phoebe and Jake, standing in the living room, holding balloons and a cake, and smiling nervously.

CHAPTER THIRTY-FIVE

'We know your birthday is on Monday,' Phoebe said, 'but as we're both busy during the week, and you now work a couple of days, we decided to do a flying visit, and as it's Saturday, stay over tonight with you.'

'You two are so naughty,' I said, hugging them. I was, of course, delighted to see my kids, and even if I didn't feel like celebrating, it was lovely to have them home. They'd both told me they couldn't get back to Cornwall for my birthday, and with everything going on, I didn't question it.

'We weren't going to leave you on your own for your birthday, Ma,' Jake said, already going through the cupboards looking for food.

Ryan had gone to the hardware store for nails, and I'd just been going to make lunch for us. He would walk back into the house at any moment, and I wasn't quite sure what to do. I really didn't have the energy to break it to the kids that one of 'the Jarvis Brothers', as they referred to them, was sleeping in Jake's room. Except he wasn't, he was actually sleeping in mine. I didn't know which was worse. I may have to explain why he was here – but not tell them *everything*.

'Fabulous,' I said, then suddenly realised that Jake would be taking his stuff up to his old room, and he'd see Ryan's stuff there. And I may in fact have to tell them *everything*.

My children laid out gift bags on the kitchen surface, and Phoebe opened a bottle of fizz.

'Oh, you are both so lovely, I'm really touched,' I sighed, taking the glass Phoebe was proffering.

'It's good to be home,' Jake sighed, and Phoebe and I caught each other's eye.

'You okay, dickhead?' It was Phoebe's affectionate nickname for him, which was fine until we had company. I remembered Mark's sister finding it rather 'disgraceful'. It always made me smile.

'Yeah, I'm good,' he said.

'Have you heard anything from her?' she asked, referring to the girl who had broken his heart.

He shrugged. 'No, and she can piss off,' he said, topping up our glasses, as he'd always seen his father do. 'Happy birthday, Ma,' he said, and echoing this, Phoebe lifted her glass and we clinked them together.

'Here's to plenty more fish in the sea,' I said, and we clinked again.

'That applies to you too, Mum,' Phoebe replied, 'now you're young, free and single.'

Just as she said this, I was aware Ryan had come in through the glass doors. The kids were looking from him to me and back again, a bemused expression on both their faces.

'Hey, Ryan,' Jake said, and Phoebe immediately got another glass.

'Are you going to celebrate Mum's birthday with us?' she asked.

'Oh, I didn't know,' he said, standing awkwardly by the doors, his hands in his jeans pockets. 'You never told me, Carly,' he said, obviously feeling bad.

'It isn't until Monday,' I said, still wondering how the hell I was going to break it to them that he was staying now, and kicking myself for not just telling them over the phone when we first arranged it. I just never thought I'd be in this position. Jake had told me he had summer work in Exeter, and Phoebe didn't visit often, and they both usually told me beforehand when they were coming home.

'So, what shall we do tonight?' Phoebe asked, looking around.

My heart hurt a little as Ryan looked down, obviously excluded from this conversation, and I wanted to put my arm around him. He was my partner, however temporary, and he should be celebrating my birthday with me and my family.

'Let's do a takeaway and stay here. We can sit in the garden?' Jake suggested, always keen to be home.

'Okay, are you happy with that, Mum?' Phoebe asked.

I nodded. 'Yes, that would be lovely…'

I shot a look at Ryan, who made an 'I'm fine' face. But I couldn't help feeling bad that he wouldn't be part of this.

He was soon talking to Jake about the work he'd been doing on the house, while Phoebe took the takeaway leaflets from the drawer.

'What do you fancy, Mum?' she asked.

'Chinese?' I suggested, still wondering how I was going to introduce the idea that not only should we invite Ryan to share the takeaway, he was also sharing their mother's bed.

'I think we should order now, for later,' Phoebe was saying. 'That way we can just relax, have some more drinks; you can open your present.'

'That sounds good,' Jake said, turning away from his conversation with Ryan.

'So,' Phoebe said slowly, as she read the leaflet, 'I'm thinking Banquet A for four people?'

'Four?' I asked.

'Is there one for three?'

She looked surprised. 'Why, isn't Ryan staying?'

He looked over at us, and I looked back at him. 'I'd love to,' he said, 'thanks.'

'Great,' I said, surprised, but touched at the way he'd been included.

Ryan and Jake went outside to look at the work he'd been doing.

'So, you're okay with Ryan staying for dinner?' I asked Phoebe when we were alone.

'Yeah. Mum, we're obviously going to vet him, and give you our verdict. But we're not stupid, Jake saw his socks on your bedroom floor when he came home to get his books – and I saw his bedroom eyes every time he looked at you when I was last home. I wasn't sure about him at first, but I trust your judgement, and he seems to make you happy, which makes me and Jake happy. And, of course, like all good children, we have gone through his social media like Google detectives.'

'And?' I asked.

'And so far, there's nothing to report. But we're watching.' She pointed her fingers at her eyes then mine, and I thought how strange it was to have my kids looking out for me, when it had always been me looking out for them.

The evening was better than I could ever have hoped; there was suddenly no awkwardness about Ryan being around. Jake, being the lovely kind soul he was, had no problem with Ryan's stuff being in his room. 'It's like having a big brother,' he said to me quietly as we gathered the plates together for the Chinese food. 'I always wanted a big brother.' I was relieved and happy, and that Jake saw Ryan in those terms was a bonus – here was a role model, someone who worked hard and genuinely cared for people. Ryan didn't always put himself first, and hopefully, was nothing like Mark, the father Jake had hero-worshipped most of his life.

That night, the four of us sat around the garden table, talking, drinking, eating and, of course, laughing. Candles flickered in jam jars, and the scent of honeysuckle wafted around us, mingling with the laughter, dancing around the flames. It was a warm night, the sea like black glass, the sky a velvet canopy, studded with stars, and my kids not only accepted him, but they *liked* Ryan. They'd drawn him in, included him in our family; they'd laughed at his jokes and listened to his stories. But, more importantly, he'd listened to theirs, he hadn't dominated the conversation, made us feel like a decorative background. He asked questions, was interested in their family memories and laughed along with us. How different things were turning out to be. I had no money, and probably quite a struggle ahead to keep the house, to pay the bills; life was going to be hard. But that night, I'd never been happier.

Our lovely family evening under the stars kept me going long after the kids had gone back to their respective lives. I did some more days at the shop, enjoying the structure it gave to my week, and growing fond of Maureen, who I worked with most days.

Ryan didn't seem to have found any extra work, so spent the time working on the house. Life was quite blissful, and I rarely thought about Mark, or Erin, apart from one evening when Ryan mentioned something his brother had told him.

'Max says he saw Mark with some redhead the other night.'

'Redhead?'

'Yeah, really young, someone said she's a journalist. She's going to America with him to write about his new show.'

'Really? That's interesting, I wonder if it's Charlotte,' I said, 'and I wonder if Erin knows.' I raised my eyebrows, remembering the pretty young reporter from the interiors magazine. 'I should have known when he invited her to our silver wedding party. He might have been seeing Erin then, but looks like he was already lining up the next one!'

'He really is something else, isn't he?' Ryan said, shaking his head.

'Yes, I imagine that's where the money from our joint bank accounts went; he probably took Charlotte on weekends to Paris and New York in the best hotels.'

'Wouldn't Erin find out?'

'No, he's a bloody expert at cheating, he's been doing it for years. He'd tell her it's work.'

That conversation reminded me that Mark was about to leave for America, and I felt it only fair to myself that I try one last time to ask him to give me the money he owed me. So I called and left a message.

I left several more voicemails to him over the next few days, each one more angry than the last. As usual, I received no response. So when my phone rang one afternoon while I was at work, I was amazed to see his name come up. I asked Maureen if I could take it outside, said it was 'the doctor' and just hoped she didn't see the 'dickhead' flashing across my phone screen.

I hadn't heard from him for a couple of weeks, but had been kept updated indirectly by Lara, who called me now and then to complain about him, like he was *my* errant child. Most of her calls began with, 'You won't believe what he said to her this morning…' and she'd go on to regale me with some repeated conversation that Erin had taken offence at. I didn't particularly want to hear it. I still felt a bit of a disconnect between us, since the day we'd met for drinks.

'Carly, why do you spend your time stalking me on my phone? Don't you think I've been through enough? All that stuff with Erin, when she decided to go AWOL. She is blabbing to anyone who'll listen, saying I'm out all night, having affairs. Estelle and I are trying to keep stuff out of the papers every day. Last night, I almost had to call an ambulance I felt so ill.'

'Oh, something serious, I hope?'

'I *thought* I was having a heart attack. But it turned out to be heartburn,' he explained, like I'd care.

'So, my messages, can you please answer the question, when will you put the money back in our accounts? And we'd agreed twenty per cent on the US deal.'

'Here's the thing, Carly – it's all been a bit touch and go with the US deal. Trying to convince the streaming network that Erin isn't a fruit loop is a full-time job in itself after that stunt she pulled. I've had enough, Carly.'

I wasn't surprised this was causing some problems. TV networks won't play ball with high-risk presenters, and having virtually faked her own death, his girlfriend was a scandal waiting to happen. If the US deal didn't come off, then we'd all be disappointed, including me, but my priority was my home, and how I could keep it. My big concern was that Mark had been dragging his heels to sign the Consent Order, which was essentially our financial agreement for the divorce, and gave me back his half of the house.

'Look,' I said, 'whatever's going on, you have to sign the divorce papers. I want my house back, and you out of my life, Mark.'

'Okay, I'll sign them.' He agreed to this so quickly I smelled a rat, but I didn't want to let it go, so jumped at it.

'I can come to the cottage now?' I suggested.

'No, actually I'm staying on the houseboat of a friend.'

'Really? Since when?'

'Since yesterday.'

I wasn't aware of this new development. 'Have you left Erin?' I asked.

'No, no, I just need some space. I can't get any sleep with the baby, and I need peace and quiet.'

'You used to say that when our kids were little, and you went to a hotel,' I said, knowing he was probably with someone then, and with someone now.

'Hmm. How about we meet tomorrow evening?'

I sighed; it was obvious what he was up to. 'Okay, I'm working tomorrow, so can we say seven?' I suggested.

'Fine.'

'If you call it off or back out on our agreement in any way, that's it – I've already told Estelle, I'm going straight to the press and I will tell them everything, including the rumours I'm hearing about your little redheaded reporter.'

He snorted. 'Do you really think anyone's going to listen? You've said yourself how happy you are for me and Erin, and yet you tried to attack her in your home… You're very mixed up, always have been, Carly. Especially after your mother's death.'

I went cold. 'You can't hold that over me forever, Mark, it was a long time ago.'

'Doesn't make it right though, does it, however long ago it was?'

'Tomorrow at seven,' I said, unable to even continue the conversation, and I put down the phone.

Later that evening I told Ryan about the conversation, and what an idiot my husband was.

'If he's such an idiot, why are you always calling him? Just talk through your lawyers,' Ryan said.

'Because it costs to talk through our lawyers, and some of the things I have to say to him would make them blush,' I replied, opening the fridge and taking out salad for dinner.

He didn't answer, so I turned round.

'Are you jealous?' I was surprised.

'Yeah. I am. Is that so weird?'

'Yes, because there's nothing to be jealous of.'

'I'm not the jealous type – at least I don't think I am, but the idea of you meeting him, being anywhere near him… it *gets* to me.' He pulled a baffled face, like he'd never experienced jealousy before. I wondered if things were changing between us, and we were coming to rely on each other, to care too much, and if that was a bad thing?

'Ryan, you need to remember, he isn't Mark Anderson, the handsome, capable TV presenter you see on the screen. This is the real Mark, the alcoholic with attachment issues,' I sighed, closing the fridge door. 'He reckons the US deal is in jeopardy, and he's not at the cottage with Erin, he's staying on a boat, which I think means he's seeing someone.'

'God, he's really sunk low, hasn't he?'

'Mmm. He thought by having a younger wife he could be immortal, that she'd make him look younger in America – but she may have single-handedly wrecked everything.'

'They're like two kids,' Ryan said, shaking his head.

'I want my house back; I don't want to be married to that childish, selfish man any longer. That's why I'm meeting him tomorrow and because we need to change our wills. At the moment we're both the other's next of kin. I'll be delighted to hand that over to Erin. Lara said there's talk of a wedding.'

'But he's just moved out?'

'I know, but apparently they haven't broken up.'

Ryan laughed. 'They deserve each other.'

'Yeah – I wonder how long that marriage will last?'

Little did I know, there wouldn't even be a wedding.

CHAPTER THIRTY-SIX

The following evening, I returned late from seeing Mark. The meeting had been traumatic, in ways even I hadn't expected, and I really didn't want to talk about it. But Ryan was waiting for me when I got back.

'Where have you been?' he asked, standing in the kitchen in bed shorts and a T-shirt; his hair was a mess and he looked genuinely worried.

I walked up to him, and put my arms around him. 'I'm back now, that's all that matters,' I said, trying not to cry.

'You smell smoky,' he said into my hair.

'That's Mark and his damn cigarettes.'

'Why are you so late?'

'Oh, the usual shit. I arrived on board to find him below deck in a stupor. Took me ages to get any sense out of him. And that boat he's living on is old and it smelt vile and I wanted to vomit…' I shuddered at the memory, as he squeezed me tighter.

'So did he sign the papers?'

'No… he was too drunk.'

'But…' he looked at his watch, 'it's after eleven, you went at seven. You've been four hours, Carly.' Then his face changed expression. 'He didn't hurt you, did he? If he touched you, I'll—'

'No, no. I'm fine, just so tired.' I gave him a weak smile, but even that felt like too much effort. I just wanted to go to bed, to try and forget this evening, although I knew that would be impossible.

'Hey, what about a nice cup of coffee?' I said, feigning brightness. I just needed him to stop asking questions and was relieved when he pulled away from me and put the kettle on.

'Did you even talk?' Ryan asked. 'I mean, the house – the reason you went there was to make sure you got your half back,' he said, as he put a heaped spoonful of coffee into a mug.

'Yeah, I know that, Ryan,' I snapped.

He rolled his eyes; he seemed pissed off.

'What's the matter?' I asked.

'It doesn't add up. You're saying you spent all that time on some scuzzy little boat, and came away with nothing?'

That angered me. 'Ryan, he was drunk, anything he might have signed would be worth nothing. I'm sorry if you're annoyed I didn't get the house back…'

'I'm not saying that. I just can't believe you spent all that time with him and didn't get any further.'

'How many times do I have to tell you? He was pissed. I tried to cajole him, but he'd been drinking all afternoon; even if he had agreed to it, his signature would have been meaningless.'

'Whatever,' he mumbled, sounding like a bloody teenager.

He plonked my mug down on the kitchen unit without looking at me.

'I'm going to bed,' he sighed. 'I'll stay in Jake's room tonight; I've got a lot to do tomorrow.'

I was hurt, but after the night I'd had, a little part of me was relieved. I didn't want to have to talk any more about it, or address the timeline any further with Ryan. There were things I needed to get my head around; things I couldn't tell him.

The next morning, I was woken by a sharp rapping on the front door. I heard Ryan answer it, and sat up, half-awake, listening to him talking to a female voice, and then a male voice.

I put on my dressing gown and walked out onto the landing, where I peered over the bannister, straight into the faces of DS Sally Barker and DS Harefield.

'Ahh, there you are, Carly,' Sally said, walking to the bottom of the stairs. 'Could we have a word?'

My heart sank as I walked downstairs to join her.

'I'm sorry, love, we have some bad news – your husband, Mark Anderson, has been found dead this morning.'

My hands flew up to my mouth. 'Oh God, I don't believe it! What happened?'

'A fire, on the boat he was staying on. It looks like there were some head injuries too, but we're not sure if they happened *before* the fire, or as a result of him falling.'

'No! A fire?' I felt unable to say anything else.

'Yes, very sad, and probably an accident that could have been avoided. A lit cigarette perhaps?' she suggested.

'Yeah, he sometimes smoked.' I nodded.

'My colleagues are with his… partner?' She cleared her throat. 'But as you're still his wife on paper, I felt it only fair to come and tell you in person,' she said, searching my face.

Ryan offered them coffee.

'They drink tea, I think, don't you?' I said, looking back at Sally and DS Harefield's rather blank faces.

They both nodded, and Sally dragged her eyes away from mine to study Ryan, who was now in my kitchen. In pyjama bottoms. I looked down at my own night attire, and, embarrassed, pulled it around me, covering my cleavage.

'When did you last see Mr Anderson?' DS Harefield started before we'd even sat down. He was getting out his notebook, and my heart sank as I was lurched right back to Erin's disappearance, the questioning, the dark, dank little office with only a desk, and the constant questions. I couldn't go through that again.

'I haven't for a while… Actually, I spoke to him on the phone, the day before yesterday,' I added, realising they might check his phone records.

Ryan shot me a look, but I ignored him, keeping my eyes firmly on DS Harefield's eyes.

'Oh – and did he seem… any different from usual?'

'Any different from his usual drunk and depressed? No.'

'Has he had a *diagnosis* of depression?' Sally asked.

'No… Oh, I don't know. Ask Erin, ask Lara, they know more about his recent mental state than I do. All I know is that he's always had a problem with alcohol.'

'Has he ever indicated to you that he might have considered taking his own life?' DS Harefield asked.

'Not directly, but let's face it, he was an accident waiting to happen.'

'Meaning?' he said, looking up from his notebook.

'Meaning – his big dream in LA was looking unlikely, he had the new baby, the high-maintenance younger woman, money was tight; it's no surprise that his alcoholism had worsened. Lara, my friend, Erin's mum – she said he sometimes dropped the little one off at hers and she was horrified because he'd driven over and she smelt alcohol on his breath,' I said. I wanted them to know how bad he was. 'I think he'd given up on life,' I added, with a final flourish.

'Oh dear,' Sally said, making notes, 'you think he was suicidal?'

'Look, I'm no psychiatrist, but the last time I spoke to him on the phone he said he'd had enough…' I started, then plucked a tissue from the box to dab my eyes. 'I'm worried now that he was asking for help, and I missed it…'

'You mustn't blame yourself,' Sally said, as Ryan put down cups of tea for them both on the coffee table.

They chatted away, trying to make conversation, but I knew this was more than just chat, that they thought I knew more than I was saying about Mark's death. And just before they left, Sally was still keen to find out about Ryan's status in my life.

'So – you guys are still together?'

Ryan looked slightly panicked at this, unaware that I'd already told Sally at the last 'meeting'.

'Yes, still together.' I smiled at him, and he smiled back.

'Good for you,' she said, giving me a wink, which was all rather embarrassing, but I appreciated her support, and it felt like an indication that they were finished with me. After more small talk, which felt like genuine small talk, mostly about the house, I gave her a *Forever Home* coffee table book for her mum, who she'd said on our first meeting had loved the programme.

'Oh Carly, she'll treasure this,' she said, pink with pleasure, and asked me to sign it.

'I'm not the famous one,' I said, with a smile. 'It's Mark's signature she'll want.' Then I looked at her. 'Oh God, I will never get used to the fact he isn't here…' And I burst into tears.

Sally comforted me, told me 'sometimes things happen for a reason, and who are we to know what goes on in someone else's head'. I stopped crying, and, satisfied I wasn't able to tell them anything they didn't already know, I walked them to the door, and they left.

'What the hell are you doing lying to the police?' Ryan hissed as soon as their car had left the driveway.

'I didn't *lie*.'

'Carly, you so did,' he said, his face red. 'You were *there*. You were with him for four hours last night, and today he's dead. WTF?'

'You heard them. He killed himself. He set light to his boat, either by accident or suicide – he did it, anyone can see that,' I said, gathering the cups together to wash. 'I didn't *need* to tell them I was there.'

'I think they came here because they were convinced you knew something. I just worry for you. I don't want to be collecting you from bloody police custody again, or worse.'

'Look, Ryan, this isn't helping. Believe it or not, I'm sad about Mark, he's the father of my kids – and now I have to tell them,' I said.

'Okay, so perhaps you'd better make those calls.' He shrugged, leaving the room.

'Ryan,' I called, 'stay with me while I call them. You're one of us now.'

He wandered back into the room and, sitting down next to me on the sofa, held my hand as I called them.

Phoebe didn't cry. She was surprised, but as I said to her, 'In some ways, darling, it was inevitable, he was so unhappy, and his drinking had got so much worse.'

The phone call to Jake was harder though. He cried a lot and asked me how I was and said he'd come over. 'Stay at uni, darling,' I said. 'Don't drive back, you're in no fit state. Come when you're ready and feel strong enough to face all this. The police have been and I just don't want you or Phoebe having to deal with them.' I wanted my kids as far away from this as possible. I had to protect them.

That evening, as Ryan and I sat on the sofa, staring out onto the ocean, we were both quiet. 'Are you okay?' he said.

'Yeah, I think it's just hitting me now what's happened,' I said quietly, although in truth, my mind had been non-stop all day. 'Talking to the kids was the worst. I'm glad that's over,' I said, knowing I'd be there for them as I always had been, where their father hadn't.

'Who gets this house?' he suddenly asked.

'You mean now Mark's died?'

'Yeah – does half of it automatically go to Erin?'

'Not sure, it depends,' I lied. I didn't want Ryan to know I was still next of kin. Mark's will hadn't been changed, and therefore everything would be left to me, including the half of my house I gave to him all those years before. I had to know if Ryan wanted me for me, and if I didn't have the house, or any money, that would be a test. 'Why do you ask?' I said.

'No reason, just wondering,' he said, then immediately changed the subject – which made me feel even more uneasy.

CHAPTER THIRTY-SEVEN

The next few days were a blur; the children arrived and brought with them fresh sadness, but also some happy memories of their dad. Jake was a mess, but Phoebe was still surprisingly strong. I wondered if she was just hanging on and would collapse in a heap of grief at the funeral or after.

Interestingly, the memories they wanted to talk about were from way back, when they were very small, and I suspected there was a lot of rose tint to those memories. Meanwhile, the newspapers covered the story in style, lots of splashy headlines about his 'amazing career' and the 'tragedy' of his death. One particular in-depth piece that really seemed to get to the heart of the man was written by a journalist called Charlotte Cooper, who referred to him as 'a good friend', which I took to mean far more. The most surprising though, perhaps, was an interview in the *Daily Mail* with Gemma Hough, the lead groupie and yummy mummy who virtually accosted me at the hair salon. According to Gemma, she'd 'enjoyed' a 'torrid' relationship with Mark Anderson several years before, when they'd spent 'whole days' in bed together. I wasn't surprised, but I knew Mark, and I doubt it was an affair, just a string of one-night stands with the same woman, and meaningless to him.

'Disrespectful bitch,' was my daughter's comment. But I was past caring; this was just the tip of the iceberg. I was sure there were plenty more women ready to sell their stories to the tabloids. I hated the kids seeing it, but there was little I could do. I couldn't stop that tsunami; even Estelle couldn't staunch that flow, though, God help her, she'd try. She'd sent flowers, and a card, and would, I was sure, be firefighting and grieving all at the same time – it would be quite messy. Meanwhile, all this bad press would have Mark turning in his grave, I thought, and tried not to smile.

The days after someone's death are a kind of limbo, waiting for the funeral, a veil of sadness over everything, and I just had to get through that, as I'm sure Erin did. Lara called a few times, but her sympathy didn't stretch very far when it came to Mark.

'It was the *only* way, we all knew where he was heading,' was the closest she came.

Erin was, of course, at the wake, which I was happy to host at our home – our forever home. This was preceded by a service at the village church, where several unidentifiable blondes appeared on their own, accessorised by tears.

'I wonder what number she was,' Lara murmured in the cemetery, as one of them placed a rose on the grave.

Then, out of the corner of my eye, I saw her, Charlotte Cooper, the reporter I was convinced Mark was seeing when he died. She was dressed in black, carrying a red rose, and tears were streaming down her cheeks. They had *definitely* been more than friends.

'What the hell is she doing here?' Phoebe hissed, under her breath, on the other side of me.

'I think she was his final hurrah,' I said.

'*Dad's?*' Phoebe looked horrified.

'Yes, she's the journalist, Charlotte. Ryan's brother saw your dad with a redhead in the pub the night Erin went missing.'

'Oh Mum, that's fucked up.'

'I know, she's very young.'

'Not just that. You know that was Jake's girlfriend, don't you?' I almost collapsed at the side of the grave. 'No…'

She sighed. 'Poor Jake, I hope he doesn't see her.'

But looking at Jake's face, I think he already had.

Later, when most of the guests had gone, we all walked down to the beach, where Phoebe, Jake, Erin and I scattered Mark's ashes on the sea, watched by Ryan and Lara. The moon lit our way, and Erin said something about 'an extra star in heaven tonight', and Lara rolled her eyes and muttered, 'More like it's hot down below.' I didn't acknowledge this, but Phoebe had obviously heard. When we finally returned to the house, and Lara and Erin had gone home, just me, Ryan, Jake and Phoebe remained.

'I can't help but feel that Lara's glad – about Dad,' Phoebe said.

'Well, she worried about Erin, and the baby – she saw Dad as an albatross around all their necks really. She never liked him.'

'That's not true – I remember her kissing Dad at one of our Christmas parties – with tongues,' Phoebe added, and Jake nodded.

'When was this?' I asked, feeling the familiar thump of my heart when someone imparted a new story about my husband.

'Years ago. I was only about ten, but I remember it really clearly. We saw them, didn't we, Jake?'

He nodded, clearly uncomfortable, not wanting to hurt my feelings.

I just rolled my eyes and said, 'Well, you know your dad, he was always kissing the girls.' I then said I had to go to the bathroom and allowed myself to hurt over Mark's betrayal for the very last time.

And later, after Phoebe and Jake had gone to bed, and Ryan and I were alone, he asked me how it made me feel to hear that about Lara.

'It hurt,' I said, 'but I think I've probably always known, but chose not to see it – because, if I faced it, I'd have lost my best friend.'

'Best friends like that, you don't need enemies,' he sighed.

He was right. 'Now I know they had a fling, it makes sense now why she hated him so much. He obviously dumped her.'

'Your husband and your best friend. That would freak me out,' he said.

'If I'd known at the time, it would have freaked me out too, but I trusted her. And you know what – I also think Lara was the one who put the petals on our bed all those years ago.'

'What?'

'Yeah, it wasn't "a stalker", as Mark had insisted. I had a feeling he'd overdramatised it to deflect from what was really going on. I guessed "the crazed fan" was actually just someone he was seeing, but he didn't want me to know, and let's face it, whoever she was, "a stalker leaving rose petals" made a great story for the tabloids.'

'But what makes you think it was Lara?'

'That night, I had the chance of showing my work at an art gallery in Devon. It was over the school summer holidays and had been booked for months. It meant a lot to me, and Mark knew that. So, when at the last minute he suddenly said he had to be on location and couldn't stay home with the kids, I'd called the gallery and they'd said "bring them along", so I did. I booked a little bed and breakfast and me and the kids were going to stay over. But Phoebe wasn't well, so we didn't stay over, we came back early. But when we got back, Mark was here; he said the shoot had been cancelled. I didn't think twice and we all went to bed, but the next morning, we woke up, and I saw something on the duvet. At first, I thought it was bloodstains on the white cotton, but when I touched the red, it was fake rose petals. I freaked out, knowing someone had been there while we slept, and Mark immediately started saying it was his stalker, and called the police and everything. It was soon all over the papers, and that week the viewing figures went through the roof. I was interviewed by the police and the press and it was crazy. Lara had keys to the house then, we were best friends. I had my suspicions, but what could I say? But now I know he'd never been working, it was a lie, he and Lara had planned to spend the night together here, in our bed. And I ruined it by coming back early. He probably didn't get chance to warn her, or perhaps he did and she came over because she thought he had someone else over instead of her? Either way, she'd come over during the night with the petals and love note and was about to lay them on the bed, or even get in with him, when she must have realised I was there, dropped them and ran. I think Lara came over late that night to check up on him, the way Erin came here to check up on him the night she went missing.'

'They've both got a screw loose if you ask me,' Ryan sighed.

'There was something else too. When we met for a drink recently, we were talking about my thirty-fifth birthday and how Mark hadn't been there with me. "I remember your thirty-fifth, he sent you a bunch of lilies," she said, "and told you he was working late, couldn't make it home. And all the time he was down the road, in *this* hotel with someone else."'

'Nice of her to remind you,' Ryan murmured.

'Thing is though, I'd never told Lara that he'd sent me last-minute lilies, and worked late on my birthday. I'd lied to all my friends, including Lara. I was embarrassed, couldn't bear their sympathy, their assumptions that he must have been up to no good. So I made up this elaborate story telling them that after work he'd driven through the night, arriving home at four in the morning to give me a beautiful diamond bracelet. But somehow, Lara had forgotten my lie, and only remembered what really happened. She *knew* he hadn't made it home that night – because the woman who was with him in the nearby hotel on the night of my birthday *must* have been her.'

'Christ. That's messed up, your best friend was shagging your husband?'

'It isn't unheard of.' I gave a weak smile.

'But what about *her* husband?'

'Mmm, I've been thinking about that too. Steve killed himself not long after the rose petals incident. Lara told me when we met recently that she'd hurt Steve, and that he always felt like a loser next to Mark. Well, he would, wouldn't he, if Mark was sleeping with his wife? It would explain why she suddenly hated Mark so much and couldn't bear it when he tried to comfort her at Steve's funeral. Steve must have found out about Mark, and his wife. He adored her, probably couldn't take the pain, and walked into the sea.'

'Wow!' Ryan said under his breath. 'Are you going to talk to her about it?'

I shook my head. 'No, I've lived with it this long, no point raking it all up. Lara's suffered enough, and if there's such a thing as karma – the fact Mark hooked up with Erin just a few years after he'd been having an affair with her was probably punishment enough.'

'All these people and their secrets,' he said, pouring the remainder of a bottle of wine into both our glasses. 'So,' he said, moving round to face me fully, 'what secrets are *you* keeping?' He was looking at me in a strange way; his eyes were cold.

'What?' I said, smiling.

'I think you're keeping a really big secret… that Mark's death *wasn't* an accident.'

CHAPTER THIRTY-EIGHT

'So, will you trust me with your secret?' Ryan asked.

'What do you mean?' I replied, my heart slowly starting to thump.

'I *know*,' he said, looking at me intently.

I laughed, and took a gulp of wine.

'I *know* what happened to Mark,' he repeated.

He couldn't possibly… could he?

'Yes, he had too much to drink and set fire to the boat…' I started, hoping he couldn't see the truth in my eyes.

He put his glass on the coffee table, and faced me. 'I care about you, Carly, but I can't be with someone who isn't being *honest* with me.'

I took a deep breath. 'And what happens if I don't want to talk about it?'

'Then I leave tomorrow.'

I sipped my wine and wondered what I should tell him.

'I don't understand why you think Mark's death *wasn't* an accident?' I said, in a last-bid attempt to keep this secret to myself.

'Because you didn't want the police to know you'd been there that night.'

'I *told* you, Ryan, I didn't want to go through what I went through with Erin, all the questions, the police station – it was horrible.'

'Okay, so tell me this. Why did you call my mate Simon on the night Mark died?'

Shit. I tried not to let the horror show on my face. 'How do you know I—'

'He told me you'd been in touch, said you'd asked him to delete CCTV or something from the boatyard.'

No, no, no.

'You didn't answer *my* calls.' He was staring at me, his eyes cold. 'But you called Simon.' He paused. 'And something else… The *baseball* bat,' he was nodding now, 'there used to be *four* baseball bats in Jake's room, and now there are only three.'

'I don't remember how many baseball bats there were,' I said. 'God, Ryan, the police are happy with it. I don't see why *you* have a problem, Miss Marple.' I tried to lighten the moment, but deep down I was thinking, he knew. Would he go to the police and tell them? If he didn't go this week, would he go next? Would he go next year if we broke up?

'The deleted tape, the baseball bat, it's obvious. Who *loves* using the baseball bat?' He half-smiled at this. 'I don't know why you're even trying to hide it.'

'Jake was in Exeter, over 100 miles away—'

'*I know!* I'm not talking about Jake! I'm talking about *you!*' he said. 'Don't you remember, on one of your rants down the phone, you threatened to chase Erin with one?'

'That was a figure of speech.'

'Whatever, but when they came here that morning to tell you, the police said Mark may have died from head injuries *before* the fire.'

I couldn't continue with this charade. I had to give him something. He wasn't stupid, he'd heard me lying to the police, and he knew I was at the boatyard that night.

I took a deep breath. 'Okay, so you want to know exactly what happened?'

He nodded.

'But if I tell you, how do I know I can trust you never to say anything? Ever.'

'You have my word. I love you, Carly. And you can trust me. I'm not Mark Anderson.'

I started to cry. It wasn't just the memories of that night, but he'd just said he loved me, and he so wasn't Mark Anderson, he was my future. I was finally free of Mark, and the shadow he cast over me, and he couldn't tell mine and my mother's secret; it was safe in my heart where it would stay.

'If I tell you, will you be able to forgive me? It might change your feelings,' I said, feeling tearful. It would be so sad to lose him now.

He shook his head. 'Never. I don't think anything could change how I feel about you, Carly. I told you, I've loved you forever.'

I took a deep breath. 'I thought about it long and hard, but when the police seemed happy to accept it was an accident, why ruin another life?'

He nodded. 'You did the right thing, Carly. Mark was a cruel bastard, he ruined yours and your kids' lives.'

We sat in silence for a few seconds, and then he said: 'I don't want details, but I'm guessing that night, you'd turned up there hoping to get your divorce. You took the baseball bat with you to protect yourself, but when you got there he was incapable of anything and you were frustrated – I get that.'

I nodded, slowly, unable to even think about that night.

He touched my face. 'No one could blame you for killing him after all he put you through,' he said gently. 'And it doesn't change how I feel about you.'

'I've no money, and I killed my husband. I'm not exactly a keeper, am I?'

'I don't care about money. I'll save up enough to take us both to Thailand and live on fish from the sea.'

After everything, that sounded like heaven.

'You don't hate me?' I asked.

'No… I told you, I love you.'

CHAPTER THIRTY-NINE

THE NIGHT MARK DIED

The boatyard was horrible – rusty old boats, machinery that hadn't worked for years just lying around. No one was about, and I didn't know where the boat was. I wandered around for a while looking for it. Eventually I found it, and climbed on board. It was filthy, and I didn't even want to get on, but as I said to Ryan, I had to make this meeting positive, and get what I needed and go. I called out to Mark and eventually he responded, 'Down here.'

My heart was in my mouth; there was no one around, and I was climbing down into this foetid vent of hell to meet up with someone I really didn't want to.

As soon as I stepped into that dark, sweaty cabin that reeked of piss and whisky, I knew: he wasn't in any fit state to talk to me about money, nor was he going to sign the divorce papers. It looked to me like he'd been down there all day, drinking and becoming more and more angry.

When he saw me, he tried to stand up, and he couldn't, he had to hold on to the side of the boat. I hadn't seen him like this for years, but was immediately triggered, memories of the past flashing before me.

'I'm not staying Mark,' I said, readying myself to leave. 'There's no point trying to talk to you in this state. I want the divorce, and I want my home, and from now on we'll deal with each other through our solicitors.'

The look on his face told me I was in danger, I'd seen it often enough. But as I turned to go back up the stairs, I was grabbed roughly from behind by my hair, and with a roar, he pulled me back down into his horrible dungeon by my legs.

I screamed, and kicked out at him, but there was no one around to hear me, and he seemed to find the strength from somewhere to overpower me. As he knocked me to the ground I realised, this was so much worse than it had ever been before, he was like a wild animal. He'd totally lost control, the last few months had tipped him over the edge, Erin missing, his American dream hanging in the balance, everything was falling apart. I couldn't believe I'd walked into this, it was like he'd been waiting for me to arrive so he could inflict all his disappointment and rage. I was face down in the putrid water on the floor of the boat, all I could hear was the creaking of wood on water, and his rasping breath. I closed my eyes, cringing, just waiting for the crunch of his fist. But after several seconds that felt like hours, I slowly dared to raise my head. I tried to move my arms in an attempt to get up off the floor, but with the heavy thud of his foot on my back, I was down again.

'Don't even think about leaving,' he hissed. 'YOU, YOU, you're like the rest of them, think you can do better without me. You CAN'T! You NEED me!' He was shouting, and lurching over me, the rocking of the boat and the whisky impairing his balance, and when I eventually strained my head to see a way out of this, I whimpered. He was holding a chair that I could only assume was for my head.

'NO! NO! MARK!' I yelled as loud as I could, desperately trying to crawl away, but his foot was on my back again, and as I was pushed down into the damp floor, the boat rocking from side to side, I doubted I would live through this night.

I closed my eyes and shielded my face, knowing the chair would land on me at any minute. And I heard the roar again, loud, angry, full of pain. I was shouting 'NO!' as he roared, but even in all the human noise, I heard another voice. Someone else was there, on the boat. Mark was roaring, but so was someone else. Eventually I was brave enough to open my eyes, and I'll never forget what I saw. My son, was standing over his father. 'Jake?' I murmured, unable to process what I was seeing. But then to my horror, I realised, he was holding a baseball bat high in the air, over Mark's head.

I had to stop it and, in an instant, I propelled myself forward with all my might, shouting, 'NO, Jake!' But as I cried 'No' again, he brought the bat down on his father's head screaming, 'Bastard, bastard!' Mark dropped the chair he was holding, stunned, he tried to move, but Jake brought the bat down again, with a cracking thud. After a third time, he stopped. It was as if he finally heard me calling his name, begging for him to stop. He looked down at his father twitching on the floor, blood pouring from his head. I didn't care about Mark, I only cared about Jake, and avoiding the fresh streaks of blood now snaking along the floor, I crawled through the wetness to reach him. He was on his knees, crying now, and I held him in my arms, telling him it would be okay, just as I had when he was a little boy. But as sure as I sounded to him, inside I was screaming with fear. My son had just killed his father, and we were on a boat, with the body. And I didn't know what to do.

We held each other and both sobbed. What kind of harm had we caused our child for him to do this?

'Why, darling?' I cried, as I rocked him, sitting in the fading light of a small shaft coming from the half-open door above.

After a while, he was able to tell me, to vocalise his feelings and explain. 'It was Dad's job to look after you, and he just left you there. I wanted him back in our home, our family home. I called him, leaving messages, telling him how lonely you were, but he never called back, he was too busy with her. He'd always been too busy with someone else,' his eyes were fixed on the blood now trickling along the floorboards.

Despite all the hurt Mark had caused me, he'd hurt our children far more. All this time I thought I'd protected them, stayed with their father playing happy families, but we hadn't fooled the children. And I hadn't protected them at all. By staying with Mark, I'd exposed them to all the pain that was enmeshed in life with the father they'd both once adored. My children had been damaged: Phoebe couldn't find her feelings, she couldn't commit to anyone, and I doubted she ever would, because Daddy had already smashed it. Jake had found his feelings, but couldn't control how he felt.

'I hate Erin,' he said. 'I set up an anonymous account to send her threatening messages, telling her to leave Dad alone. She thought it was you Mum, she sent vile messages back. I was shocked at how horrible she could be, but realised I could get at her if she thought I was you. She asked me, "How did you like the gift?" I wasn't sure what she meant, but I knew she had something to do with that sand on the floor.'

Jake didn't know about the rat, I'd never told the kids; I didn't want to scare them. So, at times, it seemed their messages became slightly confused, but Jake continued to goad her, it was him who sent the spiders in the post, sent messages telling her Mark would leave her, that he didn't love her. Remembering the vase that had been smashed, the picture that had been moved, the note in the blue envelope missing from the kitchen drawer, which she knew the police might check for fingerprints. I asked Jake if she'd ever mentioned that. He said it made sense; she'd sometimes say things like, 'That vase was SO ugly,' or 'I think that picture looks so much better over there,' assuming she was talking to me. She must have used Mark's keys to get in when I was asleep, or out, haunting me, goading me with how she'd rearrange the house when it was hers. It was just a game to Erin.

Even more worryingly, she also apparently sent messages detailing her sex life with Mark. Jake said it was 'messed up', and he didn't read them, but I could see it upset him. From what he said, it was when she told him how much Mark adored the new baby that things were ramped up. She said that Mark had told her, 'I messed up with the other two. I've been given a second chance with Billy, and already I love him more.'

Who knows what the truth is? Perhaps Mark did say words to that effect. He was probably drunk and telling her what she wanted to hear – or perhaps Erin said it trying to hurt me? We'd never know.

Meanwhile, Charlotte the journalist dumped Jake, and started seeing Mark. Now I realise she probably used him to get to Mark, something that Jake was no doubt aware of. But to find out his girlfriend was now sleeping with his father, must have felt like the ultimate humiliation, and the ultimate betrayal.

When Jake heard Mark and Erin were trying to take the house from me, and that I was going to meet Mark at the boatyard, he decided to drive over from Exeter. 'I wanted to protect you,' he said. 'I'd spoken to Dad on the phone. He said you were coming over, but he couldn't let you have the house; he said it was the only way he could get Erin back – if she could live there. I knew she'd all but left him and he was desperate. I wanted to come and plead for the house, to stop him taking it from you… from us, so I came along, but I also called home, for the bat, just to threaten him. I never meant to use it Mum, but when I saw him holding that chair over your head…'

'It's okay Jake, you were protecting me,' I said, and hugged him close, we were both in tears, and inside my heart raged at myself and my husband. My teenage son, who I'd tried so hard to protect, had been caught up all along in our mess, and in trying to protect me, he'd now found himself in an impossible place. How had it come to this? I hadn't kept him safe after all, but I would make sure he was safe now.

It was dark by the time we'd worked out what to do. By then the blood was in the wood grain of the boat, and even with all the cleaning fluids in the world, we'd never hide the evidence. So, I told Jake to get into the water, to wash away any blood that might be on his clothes. 'Don't hang around, your clothes will be wet, but get straight in the car and drive back to Exeter. Don't stop anywhere, and if anyone sees you or your flatmates ask why your clothes are damp, you fell in the sea.' He was shaking, and I was so worried about him driving back, but had to get him away.

When he'd gone, I found some boat fuel stowed on the upper deck, and sprinkled that all over the boat, adding a final flourish with the remainder of a bottle of Mark's whisky all over him. Then I turned on the gas hob, and sparked up his lighter. I then dashed from the boat with minutes to spare before it set alight, and standing from a safe distance, watched the explosion, followed by bright orange clouds. The surrounding water looked like liquid fire and the air was thick with smoke. I couldn't stay for long, but I said my goodbyes and felt nothing. After twenty-five years and two children, you'd think I'd at least have felt loss or sadness, but I felt only liberation. The sky had lit up like bonfire night, and I was finally free.

The smoke and flames must have been seen miles away, and someone somewhere would have called the fire brigade, who were probably on their way. So I climbed into the car and drove off quickly, parking a couple of miles down the round to gather myself together. I reeked of smoke. I checked my clothes for any bloodstains. They were damp from the floor of the boat, but there was nothing too obvious, and I'd change as soon as I got home so Ryan wouldn't question anything. I took my phone from my bag: about six missed calls from Ryan, he was probably worried about me. I was almost tempted to call him, tell him everything, but something stopped me – I'd been married to a man I told my secret to, and he held it over me all my life. No, I would just drive back and wait, and hope. The boat was now in flames, no one had seen us, we'd left nothing behind, there was nothing or no one to tie me, or Jake to what happened. But then a horrific thought occurred to me – what if there was CCTV at the boatyard? Then I remembered, of course there was. Shit! Simon who'd installed my own CCTV camera, had boasted about working at the boatyard and fitting the security equipment.

I fished around in my bag, and there they were. 'Every breath you take, every move you make, CCTV is watching you.' Who knew CCTV Simon's gaudy business cards would come in handy? I called Simon straight away, and told him that my husband had invited me over to his boat at the yard to discuss our divorce. 'While we were having a drink and talking through things, he lit up a cigarette,' I said, 'but he must have left the gas hob on, because as soon as I said goodbye and left him, the whole thing went up.'

'Oh no, I'd better get down there – I'm their security advisor…' he started.

'No, it's all fine, the fire brigade are there,' I lied.

'Oh good, glad the lads have arrived. But are you okay, Mrs Anderson?' he said, sounding genuinely concerned.

'I'm fine thanks… but, I have a bit of a problem.'

'Problem? I could almost hear him salivating, Simon was definitely one of life's problem solvers.'

'Yeah, thing is, the fire was raging, so obviously I couldn't go back in and try to save him. But I'm worried how this might look to the police. You know how these things work, so I was ringing for your advice, Simon,' I lied again, playing the damsel in distress.

'Ah, my advice? I see,' he said, sounding flattered.

'Yes, I'm worried I might be implicated in some way, when obviously I'm innocent. You may have seen all the stuff about the missing girl?' I said, referring to Erin. 'I was innocent then too, but… Simon, I think the police might try to frame me. What can I do?'

'Well…' he started, as I imagined his chest puffing out with pride; here was Mark Anderson's wife asking for his advice. 'You Mrs Anderson, could be in very tricky waters…' he continued, and went on for far too long about arson, murder, and his time, 'with the security services.' But eventually he arrived at the information I was interested in. 'In a nutshell Mrs Anderson, it always comes down to surveillance – and it depends what exactly is on the CCTV.'

'Oh Gosh, I hadn't even thought about that!' I lied, feigning surprise.

'Well,' he said, lucky for you, I have.' I could hear the swagger in his voice, 'You might recall, that I just happen to be in charge of the CCTV at the boatyard.'

And my lies kept coming; 'I'd completely forgotten, I mean what are the chances? Oh Simon, is there anything you could possibly do to help me?' I asked, adding a little extra pleading in my voice.

'Can I make it go away you mean?'

'Well, I wouldn't want you to get into any trouble, Simon.'

'Hey, trouble is my middle name,' he said proudly. 'Let's put it this way, from the minute you picked up your phone to call me, your problems with the police were over, I know what the boys in blue are like, once they get the bit between their teeth there's no stopping them. So, you go home, get a good night's sleep and worry no more. Consider tonight's recording deleted.'

I thanked him profusely, said I'd trust him with my life, and would be eternally grateful. Then I called Jake to make sure he was back in Exeter, and when he said he was safely back, drove home to Ryan.

EPILOGUE

It's late autumn, the trees are golden, and the foam-laced sea is more boisterous and bracing after the glassy summer months. The house is looking good too, Ryan's put Thailand on the back burner and continued to work on it. The care and attention he's paid is really starting to show. I think the same can be said for me; someone told me yesterday that I looked ten years younger, and I have to say, I've never been happier.

Thanks to Mark dragging his feet with signing the divorce papers, I remained next of kin and inherited everything when he died. So I'm now the owner of my beautiful white, art deco house that lives precariously on the edge of a cliff in Cornwall – my forever home. It's all I ever really wanted, and whatever happens in the eb and flow of life's tide, I intend to stay here. The US channel still want to use the *Forever Home* idea, even without Mark, and have offered to pay me a retainer for use of the Forever Home brand. I feel like I'm finally climbing out from under Mark's shadow.

I still have the recording I made detailing my emotional pain, and close-ups of my injuries, and I may, in the future, release this into the wild, because I think Mark Anderson, and men like him, have been protected long enough. I'll donate some of the retainer fee from America to a domestic violence charity – if I can save one woman from what I went through, it will be worth it.

The inquest into Mark's death has now been carried out and the coroner recorded it as 'Accidental', describing his death as 'a tragedy, and a great loss'. The inquest revealed that Mark, a heavy smoker, had apparently turned on the gas hob on his boat while smoking. It was apparently his 'bolthole, where he spent quiet time working on his scripts' – a line straight from Estelle's playbook.

Meanwhile, Erin has got herself an agent, and under Estelle's tutelage has been paid well for her 'open and honest' interviews with the media. She plays the grieving girlfriend so well; I particularly enjoyed an, 'exclusive' with *OK!* magazine, who took her, Lara and Billy to the Seychelles. It seems that only by the infinity pool of a five-star hotel could she 'begin to heal'. And in a lavish, six-page spread, Erin and Lara continued their grieving journey while sporting tiny designer bikinis from Lara's company.

However, Erin's real focus of grief is that, as Mark's next of kin, I received everything in his will. But I think she's finding solace in those lucrative magazine interviews, and hear she's been approached by a reality show. I hope she achieves all her dreams, I'm just glad she's stopped stealing mine. Meanwhile, I've set up a trust fund for Billy, because he is Mark's son, my children's sibling, and I hope one day, when Erin grows up, they can all be family. Mark failed all his kids one way or another, and I want to make up for that, to *all* his children. Even after his death.

Lara called me a little while ago; she wanted to meet up, go out for drinks again, and re-establish our friendship. It broke my heart, but I had to say no. I'd loved her, trusted her, she was supposed to be my friend, but while I'd been sharing everything with Lara, she'd been sleeping with my husband. How could I ever trust her again? As Ryan said, with friends like that, I don't need enemies.

As for me, I have new adventures ahead, I'm about to open my own shop selling those ice cream paint shades and candles that smell like the sea. I'm bringing *The Forever Home* back, now it's completely mine again, and this time, it will be real, with no dark shadows behind those white shuttered windows.

As for Jake, he and I will spend the rest of our lives looking over our shoulders, but it's a price I'm prepared to pay. I didn't realise how much our flawed marriage had impacted our child. He's not a bad person, but even if he were, I'm his mum and it's my job to protect him until the day I die, and if that means living a lie – then so be it.

So, in spite of everything that's happened, life is good. Ryan and I are happy, I think I may have even fallen a little bit in love with him. But experience tells me I can't ever rely on one person – unless that person is me. Who knows what's round the corner for any of us? But if ever Ryan and I break up, or he proves not to be who I *think* he is, then he can take my 'secret' to the police. As long as he believes it's *me* who killed Mark, then Jake is safe. And ultimately, that's all anyone wants, isn't it? For their kids to be safe – and happy, forever.

A LETTER FROM SUE

I want to say a huge thank you for choosing to read *The Forever Home*. If you enjoyed it, and want to keep up to date with all my latest releases, just sign up at the following link. Your email address will never be shared and you can unsubscribe at any time.

www.bookouture.com/sue-watson

I wrote this book during a very cold winter and a second and third UK lockdown. The frosty mornings, short dark days, and lack of sunshine made me long to go to the beach and feel the sun on my face. This was impossible in the landlocked Midlands where I currently live, so I decided to set this book in a beautiful house in Cornwall, and it was a pleasure to spend so much time there – at my desk. I also wanted to bring the sunshine and seaside loveliness to you, my readers, who I'm sure, like me, are longing to see the sunshine, and the sea again. So, among the dark shadows, and twisted relationships, I hope this book also gives you hope of better days to come, when we can enjoy a sea breeze, and sunshine on our faces once more.

I hope you loved *The Forever Home* and if you did, I would be very grateful if you could write a review. I'd love to hear what you think, and it makes such a difference helping new readers to discover one of my books for the first time.

I love hearing from my readers – you can get in touch on my Facebook page, through Twitter, Goodreads or my website.

Thanks,
Sue

 suewatsonbooks

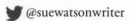 @suewatsonwriter

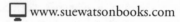 www.suewatsonbooks.com

ACKNOWLEDGEMENTS

As always, my huge thanks to the wonderful team at Bookouture, who are there for me every step of the way; from romcom to thriller killer, they always have my back.

Thanks to my editor Isobel Akenhead who brings my ideas to life with her inspiration and guidance. Special thanks to Jade Craddock, my brilliant copyeditor, who always makes sense of my ramblings, and turns them into books, and to Sarah Hardy, for a fabulous first read.

Extra special thanks to my friend and reader from across the pond, Ann Bresnan, who goes through my writing with a forensic eye and always provides brilliant insight. Ann is unstoppable, and has been known to work on my books in the eye of a hurricane – literally!

As a BBC TV producer, I once worked on DIY programmes similar to *The Forever Home* that Mark Anderson presents in this book. I have such happy memories of those times, and especially two brilliant and talented presenter/designers, Colin McAllister and Justin Ryan, who now create home happiness on Canadian TV. I want to thank them for their continuing inspiration, friendship and support, which has meant so much to me over the years. But, perhaps most of all, I have to thank them for introducing Nick Watson ('awesome hubs') and I to the Toronto skyline, and the Boulevardier cocktail. Cheers, boys!

Made in the USA
Monee, IL
30 December 2021

87588797R00201